A Dance of Light and Shadows

Haley Davis

THE STORMY QUILL

Book Cover by Devyn Shank

Edited by Grace Fabbri

1st edition 2025

Dedication

To my husband's unending support, to my girls who made me believe again, to my father who I wish could be here to see this, and to all of my amazing friends and family. None of this would be possible without you.

To my readers, remember, it's never too late to start dreaming again.

And to younger me, we finally wrote that damn book.

Prologue

LANA

*T*wenty-one years ago...

"Please Fenn, don't hurt her!" Lana's voice cracked, tears streaking down her face as she stood before the sleeping infant. "She's just a baby!"

Sweat glistened on her brow. With each frantic incantation, she called out to Zaria, pleading for her aid—but it felt as though even her god had forsaken her, her pleas falling upon deaf ears. Horror clawed at her chest as she witnessed Fenn absorbing the spells she cast,

1

the murky aura surrounding him swelling with each futile attempt. This was her end; nothing would save her tonight.

She stood before the wooden cradle, clutching the silver dagger Fenn had gifted her on their fifth wedding anniversary. Even if she knew how to wield it, it would do her no good. She had never acquired the skills necessary to defend herself without the aid of magic, nor had she ever envisioned a time when that magic might fail her. Her mind was clouded with a singular hope: that her sister would burst through those doors at any moment. Yet it seemed that even her sister had turned her back on her. How else could he have shattered the wards and remained unharmed? After all, they had never been fond of half-breeds, and she supposed that's what her baby was to them.

Fresh tears brimmed in her eyes as she pressed the dagger's tip into her palm, carving the final slash of a runic symbol, praying to Zaria and any other gods willing to listen that it would work. A life for a life. She might not make it out alive, but with her dying breath, she would ensure her baby did.

"She's an abomination," Fenn snarled, a beastly growl erupting from deep within him, sending an icy chill racing down her spine. The man before her bore little resemblance to the man she had wed all those years ago. He had his face and tall, muscular body, but his eyes, once an oceanic blue, now burned with crimson rage, darkened by corruption.

Lana had never truly loved him in the way a wife was meant to love her husband. Their marriage had been one of convenience, dictated by the elders in the coven. Over time, they had forged a bond, one full of compassion and care. He had always been kind, with a gentle touch and even softer words. But the man standing before her was merely a vessel of pure fury and madness, stripped of all reason. A dark fear clawed at her, whispering that he might not be a man at all.

"Fenn, listen to me. It's Lana," she begged, her voice trembling, hoping that somehow her words would pierce the madness consuming him. But he prowled closer, his lips drawing in an upward curve, reveling in her fear. "You don't want to do this." She took a step back, holding the dagger out before her, the metal trembling in her grip.

"It must be done," he said, and with a flick of his fingers, the dagger was wrenched from her hand and sent clattering across the room. Lana's heart thundered in her chest, but she remained resolute, planted firmly between him and her child.

Fenn's eyes gleamed wickedly in the moonlight that fell through the parted curtains as he began to stalk towards her, each step echoing on the wooden floorboards. His lips twisted in an ominous chant, words dripping with malice as a dark, red-tinged aura coiled around his body like a predator preparing to strike.

She had suspected he had fallen victim to some sort of dark magic the day she had found him murmuring to the shadows in her sister's study, but she hadn't wanted to believe it. Didn't want to believe that the man who had fathered her eldest daughter had succumbed to the corruption of dark magic that now consumed him, eating away at his soul—if there was even a soul left.

Fenn stood before her, savoring her grief like a rare delicacy. "I'm going to enjoy this," he sneered, his lips curling with delight as he held his arms out wide, the cloud of darkness erupting from his sides in an eagerness to be unleashed upon her.

"Fenn, no, please. I can—"

A flame of darkness consumed her. Agony burned through her body, silencing her final plea as it coiled around her like a serpent, snatching the very air from her lungs. A vice-like grip held her in a tormenting stillness, her arms falling limp to her sides. She was defenseless, at the mercy of a man who could no longer be reasoned with.

Her heartbeat thundered in her ears, frantic and desperate, as the suffocating pressure closed in. She struggled against the grip binding her, but each attempt was met with another searing pain, leaving her gasping for breath that would not come. Her vision blurred, darkness creeping in around the edges, threatening to swallow her whole.

With each fading heartbeat, she felt the crushing weight of her own mortality. Yet in that despair flickered a thread of hope; her death would give her child a chance—a chance to breathe, to laugh, to love. As she closed her eyes, surrendering to the encroaching darkness, a bittersweet warmth flooding through her. She was leaving this world, but in her heart she cradled the certainty that her precious *baby girl would live. She would live, and Lana knew that when the time came, she'd burn the corruption from this world.*

Chapter One

The wind howled, sending wisps of her hair twirling upward in a dance. The briny smell of the ocean enveloped her as the gritty sand clung to her dampened toes. Thunder cracked in the distance, swallowing the nearby hum of the windmills, followed by a jagged bolt of lightning that illuminated the seascape before her. As another crack of thunder sounded above her, she knew it would be mere seconds before she'd be drenched in the icy rain. Yet she still couldn't bring herself to move.

When she was younger, she would have run home and hid under her covers at the slightest rumble through the air. Now, she found herself almost comforted. She didn't know when her fear had vanished, but she couldn't have felt more alive standing there on the shore as the sky grew angry and the ocean danced in anticipation.

Another crack of thunder echoed across the shore as she felt the first drop of rain pelt her forehead. She sighed a smile. *This was why she had come.* While most would be running to find the nearest dry shelter, she let herself fall backward into the cool sand, arms splayed out wide as if to say *welcome*.

The cold rain drummed against her skin, each droplet an icy finger prying her thoughts away from the manor, from the suffocating weight of her reality. She lay there, water soaking through her clothes, and shivered—not just from the chill, but from a sense of something she had forgotten: *freedom*. For the first time, the absence of expectations brought her a breath of relief.

Above, the moon peeked out from behind swirling clouds, casting beams of silvery light that danced upon her casting ring. Its glimmer mocked her with unfulfilled promises and looming challenges. Whispers of judgment caressed her ears, swirling in the night air; yet they felt distant now, like echoes from a forgotten past. Exhaling heavily, she turned her gaze from the ring, closed her eyes, and surrendered to the rain as it stung her skin, a bittersweet reminder of the freedom she feared would always remain out of reach.

The silver casting ring glistened in the sun, its once-concealed needle now tinted red from Ivy's blood as she tirelessly recast the blocking spell. She didn't know what she was doing wrong, or why her magic always failed her. Iverlyn could feel it begging to break free, but perhaps that was wishful thinking. Sometimes, she wondered if it was cosmic karma brought onto her by her mother's death.

Her shoulder jolted back when yet another invisible brute force collided with her, sending her staggering backward. That would bruise later. She had lost count of how many times she'd been battered into, lost track of how many times the needle had pressed into her aching fingertip as she chanted the spell meant to protect her and failed. But Seraphina wouldn't stop. She never stopped.

"You aren't trying hard enough," her aunt gritted out as she sent another spell hurtling towards Iverlyn, not even bothering to give her enough time to prepare. She was mad. She always grew angry when Iverlyn continued to fail at spells everyone else her age seemed to excel at. Each time they trained, her anger grew, and it showed in the growing strength of each spell being thrown at her.

"*Try harder,*" she bellowed, her voice echoing along the empty shore.

Just as Iverlyn raised the casting ring needle to her fingertip, a blast from the following spell slammed into her stomach, forcing the air from her lungs and sending her sprawling onto the harsh, unforgiving sand and jagged seashells. Gasping for breath, Iverlyn lay there, feeling the cruel bite of each shell against her skin, while the sound of Seraphina's footsteps grew nearer. Would she ever be worthy in her aunt's eyes? Would this ever end?

"*How many more times must we do this before you start taking it seriously?*" *Seraphina's voice cut through the air like a dagger, dipped in bitterness. Each word lashed into Iverlyn like a wound she knew would never truly heal. Seraphina was convinced that Iverlyn's failures stemmed from a lack of motivation and drive, unable to accept the possibility that Iverlyn's blood might simply lack the potency to cast the spells successfully.*

"*I. Am,*" *Iverlyn forced out through clenched teeth, pushing herself to stand defiantly before Seraphina. A fierce determination ignited within her, an inferno that mirrored the distant rumble of thunder. She steadied herself, her fingertips trembling as they brushed the casting ring, preparing for another strike.*

Seraphina's eyes narrowed, cold and unyielding, fixed on the casting ring that adorned Iverlyn's left hand. "*You don't deserve that,*" *she spat, her voice laced with venom as her gaze seared into the ring.*

She had always been unhappy with the idea of Iverlyn having her own casting ring. They were considered symbols of power, with only esteemed coven members having them. Iverlyn's mother had her ring crafted for her during the last month of her pregnancy and had it enchanted so it would always be with her, making it impossible for Seraphina to take, despite her many attempts to do so. She recalled her aunt once taking the ring and throwing it into the ocean, only for it to reappear in Iverlyn's pocket seconds later.

These rings were crafted to aid in the ease of spell casting, each housing a needle to draw the necessary blood to cast a spell. The rings were always worn on the left hand, replacing the traditional spot of one's wedding ring, because in Salus, there was no greater devotion than to the magic that coursed through their veins. While marriage was sacred, it would never come before the magic they all held dearly. The ring, while beautiful in its intricacy, was bulky. While most members of the coven loved to wear theirs for everyone to see, Iverlyn preferred to keep hers tucked safely away in her pocket, with the exception of her training sessions with Seraphina. In Salus, magic was not just a skill but a way of life, and the ability to cast powerful spells was a measure of one's worth and status.

"Fucking sand." Mumbled absurdities sounded from behind her, shattering the symphony that the crashing waves and now-slowing storm had played. She didn't need to look to know that Theo, her long-time friend, was stumbling towards her. Despite growing up on an island, he had a rather large distaste for the beach shores.

A small chuckle escaped her as she heard what seemed to be a struggle behind her, followed by another slew of curses. It wasn't long before Theo collapsed beside her, tossing a warm blanket in her direction with an exasperated sigh.

"Out of all places you could have come. Why here, Ivy?" he huffed, using the nickname only he used for her. He grabbed the blanket he had dropped into her lap and draped it over them, shielding them from the slight drizzle of rain.

"I told you, it's peaceful," she responded with a shrug, tugging the blanket tighter around her, thankful for its warmth.

This had become a routine of theirs. When feeling overwhelmed, Iverlyn would find herself in the same spot she sat in now, and when ample time had passed, Theo would show up to retrieve her and ensure that she returned home safely.

She didn't need the shimmer of the moonlight peeking through the clouds to know that Theo's soft, yet sculpted features ticked in annoyance as he shifted uncomfortably on the ground beside her, or that his sandy blonde hair was already curling up on the edges in a way that only the salty air seemed to cause.

"Are you ready for tomorrow?" Theo asked, his voice soft and weary.

Tomorrow was supposed to be the day that her life would change forever. Tomorrow would be the day that she would either finally prove herself to her family or utterly fail them. None of them would dare speak it out loud, their superstition too strong, but she knew they all expected the latter. If she were being honest, she did too—the only person who seemed to have any confidence in her ability was Theo.

"No," she answered honestly. She knew he already knew her answer from how his arm, loosely draped across her shoulder, tightened, pulling her closer into his warm embrace.

"It'll all work itself out in the end," he said, running a calloused hand down her cold arm in reassurance.

She let the quiet hum of the windmills and the soothing crash of the waves fill the space between them as she sat, willing herself to believe the words he had just spoken.

"I'm nothing like any of them," she said, breaking the silence and digging her heels into the cold sand.

"Is that such a bad thing?" Theo's question seemed to echo through the night as he spoke the words that she had found herself pondering nearly every moment.

In the ordinary world, her family thrived as successful business owners, maintaining a comfortable yet unassuming lifestyle and avoiding unwanted attention from outsiders. Something that wasn't hard to do, thanks to how secluded their island was from the outside world.

Although they disliked the term 'witches,' Iverlyn felt it was the most appropriate way to describe them. In the aftermath of the Flame War, which the rest of the world referred to as the Witch Trials, the survivors yearned for a community—a coven named Salus. This hidden sanctuary nurtured future generations, fostering their powers and shielding them from the outside world. Most coven members lived on a small island, rarely interacting with the outside world unless absolutely necessary. Iverlyn had never set foot beyond its borders. Her family regarded those of the mundane world with disdain, believing that even casual contact could sully their pure bloodline.

Though forming relationships and raising families with mundanes was technically permitted, Iverlyn's family viewed such actions as the utmost betrayal. They believed they should only marry within Salus to preserve their bloodline's purity and their powers' potency. This belief contributed to their reputation of never failing the ritual Iverlyn was destined to undertake the following day. She feared she might be the first to falter.

To maintain Salus's secrecy and safety, every young woman was required to face the sacred bloodstone on the seventh moon of their twenty-first year. The coven believed the stone was a gift from Zaria, the Goddess of the Night and mother of all witches, as a way to ensure that only those worthy of the coven were allowed to remain on the island. Passing the test meant acceptance by the community; failure resulted in exile or, in some instances, forced marriage in an effort to restore the bloodline. The inhabitants of Salus were valued for their contributions to the coven. Those with nothing to offer were banished to the mundane world, their memories of Salus and its residents erased.

Although men could carry magic in their blood and pass it to their offspring, only the women of Salus could wield it. Legend had it that Zaria cursed the men of the bloodlines she had imbued with magic as punishment for her consort betraying her trust. Iverlyn had heard tales of men driven mad by their futile attempts to harness the powers their wives and daughters controlled. None had ever succeeded.

The women in Iverlyn's family approached the bloodstone ritual with unwavering confidence, secure in the knowledge that ancient magic flowed through their veins. Her family was the cornerstone of Salus, akin to royalty, with an impeccable record of success in the bloodstone ritual. But Iverlyn was convinced this proud tradition would cast a shadow over her family's name tomorrow just as it had to so many others, as she would fail.

"What if I fail?" Her words were fragile and quiet, and she hated how weak she sounded. She wouldn't dare show this uncertainty to her family, but with Theo, she could bare her very soul to him, and he would never use it against her.

"If you fail," Theo paused, pulling her close and clasping his free hand on her knee, "then perhaps it would be proof the system Salus abides by is indeed utterly flawed."

A chill ran down her spine as Theo spoke, and she didn't know if it was from the cool breeze against her damp clothes or his words.

With her, Theo never tried to feign belief in Salus and everything it stood for. His disregard for their rules only seemed to grow as her ritual grew closer. At times, Iverlyn even agreed with him, but they could never share that with anyone else as it would be seen as the highest form of treason, and they would meet a fate far less desirable than exile.

"We really should be getting back." Theo stood, shrugging the blanket off his shoulders. "I'm sure they are looking for you by now," he continued with an outstretched hand.

She knew he was right. Her family wasn't fond of her nightly strolls, but especially on a night like tonight, she knew they would meet her at the door with their usual disapproving glares. Instead of accepting Theo's outstretched hand, she pleaded, "Just five more minutes." *Five more minutes of freedom.*

She didn't need to see Theo's face to know that a sly grin lay firmly planted there as he responded, "Five more minutes."

Chapter Two

Iverlyn's heart fluttered in anxious skips as she stood on the porch, the great cherrywood door looming before her. The soft glow of the entryway flicked on as she walked up the long driveway, signaling that Seraphina was still up and waiting for her return. Iverlyn knew what she'd be walking into when she left the beach. It wouldn't be the first time she would return home to face Seraphina's wrath, and she knew with unwavering certainty it wouldn't be the last.

The obsidian knocker, intricately crafted to mimic a crow's head, glistened as the porch lights cast a warm glow upon its polished surface. The elongated beak shimmered softly while its eyes sparkled with an almost unsettling semblance of life, watching her intently. She stood frozen, an electric tingle of apprehension coursing through her as she steadied her trembling hands before finally crossing the threshold into the house. Showing fear never did her any favors, as Seraphina saw it as a weakness, and nothing angered her aunt more than signs of weakness in her own family.

She could run away, forget about the ritual and her failing magic. Start a new life somewhere far away, a simpler life where her last name and heritage meant nothing. It wasn't the first time the thought had crossed her mind, but where would she go? And, more importantly, how would she get there? She had never even left the confines of Salus, and the schooling they offered on the island very conveniently skipped over geography. Even if she could secure a boat, which she'd have no clue how to operate, she wouldn't even know which way to travel. Sometimes, Iverlyn wondered if the elders kept the location of the island shielded not from fear of a breach of safety as they claimed, but as a way to ensure that none of the coven members left and tried to start a rival coven of their own.

"You know, the longer you wait out here, the worse it'll be for you when you go inside. She was raging mad when you left earlier." Isodyl's voice sounded from behind Iverlyn as she and

Elara stepped onto the stoop next to her, undoubtedly returning from yet another party with their all-too-short tops and skirts that looked like they would be small for a toddler. Iverlyn couldn't help but envy their carefree confidence. Would she be like that had she received the same love and support from Seraphina that they had?

Isodyl was her half-sister, older than her by only a few years, and Elara was Seraphina's only child. When Iverlyn's mother died, and Isodyl's father disappeared, Seraphina took her and her sister in to raise them as her own.

"You look like a wet rat. Where were you?" Elara's snarky voice chirped as she looked Iverlyn up and down in disgust before turning to Isodyl, who shared a menacing snicker with her.

She supposed she looked a mess compared to the sparkling duo standing next to her. Iverlyn's clothes hung limply at her side, the fabric stretched and sodden from the rain, and her copper hair was tousled in matted tendrils from the wind.

Looking at the pair, you would think they were sisters. Both shared sapphire blue eyes that shone brightly in contrast to their olive-skinned complexion, golden locks that fell just below their shoulders in perfect loose curls bouncing with volume that Iverlyn could never achieve on her own. They even shared the same cunning smile as they awaited to see what disaster awaited Iverlyn on the other side of the door. The only difference between the two women was that Elara stood barely an inch taller than Isodyl.

"Girls, is that you?" Seraphina's voice called out as the door swung open. Iverlyn watched her aunt's warm smile melt from her face as her eyes settled on her. "Where have you been?" she demanded as she wrapped a hand around Iverlyn's arm and dragged her into the house, not bothering to slow down as Iverlyn staggered behind her.

"Do you know how important tomorrow is to this family?" Seraphina exclaimed shrilly as she came to a halt in her study, releasing Iverlyn's arm with a rough shove.

Iverlyn remained silent, only responding with a slight nod, knowing that nothing she said would calm Seraphina's rage. Instead, she kept her eyes trained on the plush maroon-colored carpet beneath her feet. Seraphina had always found the greatest pride in the fact that the Wardwells were the only family to have never failed the bloodstone ritual. Iverlyn's impending failure threatened that spotless record she used as leverage over all the other elders in the coven. But Iverlyn knew it wasn't just that her failure would forever stain the Wardwell name. Her failure of the ritual would also confirm the rumor that the whole town had been eager to solve since her birth. She was a bastard child, the product of her mother's affair with a wandering mortal man who had found his way onto the island when his boat stalled just a few miles from the shore. It was a secret Seraphina had tried tirelessly to cover up, but even she couldn't stop the rumor mill that circulated the island.

"Clearly, you do not. You struggle enough when you are *focused*, let alone when you are gallivanting around all hours of the night doing Zaria knows what with that *boy*," her aunt chided. She didn't need to see her aunt's face to know that it contorted into disgust as she referred to Theo. Seraphina had never been fond of Theo and Iverlyn's friendship, claiming that she sensed he was up to no good. However, Iverlyn suspected it was because she preferred to keep her isolated. The fewer people Iverlyn had, the easier she was to control.

At one point, after she discovered that Theo was sneaking Iverlyn books and pastries that Seraphina had maliciously banned from her when she continued to fail, she tried to turn the whole island against him, claiming he had nefarious reasons for growing close to Iverlyn. For a while, it worked. Seraphina had always been gifted with the ability to influence others to do her bidding, and if it wasn't for Iverlyn knowing the truth, she supposed she, too, would have believed the lies.

"Well, don't just stand there, girl. Say something," Seraphina's shrill voice demanded as she stood before Iverlyn, hands planted firmly on her curvy hips, her perfectly manicured nails drumming impatiently as she waited for a response.

Iverlyn could hear Isodyl and Elara snickering from the other side of the closed door. They seemed to delight in listening whenever Iverlyn found herself at the mercy of her aunt's wrath, which was more often than not these days. She could picture their cunning smiles plastered on their perfectly olive complexions, their blue eyes glowing in delight at Iverlyn's torment. She knew Elara was more of a sister to Isodyl than she ever had been and likely ever would be. It was fitting, as they seemed to share a remarkable resemblance in personality and looks.

"I'm sorry, I was just nervous and thought a walk would help," Iverlyn answered, peering up through her tangled hair. She kept her voice soft, not wanting to provoke her aunt more than she already had.

Seraphina pursed her ruby-red lips, her dark eyes narrowing in a disapproving glare. "You foolish girl, of course you should be nervous. You can barely perform the most basic of spells. Spells that your cousin and sister had been doing by the age of thirteen." Her words were cold and sharp.

Her aunt wasn't wrong. Despite Iverlyn's many hours of training and learning, she still found herself stunted. Most women in Salus came into their magic by age fifteen, and by eighteen had mastered all the basics of spellcasting. Her family had always been gifted; some of them, like Seraphina, mastered their abilities by age sixteen. They grew stronger from there, barely giving the bloodstone ritual a second thought.

She remembered the day Isodyl faced the bloodstone. She was so sure of herself, and if she had doubts, she never showed them. Her sister had always radiated confidence in a way that Iverlyn envied. Perhaps it was because not only did she look perfect, but she also *was* perfect, never knowing what it was to fail.

"You will not embarrass this family tomorrow. I forbid it," Seraphina said as she snatched Iverlyn's chin, her long nails pressing in on either side. *As if her word would trump Zaria's will.* "And if you do," she snarled, baring her perfect white teeth, "I'll make you wish you died with your mother."

Her words were sharp, dripping with malice, and Iverlyn didn't dare to think she didn't mean them. All the years of torment, all the scars that now marred her skin, they were done to her in preparation for the ritual that awaited her tomorrow, and when she failed... Iverlyn knew there would be nothing stopping Seraphina from unleashing hell on her.

Her aunt released her grasp on Iverlyn's chin as she sauntered to the plush black leather chair behind her grand mahogany desk. She settled into the chair, crossed one leg over the other, and drummed her nails against the wood as she looked Iverlyn up and down. She pursed her lips and clicked her tongue before saying, "You know, I think that when you killed your mother, you did her a service." She paused, a cruel smile spreading across her face. "While pregnant with you, she told everyone how powerful you'd be, that she could feel it. Just imagine how disappointed she'd be to know how much you have failed her."

The words hit Iverlyn like a physical blow, her aunt's voice echoing in her mind in an unrelenting loop. *When you killed your mother.* Iverlyn didn't think she could breathe as her gut twisted, and guilt settled like a lead weight. She would never know her mother, never feel the warmth of her embrace, because childbirth had taken her away too soon. Because *she* had taken her away. It had always been there, that unspoken blame, coloring every harsh word and cold glance. They'd never said it outright, but maybe they didn't need to. Perhaps she'd always known.

"Go. Get out of my sight. I can't bear to look at you," Seraphina hissed with a fling of her wrist as if she were shooing a fly.

Iverlyn wanted to say something, to tell her that she was wrong. That her mother wouldn't be disappointed in her, that she would love her, and that she would care for her. But the truth was, Iverlyn couldn't; because as much as she liked to envision her mother as someone who was kind and caring, someone who would love her unconditionally, she had no clue what type of woman she had been. For all she knew, her mother was just as cruel as the rest of them. So instead, she turned and silently walked out of the room, through the closed doors where her older sister and cousin still stood snickering, and to her room where she'd stay until they called her to prepare for the ritual.

Chapter Three

Morning had arrived with a cruel swiftness as the sun filtered through the single window in Iverlyn's room. She threw her arm across her face and groaned. She had barely slept, and the little bit of sleep she did find had been plagued with taunting dreams of her imminent failure. At one point through the sleepless night, she had even let herself think about what it would be like to be free of Salus, but she stopped the delusion before it sunk its claws deep. She knew Seraphina would never let her leave this island. Not in one piece, at least.

Hours passed, and Iverlyn still found herself in bed, staring longingly out the window, daydreaming of a different world, a happier one. One with Theo, far away from magic. They could travel the world, she could read books that didn't pertain to the coven; he could visit his home again. They could be free. She knew she was just torturing herself, but it was a well-needed distraction as the hours ticked by and the ritual grew closer. Her stomach grumbled in protest as she continued to lay in bed through breakfast and lunch, but she couldn't bear the thought of eating.

"You're still in bed?" Isodyl sneered from where she had shoved Iverlyn's door open. Iverlyn didn't bother to look at her; she knew that when she did, she'd find the look of disdain her sister always seemed to wear when she was around Iverlyn.

"What do you want, Izzy?" Iverlyn grumbled into her pillow, choosing to use the nickname that she had adorned her sister with when she was younger and had been unable to pronounce her name. Times were different then. Isodyl was too young to harbor any hatred towards her, and for a couple of years, Iverlyn was able to get an idea of what it was like to have a sister, to have a family, even if her aunt always seemed to treat her differently.

"I told you I don't like it when you call me that," her sister growled. Iverlyn rolled her eyes, pulling the plain white comforter over her head to block out the light her sister had just flicked on. Like the rest of the items in her room, the comforter was worn, and the faded and rough fabric did little to nothing to shield her from the light. When she was sixteen, she had asked Seraphina if she could redecorate her room, just as Isodyl and Elara did at her age, but unsurprisingly, her request was denied.

"Aunt Sera asked Elara and I to help you get ready for the ritual," Isodyl said with a clatter as she cleared off Iverlyn's too-small desk. "Get up," she demanded, her voice clipped.

Iverlyn didn't move. She knew she was being childish and looked pathetic, but what was the point in pretending when she knew they would all see her that way anyway? An irritated sigh sounded from Isodyl as she stomped over to Iverlyn's bed and ripped the blanket off her before grabbing her arm and dragging her over to the desk where she had strewn out an assortment of make-up and hair styling tools.

"Elara will be here in a minute to help, but we should get started," Isodyl said, dragging her eyes up and down Iverlyn's body before reaching out and picking up a lock of Iverlyn's tangled hair, her lip curling in disgust. "This is going to take a while."

They both remained silent as Isodyl untangled her wiry hair before meticulously coaxing it into copper curls cascading down Iverlyn's shoulders like falling autumn leaves. Elara joined them and began painting a thick layer of makeup on Iverlyn's face, sure to cover the freckles that dotted her nose and cheeks. Iverlyn was almost sure that once they were done with her, there would be no resemblance to the girl she was. But she supposed that was the point.

She remained silent even when Elara and Isodyl discussed what use they would make of her room once she was exiled from Salus after the bloodstone marked her impure. Both of them were so sure of her failure. Despite their forced reassurance in the days leading up to the ritual, now that they were alone, where no one could hear, they didn't feign the belief that she would pass.

"I think we've outdone ourselves," Elara mused with a proud smirk as she helped lace up the silky white gown everyone traditionally wore for the ritual. Isodyl nodded in agreement, and as Iverlyn caught a glance of her reflection, she couldn't disagree.

Before her stood a stranger: a girl transformed, her hair cascading like silk, gleaming with an almost otherworldly vitality. The once-freckled canvas of her face now bore smooth, alabaster skin, free of any blemishes, just as Seraphina preferred. Her eyes, once ordinary and dull, now sparkled with an alluring vibrance, enhanced by deft strokes of makeup that made them appear greener than ever, golden flecks against the deep emerald of her irises. A gentle blush kissed her cheeks, imbuing her with a warmth that radiated joy, while her lips, tinted a soft, rosy pink, seemed to bloom with life, drawn larger and more inviting. She would have looked like the perfect little doll if not for the gown, overly voluminous and draping awkwardly around her slender waist.

Iverlyn remembered how her sister had filled out the gown when it was her turn to wear it; despite it resembling the plainest sleepwear, she had made it look elegant. The silky cloth draping smoothly over her curves accentuated her body in a way that a bride on her wedding night could only hope for. She practically seduced the bloodstone into declaring her of pure blood. Iverlyn, however, looked like a child playing dress up with her mother's clothes. The gown hung loosely on her petite body, hovering barely half an inch from the floor as it skirted across the top of her foot. Befitting, she thought, for her appearance to be so lackluster on the day she would be declared impure.

"Tonight, we stand before you, Zaria, Goddess of the Night, and ask you to lay judgment down upon us," Seraphina's voice echoed in the night air, and the townspeople that had gathered around the altar fell quiet. "Tonight, we offer you Iverlyn Wardwell, the youngest of the Wardwell family, and we ask that you bless her just as you have blessed us all. With your approval, she shall be welcomed into our sisterhood with open arms." Seraphina threw her arms open wide in a flourish as the crowd around them erupted in cheers.

Iverlyn combed through the sea of faces, searching for the only person who could calm her nerves at that moment, but Theo was nowhere to be found. Maybe he was running late.

"Are you ready?" Seraphina asked. A forced smile adorned her face as she reached out and gingerly tucked a strand of hair behind Iverlyn's ear. Iverlyn resisted the urge to flinch away from her aunt's touch as her hand lingered on her cheek in a gentle caress. To anyone else, it would seem that her aunt was calming her nerves and reassuring her that all would be well. It was all an act, of course, and a good one at that. Seraphina had always been talented at making people see what she wanted them to see. And tonight, as they stood on the white, ashen altar with the eyes of the entire coven on them, her aunt wanted them to see that she was loving, caring, and supportive. Three words that Iverlyn didn't think she'd ever use to describe Seraphina.

Iverlyn had attended a handful of bloodstone rituals over the years, but as she stood there staring at the altar where the stone glimmered in the moonlight, she felt different—eager. A chill ran down her spine as a warm breeze wrapped around her, almost pulling her toward the large, jagged stone. It was a beautiful sight to behold. Iverlyn couldn't deny it.

Seraphina nudged Iverlyn up the marbled stairs leading to the stone. With each step she took, she swore she could feel power rolling off the stone in anticipation. Or perhaps the power was from the group of elders who awaited her. They were clad in black cloaks that cast daunting shadows over their faces, making it nearly impossible to tell one apart from the other. Iverlyn couldn't see their eyes, but she knew their gazes bored into her as they waited with interlocked hands, only leaving a gap large enough for her to walk through, where Seraphina would take her place as the thirteenth and final elder before the ritual began.

"Do you remember what to do?" Seraphina asked as Iverlyn cleared the final step and stood before the stone. She had only seen it from afar, but it was a sight to behold up close. Each jagged edge of the large stone looked like a blade ready to be wielded. Standing next to it, Iverlyn felt small and weak. It gleamed wickedly, turning Iverlyn's blood to ice as the red streaks on the blackened stone seemed to beckon to her.

"Iverlyn." Seraphina's clipped tone snapped her out of the trance she had fallen into. "Are you ready?" she repeated, and Iverlyn could see the irritation flare in her eyes despite the calm voice and gentle smile she wore.

Iverlyn nodded, her voice caged by the trembling nerves coursing through her. *This is it. Everyone's eyes are on you. You can not fail. You* will *not fail.* She locked eyes with Seraphina as she clung to the mantra, repeating it in her mind. Maybe if she believed it hard enough, it would be true. Iverlyn knew it took restraint for her aunt not to show annoyance and distaste towards her as they stood there. She never allowed anyone to see anything but a united front regarding her family. *Conflict within the family is a weakness; we must never show weakness,* Seraphina would say, her head held tall in a way that emanated excellence.

The moon was directly above them now, and the elders began quiet chants as Seraphina pulled the ritualistic blade from within her cloak, offering it to Iverlyn. "*Sanguis ad lapidem,*" Seraphina intoned, her voice a silken whisper that entwined with the cool night air. She lifted her hood, pulling the dark fabric closely around her face, concealing her features in shadow, just as the other elders had done.

Iverlyn's fingers curled around the black obsidian handle as she tried to contain the tremors coursing through her body. *You can not fail. You will not fail.* Seraphina gave Iverlyn one final clipped nod before she stepped back and took her place in the circle. A black veil grew around them, shielding the view of the townspeople who had gathered below.

It was a stunning blade, one that Iverlyn had admired countless times in Seraphina's study, where it was prominently displayed. The hilt felt cool against her skin, its obsidian surface interlaced with shimmering streaks of silver that danced in the moonlight. To her surprise, the dagger felt heavier than she had anticipated; and with each incantation echoing around her, the hilt began to warm, a mysterious shadowy aura clinging to it. As she unsheathed the weapon, it revealed itself as a gleaming silver masterpiece, decorated with intricate swirls and bearing the Latin inscription *en sanguis eius exquiritur* meticulously etched into the blade.

Gripping the handle firmly with both hands, she raised the blade high above her head toward the starlit night sky, following the precise instructions given earlier until the solemn chanting ceased. With deliberate care, she lowered the blade, holding it tightly in her left hand as she hovered her right hand over the ancient bloodstone. Bringing the blade to her palm, she felt a sharp, chilling sensation upon contact, wincing as the cool edge traced through the lifeline on her palm. Her breath hitched, mingling with the collective gasp of everyone who had been watching silently below around the altar as her blood trickled down her hand, splattering onto the sacred stone below.

She watched as her blood rolled down the stone. Iverlyn felt as if she had been suspended in time, being held captive as she willed the stone before her to glow. Silently praying, *begging* her ancestors for acceptance. Everyone around her remained trapped in a stillness of anticipation. Breaths were not drawn, hearts did not beat, and even the wind didn't dare to howl. *You can not fail. You will not fail.*

As the seconds stretched on and the stone failed to glow that red hue of acceptance, Iverlyn felt her heart plummet to her stomach. The black veil that had risen during the ritual fell, revealing the townsfolk who watched with wide eyes. *I'll make you wish you died with your mother.* Seraphina's threat from the night before loomed over her with a taunting surety. *She had failed.*

The blade clattering to the floor shattered the heavy silence as Iverlyn stood frozen, fearing what awaited her in the coming moments. *She had failed.* Blood continued to spill from the small cut on her palm, staining the once-pristine white dress she was wearing, marking even the clothes she wore as imperfect. The silence was so heavy that Iverlyn could almost hear the splat of her blood as it landed on the stone at her feet. Zaria had marked her as impure.

Chapter Four

Failure. Disgrace. Impure. Iverlyn was numb. The world buzzed around her as her fate was determined, but she didn't hear anything aside from the few words that broke through the sound of her pounding heart, looping in her head. *Failure. Disgrace. Impure.*

The walk home from the ritual was a blur of hushed voices, and Iverlyn found herself in a daze. The shocked whispers of the town echoed unrepentantly in Iverlyn's mind, forcing her to replay the events. The night air, usually heavy with humidity from the relentless seas, was frigid as she began her descent from the altar—almost as if it, too, were disappointed in her failure. The indistinct murmurs of the town held her hostage at the bottom of the dais until Seraphina's biting grip cut into the flesh of her upper arm, dragging her through the crowd.

Still, she didn't know how she had come to be sitting in the dimly lit living room while the rest of her family discussed her fate the next room over. The gnawing ache from her hand persisted, although it had stopped bleeding thanks to the white cloth tightly wound around it. *When had that happened?* The panic of desperation still clung tightly to her chest as she wondered why Theo wasn't at the Ritual, remembering how she had feverishly searched the crowd only to be met with the judging eyes of the town. *He promised he'd be there.*

"We can't stand for this. She's made a fool out of us all." A voice she thought belonged to a distant cousin boomed across the room. Why was he even here? Had she caused such an uproar in the family that they needed a debate on such a large scale? Or maybe this was normal when one failed the bloodstone. She caught Isodyl's gaze and could have sworn that she saw something of sorrow in it, but it was quickly masked with her usual cold look.

No one bothered to move to comfort Iverlyn; as far as they were concerned, she was nothing more than an inconvenience they needed to deal with when the bloodstone failed to glow. To them, being marked by the bloodstone as impure meant that you were no longer their blood. Instead, she was a pesky annoyance similar to the vermin that Seraphina poisoned if they dared enter her yard each summer; but something in Iverlyn's gut told her that whatever Seraphina decided to do with her would be far crueler than the fast-acting poison she used to get rid of them.

"Iverlyn. Come." Seraphina's curt words brought her attention to the scouring faces before her, summoning her like a dog.

She stood up slowly, wishing her trembling limbs to be still. *Don't be such a coward,* she scolded herself, hating that she was only further proving to the judging faces that stood before her that she didn't belong.

It'll all work out in the end. Iverlyn remembered Theo's words. He had been so sure that no matter what happened, she would be okay, and things would improve. But where was he now that she had failed? Theo had promised Iverlyn he'd be there at the ritual, knowing how much a friendly face would mean to her. She wondered if the news had even reached him yet. Surely, it had. The one family in Salus that never had a daughter marked as impure had finally failed. She imagined the news was buzzing all over.

"We've decided," Seraphina began, her lips drawn in a taut line, "that while many of us wish to see you exiled for the catastrophic embarrassment you have brought onto this family, we as a whole," she paused, sending Iverlyn's brutish cousin a pointed look as if she were daring him to step out of line and object, "believe that while you may be beyond saving, perhaps you still have a chance to make things right." Iverlyn's blood ran cold at the malicious gleam in her aunt's eyes and the hint of a cruel smile that tugged at her lips. *I'll make you wish you died with your mother.*

"As I'm sure you've heard, Alastair Proctor has been looking for a new wife, as his first wife passed away earlier this year, leaving the Proctor family without an heir." Iverlyn's heart seized in her chest. *No. No, anything else. Anyone else.*

"We think this is the perfect opportunity to merge our families. While the magic may have failed in you, we still believe it's possible that with the help of his bloodline, your children..." Seraphina was still talking, but Iverlyn could hear nothing but the rushing blood in her ears. *They wanted her to have his children.*

Chills ran down Iverlyn's spine at the thought of being in the same room as that man, let alone being *married* to him. He was the last of the stronger bloodlines, her family being the strongest. Rumor was that he killed his wife once he learned that she couldn't bear any children. Marriage was sacred in Salus, and once married, one did not divorce, only remarrying on the rarest of occasions. It was suspected that Alastair killed his wife so he would be able to remarry and grow his bloodline, his mother being the last female in his family to be gifted, and him being her only child.

Although Alastair's family lacked a female heir, the power that ran through their veins and the vast wealth they flaunted at every social event was second only to her family's. She imagined that they had fetched a pretty price for her. Regardless of her failure, she was still a Wardwell; and no matter how much she wished otherwise, the Wardwell magic still ran through her, even if she could not wield it.

"He will be here soon to discuss the details of our arrangement, so go change. Isodyl has picked a dress for you to put on," Seraphina continued, her words breaking through the panic vibrating Iverlyn's body.

Iverlyn felt numb as the words sank in. She realized that she had been reduced to nothing more than a pawn for her family to win the favor of a man who might have murdered his wife. Any hope she had for a better life had been ripped away. While Seraphina spoke as if they were doing Iverlyn a favor by allowing her to marry Alastair, Iverlyn knew this was her aunt's way of fulfilling her vow to her last night in the study. *I'll make you wish you died with your mother.*

Alastair's footsteps reverberated through the all-too-quiet room as he stalked around her, circling her as if she were his prey. By the time she had returned from changing, Alastair had already arrived, and the rest of the family had been dismissed; but Seraphina remained, silently observing in the corner, no doubt relishing in the fear that was trembling through Iverlyn's body as the man scoured her up and down.

He towered above her, standing nearly a foot taller than her petite frame. His hair, a sophisticated blend of salt and pepper, was meticulously slicked back, every single strand obeying his command and refusing to betray even the slightest hint of disarray. Clad in tailored slacks that whispered of elegance and a black shirt perfectly tucked into his waistband, he presented an image of immaculate grooming—his attire unblemished by so much as a hint of a wrinkle. To any passerby on the street, he would have easily passed for the quintessential gentleman, embodying charm and sophistication with every calculated movement he made. But as Iverlyn dared to meet his gaze and saw the same dangerous gleam in it that Seraphina often had, she knew it was all an act.

The dress that her sister had helped her into was by far the nicest piece of clothing she had ever worn. It hugged her in a way that made her petite body seem *seductive*, accentuating features she hadn't realized she had. It even covered the scars that littered her body, leaving only the ones that wrapped around her collarbone visible. The emerald green fabric perfectly complemented her pale skin and copper hair, which Isodyl had teased into soft curls. This dress hadn't simply been chosen for her. No. It had been made for her, molding her body into one belonging to a seductress.

Alastair's fingertips caressed the exposed expanse of her upper back, bare from the low dip in her dress, halting just above the small of her spine. A shiver rippled through her body as his eager fingers traced a path across her front, skimming her collarbone and leaving a constellation of goosebumps in their wake. His fingers grazed the scarred skin, remnants of cruel punishments inflicted by her aunt, prompting his lip to curl into a snarl.

"Such a pity," he murmured, shaking his head in disapproval.

Her breath caught as he continued his meticulous examination, his fingers traveling up the curve of her neck. He cupped her chin with his bony, clammy hands, his grip almost bruising, compelling her to meet his gaze before planting himself in front of her.

"You are a pretty thing," he purred lustfully, his crooked smile revealing a vile intent. His eyes, filled with wicked desire, moved languidly over her body, taking in every detail with unsettling intensity. They narrowed as they settled on her marred skin. "Well, almost," he added with a snarl, the word dripping with contempt. Alastair was a man obsessed with perfection, priding himself on an ideal that left no room for flaws. Despite her fear, a tiny spark of hope flickered in Iverlyn's belly as she watched his gaze linger disparagingly on her scars. Could his disdain for her imperfections be enough to make him decline her family's offer?

She felt naked under his sinister gaze, and the longer his eyes raked over her, the more the dread built inside of her. His hands traveled to her waist, gripping her tightly and pulling her closer to him. She could feel his hot, heavy breath on her forehead, but she didn't dare look up.

"So," Seraphina started. Iverlyn had never been more thankful to hear her voice as Alastair loosened his grasp, and she quickly took a few steps back, creating some distance between them. "Are you satisfied with our arrangement?"

A few moments of silence stretched out, weighed by the thick tension in the air. She could almost feel the searing intensity of his gaze piercing through her as he reached out slowly, deliberately, twirling a strand of her hair around his finger. The very thought of meeting his eyes made her shudder; she had no desire to confront the unmistakable lust lurking within those dark chocolate orbs. A wave of disgust surged through her, twisting her stomach into tight, painful knots. How could her family hold her in such disregard, to the extent of condemning her to a life bound to this vile, loathsome man?

"She'll do."

The words echoed in her mind, thick with the weight of his intentions. She could feel his hot and oppressive breath sliding down her neck like a warning. His body was tense, a coiled spring ready to snap, and in that moment, the realization seeped through her. *She was in trouble.*

Chapter Five

I'll come collect you tomorrow, my bride. Alastair's parting words played on a loop as Iverlyn entered her room. *Collect*, as if she were nothing more than a prized doll for him to add to his collection.

You should be thankful, Seraphina told her as she saw the look of horror Iverlyn could not contain after Alastair had left. Perhaps a part of her should be relieved; she wouldn't put it past Seraphina to find some other ways of horror that would make her marriage to Alastair look like a dream. But as Iverlyn found herself in her room still shuddering from Alastair's gaze, skin aflame from his unwanted touch, all she felt was rage. Red hot rage that she had been diminished to nothing more than a pawn at her family's mercy—a womb for purchase. She didn't know what they gained from their arrangement with Alastair, but nothing was worth the virtue of her free will.

She studied herself in the mirror: how the emerald dress clung to her like a second skin, molding certain areas of her body to look more pronounced. It was the dress of a seductress, and she *hated* it. It was no coincidence that this was the one that had been chosen for her tonight. Seraphina wanted to be sure that Alastair lusted after Iverlyn, and judging by his groping hands and lingering stares, she had succeeded.

Disgust roiled in her stomach as she remembered the way his hands had wandered over her body; the way his breath, heavy with need, had washed over her skin; the way his lustful eyes had undressed her and marked her as his own. Tears welled behind her eyes as she stared at her reflection, stared at the body that he had seemed to crave so much. This couldn't be her life. She needed to get out. Get out of this dress, out of this house, out of Salus.

A strangled sob escaped her lips as she clawed at the zipper on the dress, desperately trying to pull it off, but she couldn't reach it. *How was this her life?* She kicked off one of the black heels that Isodyl had insisted she wear and threw it at the mirror before her, watching as cracks spiderwebbed their way across it, a few shards breaking free and clattering to the ground.

She sank to her knees as another sob wracked her body. She had to find a way out. *Any* way out. As if answering her plea, the moonlight snaked in through her window and glimmered in the shards of glass that had broken free. They stared back at her, a silent siren's call that promised relief—promised *freedom*.

She reached out and gingerly grasped one of the shards, catching her reflection in the shattered mirror. Tears streamed down her face, and the makeup that Isodyl and Elara had expertly applied ran down her cheeks in black rivers of desperation. She wondered if Alastair saw her now, broken and crumpled on the floor, if he would think she was such a prize.

She turned the shard of glass over in her hands, studying it as it twinkled in the moonlight, promising her the freedom she craved.

"Ivy?" Theo's tender voice sounded out from behind her. She jumped, a small scream escaping her lips as she tumbled forward in surprise, cutting her hand in the process. "Ivy, are you okay?" Theo asked. He knelt beside her and placed a warm hand on her back that she instinctively flinched away from.

She stumbled to her feet, not bothering to pay any mind to the bleeding gash at the base of her palm. "What are you doing here?"

Theo watched her with weary eyes as he walked towards her slowly, pulled the glass shard she was still clutching out of her hand, and placed it on the desk beside him. "I came to get you," he said as his eyes swept over the shattered mirror and the discarded heel that she had speared towards it.

"Get me?"

"I found a way off the island. I'm taking you somewhere safe, but we have to be quick. We don't have much time." He walked over to the closet and started rummaging through it, but Iverlyn was too shocked to move. Too stunned to comprehend what was going on. *He found a way off the island?* How was that even possible?

"You'll have to pack light, so only take what's necessary. We'll get you whatever you need when we get to where we're going," Theo continued as he dumped out the contents of her old school bag, which had been stuffed in the back of her closet, and started filling it with items.

"Ivy? Are you hearing me? We don't have long."

"H-how are you here?" she asked.

He walked over to her and cradled her face in his large hands, rubbing away the tears that had stained her cheeks. "I promise you I'll explain everything later." He paused, taking her still-bleeding hand and wrapping a piece of fabric around it. "But for now, we really need to go."

"Is there anything you want to bring?"

"No." Iverlyn looked around the room. It was plain; Seraphina had destroyed everything that had meant anything to her out of spite. Her only personal belonging was the casting ring that still adorned her finger.

"You're going to want to change," he said as he thrust clothes into her hands. She stared down at them and then at the bag that he held. *Was this really happening? Would she actually be free?*

"We've got to go," he urged again, snapping her out of her gaze.

"My dress, I can't unzip it," she said sheepishly, her cheeks burning in embarrassment.

Theo cleared the room in two strides and gingerly unzipped her dress before facing the window, giving her the privacy she needed to change.

"Where will we go?" she questioned him as she peeled the emerald dress off, slipping into the clothes he had laid out for her. She did not miss that he had chosen her favorite t-shirt—one that had once belonged to him, one that she found herself sleeping in whenever she needed a little extra comfort from the harsh realities of her life.

"Somewhere safe. There's a lot I need to explain, and I promise I will. But first, we need to go," Theo urged as he walked over to her window, flinging it open, where a ladder was waiting.

Iverlyn felt a blossom of hope flutter in her chest as she stared at her friend's outstretched hand. *It'll all work out in the end,* he had promised her, and as she placed her hand into his, he guided her out the window and onto the ladder, she finally allowed herself to believe him.

"Don't," Seraphina's voice thundered over Iverlyn in a staggering command, "take another step."

Iverlyn stilled one foot on the dock and the other on the small ramp leading to the boat, her freedom only a few steps away. So close she could almost taste the sweet promise of it, but she couldn't bring herself to move as she turned to see Seraphina stalking towards them with predatory intent. Iverlyn didn't know if it was the fear of what Seraphina would do when she reached them or if her aunt had used her magic to root her to the swaying dock; but Iverlyn was frozen, her eyes wide, heart thundering in her chest as Seraphina's lips curled into a smile that made her skin crawl.

"You stupid, stupid girl," Seraphina seethed as she prowled closer, "I've always known you to be a failure, but I didn't expect you to be a coward." She spat the word, her lips curling in disgust.

The flare of the boat engine roaring to life filled the air. Theo had reached the boat.

"Ivy, we can still make it," Theo called behind her. He thought they still stood a chance. *Oh, how wrong he was.* Seraphina wouldn't let her off this island, even if it meant killing her. Her magic was formidable to even the most practiced witches, and Iverlyn was not a practiced witch. She should tell him to go, leave her, save himself. But even her voice seemed trapped by the vice grip of the fear that sounded through her. *There was no way out.*

"You thought you were clever, didn't you?" Seraphina took another menacing step towards them, the inky burgundy tendrils of her magic snaking towards them like snakes preparing to strike. Iverlyn knew Seraphina had them cornered, knew that even if they did try to flee on the rumbling boat, all it would take was a simple incantation from Seraphina to stop them.

"Ivy, just get on the boat," Theo called out, his hand outstretched to hers. He seemed so sure and so valiant in his efforts to save her, but Iverlyn knew all he did was condemn himself to face Seraphina's wrath. Wrath that she knew he wouldn't survive. Seraphina had never liked him, but now that he had tried to help her escape, he wouldn't be leaving this boat ramp alive. Not unless he left her behind.

Tears welled in her eyes as she turned to face her friend. She couldn't go with him, but she could ensure that Seraphina was focused on her long enough for him to escape. Theo shook his head as their gazes met, as if he saw the words she failed to speak. *Go. You have to go.*

"Get on the boat," Theo pleaded, his eyes wide.

A tear rolled down Iverlyn's face as she looked at her friend one last time. "She won't kill me, but she will kill you. You have to go,

Theo. Please," she begged, her voice cracking over the last word, a heavy stream of tears rolling down her cheeks. She couldn't live with herself if something happened to him.

The panic was setting in, and Iverlyn could feel her limbs begin to quake; but she refused to give into it, not this time, not when Theo's life depended on it. "Take me and let him leave."

"Oh, isn't this touching," Seraphina mused from where she stood a few feet away. She hadn't moved any closer, but her magic snaked from her body and was coiled just inches away from Iverlyn's feet, ready to strike. "The little mouse has finally found her courage, and for a boy who isn't a boy after all. Isn't that right, Theo?" Seraphina's gaze locked on Theo as she studied him, as if trying to unravel a mystery. "It seems that you really are your mother's daughter," she tsked, turning her gaze back onto Iverlyn.

She knew what her aunt was trying to do, and she wouldn't fall for it. She had always claimed that something was off about Theo, that he had nefarious reasons for growing close to Iverlyn, but it was all attempts to shatter the relationship they shared. Iverlyn had never fallen for them before, and she wasn't about to now.

"Just let her go. I can take her far away from here. You'll never have to see her again." Panic surged through Iverlyn as she watched her aunt's heated gaze return to Theo. He was going to get himself killed.

Seraphina's eyes lit up with dangerous humor as she chuckled. "Tell me, Theo," she began with a raised brow. "Does our little mouse here know who you truly are? Do you think she'll still want to go with you when she finds out you have lied to her all these years?"

Theo's jaw ticked, and his hands clenched into fists at his sides. He glared at Seraphina but didn't object to what she said.

"Tell me." Seraphina's magic flicked upwards, snaking its way up Iverlyn's legs and past her torso until it became a loose collar around her neck. Iverlyn felt the familiar bite of her aunt's magic as it settled over her skin. "How did you hide yourself so well all these years?" Seraphina's gaze was still fixed on Theo as if he were a puzzle she was trying to piece together.

Theo remained silent, his jaw tense as he met Seraphina's stare. He wasn't denying it. Why wasn't he denying it? It couldn't be true. Her aunt couldn't have been right after all these years.

"Let her go," he growled, the sound rumbling like thunder from deep in his chest. A fierce glint sparked in his eyes, one that Iverlyn had never seen before in all the years of their friendship. It was raw and primal, an unmistakable hint of something beyond human.

"And if I don't?" Seraphina baited as the magic collar flicked around Iverlyn's neck, a reminder that her aunt had the upper hand. She was playing a game with him, goading him to play along by using Iverlyn as a pawn.

"You don't want to find out." Theo's voice was icy and no longer his own.

"Oh, but I do," Seraphina purred, her lips tilted in a vile grin. "I really, *really* do."

Iverlyn gasped as the magical leash grew tighter around her neck, biting into her skin.

Theo bristled, his eyes flaring in anger. "Do not do this," he warned in that same primal voice from before. *What was happening?*

Seraphina's only response was the wicked gleam in her eyes as her magic swelled, growing tighter around Iverlyn's throat until she couldn't draw air into her lungs. She tried to claw at the magic that had fused itself to her skin, but her arms were restrained at her sides, leaving her helpless as her aunt stared at Theo, waiting, baiting him to act.

Iverlyn's vision began to blur, a kaleidoscope of darkened spots dancing before her eyes. Each frantic beat of her heart reverberated through her ears, the wild rhythm gradually slowing with each passing second. Her lungs ached, burning with an intense, desperate need for air. Iverlyn's knees buckled beneath her. The only thing keeping her upright was the magic-trapped vines around her body. Was this the end? Was this how she was going to die?

A slew of curses left Theo as a bright orb of light exploded from his position. A surge of power rushed forward, crashing into Seraphina and sending her sprawling backward. Her magic faltered, retreating hastily and leaving Iverlyn crumpled on the dock like a discarded doll. Before Iverlyn could even grasp the chaos unfolding around her, Theo scooped her into his arms. In the blink of an eye, they found themselves on the boat. But not before Seraphina's magic lashed out again, coiling around Iverlyn's throat with a deadly intent, a vice grip that promised not to falter this time.

Her chest ached, her lungs burned, her head lolled to the side, and her arms fell limp; her body felt too heavy, too tired, as black spots danced before her vision, threatening to consume her.

"Just hold on, Ivy. We're almost there," Theo's voice called out to her, but as her vision grew black and her body fell to the cold, damp floor of the boat, she knew it was over—that she had lost. The last thing she heard before the blackness consumed her was Seraphina's victorious cackle filling the night air. But at least now she was *free*.

Chapter Six

As a calm wind tickled her face, Iverlyn felt like she was floating, cocooned in a sea of darkness. Was this what death felt like? Wetness dappled her cheek as she rocked, the sound of waves crashing against a shore as a lullaby for her aching body—a body she wouldn't have if she were dead.

"Ivy? Open your eyes for me." Theo's timid voice floated through the air, wrapping around her like a warm embrace. He was alive. *She* was alive.

A laugh sputtered out of her aching chest as she opened her eyes, meeting the vast expanse of the sky. The midnight colors were now bleeding into a symphony of purples, pinks, and oranges as the sun began to peek over the horizon. *This was freedom's visage.* The heavy, salty scent of the sea perfumed the air. *This was freedom's flavor.* The cool, misty breeze caressed her skin, washing away the lingering years of dread. *This was freedom's touch.* They were alive.

"Are you alright?" Theo asked as he gingerly placed a hand under her shoulder before pulling her into a seated position.

"I'm alive. We're alive," she said, not quite believing the words as they left her mouth. *She was free. She was free. She was fr—* The ecstasy of their escape began wearing off with a brutal harshness as she recounted the events that happened. Seraphina holding her hostage in her burning tendrils of magic, Theo trying to convince her to let them flee, Seraphina recognizing something in Theo that Iverlyn never had in the seven years of their friendship, and then Theo... Theo had magic. He saved her, and he had *magic.* Iverlyn shuffled away from him until her back was flush against the inner wall of the boat. Her eyes were wide as she stared at the man before her. Seven years of friendship, and she didn't know he had magic. How was it even possible?

"I... I don't understand," she mumbled, shaking her head as she remembered how a burst of light had almost seemed to explode from him, the way a wave of power so strong that it knocked Seraphina off balance had surged from him.

"I have a lot to explain," Theo said as he stood up from his crouched position and offered her an outstretched hand. "And I promise I will, but we need to get somewhere safe. If they decide to come after us, we're sitting ducks on the water."

Iverlyn peeked her head up over the wall of the boat to see that they were in the middle of the ocean, with no signs of land in any direction. How far had he taken them before she woke up? Iverlyn looked at his outstretched hand wearily as Seraphina's words replayed in her mind—a *boy who really isn't a boy after all.* Iverlyn remembered the animalistic growl that had left him, the way his eyes had gleamed with something far older and far more dangerous than the twenty-one-year-old man she had come to know.

"Who are you?" she asked, feeling a small piece of her heart break away from his betrayal.

"I'm still Theo. I've always been Theo." There was a sadness behind his eyes as he withdrew his outstretched hand and shoved it into his pocket. It made Iverlyn want to reach out and hug him, to tell him that it would be okay, just like he had done to her so many times before, but she didn't. At that moment, as her heart lay crumbling within her chest, she wasn't sure things would ever be okay again.

It had been nearly two hours since either of them had uttered a word, and Iverlyn was growing tired of her overwhelming list of unanswered questions. After a long hour of fighting a losing battle with sea sickness, Iverlyn was thankful when land came into view. She didn't know what she expected to find, but she was disappointed to see only a single car parked in an empty field with no soul in sight. In truth, it didn't look much different than Salus, with its flat, sandy shores and gulls circling above as the early morning sun filtered through the clouds. The car was for them, and Theo wasted no time before ushering her into it, claiming that they needed to keep moving. That was the last time he had spoken to her.

She sighed as she continued staring out of the window in silence. Somewhere along the way, the flat, sandy lands laid out before them had begun to mold into a patchwork of rolling hills of flourishing farmlands, a sight Iverlyn wasn't used to seeing. It wasn't that they didn't have farmland in Salus. They did, but it was nothing compared to the expansive fields unfurling before them as they drove.

"Have you always been able to do magic?" Iverlyn found herself breaking the silence, no longer able to bear it. Although magic flowed through the veins of everyone in Salus, men and women alike, it was unheard of for men to be able to wield it.

Theo glanced in her direction, surprise flitting across his features before returning to the road before them. "Yes. I was born with it. Like those in Salus, our abilities mature by age twenty-one; but unlike members of the coven, our magic is a gift that we are born with, rather than one that is taken."

Born with it. Theo had moved into her town at fourteen, where they had become fast friends, or so she thought.

"You said *our.* There's more of you?" she asked.

Theo thrummed his fingers against the steering wheel as if he were deciding whether or not to answer before he sighed and nodded. "There are, and once we get where we are going, I promise to–"

"Tell me everything. Yeah, I got that the first three times you said it," she snapped, cutting him off and laying her head against the cool window with an annoyed huff. She felt guilty for being angry with him—he had just saved her life, after all—but she couldn't help but wonder how much of their friendship had been a lie.

"The story you told me," she started, "about your parents... how they died?" Her question left her lips in a whisper. She didn't know if she wanted the answer. She and Theo had been friends for nearly a month before he had opened up to her about how his parents had perished in a gruesome car crash that had left him orphaned. With no family left, a distant relative who resided on the island and still had ties to the outside world took him in. His mom had been exiled from the island after failing the bloodstone ritual and had made a life for herself, one that Iverlyn often thought about as a reminder that there was more in the world than just Salus. When he shared his story of his grief with her, that was the first time she had felt genuinely safe with Theo. It was the first time that she had felt seen. She didn't think she would ever forget the rawness of his sorrow, the way his eyes glistened with the pain of the memory, and how his breath would catch ever so slightly whenever she mentioned his family.

She watched Theo as several moments passed, and her question went unanswered. It *had* been a lie. They bonded over the shared loss of their parents, and it was all a lie. She suspected he had concocted it for that reason precisely. *Trauma bonding.* And it had worked; Iverlyn felt alone in the world, never truly belonging in her family, constantly feeling like an unwelcome burden. Then along came Theo, orphaned and placed into a stranger's home. Iverlyn remembered the first time she learned of Theo's loss and the way she felt almost relieved to have someone to whom she could relate—then immediate guilt for feeling that way. She was drawn to him because he understood what it felt like to be alone. He knew the crushing weight of feeling as if your very existence was a burden, and she felt a sort of peace because of that; at least she wasn't alone in her misery. A sharp jab radiated through her chest, twisting her gut as she realized none of it was true.

"It was all a lie, then?" she asked, hating how her voice broke as the words passed through her lips. She hated the way her chest seemed to crack open under the weight of knowing that he had lied to her for so many years about so many things. She felt tears welling in her eyes as he remained quiet. The only sign that he had heard her question was the slight tick in his jaw and tightening of his grip on the steering wheel.

Iverlyn forced her gaze away from the man sitting beside her, and the friend she was starting to realize was just a stranger. As she stared out the window, gazing out over the endless field of trees as they drove down the winding road, she couldn't help but wonder; if Seraphina had been right about Theo all those years, then perhaps her aunt was right about her as well.

Chapter Seven

I verlyn sighed, watching Theo's back as he pushed up the rocky trail ahead. Since leaving the car, not a single word had passed through his lips—forty-five minutes of silence punctuated only by the crunch of fallen leaves and the rocky terrain beneath their feet. He had taken her bag, slung it carelessly over his shoulder, and set off without so much as a glance back.

She had never seen a mountain like this before. On Salus, the terrain was mostly flat; as she stared at the looming incline before her, rocks jutting out at every angle, large roots blanketed by layers of leaves, she realized the so-called mountain on the island had been nothing more than a large hill.

She also hadn't seen so many colors in the trees before. The canopy above was beginning to melt into an array of oranges and yellows. It reminded Iverlyn of the way the sky seemed to paint itself at every sunset in Salus, and she wondered if the sunsets here were the same, if she'd even be able to see one where they were going.

A gust of wind danced between the trees, and Iverlyn wrapped her arms tighter around her midsection. She wished she had grabbed a jacket. The air here was thinner than she was used to, and was growing brisk, the sky above them beginning to darken with the threat of rain. She swore the temperature had dropped at least ten degrees. It didn't bother Theo; he seemed almost eager as he continued climbing the steep mountainside. Her legs ached, and her lungs burned with each inhale as she battled her way up, wishing she found the trek as easy as the man before her did.

The old Theo would have stopped for her, let her find her footing, and extended his hand for those tricky moments. In truth, the old Theo wouldn't have needed to stop at all because he would have stayed right by her side. But this Theo? This Theo was something else entirely. He was a powerhouse of muscle and grace, forging ahead with relentless determination, hardly sparing a glance backward. Not that he needed to. She imagined the sound of her stumbling steps and labored breaths were enough to assure him that she was still following along the path he had forged for them.

"Are we," *huff*, "almost," *huff*, "there?" Iverlyn wheezed out as she collapsed forward, bracing her hands on her knees. If you had asked her if she was in shape before this hike, she might have said yes; but now, as her lungs burned and her legs quaked beneath her, she felt quite the opposite.

The crunch of the fallen leaves stopped before her as she heaved air into her lungs. She was sure she looked pathetic and didn't dare meet his gaze.

"It's not too much farther," Theo said. His voice was distant, lacking the gentleness it usually carried when he spoke to her. She tried not to take it personally—after all, the man before her was no longer the Theo she had grown to love over the years—but she couldn't help the stabbing pain in her chest as she heard him speak to her in a tone that she had only ever heard him use with those he didn't care for. Iverlyn had never been one of those people, not with Theo. Was he disappointed in her because she failed, and he had to expose his secrets to save her? Or was there something else she was missing?

Another brisk breeze brushed across her skin, causing a shiver to run up her spine. She heard the crunch of leaves as Theo advanced towards her, but she still didn't dare to look up—not even when his muddy boots stared up at her from where she hunched over, lapping the air into her lungs.

"I know you need a break, but we can't afford to stop," he said in that emotionless voice. "It's going to storm, and if you think this is hard now, it's about to be a lot worse when the ground is slick from the rain." A clash of thunder rang out in the distance as if to prove his point.

Iverlyn sighed as she shoved herself forward, still not bothering to look at the man who stood before her. She walked around him, willing the tears away, ignoring the quake in her bones and the chilling pain from the blistering bruises around her neck.

"Ivy, wait," Theo said with a defeated sigh, his fingertips brushing her back.

She stilled but didn't turn to meet his gaze. It wasn't that she was trying to be difficult; Iverlyn just didn't think her heart could handle seeing his gaze so devoid of emotion, like the Theo she had grown up with had disappeared entirely, and she was nothing more than an inconvenience.

A shuffle behind her broke through the tense silence, but she remained with her back towards him, and he opted to remain quiet, letting the silence hang heavily between them. It remained that way even when the warm, earthy scent of vanilla and sandalwood enveloped her in a gentle caress. It was his scent. The same one she had gifted him just last year on his birthday. If it even *was* his birthday. If he'd lied about his parents and his magic, then she supposed he could've lied about that too. The aroma only embraced her further as Theo tugged a warm hoodie over her head, *his hoodie.* Her heart swelled at the act as she stifled the urge to bring the soft, warm material to her nose and breathe his scent in. Maybe the old Theo was still there.

"We're here," Theo said as he stopped before a large stone wall. Iverlyn glanced up at it with wide eyes, its stones slick from the slight drizzle of rain that had begun just moments ago.

"We aren't going to climb that... right?" she asked.

Humor sparked in Theo's eyes. He seemed more relaxed now, like the Theo she had grown up with. "No," he answered through a chuckle.

Iverlyn nodded slowly, looking around to see if she had missed anything, but the rock wall before them stretched as far as the eye could see. "I don't understand."

Theo's grin widened, and his eyes lit up with childlike enthusiasm. He reached his hand out and placed it on the wall—no, he placed it *through* the wall.

Theo reached out, grasping her hand in his, and gently pulled her along. The wall before them shimmered and then vanished, revealing a mesmerizing panorama. She was perched on the peak of a majestic mountain, overlooking a landscape that seemed plucked straight from a fairy tale. The world below thrummed with life

64

and vitality. The sky, now clear of clouds, bathed the scenery in a radiant glow, with the sun casting its golden rays across the horizon. Small, quaint cabins dotted the landscape, nestled alongside sparkling brooks that meandered into a large, serene river, its waters glistening in the sunlight. Farm animals roamed freely, grazing on verdant pastures, while birds filled the air with their melodic chirping. If she listened closely, she could hear the distant sound of children's laughter, adding to the enchantment of the scene. At that moment, an overwhelming sense of peace and warmth enveloped her like she had entered a new world.

Iverlyn had heard of cloaking spells before, but to hide an entire realm? The amount of magic and sheer power it must take to conceal it from prying eyes... she couldn't even begin to imagine.

"Welcome to Arbor. Welcome to my home."

Chapter Eight

"It's beautiful," Iverlyn mused, unable to tear her eyes away from the view before her.

Iverlyn didn't know where to look, didn't know how to process the whole new world she had just walked into. It had been a wall of stone, and a large one at that, and now... well, she was breathless from the sight before her.

"How?" she asked, her voice trembling as her gaze was stuck on the landscape before her.

"Some ancient, very powerful magic," Theo answered from beside her. All tension had melted away from him when they stepped over the barrier. In all her years of knowing him, she didn't think she had ever seen him so relaxed, so relieved.

"No one in Salus could ever do something like this," she mused, primarily to herself. If her family knew that magic so powerful existed, they would go to any length to attain it. Iverlyn didn't even want to consider the type of havoc they'd cause.

"The power that Salus was built off of is nothing compared to this."

"And this power," Iverlyn started, allowing her eyes to sweep across the vast world at her feet. "Is it how you were able to stop Seraphina?"

Theo nodded, his hair flopping down into his eyes from the movement. Iverlyn took a deep breath as she moved to a nearby boulder and let herself sink onto it. Theo had magic all those years. He had magic rivaling Seraphina's, which could have saved her from the years of torment. Not only that, but he had somewhere he called home; somewhere that Iverlyn felt would soon become her home.

"Why now?" she asked quietly, "Why bring me here *now*?" All those times they had fantasized of running away, of escaping the horrors she faced on that island—they could've escaped years ago. She could have been safe.

Theo sighed, sitting down beside her, "I know you have a lot of questions—"

"Questions you promised to answer when we got here," she said with a pointed stare.

Theo nodded and ran his fingers through his hair. "I did, and I'll answer them all, I swear, but we have a little farther to go."

Iverlyn sent him an icy glare and threw her arms across her chest. As childish as it might have seemed, she would sit on that boulder until he gave her some answers. "I'm not going anywhere else with you until you tell me what's happening."

Theo stared at her as if trying to determine if she was serious. Iverlyn tucked her legs onto the boulder, crisscrossing them underneath her, planting herself firmly. "I'll answer one here and the rest when we get to the cabin," he said.

"Two. You'll answer two now," Iverlyn said firmly. She had never been good at bargaining on her behalf, something that Theo had been telling her to work on for years now. Judging by the hint of a grin that spread across his face, he saw the irony in it as well.

"Fine, two questions, and then we start walking again."

Iverlyn smiled triumphantly as she fidgeted with the casting ring on her finger, trying to figure out what questions to ask when the faint scar on her wrist glinted in the sunlight.

"You know," she stared, tracing her fingers across the scar, "the night I got this scar, I thought I was going to die, and I expect I would have had it not been for you. Seraphina was so mad that ni ght..." Iverlyn mused, shaking her head as the chill of the memory snaked up her spine.

The rest of the elders had just opposed her aunt at a coven meeting, which rarely happened. They all knew and respected that Seraphina held more power than any of them, and Iverlyn had always suspected that they were afraid to go against her. But that night was different. Iverlyn didn't know why they had opposed Seraphina's rule or what it was for; all she remembered was the blazing anger in her aunt's eyes when she ripped Iverlyn from her bed and demanded that they train despite it being nearly midnight. Seraphina had blamed her for the other elders not bending to her will. Her aunt had claimed with so much certainty that the only reason they would ever dare oppose her was because they saw weakness in the fact that Iverlyn was still unable to wield her magic at the age of sixteen.

Seraphina had ordered Iverlyn to spill more blood when trying to cast the spell, had told her to slice her palm rather than use the small needle on the casting ring, and when Iverlyn hesitated...

Iverlyn shook the memory from her mind, clearing her throat, "That night, you found me half dead on the beach, and do you remember the words you said to me?" Iverlyn asked, pulling her gaze to meet Theo's. "You told me that you wished you could take me away from the island, that we could build a life somewhere far away."

A haunted look passed over Theo's face, and he almost seemed to pale as the words left Iverlyn's mouth.

"So, my question is," tears bristled at the corner of her eyes, threatening to spill over, "why now, Theo? Why now and not *then*?"

Theo inhaled sharply as his gaze drifted to the scar Iverlyn was still tracing over her wrist. It was one of many, and he knew as much. "Ivy, I—" he started, standing up from the boulder and pacing before her. "You don't know how badly I wanted to get you out, but I—" he stopped short, a strangled sound coming from his throat, "I couldn't." The two words held so much anguish as they left his mouth that Iverlyn's heart nearly broke. *Nearly.*

"You couldn't, or you wouldn't?" She regretted the words the second they passed through her lips. She regretted them even more as she watched him recoil from them as if she had landed a physical blow.

"That's not fair. You don't know how hard it was for m—"

"How hard it was for you? *You!?*" Her words echoed through the forest, and everything around them seemed to shush into an eerie silence as the anger simmered in her belly. "Gods, Theo, how could I not have thought about how years of *my* abuse affected *you*," she seethed, every word lashing from her like a venomous strike.

Theo flinched at her words. "I didn't mean it like that."

"Then what? Tell me, how was this so hard for you?"

"You don't understand," Theo said, shaking his head, "I had no choice. I had orders, and I—"

"Orders?" Iverlyn's heart froze in her chest.

Theo grimaced as he noticed his mistake. He had said too much, letting Iverlyn hear something he wasn't ready for her to hear yet. "Let's not do this here. Let me get you to the cabin, and then I promise I will tell you everything."

"You promised two questions. What do you mean you had orders?"

"Come on, Ivy, please. You know I'll tell you everything," Theo pleaded, holding out a hand to her.

She stared at the hand before her, and for a moment, she considered taking it, but the sting of his betrayal bit back at her. She had every right to be angry with him. He owed her answers.

"Tell me," she insisted. "What do you mean you had orders?"

Theo's shoulders sagged in defeat as he threw his head back and sighed. "Fine, but you have to let me finish explaining it and promise not to get angry with me." He paused, his gaze sweeping over her tensed body. "Well, any angrier than you already are," he added. Iverlyn nodded. She didn't know if she could make any promises; but she would at least try if it got her the answers she was looking for, she was willing to try.

"What do you know about your father?" Theo asked. His questions almost seemed to echo off the surrounding trees as an icy chill washed over Iverlyn.

Her father. In the seven years she and Theo had known each other, he never asked her about her father. Not that it was a secret, but the whole town knew—or, at the very least, suspected—that she was the product of her mother's affair. Those suspicions only continued to grow when Fennrick, her sister's father, abandoned the island and Isodyl after her mother's death. She supposed any doubt Seraphina had been able to cast over the situation was gone now that Iverlyn had failed the bloodstone ritual. But none of that changed the fact that she knew very little about the man who sired her.

"I know he was mortal, that his boat had stalled just a mile offshore, and that's how he found himself on the island. I know he and my mother had an affair and that he left when he found out she was pregnant with me." Iverlyn recited the only information Seraphina had ever been willing to give her about her father whenever she asked.

"That's it?" Theo asked, his voice tinged with disbelief as his eyes furrowed.

"That's it. Seraphina would never talk about it. She thought it made our family look weak."

Theo shook his head, lips lined in disappointment. "Of course."

"Why? Why are you asking about my father?" Iverlyn asked as she eyed him wearily. He was pacing, as he always did when something was bothering him. "You know something," she said, tracking his movements with her eyes.

"I really would feel better if we had this conversation at the cabin," he said, raking his fingers through his hair, a gesture he always did when he was anxious about something. *Good to see that not everything was a lie.*

"Theo," Iverlyn warned, the agitation flaring in her voice. She stood from the rock and grabbed his hand, pulling him to a stop. "I know you know something. Just tell me, please."

Theo hesitated as if he were trying to decide whether to answer before blurting, "Your father. I know your father."

Iverlyn felt like the air had been sucked from her lungs, and the ground she stood on had been ripped from beneath her feet. She dropped Theo's arm from her grasp and stumbled backward until the back of her knees brushed against the boulder before allowing herself to fall backward onto it. *Theo knew her father?*

"It's a long story, and I will tell you everything, but he didn't know about you—not at first. He's not some horrible man who abandoned you and your mother. You have to believe that," Theo continued, walking towards Iverlyn as he spoke.

Theo knew her father? A clang of thunder rang through the air as the sky above them grew dark. "I don't understand." She shook her head. This couldn't be real. Theo couldn't know her father. He had lied to her about his magic and his parents, but to be her friend for all these years... he couldn't know her father. This was a horrible dream, something that her mind concocted to make her forget about Alastair and the ritual. This couldn't be real.

Theo knelt before her, one hand on her knee and another cupping her cheek. "I know this is a lot to process, but I need you to calm down. Just breathe, and I promise I will make this all make sense."

She hadn't noticed she was drawing in quick, uneven breaths, her chest rising and falling with a sporadic panic that seemed to overtake her body. Theo knew her father. She squeezed her eyes shut, willing herself to wake up from this nightmare. When she opened her eyes, she knew an entirely different nightmare would be waiting for her, but at least in that one, her only friend wouldn't have betrayed her.

Another clash of thunder rang above her, and an icy drop of rain splattered on her forehead and ran down her face, mingling with the tears she hadn't noticed she had been crying. She opened her eyes to see Theo still kneeling before her. The sky had darkened as billowing gray clouds circled above them, the wind howling and rain pouring. Yet, just a few yards away, the sun was shining. It was as if the storm was only for her.

"Just breathe, Iverlyn," Theo coached as he cupped either side of her face, pulling her gaze to meet his own. "I know this is a lot right now. But it'll all work out in the end."

It'll all work out in the end. The exact words he had spoken to her all those times when he was comforting her on the beach.

He had never been supportive of Salus or the rituals they held, but she had always assumed it was because he didn't have magic himself. He wouldn't have been the first male on the island to have animosity towards the coven. But he did have magic, and he was the only person to believe that it would all be okay despite her lack of magic. He never assured her she'd pass, only promising it would all work out.

"You knew I would fail," she breathed, her voice barely audible in the howling wind. Icy droplets of rain rolled down her cheeks as tendrils of her hair clung to her neck.

Theo remained silent, but the weight of guilt etched into his face spoke louder than any words would have. It was how he was always so sure she'd be okay after the ritual, how he just so happened to have a boat and car waiting for them right when they needed to escape. It was why he wasn't at the ritual despite his promise that he would be. Theo didn't need to see the outcome when he knew with certainty what it would be.

"You *knew* I would fail!" she shouted, leaping to her feet, flinging Theo's lingering hands away as if they burned. Her voice roared through the space around them. "How long did you keep this from me? How long did you know?"

Theo averted his eyes, shame mingling with resignation as he replied, "We all knew, Ivy. Deep down, you knew it too."

Iverlyn recoiled away from him as the words taunted her. It was true, she had never expected to pass the ritual; but hearing those words from Theo hurt more than she was willing to admit. The wind whipping around them slowed as the heavy downpour turned to a drizzle.

"It was more than that, though. You were so sure that you had an entire escape plan put together. People don't just do that out of precaution." She refused to believe that there wasn't more that he wasn't telling her.

"You're right," Theo said, surprising her. "Your father didn't know about you when he left Salus, and when he found out about you, it wasn't safe for him to return. So he sent me instead."

"So, when you said you had orders?"

Theo nodded. "Orders from your father. He knew you wouldn't pass the ritual. The bloodstone would sense his blood in you, and he knew it would deny you covenship because of it."

Iverlyn didn't respond. She didn't know if she could. Her tongue felt heavy, weighed down by everything she had just learned.

"You could've told me," she said quietly, "and we could've left before the ritual, before…" *Before Alastair.*

Theo stilled as Iverlyn's words faltered to a stop. She felt pathetic—it could've been worse, and it *would* have been had it not been for Theo saving her when he did. But she couldn't help but feel so discarded, so… *violated.*

"What happened after the ritual?" Theo's voice deepened.

"Nothing." She crossed her arms across her belly as a shiver wracked through her body. The rain was gone now, but the heavy blanket of clouds above them still cast out the sun's warmth.

"Ivy, I saw you in your room. I kn—"

"How far is the cabin?" she asked, silently pleading with Theo to drop the subject. What he saw was a moment of desperation. A moment when she had been backed into the corner with no promise of a better life. A moment when the promise of death looked like the only solution that allowed her even a sliver of control. But that's all it was—a moment.

Theo sighed and looked as if he would say something more but stopped when he dragged his eyes to meet Iverlyn's gaze. "It's not that far."

Chapter Nine

T he cabin that Theo guided them to exuded a quaint charm, whispering tales of warmth and welcome. Though Iverlyn couldn't help but notice that even the garden sheds back on Salus towered over this modest dwelling, an undeniable sense of homeliness enveloped her. The cabin was shrouded beneath a verdant canopy of leaves, tucked snugly between two grand oak trees, their impressive trunks standing like ancient sentinels. Sunlight streamed through the foliage in delicate slivers, dancing upon the surface of a small stream that babbled contentedly behind the structure, its shimmering waters sparkling like diamonds as it flowed. Vines of ivy wove their way up the sides of the house, tenderly framing each window as if the cabin had leapt directly from the pages of a fairytale.

Yet, upon stepping inside, the narrative took a stark turn. The air was thick with neglect, a heavy blanket of dust cloaking the furniture, while abandoned boxes huddled haphazardly in corners as if they had been forgotten by whoever used to call this place home.

"I think it's time you finish explaining everything," Iverlyn said as she hugged her knees to her chest. She had been disappointed to find the small cabin had no electricity but was thankful for the small hearth before her that Theo had nursed to life when they arrived. The sun was beginning to sink below the horizon, and with that came a brisk chill that seemed to almost seep into her bones, even after she changed out of her dampened clothes.

Theo nodded. "I agree." He draped a heavy woolen blanket across Iverlyn's shoulders before sitting next to her on the couch, angling his body so he could face her.

"How do you know my father?" Iverlyn asked as she tugged the blanket around her body, thankful for its warmth.

"I grew up here in Arbor, and I guess you could say your father took me under his wing and gave me a place to call home when I had nowhere to go."

"So, your parents?"

"Didn't die in a car crash. I never knew them. I lived with my grandmother until she grew too sick to care for me, and then your father took me in. Helped me learn how to control my magic." Theo reached into the bag at his feet and handed her an apple as he spoke, grabbing one for himself as well.

Iverlyn frowned. She really didn't know the man sitting before her. "Why lie to me about that?"

"I needed you to trust me," he confessed. "You were so closed off to everyone. I needed it to be different with us."

Iverlyn nodded, her voice trapped in her throat, and a heavy wave of betrayal fell onto her.

"Your father sent me there to keep you safe. He wanted you to have a friend, someone you could trust," Theo continued in her silence. Iverlyn stared at the flames as he spoke. She had always wondered why Theo continued to be her friend even when the rest of the town had seemed almost afraid to be.

"I still don't understand why you couldn't tell me the truth." She wanted to understand, wanted to know why they felt lying to her all these years was the only option.

"I wanted to, but it wasn't my call. Your father gave me a job to do, so I did it." He shrugged.

A job. Was that all she was to him? Seraphina had warned her that he wasn't someone she could trust and that he was hiding something. Iverlyn had refused to believe her, instead choosing to believe that her warnings were nothing more than attempts to isolate Iverlyn from her only friend. But now... perhaps that was the only nice thing her aunt had ever done for her.

"I never meant to hurt you," Theo said quietly as he placed a hand on hers, where she fidgeted with her ring. "Your father just wanted to ensure you were safe, and we did that the only way we could."

Iverlyn pulled her hand from his. She didn't know if she had ever really been *safe*, and she had the scars to prove it. Scars that Theo had helped her bandage more times than she could count.

"He's an important man, Ivy. Because of that, there are people who would do anything if it meant seeing him fall. He couldn't afford to take the risk of bringing you here and having you be used as a pawn," Theo explained.

Iverlyn was at a loss for words. The simmering anger coiled tightly in her stomach, threatening to spill over. Theo claimed her father didn't want her to be a pawn in anyone's game. Yet, there she was, left in Salus, with someone planted in her life to earn her trust and affection over the years—all of it a delicate dance of deception. Wasn't that the very definition of being a pawn, just one under his control? She could see that Theo believed what he did was right, that his revelations would somehow ease her pain. But instead, they only made the already shattered fragments of her heart feel even more fragile. All she wanted from this life was to be important to *someone*. To be loved by someone so fiercely that they would do anything to have her by their side. She used to think that one day, that person would be Theo.

"So, what changed?" Iverlyn asked when she found herself able to speak. "Why did he have you bring me here now?" She couldn't help the bite of bitterness in her voice as she asked.

"He knew you couldn't stay in Salus once you finished the ritual, and now that you're twenty-one, with some training, we can teach you how to use your magic to protect yourself."

"But I don't have magic," Iverlyn said, shaking her head, the slice in her palm from the ritual almost tingling as a reminder.

Theo raised a brow and gave her a small smile. "Are you sure about that?"

Iverlyn's brows furrowed. "Theo, you know I failed the ritual. I don't have magic."

"You don't have the type of magic that the coven recognizes as one of their own. But you do have magic, Ivy."

Iverlyn shook her head. She couldn't have magic. All those times she had begged for her magic to answer her calls, all those times she thought maybe she felt it stir inside of her, and every single time, it damned her to the wrath of her aunt. She didn't have it. She couldn't.

"Your father does," Theo said, "In fact, he has quite a lot of it, and I'm willing to bet that you do too. I've seen it in you."

"Then why can't I use it?" Iverlyn asked, frustration brewing in her voice. Just because her father wielded magic didn't guarantee she could; and if that were the case, wouldn't she have inherited her mother's powers too?

"Have you ever noticed how storms erupt when you're upset or your feelings run high?" Theo inquired, his tone serious.

"I mean, we lived on an island, Theo. It stormed all the time," she shot back.

"True, but what about the storm that rolled in earlier?" he asked, undeterred.

"That was just a storm, Theo!" she insisted, a hint of exasperation creeping into her voice.

"A storm materialized when you started to panic, a storm that lingered directly over you and nowhere else. You honestly can't tell me that you don't see it or feel it?" he pressed, leaning forward.

Iverlyn leaned back onto the couch, letting her gaze fall to the crackling fire before her. Did she feel it? Sometimes, when she was training with Seraphina, she thought she felt it, and a few times—had even begged for it to answer her, but it never did.

"If I had magic, then wouldn't it have answered me all those times with Seraphina?"

"No, not necessarily." Theo shook his head. "Our magic is weaker outside of Arbor. Some can't even access their magic outside of the realm."

Iverlyn raised her brow. "But you did. Right?"

"I have a lot more practice than most. But that's beside the point. You have magic, and whether you realize it or not, you've used it before."

Iverlyn eyed him as he spoke, dragging her hands down her face. This made no sense to her. "You can't honestly expect me to believe that I somehow summoned a *storm*, yet couldn't manage to have even an ounce of magic when I was with Seraphina. That's crazy, Theo."

"Is it? Do you remember the first night I found you on the beach? Do you remember what you said to me?" Theo asked.

Five Years Ago...

Iverlyn couldn't believe it. Pain laced its way up her arm as she stumbled through the sand, discarding her sandals with two aggravated kicks before she continued walking. She'd find them later. Or not. If she was being honest, she didn't care. All she cared about was getting as far away as she could.

Seraphina had struck her, had let her magic lash into Iverlyn's skin with a blistering bite that Iverlyn was almost sure would scar. With proper care, it could be healed. Quite a few people in the coven had chosen to take up the art of healing, but Seraphina forbade it. She wanted Iverlyn to have a reminder of her failure seared into her skin.

'Perhaps this is the motivation you need,' she had said, towering over Iverlyn's cowering form. Her aunt hadn't felt an ounce of re-

morse from the blow she had delivered; in fact, Iverlyn suspected that she rather enjoyed it.

The braid Iverlyn had tied her hair back into was unraveling in the wind, tendrils breaking free. Dark clouds rolled in from the horizon, covering the moon that had illuminated the sky in a thick blanket of black as a loud clang of thunder echoed across the shores. Silhouettes of the crashing waves flashed as lightning danced on the horizon. She didn't think she had ever seen the ocean so angry, or the sky for that matter. Despite living on an island, they never really had storms like this.

A gust of wind howled, spraying grains of sand into her as she continued staggering forward. She knew she shouldn't have been out here, but something about the storm as it rolled in over the shore, its rain soaking through her shirt in seconds, called to her, almost as if it had felt how alone she was.

She continued staggering through the sand, reveling in how the warm wind tugged and pulled at her body, her hair twirling around her in spirals. The tie that had once held it together was now lost somewhere on the sandy shore. She kept walking even when her feet met the water, ignoring how the shelled ground bit into her heel as she pushed forward until the water rested just above her knees.

The current tugged at Iverlyn almost impatiently, desperate to whisk her away. Thunder rumbled overhead, echoing ominously, while a flash of lightning lit up the ocean, unveiling a looming wave charging toward her. Iverlyn stared, her eyes wide with disbelief, as the wave seemed to split apart just for her, morphing into two smaller ones that curled around her. The frothy white foam burst forth as it crashed upon the shore.

She understood the risk of standing in the ocean on a night like this. It was as if she were tempting fate—offering a plate of food to a starving child and insisting they resist the urge to take it. Yet, despite the dangers, she felt an unwavering certainty that the ocean could never claim her. Or maybe it was that she didn't care if it claimed her. Didn't care if this was the end she was meant to meet. The might of the storms didn't instill fear. It was hard to explain, but amid the raging winds, the booming thunder, and the flickering lightning overhead, she felt truly seen, as if the elements were an extension of herself that wanted to put a show on just for her.

"When I found you," Theo started, pulling her out of the memory, "I was terrified. You were nearly waist-deep in the water, and the storm was so bad that I could hardly reach you without being knocked over by the wind, let alone the current." Theo paused, shaking his head, "But you were so still, like none of it could touch you. And you were so calm, like you knew none of it would."

Iverlyn remained silent as she watched the admiration that had sparked in her friend's eyes. She didn't know what to say or how to tell him that she wasn't calm because she knew she was safe. She was calm because she didn't care if she was safe. That night, standing there in the ocean and waiting to see if it would devour her whole or let her leave unscathed, she thought about how she had finally felt free.

"Do you remember what you told me when I dragged you from the water?" Theo asked.

Iverlyn shook her head. She didn't. She didn't remember much about that night after the storm had entranced her.

"You told me that the storm wouldn't hurt you, and when I asked why, you just looked at me, smiled, and said that it saw you." Theo's grin spread into a smile as he spoke. "That was the first time I knew you had your father's magic. I was sleeping when I felt it, and for a moment, I thought your father had figured out a way to return to the island. It was so raw and so strong..." Theo mused, his eyes lit up with wonder, which made Iverlyn's stomach twist into knots. She didn't want this. Didn't deserve it.

"It was just a storm," she repeated, yet even her voice seemed to fail as it wavered over the words.

"It wasn't just a storm. And when your father gets here, he'll—"

"My father?" Iverlyn asked, nerves bundling in her chest. "He's coming here?"

"He'll be here tomorrow; he's finally going to take you home," Theo said as he reached out and grasped her hand.

Iverlyn took a staggering breath. *Her father.* She didn't know if it was because she had no experience with a parental figure who cared for her, but the idea of meeting her father in just a few hours was terrifying and filled her with a sense of dread so heavy she thought she might sink right through the earth. *What if she wasn't what he expected her to be? What if he regretted bringing her here? What if he saw the same failure in her that Seraphina had seen all those years? What if he couldn't love her? What if...*

Chapter Ten

"So, just to be clear," Iverlyn said, her skepticism barely masked as she perched on the edge of the couch, tucking her knees beneath her. The fireplace crackled softly, casting flickering shadows that danced playfully across the room. "You're saying that you and my father are some kind of fairies, like Tinkerbell?"

Theo frowned, his expression darkening. "No, not like Tinkerbell. We are fae. But it's not just me and your father; you are one, too."

Iverlyn raised an eyebrow, disbelief etched on her face. No way could she be one of them. She recalled that book she had stumbled upon—a tale of fae she had never quite finished. It had been tucked away in her room after a training session with Seraphina, a strange gift she now suspected came from Theo. But her aunt had discovered it soon after, and she had incinerated the pages before Iverlyn could uncover their secrets. What she did read, however, painted a vivid picture of pointed ears, exquisite features, and agile forms. Iverlyn saw none of that in herself, nor in Theo.

"You're the one who left that book for me to find, aren't you?" she asked, her eyes narrowing.

He smiled at her. "I thought you might appreciate learning about your heritage."

Iverlyn hesitated, her pulse quickening as memories rushed back. "Well, I didn't," she admitted, pausing to gather her thoughts. She had never told Theo how furious Seraphina had been when she discovered the book. "Seraphina caught me with it a few days later. She burned it." Iverlyn bit her lip, omitting the part about how Seraphina had campaigned against every book in her room that didn't pertain to spells or coven history.

Theo's eyes narrowed. "You never told me that."

Iverlyn shrugged as she rubbed the palm of her hand. She had also chosen not to tell him how Seraphina had engulfed the book in flames while it was still in her hands. For days to follow, she couldn't grab anything without wincing. "It didn't seem important at the time."

His eyes remained narrowed as they trailed to her fidgeting hands, something he knew she always did when she was holding something back. They had never been able to lie to each other, both knowing the other too well. But Iverlyn supposed that wasn't entirely true. He could still read her like an open book, but the man before her was still as much a mystery as he had been the day they met.

"Were you able to read any of it?" he asked, his eyes still glued to her fidgeting hands.

"Not much." She paused, shoving her hands beneath her legs. "The only thing I remember is that they were supposed to have pointed ears and have an ethereal beauty about themselves."

"I suppose it was a bit of an outdated book." Theo chuckled before adding, "We can have pointed ears, though most can choose whether or not to show them. And then there's some, like me," he paused, motioning to her rounded ears, "and like you, who never had them at all. My grandfather was human. My grandmother always told me I had his ears."

Iverlyn dragged her hand to her ear absentmindedly, running her fingers over its soft curve. "And when you say that most can choose whether or not to show them?"

"Shapeshifting. Some of us can shift into whatever form we choose. Others only have a specific form they can shift into."

Shapeshifting... Iverlyn couldn't even begin to wrap her head around the idea of being able to change her form. "Can you?" she asked.

Theo grinned. "It's kind of my specialty."

Iverlyn couldn't help the slight punch in her gut as she was reminded that she knew nothing about the man beside her. Shapeshifting was his specialty? The Theo she knew didn't have any specialties. That was another thing they had bonded over. Neither of them was athletic and finished school with average grades, neither excelling at any topic. Sometimes, Iverlyn thought it was the secret to their friendship. The only thing either of them ever excelled at was being there for each other.

His grin fell as he watched Iverlyn. She knew he could see how much this bothered her, and she hated it. "Stop looking at me like that," she snapped, a little harsher than she meant.

Theo pulled his gaze from her and focused on the fire before them. "I'm sorry," he said so quietly she almost missed it over the sounds of crackling wood. She didn't respond. It wasn't her job to make him feel better about all the lies he'd told, especially when he'd clearly felt so little remorse about it earlier that day.

She knew she should be thanking him for saving her from the horrible fate Alastair had in store for her, but she couldn't bring herself to speak the words. He saved her, yes. But as much as he saved her, he also destroyed her. She didn't think she'd ever be able to trust again. All those years she had cried herself to sleep, wishing for a better life, and Theo was the only thing that separated her from that. Orders or not, he still could've helped her get away.

"I didn't think it would be like this," Theo said, breaking the silence.

"Like what, Theo," she sighed.

"I didn't think you'd be so angry... so hurt."

"What did you think I'd be like? Did you think I'd be thankful that my best friend lied to me for years?" Her voice trembled as her eyes shimmered with tears like fragile sapphires. "I don't know you, but you know every—" Her voice caught in her throat as she pushed up from the couch. "You know everything about me, Theo. You know how I got these scars, how alone I felt—you knew it all." Tears flowed down her cheeks as she stood before him. "You knew it all," she repeated with a broken sob.

Silence followed, only filled by the crackling of the fire and the soft pings of rain on the window. Iverlyn stood there, arms wrapped around herself, as if that could protect her already-shattered heart. Theo's warm scent filled the air just before his strong arms wrapped around her. He pulled her back to the couch where he held her in his arms, brushing his fingertips through her hair as he promised her better days, just as he had done so many times before. She wanted to push him away, to yell at him to leave her alone, and to tell him just how badly it hurt to be around him, knowing that he would never be the man she thought he was. But as he held her as she continued to cry, she found herself rooted in his embrace and decided to pretend for just one more night that the man holding her was the one she had let herself envision a life with.

Chapter Eleven

"Well, well, well," a deep, harmonious voice mused, snapping Iverlyn out of the sleep she had fallen into. "What do we have here?" he spoke, annunciating each word with growing amusement.

She was strewn across Theo's chest, his fingers woven into her hair with one hand resting on her lower back, hugging her close to his body. They must have fallen asleep like that. She shot up, pulling herself from his grasp and falling to the ground with a resounding thud. Theo, of course, was still sleeping, soft snores sounding from him. He had always been a heavy sleeper.

Iverlyn's gaze swept to the front door, slightly ajar, where sunlight poured in around the silhouette of a man standing just within the cabin. In two fluid steps, he cleared the room and towered over her, likely the tallest figure she had ever encountered. The way his muscles strained against his shirt hinted at an incredible strength. Clad in snug jeans and a black V-neck t-shirt that revealed swirling tattoos etched into his sun-kissed skin, he seemed to embody power itself. His features were striking—so perfectly formed that Iverlyn fancied divine hands had carved them. With his chiseled jaw, full lips, sharp cheekbones, and dark, smoldering eyes, there wasn't a flaw aside from the hint of a small scar just below his left brow. And there, just visible beneath the shadow of his jet-black hair, were the delicate points of his ears—a subtle indicator that he was something otherworldly, something *fae*.

He extended his hands towards her. His fingers splayed open in an invitation that felt more taunting than welcoming. She blinked, her brain still foggy from the heavy sleep she had just been in, as she stared up at him with wide eyes. Who was this man? And how had he known where to find them? He was too young to be her father. Choosing to ignore the still-outstretched hand of the stranger, she pulled her knees up under her body and pushed up from the ground.

His eyes seemed to follow her movements with predatory calculation as she reached over and gave Theo a not-so-gentle shove. "Wake up," she hissed through clenched teeth, deciding to kick the couch for good measure as she kept her eyes firmly planted on the man who loomed over her. She had always found the way Theo could sleep through anything kind of endearing, but now, as the man before her wore a smirk on his lips that seemed more dangerous than friendly, she really needed him to wake up.

"Who are you?" Iverlyn demanded, prodding Theo again, who was just starting to regain consciousness.

"Your father sent me to escort you the rest of the way. He's running a bit behind and thought Theo could use a little breather," the man replied, his smirk transforming into a grin as he glanced at Theo before locking eyes with Iverlyn. "Guess he was right about that."

Iverlyn rolled her eyes, practically hurling daggers at the stranger. Theo groaned groggily as he swung his legs off the couch, rubbing the last remnants of sleep from his eyes.

"Theo," Iverlyn warned, punctuating her words with a sharp kick to his foot. Her gaze fixed on the unknown man loitering nearby. "We have company."

In an instant, Theo leaped off the couch, his body coiling in front of Iverlyn like a protective barrier. "What the hell are you doing here, Zainiel?" he barked.

Zainiel merely shook his head, a knowing smirk playing on his lips. "Oh, Theodore, is that *really* how you greet an old friend? After all this time, I had hoped the company of those witches might have softened that stick lodged up your ass."

"Why are you here?" Theo's voice cut through the air, sharp and unwavering.

Zainiel let out an exaggerated sigh, raising his hands in playful surrender. "Well, let's not waste time, then. I'm here for the girl." He gestured towards Iverlyn, a smirk playing at the corners of his lips. Iverlyn's heart plummeted. He was undeniably striking, but the way Theo's eyes blazed and the dangerous aura around Zainiel made her uneasy. She had no intention of going anywhere with him.

"She's not going with you," Theo growled, each word laced with warning.

Zainiel chuckled darkly, his voice like silk. "You plan to defy Kalec's orders? Come on, we both know you're such a good little *pet*."

Kalec. Was that her father's name? She had been so overwhelmed by everything else that she hadn't even bothered to ask. If it was, did this mean that Zainiel also worked for him in some way?

Theo remained silent, but Iverlyn could feel the tension rolling off his body in waves. It was clear that there was some bad blood between the two men, and it seemed she'd found herself right in the middle of it.

"Kalec has been delayed. He asked me to bring her to the estate," Zainiel continued.

"Why would he send you? Why not Ria?" Theo pressed, his shoulders still drawn tight as if expecting a fight.

"He didn't know what state she'd be in and needed to know that someone would be here who could…" he paused, his eyes flicking over to Iverlyn, "neutralize the threat, if necessary."

Iverlyn didn't know what he meant by *neutralize,* but judging by the way Theo bristled at the words, it wasn't good. Did her father believe she could be a threat?

"Everything's fine," Theo said.

"Perfect, so she's in control of her powers, then? And I assume that means you've filled her in on everything?" Zainiel said as he stalked over to the fireplace, dragging his fingers across the mantle before flicking the dust off them.

Theo angled his body so he remained between Iverlyn and Zainiel, but he said nothing.

"I'll take that as a no, then. Do you care to fill her in, or shall I? If she has a fit and loses control of her powers, I'd much rather it happen here. We both know how upset Ria would be if her garden were to be destroyed." Zainiel continued to stalk throughout the room, trailing his fingers over the various stacks of boxes.

"I've told her what she needs to know."

Iverlyn glared at the back of Theo's neck. If he thought his shortened version of the truth could be classified as everything she needed to know, then perhaps he didn't know her as well as she thought.

Zainiel raised a brow. "So you've told her *everything*, then?"

"Told me what?" she demanded, side-stepping around Theo so she found herself positioned between the two men. She didn't care who answered, but the way Zainiel stepped back and motioned to Theo that the floor was his, she knew who to turn to. Regret seemed to roll off of Theo as he looked anywhere but where she stood.

"Told me what, Theo?" she gritted out.

"I was going to, I swear. I just—I just hadn't had the chance," he stammered, rubbing the back of his neck, something he had always used to do when he found himself in an uncomfortable situation.

"You had seven years of chances, Theo. Seven years." The trickling sound of rainfall sounded against the outside of the cabin walls, and a wave of anger flooded her. She had been stupid to let him console her last night; she should've pushed him away and demanded that he answer all her questions. "I don't want any more excuses. I just want the truth."

"Go on, Theo, tell her," Zainiel baited, clearly enjoying the show.

"Your dad wanted to keep you safe. You have to understand that everything I—everything *we* did was to keep you safe. Please tell me you can understand that," Theo pleaded as he finally turned to meet her gaze.

Maybe she would find a way to understand tomorrow, but as he stood in front of her, revealing yet another lie, all she could feel was the sting of betrayal and hot rage burning through her. Theo waited for her, begging silently for her to tell him that she understood, but this time, it was her turn to remain silent.

"Your dad and I knew that infiltrating Salus wouldn't be easy. You know how tight-knit of a community they are. We wanted someone trained and experienced to keep you safe without drawing attention to themselves and to you. Sending a man into Salus wasn't an option, not without drawing attention, and you know that sending a woman wouldn't have even been an option to consider. So, we devised a plan, and the only way that plan would work was if it was a child, preferably someone close to your age—someone who could serve as a friend. You understand that, right?"

We. This whole time, she had thought that Theo was simply following orders, that he had been sent away to do a job, to protect her. But now... *we?*

"What are you saying?" She forced the words out even though it was growing hard for her to breathe. She didn't know how much more of this she could take. The windows began to rattle as the storms grew outside.

"To go into Salus as I am now would have drawn too much attention and left me with limited opportunities to gain your trust. Having your trust was paramount to the success of our plan. So, it—I had to be a child." Theo had taken a step closer to her as he spoke, reaching out to place a hand on her shoulder, but she flinched away, bumping into a stack of boxes and scattering their contents.

I had to be a child. The words echoed in her mind, each repetition amplifying her confusion. *I had to be a child.* As if being a child was a disguise, a role in some twisted play. But how could that be? Iverlyn's thoughts darted back to their conversation last night. *Some of us can shift into whatever form we choose. It's kind of my specialty.*

Iverlyn felt like she was going to be sick. *I had to be a child.* It couldn't be. He couldn't have pretended to be a fourteen-year-old boy just to gain her trust, could he? And if he had, why did he only look to be in his twenties now? Growing up, Iverlyn remembered hearing rumors of a coven who didn't age like everyone else, one who seemed to stay young while the people around them grew older. When she had asked Seraphina, her aunt told her it was nonsense—but given what she knew now, perhaps it hadn't been. The room felt like it was spinning around her as a rough breeze ripped through the cabin, slamming the front door shut.

Her stomach churned as she stared at the man before her, saw the guilt etched onto his face as he seemed to cower away from her gaze. Growing up, she had always thought Theo seemed older than he was, but she had always assumed it was from the loss of his parents at such a young age. Grief had a way of aging a person more than any amount of time could. But now... *no*. It couldn't be true. He was her best friend for *seven years*. She would've noticed, *should've* noticed.

Her heart pounded in her ears, and her breath came quickly as she shook her head. It couldn't be true.

"No." The word left her lips in a whisper so quiet she wasn't even sure she heard it herself.

Theo took a small step towards her, with an outstretched hand, "Iv—"

"No," she repeated, her voice loud, cracking with frantic urgency as she backed away from him. A clang of thunder erupted through the air, so loud that the walls shook.

Suddenly, the room felt all too small, and she needed air, only none was coming. The storm was battering the cabin walls, and thunder shook the ground, but she was too frantic to notice. Dodging Theo's outstretched hand and shoving past Zainiel, she raced to the door, fumbling with the knob before ripping it open and propelling herself outside. *She needed air.* Her vision was becoming hazy, the deafening sound of her quickening heart the only thing she could hear. The raging storm seemed to swirl around her in a cyclone, ripping away any air that she could will into her lungs.

She stumbled farther away from the cabin before her legs collapsed, and she fell to the forest floor, the ground puddling around her.

Chapter Twelve

ZAINIEL

The girl was still unconscious. Her copper hair was splayed out to the side in a tangled mess, and her pale skin seemed almost sickly, contrasting with the mud smeared across it. He supposed he could have changed her, cleaned her up at least, but he didn't want to risk waking her and having her panic again. Even through the mud, he could see the darkening bruises around her neck and some old scars peeking out from underneath the collar of her shirt, but when he asked Theo where they had come from, all he was met with was a cold stare.

"What in Caledonia's name happened, Zainiel?" Astaria's voice rang out as the door to the large bedroom swung open. He sighed and raked his hand down his face before turning to meet his sister. He had been hoping to avoid this confrontation for a few minutes longer.

"She can't control her powers," Zainiel answered gruffly, not having the energy to explain further. Besides, he was sure Theo had filled her in on his version of the story the second he found Ria. He always liked getting the first word in.

He watched as a look of horror settled onto his sister's face. "Gods, Z, tell me you didn't—"

"I didn't," he growled, cutting her off. "Give me some credit, Ria. The girl did it to herself," he said, flinging his arm towards the sleeping figure. He didn't know how he got himself into this mess. She was supposed to be Theo's problem.

"Sorry," she mumbled. "What happened, then?"

"Kalec was right. She inherited his powers. She lost control, and..." he trailed off, searching for the right words to describe what he had seen. "Ria, I've never seen anything like it. She panicked, and it started storming, and then it surrounded her. I think she suffocated herself." Zainiel had seen people lose control of their powers before. It happened to all of them. It even happened to him. But he had never seen someone's powers lash out against themselves, especially when the person they were angry at was mere feet away.

"You should've let me come. I could've helped her," Ria said.

"No," Zainiel said sharply. He *knew* his sister could help her. She was an empath and had always come in handy when calming down those who lost control of themselves. But the raw power Zainiel had felt coming from this girl... He wanted Ria nowhere near it. She was dangerous. "I don't want you or anyone else around her. Not until she learns to control herself."

Ria scowled at Zainiel. "You may be able to intimidate everyone else into listening to you, but it won't work on me. The girl needs a friend."

"I can be her friend." The word felt wrong as it fell from his lips, and judging by Ria's arched brow, she felt the same.

"Don't take this the wrong way, but you aren't exactly friendly." Ria shoved past Zainiel and walked towards the girl. He didn't even know her name. He supposed he could've asked Theo, but talking to that man even a second longer than necessary was about as tempting as throwing himself into a pit of spikes.

He watched as his sister tenderly touched the girl's shoulder, her own shoulders tensing as she read her emotions. Zainiel had never envied his sister's gift. It didn't matter how much control she had over the powers. She couldn't place her hand on anyone without being flooded by whatever emotions or pain they were feeling, sometimes even seeing their memories. He supposed that was why she spent so much time alone in the library, the one place besides her room that Kalec had warded against her ability, allowing her some reprieve.

Ria's face contorted into one of grief and sadness, a look he had seen on his sister's face more times than he could count. More times than one person should have to endure. If it wasn't her pain and loss she felt, it was someone else's. There was plenty of it to go around. But he supposed that's what happened when you lived the lives they did.

"What'd you see?" he asked as Ria pulled her hand away from the sleeping girl.

Ria's brows furrowed in deep thought as her eyes scanned the girl's body. "There's so many," she mused, so quietly Zainiel nearly missed it. Ria forced her gaze away from the girl and turned to Zainiel, tears shimmering in her eyes. "I thought Theo was there to protect her."

Zainiel's jaw ticked at the mention of Theo's name. Of course he had failed to do the one thing he was sent there to do. "What did you see?" Zainiel repeated.

"Not a lot," Ria admitted, "but enough to know she wasn't cared for. Not in the way she should have been." She turned her gaze back to the girl, reaching a tender hand out before brushing a stray lock of hair away from her cheek. "Her name is Iverlyn."

Iverlyn. He had imagined it to be something... more. Something chaotic. She might've seemed like a scared little girl now, but he knew that there was a raging storm inside her, waiting to be unleashed.

"And the scars?" he asked, unable to drag his gaze away from the girl's face. Even in sleep, fear lingered as if it clung to her like a shadow.

"From what I saw, my guess is her aunt," Ria answered.

Zainiel fisted his hands at his side. What the hell had Theo been doing all those years if not protecting her? He turned, forcing his gaze away from Iverlyn and marching towards the door.

"Zainiel," Ria called after him, her voice pitched with a warning. "Maybe you should sit here for a few minutes."

He paused, considering heeding his sister's advice. He wouldn't pretend that she hadn't just read what he intended to do. But when his gaze fell back onto the sleeping girl behind her, he felt that simmering rage building inside. He needed answers. Needed to know what had happened on the island all those years; needed to know who had hurt her so badly that even now that she was safe, it still burdened her so heavily that the pain of it nearly knocked Ria off her feet.

"Zai—"

"Don't, Ria," he snapped, holding up a hand. "Just stay with her, okay?"

His sister looked like she would object, but she just nodded and cast another sorrowful look at the girl, their future queen.

Seven Years Ago

even Years Ago

Iverlyn sighed as she squinted at the blinding pages before her. Last night, Seraphina came to her room and declared they would have a family outing today at the beach. Something that they hadn't done together in years, unless it was for a gathering of the coven or a ritual. But upon arriving at the sun-dappled shore, Seraphina tossed a heavy tome into her palms, instructing her to read it from front to back before joining in the festivities of the beach day.

The sun blazed in the clear blue sky, its fierce light reflecting off every grain of sand and the rippling waves, turning the pages of her study book into blinding mirrors. Behind her, Isodyl and Elara lay reclined on their sunbathing towels, their shrill laughter dragging down the inside of her skull like nails on a chalkboard. She never understood the point of coming to the beach only to lie on a towel. She could do that anywhere. She longed for the cool waves upon her skin, wanted to feel the silky touch of the salt water as it pulled her deeper in its embrace, and she suspected that was precisely why Seraphina chose to bring her today—a punishment cloaked in the guise of a reward.

Nearly an hour had passed with Iverlyn stewing in her envy and frustration, watching with longing as Elara and Isodyl reveled in their freedom. Her mind felt numb, dulled by the hours of relentless study. If she could have one moment, just one moment of lighthearted fun like the other children who played along the shoreline, splashing around in the waves as they lapped onto the shore, gathering iridescent seashells to use as decoration on the sandcastles that they had constructed, only to joyously demolish them moments later. Their carefree laughter and cries mocked her, a constant reminder of the simple pleasures she would never be able to enjoy. At least not until she proved herself to be worthy.

"What are you reading?" a boyish voice sounded from her right.

Iverlyn looked up from the blinding pages, thankful to have a distraction. She searched for Seraphina on the beach to find her deep in a conversation with one of the elders, too engrossed in conversation to notice the boy. What harm could a little break do?

Water dripped onto Iverlyn's shoulder from where the boy crouched beside her, peering at the book. His blonde locks, wet with salt water, curled at the ends, and his pale skin almost seemed to glow in the sunlight, almost as much as the pages she had in her lap. It was clear he didn't see the beach much. Salus wasn't a very large place. The elders preferred to keep their community as closed off from the rest of the world as possible, so it was uncommon for anyone to be strangers to each other, but this boy, with his goofy smile and warm eyes, was just that—a stranger.

"I don't know you." The words slipped from Iverlyn as she continued to study the boy. He clearly didn't know who she was, or he would have left her alone. Everyone left her alone, and at times, the loneliness was awful, but she had become used to it—so used to it that she hadn't realized how rude she had sounded when she spoke.

"I'm Theo," the boy chirped with a broad smile, dimples on display. Unfazed by her lack of friendliness, he extended a hand to her. She continued to study the boy, unsure why he had chosen to come to speak with her when there were plenty of other kids around for him to approach.

"What's your name?" he asked, dropping his extended hand before falling out of his crouch and onto the sand beside her. Did he truly not know her? Everyone in Salus knew her family. Seraphina

always took pride in that, while Iverlyn preferred to blend into the background.

"Iverlyn," she answered quietly before turning to see Seraphina still captivated by her conversation.

"Iverlyn," the boy repeated with a smile. Did he ever not smile? "Can I call you Ivy? You look like an Ivy," he continued.

She had never had a nickname. She supposed no one had ever really cared to give her one, but the idea of this strange boy giving her one felt warm.

"Sure," she responded with a small smile.

"Is that homework?" he asked, leaning over once more to peer at the book in her lap, this time a droplet of water splashing the open page. "Looks like homework. Who does homework at the beach?"

She just shrugged her shoulders in response, unsure what to say or how to say it. Socializing was something she never had to worry about. Seraphina always preferred it when she stayed quiet. She expected the boy to get up and leave but was surprised when she glanced up from the pages to see that he had nestled himself into the sand and reclined back on his elbows, a broad smile still on his face.

They sat on the shore, the silence punctuated by Iverlyn's racing thoughts. What was she supposed to say? The words seemed trapped in her throat, tangled with fear and uncertainty. Yet, as she glanced at him, his warm smile washed over her like a gentle tide, and for once, she felt the stirrings of normalcy within her. Was this friendship? If it was, she realized, she wanted more moments like this—moments where silence spoke louder than words, and his presence felt like a comforting embrace.

Chapter Thirteen

I verlyn groaned as she rolled over on the plush mattress that almost seemed to wrap around her. Her whole body ached, and she opened her eyes only to slam them shut again when the blinding sunlight made her head pulse with pain. She didn't know where she was, but at the moment, she didn't particularly care, as long as it meant that Theo wasn't anywhere near her. The betrayal she felt from Theo—who had lied to her all those years and had even helped to orchestrate the lie that was her life—was a heavy weight on her heart.

For a moment, as he held her last night, she let herself imagine a world where she could forgive Theo because he was just doing a job. She knew that most of it was a lie, but learning that Theo was the one who had helped her father orchestrate how best to go about her deception stung more than she wanted to admit. How desperate had she been to fall for all those lies with ease? And how gullible must she be to have fallen for Theo's act of being her best friend while being disguised as a boy all along? She was disgusted with the idea of how easy she had made it for him to enter her life. The depth of her feelings for Theo, which she had thought were genuine, now felt like a cruel joke. A cruel joke that she knew Seraphina was reveling in. She had been right about him.

Iverlyn had always admired Theo's wisdom, his seeming maturity, and his refusal to be cruel like the other teens on the island. She had always wondered why, but had just assumed it was because of his past. After all, he had lost everything he knew at such a young age and had been thrust into life on Salus. That sort of change would mature anyone. But perhaps her desperation for a friend blinded her from seeing the signs that Seraphina had seemed to see so clearly. The day they had met, she felt so isolated and alone that when he chose to sit next to her on the beach, even if it was just in silence, that feeling of loneliness seemed to disappear entirely. She had forgotten how debilitating that feeling was, and now it seemed to engulf her once more.

"I don't want to startle you," a soft feminine voice called out, nearly causing Iverlyn to jump out of her skin. "But I also feel creepy just sitting here without you knowing," the voice continued with an awkward chuckle as Iverlyn sprung from the bed, moving so quickly that a wave of dizziness washed over her. She stumbled backward onto the bed, her gaze locking on the woman a few feet away, who wore a small but apologetic smile.

"I'm sorry. I didn't mean to startle you," the woman said softly, reaching for a glass beside her and filling it with water from the pitcher. "I'm Astaria, Zainiel's sister."

"I'm Ive–" she stopped herself short. Iverlyn didn't seem like the right name anymore. Iverlyn was the scared little girl who let Seraphina control her, the naive girl who fell for all of Theo's lies. She didn't want to be that girl anymore. "Ivy. I'm Ivy."

"It's nice to meet you, Ivy." Astaria offered her a warm smile before extending the glass of water.

Ivy took the glass into her tentative grip, studying the woman before her. *Zainiel's sister.* She was breathtaking, an ethereal beauty that made the air shimmer around her. While she had the same sun-kissed skin and full lips as Zainiel, the contours of her face were gentler. Her jawline was delicately curved, highlighting her high cheekbones and petite nose. Dark waves of hair cascaded down her shoulders. Yet it was her eyes that captured Ivy's attention most. Where Zainiel's dark eyes felt like an unfathomable abyss, Astaria's were a striking blue that reminded Ivy of the sun-dapped shores on a summer day. She didn't know if it was because of her love for the ocean or some other reason, but Ivy felt calmer as she looked into the woman's eyes.

"Where am I?" she asked, bringing the glass of water to her lips.

"The estate. This is where you'll be living from now on," Astaria answered with a warm smile. "Your father had the room prepared for you."

Ivy gazed around the expansive room, marveling at how it could easily contain her old bedroom at least five times over. Behind her, a magnificent window framed the scene, allowing warm, golden sunlight to spill through delicate lilac curtains. She sank into the plush white bedding of the large bed, its softness surpassing anything she'd ever touched.

Before her, Astaria sat near a generous couch, flanked by two chairs that faced each other across a small table where a pitcher of water rested. Ivy's eyes wandered to a corner of the room, where a desk and a nearly empty bookshelf caught her off guard; she couldn't help but wonder if she'd be allowed to fill it during her time here. She was relieved when she spotted a lamp emitting a soft glow and a cord winding its way from it to the wall. *Electricity.*

Everything around her radiated elegance and wealth, but nothing captured her attention quite like the grand marble fireplace to her left. Its mantle was a stunning swirl of gold and green, and Ivy wondered whether it was a beautiful coincidence that it reflected the colors of her own eyes or if her father had planned it all along. Who was her father to be able to afford this sort of place?

"Is he here?" Ivy inquired, her voice a fragile thread woven with eager anticipation. "My father?"

Astaria's smile wavered, a fleeting shadow of sorrow flitting across her gaze before she replied, "he's not, but he has asked us to keep you company until he returns."

Ivy nodded, grappling with the sharp sting of disappointment that gnawed at her heart. Despite all the effort he had exerted to bring her to this place, crafting this extravagant room far bigger than anything she could ever imagine needing, he couldn't even find the time to be here when she arrived.

"There's a bathroom just through that door," Astaria said, gesturing to her right. "I had some of my clothes brought up for you. I figured you might want to freshen up and change."

Ivy looked down at her mud-covered clothes and grimaced as she ran her fingers through her tangled hair. She felt like a complete mess.

With a warm smile directed at the woman before her, she replied, "I'd really like that."

"It's not a problem. They'd be happy to help," Astaria said as she handed Ivy a warm pastry before sitting across from her on one of the plush chairs. When Ivy had returned from her shower in the equally-extravagant bathroom, Astaria had insisted that she let one of the estate healers look her over. Ivy denied it, then denied it once again, only moments later. She didn't know much about the woman who sat across from her, but one thing she knew for sure was that she was persistent.

"I'm fine, but thank you," Ivy refused with a small smile. She appreciated that Astaria seemed kind enough even to consider offering a healer to her; and judging by the darkened bruises that were scattered across her collarbone and throat and the small patch of scratched skin on her temple, no doubt from a stumble she took in the forest, it probably wouldn't hurt. But, if she were being honest, the last thing she wanted was a healer to look her over and uncover the many scars that littered her body. That would only lead to a mountain of questions Ivy hoped to avoid.

Astaria hesitated, her lips parting as if to voice a different thought. Instead, she offered Ivy a faint smile that never quite illuminated her eyes. "Well, if you reconsider..."

Ivy nodded before taking a bite of the pastry. As the delightful blend of berries and citrus danced on her palate, she felt her body relax, the heaviness of hunger lifting momentarily. Perhaps it was the stark contrast to the bland meals Seraphina deemed acceptable, but this pastry felt like pure magic. She indulged in another bite, a soft sigh escaping her as delight washed over her body. Her cheeks burned red when she opened her eyes to see Asatria watching her. Her lips pulled upward in an amused smile.

"Don't be embarrassed. These pastries are my favorite, and I'm glad to have someone to share them with, finally," Astaria said before taking a bite of her own. "Zainiel doesn't eat them," she added with a roll of her eyes.

It was hard for Ivy to imagine Zainiel as a brother to anyone, let alone someone like Astaria. The few moments they had shared at the cabin before everything went to shit, he seemed so gruff, like someone who preferred to walk through life alone.

"You know," Astaria began as she passed Ivy another pastry. "I used to travel two hours one way each week just to get these pastries. I discovered them a few towns over, and they were like nothing I had ever tasted before. When your father noticed what I was doing, he offered to hire the pastry chef to work here at the estate, even offering to house her family. He's eccentric. Sometimes, he makes decisions the rest of us don't quite understand. But he is a good man."

"Can I ask how you and Zainiel ended up here?" Ivy asked.

"Our parents died when we were young, too young," she started as she ran her finger around the rim of the glass she held. "Zainiel and I did our best to fend for ourselves, but neither of us had much control over our magic, which made things even harder. We lived alone for almost a month before your dad found us. Zainiel had just been caught stealing bread for us from a local vendor, and your father paid for the bread and brought both of us to the estate with him. He trained us both when he had spare time, made it so we could control our powers, and when we were old enough to decide whether to stay or leave, we stayed."

Ivy picked the skin around her finger while listening to Astaria's story. Her father couldn't bring her here until now, but he somehow had time to raise kids that weren't even his own. She knew it was wrong of her to feel bitter, but the idea that he might have chosen them over her gnawed at her.

"I don't understand any of this," Ivy admitted with a heavy sigh.

Astaria got up and moved over to the couch where Ivy was sitting, placing a hand on her knee. "Okay. So, tell me, how much do you understand?"

Ivy's voice dripped with bitterness as she replied, "Not as much as I should. I know that you, or rather we, are fae. However, I don't really know what that means. I know that it supposedly wasn't safe for me to be here, and that Theo was sent to protect me. I know that I suddenly seem to have magic even though I have *begged* it to answer my call for years, and it never did." Ivy sighed, shaking her head in disbelief. How was this her life? "I know that my best friend lied to me for years, and as it turns out, the only truthful thing about him was his name. And my aunt? She was right about him lying to me all those years, and now I'm wondering what else she might've been right about. I mean, truly, how gullible must I—" Ivy caught herself mid-sentence. It was like her emotions were a tide swelling inside her, begging to break free, begging to be revealed to Astaria. Why? Why would she be saying these things to someone she barely knew?

"I—I'm not sure why I just said all that," Ivy mumbled, her gaze fixed on her trembling hands, her brows knitting together in confusion.

"It's okay," Astaria coaxed gently, giving Ivy's knee a reassuring squeeze. "You can share anything with me."

Ivy pressed her lips together, biting back the urge to let everything spill forth. Deep down, she feared that if she spoke, she would bare her soul entirely to the woman beside her. Whether it was lingering paranoia or the strange magic that flared within her under Astaria's touch, a quiet voice warned her not to say anything more.

Chapter Fourteen

"**Y**ou know, your father really hated that it wasn't safe for you to be here," Astaria said after a few moments of tense silence.

Ivy raised a doubtful brow and, before she could stop herself, said, "But it was safe for Theo, and for you and Zainiel."

Astaria cocked her head to the side as she studied Ivy. "How old do you think Theo is?"

"I thought he was my age, but now..." her words trailed off. He still looked like he was in his twenties, but she knew he wasn't. He couldn't be.

"Your father didn't have to worry about our safety because we are capable of taking care of ourselves, and have been for many years," Astaria started, briefly pausing to take a sip of water. "Being fae means a lot of things, but one of the biggest things that separates us from humans, or other magic wielders, is that we experience age differently."

Ivy's brows furrowed in confusion. "You age differently?"

Astaria nodded. "We age like humans until we are somewhere around twenty, and then it slows. Your father is centuries old, but he looks like a man in his early forties."

Centuries old? Her father was centuries old? Had her mother known that? Had her mother even known he was fae? She felt a rising tide of panic inside her belly, but as if she could sense it, Astaria placed her hand back on Ivy's knee. Her touch almost seemed to send a wave of calm washing over Ivy, one that she didn't quite understand, but was thankful for nonetheless.

"So, Theo? You and Zainiel?" Ivy asked.

"Old by human standards, but still relatively young by fae standards."

Ivy resisted the urge to ask her just how old that was. She wasn't sure she wanted to know. Her mind was reeling. All this time she had spent with Theo, thinking he was just like her, an orphaned child who didn't belong anywhere, when really, that couldn't have been further from the truth.

"Does this mean that I will age differently, too?" Ivy asked as she twirled her ring around her finger nervously.

"I imagine so," Astaria answered. "From what Theo told me, it seems that you've inherited your father's magic, and that magic is what slows our aging."

Ivy nodded as she fixed her gaze out the large window. While she had been showering, Astaria had tied open the soft curtains, letting the sunlight trickle in the window and revealing a large courtyard with rows of blooming flowers and a blossoming weeping willow in the center. Her mind reeled as she tried to piece together how her life had come to this. Just two days ago, she had been standing before the altar, begging the bloodstone to somehow see something in her that even she failed to see. And now she was being told that not only did she have magic, but she would also outlive everyone she knew, aside from Theo. How had it come to this?

"Why am I not surprised?" Zainiel's voice resonated through the room as Ivy turned to find him standing just inside the expansive doorway, his piercing gaze locked onto his sister. "I specifically asked you to fetch me when she woke up," he reprimanded.

Astaria simply rolled her eyes and snatched another pastry from the tray that rested on the table before them. "We were hungry," she stated nonchalantly before sinking her teeth into the treat.

A low, irritated growl escaped Zainiel as he shook his head in disbelief and made his way over, taking a seat in one of the chairs opposite the couch.

"Besides," Astaria remarked with a casual shrug, "When have I ever taken your advice?"

Ivy couldn't suppress the small smile creeping onto her lips as she watched their playful banter. Although her time with Zainiel had been brief, it was clear he had an ego far larger than any man should, and she found comfort in the fact that his sister wasn't easily swayed to do his bidding. But that smile fell when she noticed the slight bruising on his jaw and the bloodied cut that marred his upper lip. Had he been in a fight?

"What did you do?" Astaria's voice was icy, her gaze locked onto Zainiel's swollen knuckles as she let the pastry fall from her hand.

He shrugged, flicking his wrist and wiggling his fingers nonchalantly. "Oh, this? Just a minor disagreement," he replied, a dangerous glimmer flickering in his eyes as a smirk spread across his face.

"Zain," Astaria warned, her eyes narrowing. "This isn't the time for you to be picking fights."

Zainiel sat before them, reclining back into the chair and inspecting his nails as if he couldn't be bothered to listen to his sister's words. How could one person be so arrogant?

"Where is he?" Astaria asked. "Zainiel, where is he?" she snapped when he didn't answer. Ivy sank further into the couch, feeling she shouldn't be present for this. Astaria had been so sweet to her, but the woman beside her now looked like she could rain down hellfire without an ounce of remorse.

"Relax, Ria," Zainiel said as he dragged his gaze to his sister's. "He's fine. We just had a discussion, is all." He finished with a nonchalant shrug that made Ivy's annoyance grow.

Her eyes narrowed into slits of blazing sapphire. "A discussion that called for the use of your fist?"

"He had it coming," he shot back, his tone laced with unspoken frustration.

Ivy watched as the two stared at each other, almost as if they were having a silent duel. Were they talking about Theo? The tension between him and Zainiel was so taut she was sure she could slice it with a dull blade, but she didn't even know if Theo had returned to the estate with them. She hadn't bothered to ask because she wasn't sure she wanted the answer. If he came back to the estate, that meant she'd have to see him, and if she saw him, she didn't know how she'd be able to stop the flood of emotions that would come along with it.

"Who had it coming?" Ivy asked, deciding to break the silence.

"Theo," Zainiel answered, his lips tugging upwards into another smirk. She knew she shouldn't care. After all, he had spent so many years lying to her, but the idea of him being hurt...

"Where is he?" she asked.

"How should I know?"

Ivy glared at him as she felt her anger swelling inside her. "I want to see him." She didn't—not really—but she needed to make sure he was okay.

Zainiel locked eyes with Ivy, a mischievous spark flickering in his dark irises that made her fists clench in frustration. How anyone could tolerate his arrogance was beyond her comprehension.

"I'll show you to his room; that's more than likely where he's gone," Astaria cut in, her voice slicing through the tension. Zainiel opened his mouth to protest, but Astaria rose from the couch, fixing him with a frosty stare. "You clearly lack the self-discipline to come along. You can stay here."

Zainiel returned her gaze with an equal chill. "Fine. I'll be in the courtyard, then."

They had walked down two different stairwells and were now in a winding hall that seemed to have no end. Ivy was beginning to wonder if the term castle fit this place better than estate. Zainiel had silently stalked in the opposite direction when leaving her room, but not before sending his sister one more hardened glare as if to drive home his point that he wasn't happy about taking Ivy to Theo. But Astaria didn't seem to care, and neither did Ivy.

"He's not always such an ass," Astaria said, breaking the silence. "He and Theo have a way of bringing the worst out in each other, and I think, given the circumstances, everyone's emotions are running high."

Ivy suspected the circumstances Astaria referred to was her arrival in Arbor, but she didn't understand why it seemed to have everyone so on edge. "What is it between those two?" she asked, remembering how Theo had immediately gone on guard when seeing Zainiel at the cabin.

"It's a long story, and not mine to tell," she answered with an apologetic smile.

Ivy shrugged. She could respect that, but one day she'd be sure to ask about it. After all, it seemed they all lived here at the estate, and she imagined they'd all be seeing plenty of each other.

Astaria halted before a large mahogany door. "This is it. Did you want me to come in with you?"

Ivy pondered her question for a moment. She didn't know if she was ready to see Theo yet, and she sure as hell wasn't prepared to be alone with him, not trusting herself to be in a room with him without losing whatever small grip she managed to have on her emotions.

"I don't plan on staying. I just want to see that he's okay."

Astaria nodded before knocking on the door and calling out, "Theo? It's Ria; I've got Ivy with me—" Before she could finish, the door swung open, revealing a wide-eyed, disheveled-haired Theo.

Ivy inhaled sharply, her eyes widening as she took in the sight of the man before her. He was never one to take pride in his appearance, but this—this was beyond anything she had ever seen. His face was a canvas of bruises, far worse than Zainiel's. It was clear who had come out on top in their clash. His left eye was a dark shade of purple, swollen to the point of almost closing, while a bloody gash lay just above his brow. The shirt he wore hung in tatters at the shoulder, and as he shifted his weight to the right, Ivy caught the flicker of pain that crossed his face, despite his attempts to hide it. This was not a simple brawl between two men with a vendetta against each other. It was evident that Theo had been brutally beaten long after the fight had ended.

Her blood boiled as she took in the sight before her. She was angry at Theo, and part of her didn't know if she'd ever find it in herself to forgive him. But this? This was too far. No one deserved this type of brutality.

"Take me to Zainiel," she demanded, her voice coiled with barely controlled anger.

Astaria shifted uncomfortably next to her as she reached out to place a hand on her shoulder. "Ivy, I don't think—"

"Take me to him—now," she hissed, her voice low and fierce as the air around them shimmered with electric tension. Ivy yanked her arm away from Astaria's grasp, a wave of heat rising within her threatening to overflow. She could almost taste its bitterness, a sharp tang that accompanied the boiling energy surging through her blood like molten lava. Yet she held it at bay, her determination unyielding, whispering promises of retribution. All she needed was the right target to unleash the storm brewing inside her, and Astaria was not that target.

Astaria lifted her hands with wide eyes before taking two measured steps back. Theo remained silent through the exchange, his eyes glued on Ivy. "He's in the courtyard," Astaria said softly, as if she were trying not to startle a feral animal. But Ivy, electrified by the exhilarating power coursing through her veins and the promise of the ecstasy of release, couldn't bring herself to care.

Chapter Fifteen

"Oh, what's this? Are we having a little friendly outing?" Zainiel taunted as Ivy stopped before him, Astaria and Theo trailing behind. She had found him leaning against the side of the garden wall, one leg kicked back with his arms casually draped across his chest, his signature cocky grin on display, which only made the anger in her boil even more. The sky above them was churning as the clouds began to darken, and birds flitted away as the cool breeze dancing through the yard stalled, leaving only a chilling silence behind.

"You hurt him," she snarled in a voice that did not quite sound like her own.

Zainiel's eyes flicked to Theo, who stood behind Ivy, before meeting her gaze once more. "As I said before, he had it coming," he said without an ounce of remorse, holding his head high in the same blameless fashion that Seraphina had always done.

She narrowed her eyes at him, her limbs trembling from the power beating through her veins, and a voice inside her begged her to release it upon him—begged her to *destroy*.

"It's not as if he didn't get his fair share of punches in, too," Zainiel said, motioning to his split lip as he kicked off the wall and began to stalk towards her. "Where's your concern for me, princess?"

Ivy clenched her fists at her sides as she tried to focus on the energy that was buzzing through her body. *Oh, how she wished she knew how to control it.*

"Besides, do you think he would show the same concern for you? After all, you were just a job to him, right? Tell me, princess, did he ever stand up to whoever left those bruises littered all over your body?"

Ivy recoiled from the words as if they were a physical blow thrown at her. She had never questioned why Theo never stepped in to help her in the past. After all, Seraphina was easily the strongest witch on the island and not many dared to speak against her, let alone come between her and her unorthodox style of teaching. But that had been before she knew he had magic—before Theo was more than just a boy she had grown up with.

"Hmm, no?" Zainiel tsked. "What a *shame*."

"Z, I don't think now is the time to taunt the girl," Astaria warned from behind Ivy.

"Go inside, Ria, and take him with you." The teasing notes in his voice were gone as he commanded his sister, and somehow, that made Ivy's anger grow. *He thought he was better than them all.*

"I'm not going anywhere without Ivy," Theo called out.

"Are we doing this again?" Zainiel sighed, and with a wave of his hand, a wall of darkness erupted from the ground, shrouding Theo and Astaria from view.

Ivy's heart thundered in her chest as she stared at the black obsidian wall, shadows swirling and shimmering in the sunlight. "What did you do?" she ground out through clenched teeth, holding her fists tightly at her sides.

"Don't worry, princess. I just gave us a little privacy. We don't want you to lose your cool and hurt them by accident, do we?" His tone was cocky, and it made the anger in Ivy boil. She *hated* the confidence and arrogance that he exuded.

Dark storm clouds formed above them, obscuring the sun from view and casting an eerie light over the garden. A low rumble of thunder sounded as icy rain began to fall in thick droplets.

"Oh, come on, I know you can do better than that. You have all that power inside of you, begging to be released. Why don't you show me what it can do?" Zainiel was circling her now, a predatory glint in his eyes as if they were playing a fun little game of cat and mouse.

Ivy felt like her skin was vibrating, and heat exploded through her veins, rushing to her fingertips and toes. *Who did he think he was?* She heard a crackling sound and saw her hands webbed with lightning, the ground beneath her feet scorched.

"Now we are getting somewhere. Let's see what you've got," he mused, a dangerous glint in his eyes as he rocked back onto his heels, planting himself firmly in front of her. He wanted her to react, wanted her to *fight*.

"I'm not going to fight you," she said through clenched teeth. As much as she wanted to see his ego knocked down a few pegs, she refused to stoop to that level. Fighting him was something Seraphina would do, and she wasn't her aunt.

"Aw, where's the fun in that? Afraid you'll hurt me?" He tilted his head in a mocking concern before he extended his arm, motioning towards her with two fingers. "Come on, darling, do your worst," he baited. At his feet tendrils of darkness sprouted from the ground, winding up his leg and looming behind him, swishing in an eager dance of anticipation. The power he must have to be able to control all of this so effortlessly would've been impressive if not for his cocky attitude.

Ivy focused on the ground before her. Her hands clenched tightly at her side as her arms quaked from the raw power coursing through her. She didn't know how to control it, and already a bead of sweat trickled across her temple from the fight she was waging within herself to keep it from lashing out at the man who stood before her.

"Or perhaps I should bring Theo back out here? I'm sure he'd happily go another round with me."

Ivy's gaze shot to his from across the courtyard as lightning rattled through the air, striking just mere inches from where he stood. A warning shot, albeit one that Ivy hadn't directly intended. The still-pouring rain no longer weighed down her hair; instead, it seemed to stand on end, electrified by the current running through her.

"You will not touch him again," she growled, her guttural voice crackling through the air as it left her. *It was not her own.*

"Then stop me," he taunted.

The anger she felt was raw and intense. It weighed her down like a stone as it begged to be unleashed. Every emotion from the past couple of days beat against her: the sting of failure, the burn of betrayal, the realization of the deception by which she had so easily been tricked, and worse, the weakness that haunted her. She had all this power thrumming beneath her skin, yet she couldn't control it. *She was too weak.*

"Unless," he said, stalking around her with long, graceful strides, his shadows moving with him, "you don't know how." His grin was wicked, and for a moment, she felt like she was right back on the beach with Seraphina, hearing her promise of failure echoing in her mind.

The wind howled violently around them, yanking flowers from their roots and stripping long willow leaves with brutal force. Ivy's body vibrated with fury, her vision narrowing to lock onto his infuriating grin, drowning out the piercing ring of Seraphina's taunts echoing in her mind—that she would never be good enough, that she was destined to be nothing more than a stain on her family's name, that she was a disappointment to her mother. The rage simmered within her, desperate for release. *Destroy.*

A guttural scream erupted from Ivy's throat as she flung her arms out wide, unleashing an incandescent blue light that surged forth. For a heartbeat, time froze—the world hushed to silence, save for the relentless pounding of her heart. The light cascaded like a wave, devouring everything in its path, leaving behind a ghostly trail of ash where vibrant flowers had once been in bloom.

As the intense anger seemed to evaporate from her, leaving a cold, hollow dread in her chest, she watched Zainiel's shadows surge up over him, clashing with the light. The impact caused a rush of power that threw Zainiel spiraling through the air. *What had she done?* She sank to the ground, her knees digging into the still-warm ashen piles that lay before her. She braced her trembling arms, catching herself as a wave of exhaustion washed over her, and the wave of light dimmed before vanishing. In the distance, she spotted Zainiel's crumpled form lying just below the willow tree that, while missing some limbs and others having been frayed from the harsh winds, still stood.

She sprang to her feet, urgency propelling her forward as she hurried toward him with all the speed her trembling limbs could muster. Her heart thundered in her chest, each beat echoing her desperate need for reassurance. Was he moving? A flurry of frantic thoughts coursed through her mind—what had she done? No, no, he had to be fine. He simply had to be.

"Please be okay," she whispered, a fervent prayer on her lips.

A wave of relief surged through her as she caught sight of him pushing himself up from the ground, his back turned to her. His body shook in an irregular rhythm, each tremor sending fresh waves of anxiety through her. Was he injured? But then he turned around to face her, and to her astonishment, a radiant smile lit up his features, his shoulders quivering in—laughter? Was he laughing? A hearty, joyful laugh erupted, shattering the thick, oppressive silence that had fallen like a shroud over the courtyard.

She stood frozen, struggling to comprehend the bizarre scene unfolding before her. Just moments ago, she had watched his body soar through the air, flailing like a discarded toy, and yet now he was standing there, laughing as if nothing had transpired. It was utterly insane. He was completely unhinged.

"What the hell is wrong with you?" she burst out, halting in front of him, her voice a mix of disbelief and anger.

"That," he said, leaning forward and resting his hands on his knees, a grin stretching across his face, "was absolutely spectacular," he breathed.

Ivy took a step back as she observed the man before her. He was insane. Absolutely insane.

"I knew you were powerful, but *that*?" Another chuckle rumbled from his chest. "Well, let's just say it's been a while since anyone's been able to knock me on my ass, princess."

Ivy tore her gaze away from the puzzling man before her, taking in the destruction surrounding them. Everything was in ashen piles, even the bench that had been nestled between the rows of blooming flowers. She had done this. She had done this, and *he* had wanted her to.

Zainiel let out a low whistle, his gaze traveling over the damage. He shook his head, his wet hair flopping with the motion. "Ria is definitely going to kill me for this," he muttered.

Ivy's stomach twisted uncomfortably. In just her first day here, she had already given the only person who had shown her kindness a reason to resent her. She felt like she was going to be sick.

"You wanted me to do this," she shot back, her glare fixed on Zainiel as he tugged at his drenched shirt, water spilling from the fabric.

"In my defense," he replied with a shrug, brushing off the ash that clung to his dampened knees, "I never expected you could cause this much chaos. That was a miscalculation on my part."

A miscalculation? He couldn't be serious. "You're out of your mind!" Ivy exclaimed incredulously.

A deep rich laugh escaped him, rumbling from deep within his chest. "Perhaps I am," he admitted, running his fingers through his hair and tousling it further. "But someone needed to determine just how much control you had. Which," he paused, motioning to the once-beautiful garden, "we now know is very little."

"Why?" Her shoulders fell as she continued to survey the damage she had caused. Scorch marks spiderwebbed across the ground in a perfect circle from where she had stood. She could've hurt someone. If it hadn't been for his powers shielding him, she suspected that he, too, would've been nothing but a pile of ash.

"Because, if I'm to train you, I need to know what you're capable of."

"Train me? No. Absolutely not." Where was her father? He had helped all of them gain control of their powers. Why couldn't he do the same for her?

"Sorry, princess, I'm your only option."

Princess. Ivy couldn't stand the pet name he had decided on for her. She was no princess. "My name is Ivy."

He smirked, "I think I prefer princess."

He was insufferable. Ivy didn't know how Astaria had put up with him all these years, nor how she could even try to defend his actions. A chill ran through her body as a soft breeze blew around them. She was soaked. Her hair hung in wet, spindly tendrils, and the clothes that Astaria had loaned her hung heavily, the fabric stretching from the weight of the water.

"We'll start your training tomorrow," Zainiel declared. "I'll come get you from your room and escort you to the training grounds."

"I'm not training with you," she retorted, throwing her arms across her chest. "I'll wait until my father comes. He can train me."

An unreadable emotion flickered in Zainiel's eyes, but he quickly regained his composure with a shake of his head. "I hate to be the bearer of bad news, but your father's quite the busy man. Looks like it's just you and me."

Ivy felt the sting of his words, a sharp reminder of her father's absence. Was he truly preoccupied, or was it simply that he didn't care enough to see her? After all, he hadn't even bothered to be here when she arrived. "I don't need your assistance. What about Astaria, or Theo?" She felt torn; the idea of spending time with Theo again filled her with uncertainty, yet being with him felt infinitely better than enduring the arrogance of the man standing before her.

He advanced with three purposeful strides, narrowing the space until he was mere inches away from her. "What's the matter, princess? You don't trust yourself to be near me?" His fingertips grazed her skin like a whisper, but she flinched back, taking a significant step away from him. A flash of something—hurt?—crossed his eyes, only to vanish in an instant.

"Don't get ahead of yourself," she snapped, a scowl marring her features as she pivoted and marched toward the doors Astaria had led her through earlier.

"Where do you think you're going?" Zainiel called out, his voice cutting through the air behind her.

She didn't slow her pace, calling back over her shoulder, "Anywhere but here." The truth was, while her desire to escape him was strong, the weight of exhaustion bore down on her, and she longed to shed these damp clothes that now clung to her like a second skin.

"Be ready at dawn," he called out, his voice echoing behind her.

With an exasperated sigh, she raised her hand in a halfhearted gesture, dismissing him without a word. The heavy estate door creaked open under her grip and banged shut with a defiant thud as if to say she was finished with his demands. Let him come to her room in the morning. It wouldn't change anything. She refused to train with him, and short of him dragging her out of that room himself, she had no intention of going anywhere with him.

Chapter Sixteen

ZAINIEL

"**W**as it really worth it?" Ria demanded, the door slamming shut with a thud that reverberated through the air. Zainiel cracked open one eye, leisurely stretched out on his bed, surprised it had taken her this long to come find and reprimand him. He'd half expected her to storm into the gardens the moment he was alone.

"What are you talking about?" he replied, feigning ignorance.

Ria marched up to his bed, annoyance radiating from her as she shoved his legs off the edge. "You know *exactly* what I mean—fighting Theo, provoking Ivy, wrecking my garden," she shot back, her voice escalating in pitch with each fiery accusation.

Zainiel pushed himself up, arms stretching high above his head as he took a moment to loosen his stiff back. He couldn't deny that Ivy's strength had surprised him. He was still feeling the aftereffects.

"In my defense, she caused more destruction than I did," Zainiel said coolly.

Ria's only response was a cold glare that Zainiel knew all too well.

"Seriously, Z, that girl's been through enough. Don't you think you could've just lightened up for once? And going at it with Theo like that, what were you thinking?" She shook her head in disapproval.

"I was thinking that I needed to prove a point. She's dangerous, Ria." It was unfair. If they had more time, perhaps he would've been able to approach it differently. But he needed everyone, Ivy included, to see what she was capable of.

"You know, people said the same thing about you," Ria sighed as she sank onto the edge of his bed.

"And they were right." As much as he hated seeing the fear in his friends' eyes when they were younger, and even now, they were all right to keep their distance. No matter how much Ria pitied him for it, he knew she agreed.

"And what about what happened with Theo? Do I need to worry about you going after him again?"

"He got what was coming to him," Zainiel muttered, his voice gravelly as he flexed his bruised knuckles. He hadn't been searching for a fight, but after confronting Theo about Ivy's life on that island and witnessing the absence of any remorse in his eyes as he recounted the horrors he had allowed to happen, Zainiel lost all sense of restraint. He'd been sent there to protect her, yet he had merely stood by, doing the bare minimum. If it had been him, he would have whisked her away from that wretched place the moment her aunt first laid a hand on her. Orders be damned.

"I tried to get her to open up," Ria shared, her blue eyes shimmering with unshed tears. "She really needs a friend, Zainiel. There's so much hurt inside her." Her voice faltered as a tear slipped down her cheek. Zainiel felt a knot of worry tighten in his stomach; he had feared this moment, worried about his sister allowing that girl into her life and taking on the weight of years of hidden pain. Ria nervously twisted her hair around a finger, tapping her foot rhythmically against the bed—a habit that had emerged after their parents' passing. "Do you think we should tell her? About Kalec?"

"No," Zainiel replied, his tone firm. "Not yet. She has to learn to control her powers first."

Ria nodded slowly, her shoulders drooping under the weight of unspoken fear. He knew how difficult this situation would be for her, which was precisely why he had urged her to maintain some distance.

"She's going to hate us when she finds out," Ria whispered, her voice barely above a breath.

Zainiel slipped an arm around her, pulling her close as he stroked her arm gently. He longed to promise her that Ivy wouldn't harbor any resentment, that she would understand everything once she knew the whole story, but even he was having a hard time believing that.

Chapter Seventeen

"**P**ut me down!" Ivy shouted for what felt like the hundredth time, squirming on Zainiel's shoulders. He had kept his word, arriving at her room just as dawn crested the horizon, ready to whisk her off to training. But she too was determined to keep her vow of not training with him. Despite her eagerness to master the magic that she had suddenly been burdened with, she didn't want his help. She could tackle this on her own—after all, she had single-handedly taught herself a foreign language at age ten. How hard could it be to harness her powers?

"I warned you, princess. Walk, or I carry you. Either way, you're coming to training." She could practically envision the cocky smirk that stretched across his face as he tightened his grip on her hips.

"I don't like it when you call me that," Ivy retorted, her gaze fixed on the ground that blurred beneath her.

A deep chuckle rumbled through his chest. "Yeah, well, I think it's rather fitting."

Ivy rolled her eyes. He clearly knew nothing about her if he thought she was anything close to a princess. "Just put me down. I'll walk to the damn training grounds, okay?" And she would, but only because she was rather certain that the man that so effortlessly carried her could very easily catch up to her if she attempted to outrun him.

He shook his head casually, saying, "No need. We're already here," as he eased her down onto a weathered wooden bench. Before her, a sprawling field stretched out, encircled by thick woods except for the path they had traveled. Beneath her feet, the dew-kissed grass of the meadow was replaced by a patch of sand that sparkled under the soft glow of the morning sun. On her left, a fenced area sat atop the same luminous sand. Her eyes fell on a rack of weapons just outside the enclosure, their blades catching the light, positioned for swift, easy reach. Beyond, the expansive green field lay largely desolate, punctuated only by the scattered silhouettes of battle-worn targets at varying distances and heights.

It was a combat training field, she realized. She didn't know what she'd expected, but it wasn't this.

"You're going to want to put these on," Zainiel said as a pair of boots clattered before her in the sand. She had seen them in her room when she woke up that morning and had assumed that Ria had left them at some point, but didn't know what use she would have for them. She wasn't a fighter.

"I thought you were training me to use my powers. Why would I need those?" Ivy questioned as she eyed the sparring ring warily. She didn't like where this was going.

"After last night, I doubt you'll be able to muster up any power. It takes time for our magic to replenish after an outburst like that, especially when you're untrained. Today, we will focus on you learning how to defend yourself." He motioned to the sparring ring before them, and Ivy's gut twisted.

"I didn't agree to this." Ivy shook her head.

"Well, if I waited for you to *agree*, then something tells me we'd be here for a very long while." He wasn't wrong. He smirked as he nudged the boots towards her with his foot.

Ivy sighed as her gaze darted between the boots and the sparring ring. It wouldn't hurt to know how to defend herself; she imagined that if she'd known how to, it could've spared her from a lot of the things she went through on Salus. Not that she would ever have been brave enough to go against her aunt.

"I don't know how to do any of—" she paused and waved her hand at the ring and the weapons that adorned the rack beside it, "—that," she admitted, avoiding his gaze. She didn't want to seem weak to him, or any weaker than she already did.

"That's why you need to learn," he replied firmly. "The world is a cruel place, princess. You can't rely on others to take care of you; there may come a time when you won't have someone to rely on. You need to learn to do that for yourself."

Ivy nodded softly. He had a point. If it hadn't been for Theo showing up the night he helped her off the island, she didn't want to think about what she was prepared to do to herself just for the promise of not having to be married to that dreadful man. She had no other option, knew of no other way out; but maybe if she agreed to let Zainiel train her, as insufferable as he might've been, she'd be able to make a different choice next time.

Hmph. The air rushed out of Ivy's lungs as she once again landed on her back, Zainiel's foot deftly sweeping beneath her. They had been at this for what felt like hours; and no matter how many times she tried to deflect his advances, she always ended up sprawled in the sand or caged in his arms. Her cheeks burned with anger and a little embarrassment as she shoved herself upwards.

"This is pointless," she muttered, pushing stray strands of hair out of her face.

Zainiel tossed her a canteen of water. "It's not pointless," he replied, his tone carrying a hint of impatience. The sun hung overhead, blazing in the blue sky, its warmth starkly contrasting to the cool air that had been so refreshing earlier. Sweat trickled down her skin as she leaned against the fence, her body grateful for the brief respite. She uncapped the canteen and took a sip, the cold water soothing her parched throat and easing the heat that had seemed to somehow seep into her bones. The heat here was different from the heat she had experienced in Salus. In Salus, it almost seemed to envelop you like a warm, damp blanket; here it was different, dryer.

"Let's go again," Zainiel instructed as he tossed his own canteen down into the sand.

Ivy didn't bother to suppress the annoyed groan that escaped her lips. She was tired, and she didn't care if he knew. "How much longer do you expect me to do this?"

"Stop complaining and focus."

Ivy sighed as she tossed her canteen down before stepping into the center of the ring. She never should've agreed to this. Zainiel's eyes gleamed playfully as he circled around her, bouncing back and forth on the balls of his feet. He was enjoying this.

"Remember what I told you. Keep your eyes on me and keep your body ready to react." He lunged towards her in one swift movement, causing her to stumble backward. She didn't have the coordination for this.

"Keep your core engaged, it'll help with balance," he called out as he began circling her again.

Ivy sighed. What did that even mean?

Zainiel lunged forward again, but this time, she stumbled over her own foot in a frantic attempt to evade his grasp. She felt herself tipping toward the ground when his hand shot out, seizing her arm and drawing her into his warm embrace. Her back pressed against his chest, while his other arm encircled her tightly.

"You're too wound up" he teased, his breath brushing against her neck, sending shivers down her spine.

"Well, it's not exactly easy to relax when a mountain of muscle is barreling at you," she retorted, struggling to free herself from his hold, though it was a losing battle.

Zainiel barked a laugh, loosening his grip on her before taking a step back. "Mountain of muscle, you say?"

"I take it back," she grumbled as she stalked away from him. Not that it was any less true. He truly was a hulking mass of muscle, and any doubts she might have had about that disappeared when the sun shined on his sweat-drenched body, each divot and curve glistening in the light.

"I'm done for the day," she declared, glancing back as she practically limped away from the sparring ring. The ache in her muscles had settled in long before their exhausting match, but now they felt utterly spent, like jelly.

"Same time tomorrow, unless you want this mountain of muscle to carry you out here again," he shot back, a teasing lilt in his voice.

She grabbed the jacket she'd tossed aside earlier, slung it over her shoulder and, with a dismissive wave, walked back to the estate.

Chapter Eighteen

Ivy tossed and turned in her bed. Despite her body aching from the training with Zainiel, she couldn't bring herself to sleep. She had been here nearly a week and still hadn't heard a word from her father. She was beginning to wonder if he didn't even plan on meeting her here. What was the point in even getting her off Salus if he was just going to keep her tucked away in this estate?

She was thankful for the rescue, even though she couldn't help but feel that she had traded one prison for another; but at least in this one, she wouldn't be forced to share a bed with Alastair

Proctor. She shook away a shiver as the ghost of his touch lingered above her skin.

Here she had Ria, who, despite Ivy's destruction of the gardens, seemed nice enough. The more time Ivy shared with Ria, the harder it became to believe that she and Zainiel were twins. Where Ria was inviting and friendly, Zainiel had a swaggering cockiness about him that made Ivy want to master her powers, if only to see the look on his face when she bested him.

The distant chatter of voices filled the silence coming from the hall. In the week that she had been here, she hadn't seen a soul aside from Ria and Zainiel. Theo had even seemed to disappear—she hadn't seen him since the day in the gardens—but she assumed there had to be a staff of sorts. Food was always prepared and waiting for them at every meal, and after voicing her need for clothing and a few feminine products, they all had appeared neatly folded and stacked in her room. On the days that she found herself too tired to make her own bed, she returned to find it made, with fresh towels hanging in the bathing room. She wasn't sure how she felt about someone coming into her room, but she supposed she had no secrets here.

The voices grew closer. They were nearly outside her door now, and she didn't think she recognized them. There were two, one male and one female, but both seemed young and too happy to belong to Zainiel or Theo. Ivy moved to press her ear against the door, hoping to hear what they were talking about.

"Have you spoken to her?" the hushed female voice asked.

"Gods, no. Zainiel told us all not to. I don't have a death wish," the young male responded with a scoff. Zainiel had ordered them not to speak to her? Who did he think he was?

"You know his threats to us are harmless," the young woman scolded, her voice sounding right outside Ivy's door where their footsteps halted. "I think we should invite her to the party."

"Invite her? Are you insane? Zainiel's threats to you may be harmless because you are Ria's favorite, but me? He'd have my head," the young male exclaimed, fear ripe in his voice. Ivy didn't know what Zainiel had done to strike so much fear into this boy, but she couldn't help the small spark of anger that ignited on the boy's behalf.

"Come on, Luka, don't be such a baby," the girl teased, and Ivy heard an irritated groan before the sound of footsteps walking away.

"Do what you want, but I want nothing to do with it," Luka's voice called as he walked off.

Ivy remained with her ear pressed against the door, waiting to hear the girl walk off. She was surprised when a small folded-up paper fluttered beneath the door before her hurried footsteps rushed off.

Ivy bent down to retrieve the note and unfolded it to find *Bonfire at the lake tonight. Hope to see you there. Dress warm, it gets cold out. - Lilli* scrawled out in elegant but rushed writing.

The lake? This place had a lake? Gods, she really needed to do some more exploring. Ivy turned the paper over in her hands; she didn't know if she should go. Zainiel would probably be there, and she suspected that he wouldn't exactly be happy to find her anywhere but her room. But, on the other hand, she had spent her whole life never being allowed to do anything but what Seraphina approved. She was tired of living that life.

After an hour of wandering the estates, Ivy finally found the lake. It wasn't hard to find once the music started playing and the sound of distant laughter filled the air. However, what *was* hard to find was the narrow pathway that led from the garden to the lake, and she had more than a few leaves woven into her sweater and hair to prove it. Weren't fae supposed to be graceful? When could she expect that to kick in?

The lake was large, and as Ivy stood there watching the moonlight shimmer off of it, she found herself missing the beaches of Salus, and the way the salty air seemed to cocoon around her. She knew it was foolish of her to wonder if she'd ever find herself back on those beaches; even if for some reason she was sent away from Arbor, Seraphina would sooner kill her than allow her back on the island.

She had remembered seeing a few bonfires at Salus, but she was never allowed to attend. When she was young, she snuck away a couple of times to watch the partygoers from farther down the beach. She had never been brave enough to join the party herself, but she envied the freedom they all seemed to have and wished that one day she too could be as carefree as they all seemed. It wasn't until her seventeenth birthday that Seraphina caught her sneaking back in from one of the bonfires. The following morning, she forced Ivy to walk over the burning embers until her feet were blistered and the embers had grown cold. That was the last time she had ever gone.

Laughter rang out from the large fire to her left. A group of people stood around it, some dancing, others simply enjoying each other's company. Ria was standing in the center of a large crowd off to the side of the fire, a wide smile on her face as she swayed slightly to the music that floated through the air. She seemed so happy and free that Ivy began to picture what it would be like to feel that way, too. To let the music take her body as she swayed with the wind.

"You made it!" a cheerful voice rang out as a petite blonde bounded into view, her smile radiating warmth. "I told Luka you would," she added with a proud little puff of her chest.

Ivy offered a soft smile, taking in the girl who appeared to be around her age. Though Ivy supposed that didn't mean much when Zainiel and Ria did too.

"I'm Lilli," she introduced herself, extending a hand with an infectious bounce that sent her curly locks dancing. Her hazel eyes sparkled with enthusiasm in the firelight.

"I'm—"

"Ivy, right? Of course! We all know. I mean, it's hard not to, with the whole 'long lost daughter' thing, especially after what happened in the gar—" She abruptly cut herself off, her cheeks flushing a deep crimson. "Oh gosh, I'm sorry! I tend to ramble when I get excited," she admitted, her expression turning sheepish.

Ivy flashed a tentative smile, her cheeks burning with embarrassment. How many had witnessed the destruction she had caused? How many knew it was her fault?

"I'm really glad you came," Lilli said, breaking the silence.

"Thanks for inviting me," Ivy replied, trying to sound sincere; yet she couldn't shake the gnawing feeling that she shouldn't have come.

"Do you want to meet everyone?" Lilli asked, practically bouncing on her toes as she gestured toward the small gathering around the fire. Though the group was just a dozen strong, to Ivy, it felt like a bustling crowd compared to the solitude of her days with only Theo in Salus.

"I—um," Ivy stammered, her gaze fixed on the laughter and movement around the fire. They all seemed so happy—so friendly. "I'm not sure."

"That's fine. We can just stay up here until you're ready," Lilli offered before folding her legs beneath her and sitting on the ground, motioning for Ivy to follow. Ivy did, tucking her knees tightly against her chest as she watched the flames from the fire grow. When she was little, she had always thought fire was beautiful, but now she couldn't help but see how Seraphina had honed it into a weapon as she watched it dance in the cool breeze.

"I'm not very good at the whole silent thing," Lilli admitted after a brief pause. "Luka tells me I should try harder. I think sometimes my talking annoys him. He's a year older than me. We grew up together here at the estate." Ivy had wondered if Luka and Lilli were siblings, but as the blush crept back into Lilli's face as she continued to ramble on about Luka, it became clear that they weren't, and that Lilli had developed a little crush.

"Is Luka here?" Ivy asked, halting Lilli's ramblings.

"He's down at the fire, probably waiting on me, actually," she said, motioning down the still-laughing group of people.

"Why don't you go?" Ivy urged, feeling guilty for keeping the young girl from enjoying herself.

"I'll go when you go," she said firmly, planting her arms across her chest as if to prove a point.

Ivy let out a breath, glancing over at the lively crowd gathered around the fire. Zainiel was nowhere in sight, but the group seemed warm and welcoming. If she was going to be spending time at the estate, a little mingling might do her good.

"Alright, let's do this," she said, rising to her feet and extending her hand toward Lilli.

Lilli's eyes lit up with enthusiasm, and she sprang up beside Ivy. "Really? Are you certain?"

"Absolutely. Let's go before I back out," Ivy replied with a playful seriousness.

With a joyous squeal, Lilli clutched Ivy's hand, practically dragging her toward the fire. "You're going to fit right in! Everyone is going to adore you. I just know it!"

"Look who decided to join the party!" Lilli exclaimed as they neared the group. Ivy was stumbling behind, struggling to keep pace with Lilli as she practically skipped from excitement. As they neared the group, Ivy noticed that all conversations had halted, and even the music had faded into an awkward hush as everyone's eyes now lingered over her. The only sounds were coming from the crackling fire and the few daring crickets who chirped through the hesitant silence. *This was a huge mistake.*

"Ivy." Ria offered a warm smile breaking through the tension. "I'm glad you came, I should've invited you myself, it's just that..." She trailed off, looking around as if she were searching for the words to say.

"That Zainiel instructed everyone to stay away from me," Ivy finished for her, her tone flat despite the nerves that were coursing through her as everyone's gaze continued to linger.

A flicker of surprise flashed across Ria's features before she offered Ivy a small smile, as if to say *I'm sorry*. Ivy mirrored her smile and responded with a small shrug dismissing any guilt that Ria might have felt. She wasn't responsible for her brother's actions.

A bright, cheerful voice cut through the air from Ria's right. "I'm Luka," said a boy, his hand lifting in a small but enthusiastic wave. He stood tall and lanky, a figure that appeared almost spindly, as if he were still growing into his limbs. His hair was a wild bush of curls, each springy lock bouncing playfully with every slight movement he made. Despite his awkwardness, there was an undeniable warmth in his expression, one that reminded her of Theo.

Following Luka's introduction came May's, the estate's chef, and someone that Ivy had made a note to become friends with in the future, because everything she had eaten since arriving had been mouthwateringly amazing. So amazing that she had even begun to wonder if the food had somehow been magically altered to taste better. May, while still beautiful, was the oldest of them all, looking to be the same age that Ivy imagined her mother would've been if she were alive.

It wasn't long after May introduced herself that the music began to play once more, and the lively chatter returned, with even a few friendly smiles in Ivy's direction. She supposed it wasn't such a mistake after all.

Zainiel was still nowhere to be seen, but that wasn't surprising. He seemed more like the brooding type, anyway. Ivy wondered if he had ever let himself have fun; she imagined the answer was no.

A dark figure suddenly loomed over her shoulder, as if she had conjured him with her own thoughts. She had been quietly observing Luka and Lilli bickering animatedly about who would come out on top in a fight.

"You shouldn't be here," he growled from behind her, making Lilli and Luka's eyes widen in surprise before they hurried off like startled rabbits.

"I was invited," she shot back, placing her hands defiantly on her hips as she spun around to confront him.

"Invitation or not, this isn't your place," he insisted, his intense gaze locking onto her challenging stare, equally fierce.

"Yeah? And what is my place, Zainiel?" She cocked her head to the side and raised an eyebrow as she waited for his response. A few partygoers near them shuffled uncomfortably before they, too, scurried off.

"The training quarters and your room," he answered plainly as if she should already know.

"So, you mean to tell me that I'm... what? Some glorified prisoner?" she shot back, a low roll of thunder answering the rising anger in her.

Zainiel let out an annoyed growl before wrapping a firm hand around her forearm, dragging her away from the fire and speculating eyes, all of whom had been watching carefully from a distance.

Ivy yanked her arm out of his grasp as another loud clang of thunder echoed. "Let go of me!"

"I'll let you go once we're away from the party," he muttered through clenched teeth, frustration lacing his voice. In one fluid motion, he hoisted her over his shoulder, his grip firm but not unkind. Rain fell steadily around them, drenching them both as she squirmed and protested, her kicks futile against his determined stride. She was really growing to hate how he simply carried her like a sack of potatoes anytime she put up a fight. He kept walking, ignoring her protest and the growing rain around them until he had reached the outer ring of the sparring grounds before he firmly placed her down.

"What was that about?" she demanded.

"I told you shouldn't be there."

"I'm not your prisoner," she seethed, and a bolt of lightning shot through the air and struck just yards from where they stood. She had been tied to Seraphina's every demand for so many years. She refused to trade one prison for another.

"Oh, darling, if you think this is how I treat my prisoners..." he drawled with the click of his tongue as his eyes grew dark, "you have no idea just how mean I can get."

Ivy knew he was trying to get under her skin, trying to bait her just as he had done the other day, and she refused to fall into the same trap twice.

"You know, it must be a very lonely life to be such a dick all the time," she mused coolly as she tried to calm the anger that was still coursing through her veins.

He smirked in response as he tucked his hands into his pockets and leaned against a nearby post, watching her as she struggled to reign in the power thrumming beneath her skin. The wind howled around them, sending her hair twirling into sharp, wet tendrils. He was enjoying this. Enjoying watching her struggle to control herself. And the dangerous gleam in his eyes only grew with each passing second. The same dangerous gleam she'd seen so many times in Seraphina's eyes.

"I'm not going to let you do this again," she snapped.

"Do what?"

"Make me lose control," she shot back, her frustration boiling over.

"I don't need to trick you into that. Just a little spark, a flicker of anger, and you spiral." He gestured dismissively toward the bonfire's distant glow. "What do you think would've happened if you did this back there?"

A knot of unease twisted in her stomach as his words sank in. He wasn't just holding her back; he was shielding everyone from her. How had she become the threat in this situation? How had it come to this? Her hands quivered at her sides as she fought to reign in her chaotic powers. She strained to gather them, but another flash of lightning split the sky above the sparring ring, betraying her struggle.

"Until you master your own emotions, you remain a danger to yourself and everyone around you," he shouted, his voice barely piercing through the howling wind as thunder rumbled ominously in the distance.

A stone formed in her gut as a gust of wind whipped into her, causing her to stumble backwards a few steps. She could learn to control this. She had to learn to control this. All she needed to do was *breathe.* Ivy closed her eyes and clenched her hands at her sides. *Stop, just please stop*, she begged, but the wind continued to howl, and the clashes of thunder still rang.

"You can't allow it to overpower you. Seize control and demand it to obey," Zainiel urged, stepping closer. She opened her eyes, realizing he had moved to stand directly before her.

"I don't know how," she shot back, her gaze sharp enough to cut. He knew she had no control over her magic, and tonight of all nights he had chosen to lay bare that truth.

Her bones ached from the energy pulsing within her; her legs trembled, fighting to maintain strength. The magic roiled beneath the surface, eager to be unleashed, and she feared she might be unable to contain it.

"Then release it," he insisted.

"I can't." Wouldn't—because she refused to fall for his manipulation again. Wouldn't—because the last thing she wanted was to show everyone just how weak she was and how right Seraphina had been all these years.

"You can, and you will," he demanded with an intensifying gaze, his shadows flaring around him in anticipation. "Or else you're going to burn yourself out."

She clenched her jaw as another wave of pain washed through her body, the raw magic in her veins begging to be unleashed. Begging to *destroy*.

"Ivy," Zainiel warned, a hint of urgency in his voice. "You need to stop fighting it." Even though he stood only an arm's length from her, his voice seemed far away, as if a water barrier separated them. The only thing she could hear was her blood pounding in her ears as the magic continued to thrash through her body. Why couldn't she control it?

"I really didn't want to have to do this," she heard him whisper, the tremor in his voice laden with unease as his shadows surged toward her, wrapping around her like an impenetrable shroud of darkness. In an instant, she felt the weight of despair descend upon her, her lungs constricting painfully as the stale air was forcibly drawn away from her, siphoned off into the void. A desperate gasp escaped her lips, her hands instinctively clawing at her throat in a frantic attempt to reclaim the oxygen that had been so cruelly snatched away.

The ground beneath her felt as though it were crumbling, giving way to an unending abyss, and an agonizing, silent scream clawed its way up her throat. But before she could release it, the rhythmic pounding in her ears began to fade, slowing as if time itself was stretching thin, and the throbbing ache of her own magic—the potent energy that surged within her—began to ebb, slipping gently into a calming stillness. And then, just like that, she was ensconced in the depths of nothingness, the faint echo of *I'm so sorry* sounding in the distance as the darkness consumed her.

Chapter Nineteen

ZAINIEL

"I'm so sorry," he muttered as he cradled the unconscious girl to his chest. He hadn't had a choice. He had to use his magic to snuff hers out, or she would've hurt herself, would've killed herself. The very thought tore at his soul. He despised it, using his magic in that way; it always left him feeling stained, like the power he possessed was somehow not meant for this world. The more he used it, the more he felt the stain grow on his soul.

Like a blotch of ink that would never be washed away, no matter the amount of atonement he made.

He could have just left her alone at the bonfire, watching silently from the distance to make sure she kept her powers in check, but after seeing her smile and hearing her laugh... he had to be near her. But when he walked up to her and saw the fear in everyone else's eyes as they met his, he was reminded that the bonfire was not a place meant for him, and as much as he wished it for her, not a place for her, either.

So he did what he had to do. He was trying to protect her from herself, from her magic, from the burn of betrayal she would one day feel when she inevitably lost control and hurt someone she cared for. It was better for her to distance herself now. Better for her not to grow attached and then have to suffer through the pain of seeing her loved ones look at her as if she were a monster. He was doing her a favor. One he wished someone would have done for him.

"Zainiel." Ria's alarmed voice sounded from behind him as her hurried footsteps echoed through the vacant courtyard. His shoulders sagged in defeat as she reached his side, concern etched into every feature. He knew it was only a matter of time before she came running to find him. She always knew when he used his powers to consume, had always somehow felt the stain that was left on his soul through their bond.

She placed a tender hand on his shoulder, pulling him to a stop as her gaze flickered to the girl in his arms. "What happened, Zainiel?" she asked quietly, her eyes wide.

"I had to," Zainiel said, his voice strained with desperation as he met his sister's gaze. "I didn't have a choice. I had to." He had to make her understand. Had to make her see that he didn't have any other choice. She couldn't hate him for this. She was the only person who didn't see him as the monster he was. "I had to do it," he repeated in a strangled voice.

"I know, Z. Just tell me what happened." He could feel the calming waves of her power caressing against his panic, soothing his erratic heartbeat. He knew she was using her gift to calm him. Usually, he would push back against it. He hated when she used her powers on him, because while she let her goodness wash over him, there was nothing keeping the darkness he bore from doing the same to her.

"I—I pushed her too hard. She was going to let her magic burn her out just because she wanted to prove me wrong. If I had just left her alone..." He shook his head.

"So, you had to use your powers? You had to siphon her magic?" He knew the pain in his sister's eyes was for him. She knew better than anyone how using his powers in that way took a toll on him. She was there the first time he had learned that he could not only wield the darkness but also consume with it. It had been an accident. He hadn't known what he was doing, but he would never forget the horrified look on everyone's face when they realized what he had done. When they realized how much of a monster he was.

Zainiel nodded as he looked down at the girl in his arms. She had been so wary about him when she first arrived, so on guard with everyone except Ria, it seemed, and he was finally making progress, but now... "I had to do it," he said, this time more for himself than his sister.

Chapter Twenty

She felt adrift, warmth surrounding her, even as the cool wetness of her hair gathered around her throat. *What had happened?*

"I had no choice. I had no choice." Zainiel's words flitted around her as she drifted in and out of consciousness, not understanding what had happened or why her body seemed to ache so much.

"She was about to burn herself out. I didn't have a choice," Zainiel said, his voice deep and resonant, vibrating gently where her head rested against his chest. She pried her eyes open to see the night sky above her, bobbing as she was cradled in a cocoon of warmth. Zainiel's warmth. He was carrying her. Why was he carrying her? The world seemed fuzzy around her as she blinked, trying to remember what had happened.

She had been at the bonfire, and then Zainiel had shown up and taken her away. She recalled their argument in the sparring field, the throbbing sensation from her magic striving to break free, and then... darkness. *His* darkness. It had engulfed her completely, extinguishing her magic like a candle snuffed out by a breeze.

"Let me go," she rasped, pushing feebly against his chest. "You need to let me go now." She didn't want to be in his arms, didn't want to admit that it felt nice, that it felt *right*.

Zainiel halted and placed her on a nearby stone bench without uttering a word.

"Ivy, are you okay?" Ria asked as she pushed Zainiel back and settled on the bench beside her, checking her for injuries.

"I'm fine," she answered, and she was, aside from the burning ache in her bones and the headache that still pulsed inside her skull. She groaned and folded her knees to her chest as a wave of nausea washed over her. *Okay, maybe she wasn't fine.* But as long as Zainiel stood before her, she refused to admit otherwise.

"You'll feel like shit for a couple of days," Zainiel said from where he still stood with his hands shoved in his pockets. Something that looked like guilt flickered across his face before it was replaced with his normal stoic expression. "Training is canceled for tomorrow, we'll pick it back up when you've regained your energy," he added as if he were doing her a favor, and the last thing she wanted from him was favors.

"No."

"No?"

"No," she repeated plainly as she untucked her knees and forced herself to stand up despite the ache in her bones and the nausea rolling in her stomach. "I'll be there."

Zainiel raised a brow at her as she met his stare. She would love nothing more than a day to wallow and sleep, but she was done being weak, done being a pawn in other people's games.

"Ivy, I really think—" Ria started, but Ivy shook her head, cutting her off.

"I'm fine, Ria." Her voice was harsher than she intended as she spoke, never wavering from Zainiel's intense stare.

"Don't be stupid, you need the rest. If it weren't for me stopping you—"

"Stopping me? Don't you mean if it weren't from you *suffocating* me?" she seethed, venom dripping from her voice. She didn't think she'd ever forget how his magic felt as it engulfed her own or the gleam in his eyes that had reminded her so much of Seraphina's.

He recoiled as though her words were a physical blow. "I did the only thing I could do to help you. You were hurting yourself."

"Only because you were trying to manipulate me into losing control again, and I'm done playing games, Zainiel. You can either train me like we agreed, or you can leave me the fuck alone." She was angry, so angry that she was surprised when a clang of thunder didn't echo through the all-too-still night. In fact, this was the first time she hadn't felt that familiar bite of magic since she stepped foot into Arbor.

"I was trying to prove a point," he growled. "Until you learn to control yourself, you are a danger to everyone around you. I need you to see that."

"Zain, I don't—" Ria started from where she now stood behind them.

"Ria, stay out of it," he barked, cutting her off before turning his gaze back to Ivy. "Next time, would you prefer that I just let you lose control in a crowd of people?"

"I wasn't going to lose control. Not until you showed up and picked a fight." And it was the truth. She felt the calmest she had been since arriving at the estate perched by the flames, listening to the laughter of those around her. For a moment, she felt like she had finally found a place where she belonged.

"I did you a favor, and as far as I'm concerned, I did them all a favor by reminding them all just how dangerous you are."

Ivy tried to conceal a flinch as he spoke. *Dangerous.* "I wasn't going to hurt them," she said, her voice wavering slightly. *She wouldn't have hurt them. Right?*

"You don't know that," he said. This time, his voice was softer. "Right now, your magic is tied to your emotions, and you have no control over it. It would've been just as easy for one of them to upset you. The only difference is, they are all defenseless against your magic."

She felt as though the breath from her lungs had been stolen as the weight of his words sank in. She could have hurt them, and she wouldn't have had any way to stop it. She stumbled backwards before turning and walking towards the estate doors. She could've hurt them all.

"Where are you going?" Zainiel called from behind her, but she kept walking. She'd see him at training tomorrow, and then he could say whatever else he wanted to. But right now... right now, she just needed to be alone. If only so he didn't see the tears that were threatening to fall down her face.

The next morning was brutal, just as Zainiel had promised. Ivy had woken up with a pounding in her head that made even the slightest of sounds thunderous. Her body ached in ways that she didn't even think possible, and she was about ready to succumb to it when she opened her door to find a tonic, a note, and a steaming mug of coffee waiting for her. The note was from Ria, who promised the tonic would relieve some of the pain. Ria's kindness did nothing to ease the guilt that Ivy felt from snapping at her the way she did the night before. She would be sure to track her down later to apologize.

Training had been swift, and neither she nor Zainiel spoke about the events that had unfolded the night before. She was almost sure he would say something when she doubled over and vomited at the start of their morning run, but he just gave a disapproving grunt and then continued on, only speaking to her when he was instructing her on what to do next. After nearly an hour of her attempting to summon her magic and failing, he dismissed her with an irritated sigh, a wave of his hand, and a clipped, "Go."

Ivy had found herself in her room for the rest of the day, too tired and embarrassed to make the trek down to the dining room for lunch and dinner. So instead she sat and watched as the sun dipped below the horizon and the pink and purple hues of the sunset bled into night.

A soft rap on Ivy's door pulled her attention away from the grand window and over to where Ria now hesitantly slipped through her bedroom door, a plate of food in one hand, a jug of water tucked against her side, and a large satchel hanging across her body.

"I didn't see you at dinner. I thought you might be hungry," Ria offered as she set down the food and water. Ivy was just about to decline when her stomach grumbled in protest, and her mouth began watering as the smell of the warm food wafted over to her.

"Thank you," she said quietly as she made her way over to the food, trying not to grimace as she walked. In hindsight, she should've taken Zainiel up on his offer to skip training for the day, but she would never admit as much to him.

"I wanted to make sure you got the tonic I dropped off for you," Ria said as she grabbed a glass and poured some water in it.

"I did. I was hoping to see you today to thank you for it," Ivy said, feeling the blush rising to her cheeks, "and to apologize for last night. I was angry with Zainiel, and I shouldn't have spoken to you the way I did. I'm sorry."

"I know you are," Ria said with a gentle smile as she took a seat on the couch before the fireplace, motioning for Ivy to do the same. "That's actually why I came. I wanted to talk to you about last night."

Ivy's stomach fluttered with nerves as she sat beside Ria, anticipation swirling within her. It was only natural that Ria would eventually confront her; after all, Ivy had wreaked havoc on the garden on her very first day at the estate. The friendly façade couldn't last forever. Taking a deep breath, Ivy steeled herself for whatever Ria was about to say.

"Oh, gods, Ivy, I'm not mad!" Ria burst out. "You really don't have anything to apologize for."

Ivy felt a wave of relief wash over her, but the guilt lingered. "I still feel awful, honestly. If there's anything I can do to make it right—some way I can help in the garden—just let me know," she offered, eager to mend what felt broken. If Ria wasn't there to scold her, then why was she there?

"I wanted to talk to you about Zain, and what he did," Ria started, pausing to sip her water. She watched Ivy closely as if she were waiting to see how she'd react. "What he did last night was awful, truly. But I hope you understand he thought he was helping."

Ivy didn't know what to say. Instead, she found herself staring into the fire. She still didn't quite understand everything that had happened once Zainiel dragged her away from the bonfire. But she understood enough to know that he had been trying to manipulate her into losing control, just like he had the day she arrived.

"I know this has been... overwhelming, to say the least," Ria said after a brief pause. "Your entire life was uprooted, and you were just expected to jump into this new one as if you'd always been here. I know how lost you feel, how alone you think you are." Ria placed a hand on Ivy's knee as she spoke.

Ivy didn't bother to turn to look at Ria. She knew she was trying to help, and that this was Ria's way of ensuring she wasn't alone. Ivy wasn't naive enough to think that she was the only one who had had a hard life; she caught the haunted expressions on both Ria and Zainiel's faces frequently enough to tell her that there was something that happened to them that still loomed over them in the same way Ivy's past did to her. But at least they had each other. She had no one.

"Do you know what an empath is?" Ria asked.

Ivy raised her brow in surprise as she nodded. While they were rare, the coven had a few empaths who resided in Salus. At times, Seraphina had even tried to claim she was one herself. She wasn't, of course, and everyone knew it, but no one was ever brave enough to deny it to her face.

"My magic, it isn't like Zain's. Like an empath, I can sense others' emotions, but my magic allows it to go beyond that. I can't just sense it. I feel it, and sometimes I may even see it. So, when I tell you that I know what you have been through..." Ria grabbed Ivy's hand as she met her gaze, her eyes brimming with unshed tears, "I *know.* The day you got here, I—I was sitting with you, waiting for you to wake up, and there was just so much pain." Her brows creased as she shook her head. "I saw glimpses of what you went through... of how you got some of your scars."

Ivy's chest felt tight as she listened to Ria talk. She knew it was only a matter of time before they found out, and she assumed that Theo would have debriefed them on it all anyway. "Why didn't you say something sooner?"

"I knew you didn't want me to," Ria admitted.

"So why now?"

"Because I need you to understand that when I say Zainiel would never harm you, I mean it. And it's not because he's my brother, or because I'm trying to convince you to forgive him. I mean it because I know with every fiber of my being that he really does care."

Ivy eyed her warily as she spoke. She seemed genuine enough, but Ivy supposed she could always just be mimicking that emotion. After all, Zainiel was her twin, and Ivy sensed that there was very little they wouldn't do for each other.

"I know this is difficult and that you don't trust me, but just hear me out, okay?" Ria's eyes were pleading as she gently squeezed Ivy's hand.

"Okay," Ivy said with a small nod.

Ria gave her a grateful smile before she pulled her hand from Ivy's. "Zainiel has always felt responsible for all of us here at the estate. Sometimes I even think he takes our well-being a little too seriously, and at times, like last night, it causes him to cross a line. He should've seen that you were okay at the bonfire, but I think the fear of what could've happened blinded him."

She paused, taking a sip of water. "Your father, he expects a lot from Zain, and it's a heavy burden to carry. He tends to only see the danger in things, and he reacts strongly because... well, because that's just the type of guy he is. He fights hard and loves even harder. So, when he saw you at the bonfire with a group of people he cares for, all he saw was the possibility of something horrible happening."

Ivy nodded, tucking her legs against her chest and resting her chin on her knees. She could understand why he was worried to have her around those he cared for, but she still couldn't understand why he felt manipulating her into losing control was a good choice.

"When he picked a fight with you, I think that was his way of trying to show you why he was scared for you to interact with everyone. He should've gone about it differently, and he knows that, even though he's too stubborn to admit it to you. He knows he was wrong. I felt the guilt rolling off of him last night when I found both of you in the garden."

Ria sighed and shook her head. "I wish I could tell you that something like that won't happen again, but I can't. All I can do is help prepare you for it when it does. But I thought maybe if you understood his reasoning, it would help."

"What about what he did when I lost control? What was that?" Ivy asked.

Ria took a long breath as if she were steadying herself before she asked, "Do you know what burnout is? Has he explained that to you in your training?"

"I hadn't even heard the term until last night," Ivy answered truthfully. Her training with Zainiel had been nothing more than banter, snide comments, and unamused grunts from both parties. The less they talked, the better.

"The power you have is incredibly strong, so strong that if you call upon too much of it at one time without dispelling it, it can destroy you from the inside out; and in some cases, it can take you to a point that most can't come back from. When you were fighting against it, trying to contain it, that's what was happening to you. Your magic shouldn't hurt you, Ivy. That pain you were feeling last night was burnout," Ria explained.

Ivy took a shuddering breath. "So, what he did with his magic? Suffocating me... he was trying to help?" Zainiel's words from last night echoed in her mind. *I really didn't want to have to do this. I'm so sorry.*

"Zain's magic is powerful, and at times, if he wishes it to be, consuming. He used his magic to draw your own out of you. If he hadn't..." Ria trailed off, letting the unspoken words hang between them. *If he hadn't, then she could've died.*

"I don't expect you to forgive him for the way he's acted. But I know what you've been through, and I'm here to tell you that he's not a bad person. He wouldn't have hurt you on purpose." Ria paused as if she were deciding whether to say the next words. "Using his magic that way... it does things to him, takes him to a dark place. He only does it if he sees no other way out."

I didn't have a choice. Zainiel's words that he had spoken to Ria earlier echoed in her mind. *I did the only thing I could do.* Ivy took a shuddering breath and leaned her head back against the headrest of the couch. *I'm so sorry.* She thought she had imagined it, because surely he would never apologize, not to her. She had been too angry at the time, too confused by the events that had unfolded to notice the way he had cradled her in his embrace. The way he had scooped her into his arms, held her against his warm chest, and carried her until she demanded that he put her down. He could've left her in that field. Seraphina would have.

"He saved me, and I treated him like a monster," Ivy muttered in disbelief, mostly to herself. Sure, he had caused her to lose control, but she was the one who was stubborn and fought against her magic until it reached a point of no return. Zainiel was the one who had brought her back from that.

"He still played his part in everything. I didn't tell you this to make you feel guilty. I wanted you to understand," Ria said softly as she reached into the bag slung over her shoulder and pulled out a thick book titled *Tales of Arbor*, setting it on the table before them. "I brought this for you. I thought maybe you'd like to read more about our magic in Arbor."

Ivy eyed the book hungrily. It had been years since she had read anything other than the spell books that Seraphina used to make her read. She felt the rough patch of skin on her palm tingle, a reminder of what Seraphina had done when she had found her reading a book that Theo had snuck to her when they were younger.

"You don't have to read it if you don't want to," Ria added as she moved to grab the book.

"No," Ivy blurted. "No, I want to read it. It's just been so long since I was allowed to read anything other than the spell books that Seraphina would give me," she explained, her cheeks growing red in embarrassment. She must've looked pathetic to Ria. Getting emotional over a book.

Ria gave her an empathetic smile as she eyed the spot on Ivy's palm that she had been rubbing subconsciously. "You know if you ever want to talk..."

"I know," Ivy said, sending a small smile her way as she tucked her hand underneath her thigh. She didn't want anyone's pity.

"If you'd like, I can show you where the library is one day after training. Kalec has a rather large collection of all sorts of stories. Over the years, I even convinced him to add romance novels to it. I could show you my favorites," she offered.

Ivy nodded eagerly. A library. Her father had his own library? "Can we go tomorrow?"

Ria beamed at her. "Of course we can! Come find me after training."

Ivy nodded, eager with the idea of being able to read anything she wanted, as Ria stood up and made her way to the door.

"I'll leave you to get some rest. I'll have Lilli run a tonic up to you in the morning to help with the muscle aches," she said as she walked, pausing as her hand clasped the doorknob.

"Ivy, I mean it. When you're ready to talk about what you went through in Salus, I'm here." With that she slipped out of the room, not bothering to wait for Ivy's response.

Chapter Twenty-One

The estate was quiet tonight. There were no more whispers of laughter floating through the air, no more balmy smoke drifting up from the ashen pile of the remains from the bonfire earlier in the week, and no more chatter as everyone gathered together in a group, animatedly exchanging stories. She didn't know what she had expected when she decided to trek to the lake, but she was disappointed to find herself alone. Even the moon seemed to hide away from view, casting just enough light over the crystalline lake for its water to shimmer.

Ivy sighed as she fell back into the dampened grass, staring at the sky. As a child, she'd lie in the sand, tracing the constellations, weaving tales from the scattered stars—each one a whisper of an ancient history she could only hope to one day understand. Even now, with clouds dotting the night sky, the stars burned brighter than she had ever seen in Salus. Theo had once told her a story about a Goddess named Caledonia and how she had created a realm for her children. One that made even the most beautiful views in Salus seem mundane. Ivy never dreamed that one day she'd find herself in that realm—or that it even existed.

"Oh!" a startled voice pierced the silence, jolting Ivy from her reverie. "I didn't realize anyone else would be out here. I'm sorry."

Ivy stood and turned to find Luka standing there, a blanket tucked beneath his arm, his hand nervously clutching the back of his neck. A blush crept across his cheeks. "I—I can go," he stammered, the metal rim of his glasses glinting in the moonlight as he turned to leave.

"No," Ivy rushed out. "Stay."

"I don't think that's such a—"

"Please," Ivy interrupted, desperation creeping into her voice. "I know Zainiel told all of you to stay away from me. But please, just stay." She cringed at how pathetic she sounded, but since arriving, aside from the short time at the bonfire, Ria and Zainiel were the only ones she'd spent significant time with. She craved any form of normalcy, a connection, even if it was just for a moment.

"I suppose a little while wouldn't hurt." Luka offered her a small smile as he took a few steps forward, unfurling the blanket before sinking onto it and motioning for Ivy to join him.

"Thanks," she murmured, settling beside him.

An awkward silence fell over them as Luka nervously tapped his foot against the ground, and Ivy twirled the ring around on her finger. She was never great at small talk, but how could she be if no one had ever talked to her?

"I started coming here when I first came to the estate. Lilli showed this place to me." Luka said after a moment. "It's peaceful." A cool breeze flitted through the trees, sending leaves spiraling into the lake and creating gentle ripples.

Ivy nodded in agreement, leaning back on her elbows. She stared at the lake, watching the stars twinkle on its surface as the clouds began to part. "How long have you been here?" Ivy asked, recalling how little she had learned about him at the bonfire, aside from his obvious chemistry with Lilli.

"Zainiel found me when I was twelve and brought me here. That was eight years ago," he answered.

That would make him twenty—only a year younger than her. Ivy felt a flicker of relief at the realization that someone at the estate shared her age. In a way, it made her feel less alone. She still wasn't sure how old Zainiel, Ria, or Theo were—the last time she had asked Zainiel, he had responded with a snarky, "Hasn't anyone ever told you it's impolite to ask a man's age?" As if he could preach proper etiquette to anyone. It wasn't until later that Ria explained that some, namely the eldest of the fae, took offense to being asked their age, so she decided to drop it. Although, after poring over the books Ria had left her, Ivy wondered if some fae had lived so long they simply didn't know anymore.

"It gets easier, you know," Luka offered.

Ivy turned her head to him, raising a brow in question.

"Finding your place. I grew up in Arbor, but I'm not like the rest of them. My dad was human. He was a hiker and had a nasty fall just outside of the eastern gate. My mother found him and brought him to her home. They fell in love, and well, here I am. The only fae within miles who can't see more than two feet in front of him without these," he paused, motioning to the large glasses perched on his nose, "hideous glasses."

Ivy tilted her head with a playful smirk. "Lilli doesn't seem to think they're all that hideous."

Luka's cheeks flushed a deeper shade of red as he chuckled. "No, I suppose she doesn't."

Laughter bubbled up between them. She had missed this. Simply being able to sit and enjoy someone's company without the pressures of whatever expectations awaited her. Bitterness swelled in her chest. She used to have that with Theo, but she wondered how much of it was actually real to him.

"So, you and Lilli? How long have you known each other?" Ivy questioned.

"She was the first person to introduce herself to me when I arrived here. I guess you could say we've been inseparable since," he answered, his tone soft with a warm fondness.

Ivy smiled, recalling how Lilli blushed at the mention of Luka's name during the bonfire. They made a cute couple. Once upon a time, she had fantasized that she and Theo would have a relationship like that. It had been a silly fantasy concocted by a lonely girl. One he never seemed interested in; now she knew why.

"What's it like? Outside of Arbor?" Luka inquired, his eyes sparkling with intrigue. The question surprised Ivy; she realized she had never considered that there might be fae who hadn't ventured beyond Arbor's protective embrace. Yet, it occurred to her that her journey was not so different—after all, she had never stepped outside Salus until Theo had orchestrated her escape.

"It's different," Ivy replied thoughtfully. "I had never left Salus before coming here, but even back there, we had electricity and running water in every building. The coven made every effort to be as sustainable as we—well, they—could manage, relying on resources from the outside world as little as possible. So, Salus operated mainly on wind and solar energy. But we didn't have forests like this one, or really any animals unless they were raised for slaughter. They deemed it unnecessary if something didn't serve a direct purpose for the coven."

"That's..." Luka trailed off, his nose scrunching, "sad."

Ivy had never considered it sad; it had always just been her normal. But she supposed, in a way, it was. Everything seemed to work so fluidly in Arbor. She had never seen such luscious trees or vibrant flowers, and at any given moment, she could spot some form of wildlife skittering from one place to another. Even now, she could spot a family of ducklings following closely behind their mother as they paddled through the lake.

"I guess it is," Ivy mused in agreement.

"Do you miss any of the people you left behind?"

Ivy sat with his question hanging between them for a few moments. It seemed cruel to say no; after all, they were her family, though she didn't think they had ever fully seen her as such. In truth, the only person she missed from Salus was someone who never really existed at all.

"I think I miss the idea of what they should have been to me. My family was the strongest amongst the coven; every woman grew to be a powerful witch, and when I failed even to complete the simplest of spells," Ivy paused, shrugging her shoulders, "I was just a nuisance."

"You really couldn't do any spells?" Luka asked, his brows raised in surprise.

Ivy shook her head. "None."

"But what about your magic here? The storms?"

"Theo seems to believe that I was subconsciously calling them to me in Salus, but I don't think I ever really felt it like I do now,"

Ivy answered. It was a question she had been asking herself a lot since learning of her magic. She had found herself in plenty of situations where she had been desperate for it to answer her pleas, to finally prove to Seraphina that she wasn't the weak girl she always thought her to be. But it never answered. Not like it did here, at least.

"I can only imagine how heavy this all feels for you," Luka began, a light chuckle escaping his lips. "Honestly, if I were in your shoes, I might have set the courtyard ablaze myself." His laughter faded as he quickly caught himself, a touch of regret flickering across his face. "I'm sorry," he added, cringing slightly.

Ivy's lips curled into a gentle smile. Oddly enough, his words didn't bother her. She was tired of the feeling that people were tip-toeing around her; awkward as he was, Luka was quickly becoming her only friend here.

Chapter Twenty-Two

"Why do you keep looking at me like that?" Zainiel grunted as he feigned another attack in Ivy's direction, one that she surprisingly managed to dodge with ease.

Her conversation with Ria from the night before was still fresh in her mind, and she couldn't help but wonder what other dark mysteries he hid under his tough guy act. Then there was the gnawing guilt from how she had treated him after he practically saved her life, despite the fact that he was the one who had created the circumstances causing her to need saving.

"Like what?" she asked as she dipped low, avoiding another feigned attack.

"Like you don't hate me," he huffed, swiping a foot out to sweep her legs from underneath her. She moved out of the way with barely enough time, feeling the wind of his leg brushing against her.

"Would you prefer that I glare?" They both circled the ring, Ivy never allowing her gaze to leave his, following his movements just as he had instructed her to.

A slight smirk played at his lips. "Maybe. I was beginning to find your intimidating stares rather cute."

Cute. Ivy had always hated that word. It was a compliment meant for a child, and something told her that Zainiel knew as much as a teasing glint appeared in his eyes.

He advanced towards her, going for a soft jab to the side, which she successfully evaded. He smirked, happy at her success as he danced around her in a circle, preparing for his next strike. She pivoted, keeping an eye on his body. He moved like water, rigid but flowing with ease all at once.

"Hit me," he instructed.

"What?"

"Hit. Me," he repeated as he continued his dance around her, bouncing on the balls of his feet.

"You're supposed to be teaching me self-defense, not how to hit," she said.

"Lesson number three: sometimes self-defense also means knowing when to go on the offense. Stop wasting time and hit me."

She didn't know where to start or how to hit. She'd never hit anyone before.

"Come on, Storm. We don't have all day," he taunted. "I'll even make it easy for you and stand still." He stood across from her in the ring, his stance lazy and unguarded. He clearly didn't think she could land a hit on him, and it made her want to erase that smug look off his face even more.

"Storm?"

He shrugged. "You said you didn't like princess, so I'm trying something new."

Narrowing her eyes, she advanced and threw a clumsy punch aimed at his jaw. He dodged quickly, sending her crashing to her knees. She growled in frustration and jumped back up, turning to face him again.

"Try again," he teased, his cocky smirk widening.

This time, she lunged faster, targeting the left side of his torso that he had left open. He spun around her smoothly, her fist hitting nothing but air. But this time, she stayed on her feet.

"You've got to be faster than that," he tsked as she whirled around to face him again.

She glared at him, frustration simmering in her eyes. He was supposed to be training her, yet he seemed to derive more enjoyment from mocking her lack of proficiency in throwing punches. She mimicked his movements inside the ring, her feet tracing an agile path as she recalled his defensive maneuvers. Her objective was simple but daunting: land a single solid hit.

With her eyes locked on him, she circled once more, then lunged forward with a fierce determination, her fist aimed at his jaw. The moment her knuckles connected with a firm, warm surface, a triumphant smile spread across her face—only to evaporate just as quickly. To her shock, she felt herself being pulled and twisted into an unyielding embrace, her back now against his chest, his arm securely looped around her shoulders, immobilizing her.

She hadn't landed the punch she had hoped for. Instead, he had intercepted her strike, using her momentum to ensnare her.

"Nice try, but we've got to work on your form," he murmured, his breath hot against her neck. "Wouldn't want you to break those pretty little fingers of yours," he added, the hint of a teasing smile brushing against her earlobe.

She repressed a shudder as his breath cascaded down her back, willing the goosebumps that had risen on her skin to go away. She didn't want to be affected by him like this. It would lead to nothing good. But what was the harm in a little fun?

"Do you plan on letting me go? Or do you enjoy the feeling of my body against your own?" she teased.

"Oh, darling, you have no idea," he purred in her ear, tugging her closer to him. If it weren't for the feel of his curved lips against her cheek, she would've thought he was serious for a moment, the way his fingertips lazily wandered lower on her chest. This was a game, and as much as she hated games, this was one she would play.

"Besides, if you want out of my grip, all you have to do is what I've taught you. Show me what you've learned." His voice was husky as he spoke into her ear.

She grinned. That she could do.

"Ria talked to you, didn't she?" Zainiel asked from where he sat across from her in the sparring ring.

She took a sip of water, her chest heaving as she tried to catch her breath. She didn't know how he looked as if they hadn't just sparred for two hours.

"Why do you say that?" she asked, feigning innocence. While Ria hadn't asked Ivy to keep their conversation between them, she suspected that Zainiel wouldn't be happy to hear that his sister had talked to her about him.

He huffed a sigh of annoyance as he took a large gulp of his own water. "You're different today."

"Am I?" she asked with a shrug, "I hadn't realized."

He shot her a glare that said *I don't believe you* but remained silent.

"Can I ask you a question?" Ivy asked as she plucked a blade of grass and rolled it between her fingers.

"If it's about my dashing good looks or my charming ways, I'm sorry to say that it's a mystery to us all."

"Ha, ha," she responded dryly with a hint of a smile on her face. She was beginning to like this side of him.

"Why are you training me?" she asked.

His eyebrows rose in surprise before he answered with a small shrug. "I can't have you playing the part of the beautiful damsel all the time. I figured we may as well fix that while we wait for Kalec to return."

"I'm no damsel," she bristled, hating the way her stomach flipped when he called her beautiful. She had been called many things in her lifetime, but beautiful was not one of them.

He just responded with a raised brow as if to say, *are you sure about that?*

Ivy sighed. Maybe she was a bit of a damsel. "So, my father. He didn't instruct you to train me?"

Zainiel smiled at her for a moment. A smile that nearly knocked the air out of her in an entirely different way. How was he so beautiful? "No, darling, I'm doing that all on my own," he said with a puff of his chest.

She studied him with narrowed eyes. Surely, he had something to gain from helping her. Was he just using her to impress her father? Was she a pawn for him just as she was for Theo?

"What are you getting out of it?" she asked, plucking another blade of grass.

"Would you believe me if I said nothing?"

She raised a brow in response.

"Fair enough," he said. "Truthfully? Someone has to train you, and until Kalec returns, I'm the most qualified person here to do so."

"What makes you qualified?" Ivy asked.

Zainiel smirked. "You think Theo would be more qualified to help you?"

Ivy shrugged. "Maybe he is."

Zainiel's gaze locked onto the visible scars on her shoulder and the yellowing bruises still fading around her neck from Seraphina's spell. "Are you really sure about that?" he asked, his tone darkening as he focused on her injuries.

Ivy instinctively pulled at the collar of her shirt, her voice sharp. "You have no idea what you're talking about."

"Really? Seven years was plenty of time for him to at least teach you how to fight back. Tell me, Storm, did he bother?" He raised a brow, his gaze slowly raking across her body before settling on her face.

Ivy glared at him, irritation flooding her. Who did he think he was?

"Besides," he said, reclining back onto his elbows, "I don't know if you've noticed, but I'm incredibly powerful. And despite what you've been led to believe, you are too."

Ivy sighed and rolled her eyes before pushing up from the ground. She didn't think she could take any more of his vain sense of ego, and training was done for the day.

"Running away because you don't like what I have to say doesn't change the fact that it's the truth," he called from where he still lay reclined in the grass.

"I'm not running. I have plans," she called over her shoulder as she walked towards Ria's room.

Ivy had nearly reached Ria's room, her nose in the book that Ria had left with her last night as she bustled down the hall when she ran into a hard chest. She sighed, annoyed, expecting it to be Zain, but as she looked up and met a pair of hazel eyes, all she did was stare in shock.

"Ivy," Theo said warmly, "I was just coming to find you."

She stepped back, putting space between them as she closed the book, tucking it underneath her arm. He looked better than the last time she had seen him. The bruises and marred lip from his fight with Zainiel were gone, which was no surprise. Theo had always been a fast healer, something she had envied when they were growing up.

"How have you been?" he asked, reaching out to place a hand on her shoulder, which, thanks to Zainiel's lessons, she skillfully and gracefully dodged. He looked at her in confusion and shoved his hand into his pocket.

"Where have you been?" she asked, her voice heavy with emotion. It had been over a week since she had seen him, the last time being when they were all in the garden and she had confronted Zainiel.

"I, uh," he paused, scratching the back of his neck as he looked down at his shoes. "I didn't know if you'd want to see me." She didn't, but that didn't stop the sting that she felt when she realized he'd had no problem giving her that space.

"So, your solution was just to abandon me?" she asked. She tried to keep her voice from faltering, fighting off the tears that welled in her eyes; but as she looked at Theo standing before her, all of the betrayal she felt came rushing back. Was any of it true?

"I didn't abandon you," Theo argued. "You were angry with me."

"Because you lied to me for years, Theo! I have every right to be angry with you. You made me believe we were friends." Her voice trembled, swelling with emotion as she spoke.

"It wasn't all lies, Ivy. I just—"

"Iverlyn," she corrected coolly, a chill in her voice. Ivy was a name reserved for when they were friends, and those days were over.

He winced at the correction, pain evident in his expression. For a heartbeat, Ivy nearly felt a pang of guilt, but she pushed it aside. Guilt would only lead to forgiving him, and she wasn't ready for that.

"Don't be like this," he pleaded, reaching out a trembling hand.

She sidestepped his touch, her eyes narrowing. "What are you doing here, Theo?" Her voice was sharp, and she felt the familiar stirring of power awakening beneath her skin.

He sighed, raking his hand through his hair before dragging it across the stubble on his face, which was noticeably longer than usual. The dark circles under his eyes suggested he hadn't been sleeping well either. A pang of worry tugged at her heart, but she quickly dismissed it. He didn't deserve her concern.

"Look, I just wanted to check if you've settled in and make sure you don't need anything," he sighed.

"Zainiel and Ria have seen to it that I have everything I need," she retorted, her words not entirely truthful. It was Ria who had helped her the most, while her interactions with Zainiel were primarily focused on her training, followed by her wanting to throttle the smugness out of him. But Ivy knew that insinuating Zainiel had been more helpful than him would strike a nerve, and she wasn't about to let him off the hook so easily.

"Good," he muttered, the word sharp with frustration, his eyes flashing with irritation.

A pang of guilt tugged at Ivy's heart for behaving as she had, but she couldn't allow Theo back into her life just yet. Until she could discern the old Theo from the new, she needed to maintain her distance—for the sake of her own emotional stability.

"I'll just go then," he said, moving to sidestep around her in the hall.

Ivy's only response was a slight nod as she reopened the book she had stuck under her arm, feigning interest in the pages.

"For what it's worth," his voice sounded behind her, "I genuinely came to care about you. I still do," he said, his voice imbued with earnestness, followed by the sound of his retreating footsteps.

Chapter Twenty-Three

"This is useless," Ivy groaned as she threw her hands up in defeat. She and Zainiel were in the vast training field. He had instructed her to summon her magic with the goal of hitting the target he had placed a few yards away. But that was nearly three hours ago, and she had failed to summon anything other than small sparks that a bargain bin taser could've put to shame.

"You just need to get out of your head," Zainiel said for the fourth time that hour. Which wasn't helping with her frustration.

"I already told you I don't know what you mean by that," she gritted out, sending him a cold glare, which he responded to with a knowing smirk. "Care to give me any pointers? Or are we just going to stay out here all night?" She motioned to the sun, which was now barely peeking over the horizon.

"What are you thinking about?"

"Currently? I'm thinking that the idea of using you as target practice is appealing," she answered with a glare.

Zainiel barked a hearty laugh before he walked over, stopping when he was only a few inches from her. Their shoulders nearly brushed from how close he stood. "As much as I enjoy being the trigger for your magic, I think we should just stick to the actual target."

She sighed and glared at the target before her. All she had to do was hit the target, but at this point, she'd settle for any sort of sign that her magic was willing to work with her. She hadn't been able to use it since the night of the bonfire, which was nearly two weeks ago. And it seemed that tonight it was opting to remain dormant, even as she practically begged it to answer her calls.

"I don't think I can," she admitted with a defeated sigh.

"How about a break, then?" Zainiel suggested as he sat down on the grass, motioning for her to do the same. This was beginning to become a habit for them.

Ivy sighed, folding her legs beneath her. She settled on the grass next to Zainiel as she gazed out at the horizon, captivated by the sunset's colors in contrast to the heavy mountain line that lay in the distance. It was truly beautiful.

"I know it was naive of me, but I didn't think this would be so hard," Ivy admitted.

Zainiel turned to her with a raised brow. "Go on."

"I spent so many years studying how magic worked in Salus. Praying to a Goddess I'm not even sure was ever there, training day in and day out..." Ivy paused, shaking her head. "I guess I just thought that now that I have magic, using it would come easily. I mean, you all make it *look* so easy."

Zainiel chuckled softly. "Sure, we make it look easy now, but we've all been where you are."

Ivy scoffed. She highly doubted that. Zainiel didn't strike her as someone who wasn't always in full control.

"Ria still struggles sometimes when other's emotions are strong enough. And Theo?" Zainiel smirked. "Theo used to shift into a donkey anytime he got flustered. Really made an ass out of himself."

Ivy snorted a laugh at the thought. She thought she had been there through Theo's awkward teenage stage, though she now realized she never was. While the rest of them were pimply-faced, hormone-riddled teenagers, he was always just Theo.

"And you? Did you ever struggle to control your magic?" she asked.

The smirk fell from his face. "I did."

She wanted to ask him more about what happened when he lost control, but judging by the haunted look that suddenly settled on his face, she chose not to, instead letting her gaze shift back to the horizon.

"Tell me what you're thinking," he said after a few moments.

"I'm thinking that we didn't have views like this in Salus. I mean, we had sunsets, of course, but nothing like this," she mused, her eyes still trained on the way the cool orange hues of the sun melted into pinks and purples.

"Do you miss it?" Zainiel asked, surprising her with the sincerity in his voice.

Ivy took a deep breath and let herself fall backward into the grass before answering, "I miss the beach, the sound of the waves, the smell of the salty air, the way the push and pull of the current felt against my skin."

"It sounds nice."

"It was my little safe space. No matter what happened, I knew it would always be there, waiting for me," she admitted.

"Your turn," she said after a moment. Zainiel turned to her with a raised brow.

"Tell me something—something real." She had spent all this time with him, and still didn't feel like she knew him all that well. Silence followed, and for a moment, Ivy thought he wasn't going to answer her.

"I don't like the dark," he finally confessed.

Ivy's brows shot up, and a playful grin stretched across her face. Surely, he was joking. He commanded shadows, after all.

"No, really. I find it to be quite harrowing at times," he insisted, catching the skepticism in her gaze.

"But you wield darkness, don't you?"

A fleeting emotion flickered across his face, almost imperceptible before it vanished. "Even darkness craves light sometimes."

There was a bittersweet quality to his words that tugged at her heart. Ria's voice echoed in her mind. *Your father expects a lot from Zain.* Ivy realized she had spent most of her life pleading with Zaria and any other divine being to grant her magic. Yet, she had never paused to consider that for some, the very magic she yearned for might feel more like a burden than a blessing.

A few moments of silence passed before Zainiel shot to his feet and extended his hand out to Ivy. "Come on, I want to try something."

She placed her hand in his, allowing him to pull her up. He grasped her shoulders and turned her towards the wooden target, and she had to stifle a groan before he said, "Just do what I say, and trust me."

She sighed. She had really been hoping that they were done for the day.

"If this doesn't work, I promise we'll be done for now," he offered.

"Okay, fine."

"Close your eyes," he urged, his breath a warm whisper against the crown of her head. "Picture yourself on the beach."

Ivy turned her head slightly, raising an eyebrow at him. "I never took you for the meditation sort."

He rolled his eyes. Mock exasperation danced across his features, yet a knowing smirk tugged at his lips. "Just shut your eyes, Storm."

With a reluctant sigh, she obeyed.

"Now, imagine you're by the sea," he murmured, his voice low and soothing, sending a gentle shiver down her spine. "It's just you. The sand cradles your feet, and your hair flows free." She felt his fingers deftly release the tie binding her hair, allowing it to tumble down her back and frame her shoulders.

"You can feel the breeze playing with your hair, the waves crashing rhythmically against the shore, just for you. Can you see it?" he prompted, his voice drawing her deeper into his vision.

She nodded, feeling the tension melt away. Her body moved gently with the rhythm of the waves crashing against the shore. With a deep breath, she inhaled the unmistakable scent of salt in the air.

"Now, I want you to reach for your magic," he instructed. "Don't seek its approval, it's a part of you. All you have to do is grasp it."

Ivy reached into herself as another wave crashed against the shore, and she was surprised when she found that familiar tug of her magic waiting for her, dancing through her fingertips and washing over her body in a warm caress. It felt different than she thought it would. It felt freeing.

"Good, now I want you to hit that target," Zainiel said.

Ivy opened her eyes, bracing herself for the possibility that her magic might slip away, but a soft, cool glow twirled gently between her fingertips. Holding her hand out in wonder, she watched as the light playfully wove around her fingers as if it had a life of its own. This was her magic. *Hers.* A triumphant smile spread across her face as she extended her palm, and a tiny flare of sparks eagerly danced in response.

"The target, Storm," Zainiel reminded gently.

She fought the blush that was creeping up her neck. For a moment, she had forgotten he was even there. She looked at the wooden target that stood on the other side of the field, and with a subtle flick of her wrist, she watched as a bolt of lightning shot out, hitting the bullseye with precision.

She let out a delighted squeal, spinning to face Zainiel. "I did it!" she exclaimed, laughter bubbling from her lips. "I really did it! Did you see that?" Before she could think better of it, she launched herself at him, wrapping her arms around his neck. To her surprise, he embraced her, lifting her effortlessly off the ground and spinning her around. His laughter joined hers, filling the air with their shared joy.

As the world faded around them, her gaze locked onto his. They stopped spinning, yet he held her tightly, his arms securely around her waist while her arms remained around his strong neck, one hand weaving through his soft hair. Heat rushed to her cheeks as she realized what she had just done, jumping into his arms as if they weren't just at each other's throats a few days ago. But all that vanished as he gently set her down, running his arms up her back, weaving his fingers through her hair as he hugged her close to his chest. Their blissful moment lingered, only interrupted by the faint scent of smoke wafting through the air.

"Shit," Zainiel murmured, releasing her from his grip before taking a large step back, creating distance between them. With a flick of his wrist, his shadows enveloped the smoldering target, snuffing out the flames in moments.

They both stood there, staring at what remained of the wooden column in silence. But Ivy couldn't help the little bubble of laughter as she held out her hand and summoned her magic once again. Watching as the sparks danced around her fingertips. *This was her magic.* If only Seraphina could see her now.

Zainiel watched her as she flitted sparks of magic between her fingertips, obviously admiring it. Embarrassed, Ivy stopped, before saying the two words she never thought she'd utter to him: "Thank you."

"What's that you've got there?" Zainiel asked, nodding at the casting ring that she was twirling in her fingers.

Zainiel sat beside her, where she lay on her back staring up at the constellations. She hadn't asked him to stay with her; things had been so awkward between the two of them after they broke apart from their hug that she thought he would flee at the first available chance. But when she sat down and let herself fall back onto the lush grass, he simply did the same. Neither of them had talked. They just sat silently in each other's company as they watched the night sky come to life.

"It's a casting ring," Ivy answered as she pulled herself up to sit next to him, holding the ring out so it glinted in the moonlight. "In Salus, the magic they use requires blood to work. Most spells, all it takes is a needle prick." She pressed her thumb against the ring, causing the needle to spring free from where it had been concealed.

Zainiel's brows raised in surprise as he studied the ring. "I didn't think you could use their magic," he mused.

"I can't. Really, I shouldn't even have this. It made a lot of people angry that I did. Earning these rings is seen as a sort of rite of passage, and I never earned mine."

"How'd you end up with it?"

"My mother," she answered with a sad smile. "She had it made for me before I was even born. Seraphina was furious that I had it." Sometimes, she wondered if her mother had somehow known she wouldn't live to see her daughter grow up.

"Your aunt? Did she ever try to take it?"

Ivy flicked the needle back into the hidden compartment of the ring. "She did. My mother enchanted it before she died so it could never be lost or taken." She tossed the ring a few feet and opened her palm, grinning as it reappeared instantly. Zain's eyes widened in quiet surprise.

"I've never seen anything like it," he mused, his eyes still fixed on the ring in bewilderment as he reached out gingerly and plucked it from her, only to watch it disappear from his fingertips.

Ivy grinned. She would've thought a simple enchantment would have been unsurprising to him. After all, he lived in a whole world cloaked in magic. "Seraphina hadn't, either. I think not knowing how my mother enchanted it was part of the reason she was so angry about it." Ivy recalled a time when Seraphina had even tried to break the enchantment with a few different spells, only to be furious when they failed.

"She's the one that gave you the scars," Zainiel said, the smile falling from his face as his eyes settled on the patch of rough skin on her shoulder. She tugged her jacket up, hiding them from view. She knew that he knew they were there; she had caught him glaring at them during their training. Ivy suspected that he'd known about them the second Ria had uncovered them. She wasn't naive enough to believe that his sister wouldn't have shared that information with him.

"She was the one that trained me on the island. Her methods were..." Ivy paused, running a hand over her shoulder and feeling the rough skin beneath her shirt. "Less favorable than yours. These were from one of those sessions after I failed to meet her expectations all week. She would throw spells at me, hoping that if I knew I would be hurt, I would suddenly be able to block them. The more I failed, the more she threw. Sometimes, she let her anger get the best of her."

"And that scar on your wrist?" Zainiel's gaze shifted to the faint mark, so subtle that Ivy occasionally forgot it was there. "Did she do that, too?"

Ivy felt her breath catch as Zainiel gently took hold of her arm, twisting it just enough to inspect the imperfection woven into her skin. "She believed that if I bled more, I could harness the spells," she murmured, a grimace crossing her face at the memory. Seraphina had left her battered and bleeding on that beach, and without Theo's timely rescue, Ivy doubted she would have survived the night.

Zainiel's fingers glided over the scar with a tenderness that remained even as his expression darkened. "You should have never been left there."

As his fingers brushed against the scar on her skin, a warm, tingling sensation washed over her. A cool flicker of magic stirred deep within her, playfully dancing in her belly as if it was reaching out to him. Ivy sat there, words trapped in her throat, unsure if she could even muster a reply. Since her arrival, no one had dared utter those words in her presence. They simply echoed her father's commands, insisting that he had his reasons—reasons she would one day come to understand.

As if he had noticed his mistake, he jerked his hand away from her before pushing to his feet and clearing his throat. "We should probably head back. It's getting late." The gruffness in his tone had replaced any sign of the gentleness that had just been there.

Ivy nodded softly as she pushed herself up, trying to ignore the magic in her that still stirred, pulling towards him. *It didn't mean anything.* It was late, she was tired, and he had shown her a kindness she didn't think she'd ever see from him. That's all it was. She just needed some rest.

Chapter Twenty-Four

"Ria mentioned that your training is progressing nicely," Luka remarked, his voice muffled as he chomped on his sandwich. Lilli shot him a pointed glance from her spot beside him on the blanket, leading him to stammer out an apology. "Sorry," he mumbled, crumbs flying as he spoke.

Lilli let out a long sigh, shaking her head but unable to suppress a soft chuckle. Her blonde locks shimmered in the afternoon sun as she reached over, offering him a napkin.

Ivy couldn't help but smile. Meeting Luka had become a routine for her, one that she found herself looking forward to at the end of each day. This morning, he had extended an invitation for a picnic with Lilli. She nearly declined, but Luka insisted. She and Lillihadn't spent much time together since the bonfire, only offering each other the exchange of smiles in passing, and Ivy feared Lilli might have taken Zainiel's advice to keep her distance. The last thing she wanted was to make her uncomfortable.

"She also mentioned that you and Zainiel seem to be hitting it off rather well these days," Lilli added with a suggestive smile.

Ivy couldn't help the light flush that crept across her cheeks as memories of the previous night replayed in her head. The sensation of his strong arms encircling her waist, the way their laughter blended seamlessly, and the feeling of his hair, smooth and slightly tousled between her fingers. It would be untruthful to say that those moments hadn't been replaying in her mind since they had parted ways.

"He's," Ivy paused, searching for the right words, "not as bad as I thought," she finished with a grin.

"Not as bad as you thought?" Luka scoffed with a sly smile, "Is that how you describe the embrace I saw you two in last night?"

Ivy's eyes widened and she could feel her cheeks growing even warmer. "Were you spying on us, Luka?"

"I wouldn't call it spying," he said, a hint of sheepishness in his tone. "I would call it being a concerned friend. You didn't show up at the lake." He shrugged nonchalantly. "But then I spotted the two of you giggling. Him spinning you around like a feather. I mean, it seemed pretty clear to me what was happening there." He stuffed another sizable bite into his mouth.

"We weren't giggling," Ivy objected. "He was just training me."

Luka arched a brow as he shot her a sideways look. Lilli sat beside him, grinning knowingly at Ivy.

"If that is what 'just training' looks like, then something tells me Zainiel would have a much easier time with the ladies around here."

Lilli nodded fervently beside him. "He's got a point. I've pretty much grown up here, and I don't think I have ever seen Zainiel laugh before."

"He's not the giggling type, Ivy. For him to do that with you means something," Luka added, nodding.

Ivy felt the heat spread across the back of her neck as she tried to push down the memories from last night. He had taken such a genuine interest in her life and her experiences in Salus, and when she recounted her hardships, his gaze had deepened, revealing a concern that caught her off guard. It was something she couldn't allow herself to be held up on. There were more important things to worry about, like how to control her magic, and finding her father.

"Well," Ivy started, clearing her throat. "Whatever it was, it doesn't matter. It was awkward. And it won't be happening again." She could only *hope* that it happened again, but she wasn't about to confirm that to the pair that sat before her.

Chapter Twenty-Five

I vy fell back onto the couch with a groan, her body sinking into the cushions. After finally gaining some semblance of control over her powers, her training sessions with Zainiel had turned into a grueling affair, leaving her muscles protesting with every movement. It had only been three days since Zainiel had helped her tap into her magic, and already it felt like an extension of herself, flowing as naturally as blood through her veins. But with that newfound ease came an undeniable pull toward Zainiel whenever he was near. She didn't understand it, and had spent most of last night combing through the book that Ria had left her in hopes of finding some sort of explanation, only to come up empty-handed. She had almost asked Zainiel if he felt it too, and at times, when she caught him studying her with a confused expression, she wondered if he did.

A soft knock on the door echoed through the room as Ria poked her head through the small opening. "Do you have a minute?" she asked with her usual warm smile.

"Of course," Ivy said as she propped herself up from where she had strewn herself across the couch. For the past couple of weeks, it had become a pretty normal thing for Ria and Ivy to seek one another out. At first, Ivy thought it was because Ria wanted to keep an eye on her; and while she knew that was at least part of the truth, she also suspected that Ria had come to enjoy her company just as much as Ivy enjoyed hers.

Ria nudged open the door, slipping into the room with a plain wooden box tucked underneath her arm, then pushing the door closed with her foot.

"I have to confess something," she started as she walked over to Ivy, placing the wooden box down on the table before taking a seat beside her. "I may have grown impatient and done some snooping in your father's study."

Ivy raised a brow. "You snooped?"

A deep blush rose to her cheeks. "I thought maybe there would be some answers about when he would return."

"Did you find anything?" Ivy asked, trying to dim the little bud of hope that had blossomed. It had been weeks since she had arrived, and there had been no word from her father. She was beginning to suspect that Ria and Zainiel knew just as little as she did regarding his whereabouts.

Ria's face fell, but she gave Ivy an apologetic smile. That was the only answer Ivy needed. "But I did find this box," Ria said as she grabbed it and placed it between them on the couch, drumming her fingertips nervously across the top. "I didn't read them, but I think that these are letters from your mother."

Ivy's breath caught in her throat as she stared at the plain pine box. She reached into her pocket, clutching the casting ring in her palm. When she was younger, she used to dream of what her mother must've been like. She had always imagined that she was softer and kinder than the others in Salus, but she had no real way of knowing. This ring, the one she had come to despise just as much as she cherished, was the only thing she had from her mother. Seraphina had been quick to dispose of any memories of her mother; Ivy didn't even know what she looked like. But *letters?* Letters that her mother had written herself? Ivy would finally be able to know what type of person her mother was; would finally be able to know if she was as awful as Seraphina, or if she was the kind soul Ivy always wished her to be.

"If it's too much..." Ria started, eyeing Ivy with concern. "I can take them. Hold on to them for now until you feel ready," she offered, gently moving to tuck the box under her arm.

"No," Ivy blurted out, her voice hurried. "No, I do want to read them. It's just..." She faltered, grappling for the right word. How could she convey to Ria that these letters could be both a blessing and a curse? She had always imagined her mother as different from Seraphina and the other power-driven women in Salus. But what if reading these letters shattered that fantasy, revealing her mother to be just as ruthless?

"Overwhelming? Terrifying?" Ria suggested, offering a sympathetic smile. "I'm an empath, remember." Ivy didn't think she'd ever be able to get used to Ria being able to know her innermost feelings.

"I never knew her," Ivy whispered. "All my life, I dreamed that if circumstances had been different, if she had survived that night, she would have protected me. That she would've loved me, even when the rest of the family seemed to despise me."

Ria nodded, as she pulled Ivy's hand into her own. "You know, I hardly remember my parents. When we were little, we used to make up stories about what life would have been like if our parents were still alive. They died when Zain and I were young, and El—" she stopped herself with a sigh. "What I'm trying to say is that it's normal to fantasize about what might have been, and sometimes it's harmless. But allowing yourself to live in those fantasies?" Her eyes darkened with a grief that made Ivy wonder just how much she and Zainiel had gone through in their lives. "That's more dangerous than you could ever imagine."

They both sat in silence, Ivy's eyes fixed on the box that sat between them, weighted with all the answers it could possibly hold. Ria stared into the distance, her eyes clouded with grief.

"Thank you," Ivy whispered, her voice small as it pierced the quiet. She wasn't entirely sure if she was expressing gratitude for Ria's presence, for the letters she had brought, or perhaps both. What Ivy knew with certainty was that, at this moment, Ria needed a friend just as much as she did.

Ria gave a small smile, though it didn't quite reach her eyes. "I hope that if you decide to read them, they offer you some answers about your mother."

"I think I will," she replied honestly. "I've spent so many years in the dark about my life. I can't pass up the chance to get some answers, even if they might be unpleasant."

"I can give you some space if you'd rather read them by yourself," Ria suggested gently.

Ivy cast her gaze down towards the box resting between them, then back to Ria. The desire to read the letters surged within her, but the sorrow that danced in Ria's eyes tugged at her heart. It was a familiar sadness, one that Ivy had seen reflected in her own gaze far too often.

"I've got a better plan," Ivy said, her face brightening as she squeezed Ria's hand softly. "What if we head to the kitchen, grab some of those pastries you adore, and take a stroll through the garden?" The sun was dipping below the horizon, casting a warm, golden light over the vibrant blossoms. Ria had poured countless hours into nurturing the garden back to life after Ivy's chaotic arrival, and now, aside from a few lingering scuffs on the pathways, the scene was nearly perfect.

A flicker of excitement sparked in Ria's eyes, her lips curving into a grateful smile as she nodded eagerly. "I would really love that."

The Letters

My Dearest Kalec,

I know it has only been a month since you returned to your home, but, my love, I have the most wonderful news. I am with child, your child. I have not told my family yet, though I suspect that my sister knows, and it will only be a matter of time before the rest of the coven discovers it. Do you know what this means? This means we can finally bridge our communities together, *just like you wished. You have succeeded, my love. Our daughter will be the bringer of a new age.*

I know it's too soon to know for sure, but I can feel it. Our baby is going to be the most beautiful girl, and she's going to grow into one of the most powerful women. She will be our salvation.

Your Love, Lana

My Dearest Kalec,

I've tried to write to you numerous times in the past couple of months, but I'm beginning to wonder if my family has somehow intercepted the letters. They did not take the news of the baby as joyfully as I had hoped; they forbade me from telling you for fear that you might decide to return for her. Seraphina has locked me inside the manor. It has been days since I have been able to walk along the beach with my toes in the sand. She says it's for my own safety, that the other elders wouldn't react well if they knew I was pregnant with your heir, but I fear that she is planning something. Something horrible.

With every day that passes, and as my stomach swells with our daughter, Fennrick's anger intensifies. I am becoming fearful that he may do something to harm us. Even though we were already separated when you and I fell in love, he is convinced I have wronged him and has persuaded the family of this as well. You know how seriously they take the vows of marriage here in Salus, and I fear that even if I wasn't carrying your child, people would still believe him to be the innocent

one. I truly am alone here, Kal. Please come back to us.
Something bad is going to happen. I can just feel it.

Your Love, Lana

My Dearest Kalec,

I don't know if these letters have been reaching you or not. I'm choosing to believe that they haven't, because I know you would never leave me—not like this. While our time may have been brief, our love was not, and as our child grows, so does my love for you. Yesterday, I found Fennrick in Seraphina's study, poring over her spell books. I can't say for sure, but there's something different about him. Something dangerous gleams in his eyes when he looks at me, and it's far beyond hatred. I believe he has started using dark magic, and he is losing himself to it. I want to help him, Kal, but I don't know how.

I found an old book about runes in the manor library that I had never seen before. It's in an old language that I haven't been able to decipher, but I'm hoping there will be something there to help me.

Please come back to me, Kal.

Your Love, Lana

My Dearest Kalec,

Seraphina says it's only a matter of days before the baby comes, and I still haven't heard anything from you. Fennrick has gone mad. I can hear him at night, pacing in front of my door, murmuring to himself. I tried to talk to Seraphina about it, but she assured me I was wrong and that it must be the pregnancy. But I know it isn't. When I look into his eyes, a stranger stares back. He has even stopped visiting with Isodyl.

I have placed runes outside of mine and Isodyl's rooms as a safeguard, but I still can't shake the feeling that something terrible will happen. It's not safe here, Kal. I'll leave the coven. We can take the girls, and we can leave together as a family. Just please come back to me. I'm begging you.

Your Love, Lana

My Dearest Kalec,

If you receive this letter, it means that something terrible has happened. I have spelled it to find you if something happens to me. Last night, I gave birth to our beautiful baby girl. She has my eyes and your spark. I just know she's going to grow up to do amazing things. I named her Iverlyn, Ivy for short.

I don't have enough time to explain everything, but promise me if something happens to me you will save our little girl. She can't grow up on this island. My sister thinks she's an embarrassment to the family name, and Fennrick has called her an abomination. This morning, I awoke to find him standing over her crib. I think he meant to harm her.

Even though you never came for me, I know you won't fail our daughter. Find her, Kal. Protect her, teach her how to control her powers, and tell her about me; but most of all, love her. Love her for me.

Lana

Chapter Twenty-Six

I vy sat in stunned silence, her grip tightening around the letter she held as tears streamed down her cheeks, blurring the ink as they fell onto the paper. For years, she had swallowed the lies woven by her aunt—that her mother had perished during childbirth. She had borne the silent burden of being the one who ripped her mother from this world, believing herself responsible for fracturing their family. But this letter unveiled a different narrative. A tale of a mother who had lived in fear, forsaken by the man she loved, betrayed by those who should have protected her, and ultimately, murdered by the very man who fathered her first child. A reality where her mother might still be alive, had Kalec only heeded her desperate calls for help.

A fire burned in her belly, bursting forth as a tempest through the skies, the wind howling in solidarity with her. Her father knew of her existence all this time; knew the type of people he left to raise her, the pain she would endure. And yet he still left her there. Waiting fourteen years to send someone to infiltrate her life and another seven before calling them home, if this could even be considered her home. And still didn't have the decency to be here now. What type of man did that?

Ivy shook her head as she tucked the letters back into the pine box, tears streaming down her cheeks in steady currents that matched the heavy downpour of rain that had begun to saturate the ground. Were it not for the thick canopy of the willow shielding her, she would have been drenched through and through as she sat on the bench beneath its sheltering arms. She thought it'd be easier to read the letters outside, immersed in the vibrant blooms and sweet tang of floral scents—thought that maybe it would help dull the heartbreak she knew would be waiting for her. But she hadn't expected this.

Her mother had pleaded for his return, willing to forsake the only life she had ever known if he would just come back to her—to them. Ivy could almost feel her mother's heartache echoing from the pages. She didn't know if Kalec ever truly loved her mother, but it was clear to Ivy that she had loved him with a fierceness Ivy could only dream of finding one day.

And Seraphina—she had to be involved. Or at the very least complacent. After all, she was the one that had orchestrated the elaborate lie of her own sister's death. Ivy had always thought it strange that all photos of her mother had been removed from the manor. Initially, she'd suspected it was simply Seraphina's way of grieving. Now she wondered if perhaps it was a way to run from the guilt she must have felt all those years, knowing her sister had all but foretold her very own death, and in the end had been alone and terrified.

A soft drizzle began to weave itself through the sodden branches above, and Ivy felt the cool droplets mingling with her hair. An electrifying pulse surged through her veins, tightening her breath as thunder rumbled overhead like an untamed beast—a testament to the magic within her. The memory of Ria's forgiving smile flitted through her mind; the garden had borne the brunt of her magic once before, and Ivy feared that Ria wouldn't be as forgiving a second time, especially after all the care Ria had poured into its revival.

She still grappled with her magic, its wild essence swirling within her. But after that night with Zainiel, she had discovered a way to soothe the tempest. As she closed her eyes, she pictured her sanctuary—the rhythmic crash of waves kissing the shore; the sharp, salty breeze tangling her hair; the warm, grainy embrace of the sand beneath her bare feet. Yet, as the scene painted itself in her mind, it shifted. Zainiel's smile burst forth, a playful crinkle at the corners of his eyes, laughter dancing in the air between them. She felt the warmth of his skin against hers, his strong arms coiling around her like a protective cocoon. And there, mingling with her thoughts, was his scent: a captivating blend of spice and warmth, pulling her back to that moment, grounding her.

"You're getting good at that." Theo's voice shattered the memory she had found herself in. Ivy opened her eyes to see him dipping beneath the sweeping branches of the willow, sun filtering in as the dark clouds began to dissipate. He ruffled his hair, sending droplets of rain sprinkling around as he moved further within the willow's embrace. "Controlling your magic," he added for clarity at her silence.

Ivy nodded her head slowly as she hugged the pine box closer to her chest. "I've been training," she offered, choosing to leave out who she had been training with. She knew it wouldn't be hard for him to find out, if he didn't already know, but she already had enough to deal with without having to manage his frail ego when it came to Zainiel.

His gaze shifted, narrowing as it searched her flushed cheeks, no doubt stained from tears, it dropped to the box she held, his brows furrowing with concern. "You're upset. Why?"

Ivy's gaze drifted to the ground. She opened her mouth, the words poised to strike—this was none of his business, she was no longer his concern. But exhaustion seeped from her bones, and all she wanted was her friend back, even if for only a moment. With a resigned sigh, she lifted the box that had been hidden away in the recesses of Kalec's study, offering it to him as he took a seat beside her on the bench.

"What is it?" he asked as he sat it in his lap.

"Letters," she replied, her voice trembling. "From my mother." She cast a glance upward, her lashes fluttering as tears threatened to spill at the memories those letters held.

Theo's jaw tightened, a flicker of tension dancing across his features as he stared at the box, his fingers gliding over the lid with deliberate slowness. He closed his eyes, inhaling deeply, as if bracing himself for an incoming storm. Her heart quickened. She didn't know what sort of reaction she expected from him, but at the very least she thought he'd be surprised. Why wasn't he surprised? Unless...

"You knew," her voice trembled as a solitary tear traced a path down her cheek. "You knew my mother didn't die in childbirth, didn't you?"

Theo averted her gaze, stood abruptly from the bench, and placed the box beside Ivy. He opened his mouth to say something before sighing and shaking his head as if something were stopping him from speaking the words.

"Did you know?" She already knew the answer, if he didn't, he would have objected by now, but she needed to hear him say the words.

"I'm—" he paused, his shoulders slumping forward in defeat. "I'm so sorry." His words were barely a whisper, yet they were loud enough to crash through the remnants of whatever remaining trust lay between them like shattered glass.

Ivy pressed her hand to her mouth, stifling a sob that threatened to escape. A weight coiled tightly in her chest, as if her heart were being twisted into a knot. She remembered the lies he had spun before, how Kalec's commands seemed to overshadow everything else. But this—her mother?

"Why?" she gasped, tears streaming down her face like rivulets of rain.

Silence stretched between them, the air thick with unspoken words. Theo stood there, his hazel eyes flickering with a brilliance that felt almost like a flame of guilt ready to consume him.

"I had my orders," he murmured, the words slipping from his lips like ash.

Ivy's stomach churned as a wave of nausea crashed over her. Kalec commanded and he simply obeyed. "Just go," she rasped, her body sinking against the bench, the wood cold against her back. "Please," she choked out, unable to meet his gaze. For an instant, she sensed he might say something, his lips parting as if to break the silence, but the only sound that filled the air was the muted thud of his footsteps fading into the distance.

Chapter Twenty-Seven

I vy remained seated on the weathered bench beneath the willow, its cascading branches wrapping around her like a protective curtain. The warm pink glow of dusk filtered through the leaves, hinting that dinner was drawing near and the dining hall would soon fill with familiar faces. She could almost hear the soft murmur of voices and laughter, but the thought of joining them felt like a weight pressing against her chest.

Skipping lunch had been easy enough, especially considering she hadn't touched breakfast either. The prospect of entering the dining hall filled her with a tight knot of unease. She could picture it now: Ria would be on the lookout, ready to pounce with her usual warmth. It was a welcome surprise that she hadn't already tracked her down. Even if Ivy hadn't lost control of her powers for those few minutes earlier, Ria had undoubtedly felt the chaos of emotions swirling around in her head. Theo would be there too, slipping into the shadows, his gaze averted, guilt written all over his face. And Lilli and Luka, goddess bless them, would stumble over each other in their frantic attempts to lighten her mood.

At least Zainiel wouldn't return until after the sun had set. He had roused her early, before the horizon blushed with morning light, canceling their training. She had been too groggy to think to ask him why, but she vaguely remembered his promise to return after nightfall, ready to resume their daily training tomorrow. Ivy knew if he had been here he would have tracked her down long before Theo did.

It's not that she didn't appreciate their concern. She did—it was more than she ever would have received from her own family—but her mind was still reeling, and she needed time to sort it all out. Her mother had survived childbirth, albeit not for long, judging by the letters. And her father, the man that everyone she was avoiding kept telling her was a good man, had abandoned them. If he had answered her mother's pleas, maybe she would still be alive. She couldn't begin to imagine how alone her mother must have felt, left behind by the man she loved, all while carrying his child; and, if her suspicions were correct, she was betrayed by her own coven, killed by Isodyl's father.

The crunch of footfalls along the pebbled walkway of the gardens shattered the stillness around Ivy. The steps seemed too loud to belong to Ria or Lilli, and Ivy doubted Luka would venture out without Lilli, the two of them were adjoined at the hip at the end of every day. Zainiel was still gone, which only left Theo.

Ivy sighed, tucking her knees against her chest and letting her forehead fall against them. The sound of the footfalls fell quiet and was replaced with the rustle of the willow leaves.

"Theo, please, not now," Ivy spoke into her knees, not bothering to look up. What more could he possibly have to say?

"Wow, Storm, you always know just what to say to deflate a guy's ego." Zainiel's voice sounded with a playful rumble.

Ivy looked up to find him standing just a couple of feet in front of her, a picnic basket in one hand and the other hand tucked into his pocket. His usual smirk was displayed across his face, but she could see the worry in his eyes and the subtle crease in his brows.

"I didn't think you were coming back until later." She dropped her legs, scooting over to the far side of the bench, allowing space for Zainiel to join her.

"It didn't take as long as I thought," he answered with a shrug as he slid onto the bench. His hand barely brushed across hers, but that's all that was needed to send a current of electricity coursing through her as her magic responded to his presence. Ever since that night in the field, it had been like a frenzy, yearning to be near him with an intensity she wasn't sure she'd ever understand. Did he feel it too?

After a few moments of silence, Zainiel asked, "Do you want to tell me what's wrong? Ria wouldn't say why, but she practically demanded that I find you the moment I walked into the dining hall."

Ivy remained silent, her gaze fixated on the pine box positioned between her feet. What if Zainiel was aware of the letters inside, of the truths they held? The thought of him hiding this from her just as Theo had held her heart in a vice grip.

"Ria also sent this along," he continued, as he placed the picnic basket in his lap and began to sift through its contents. "Sandwiches and those pastries the two of you love so much." He held a sandwich out toward her, raising an eyebrow in invitation.

Ivy nearly declined, but before she could, her stomach rumbled in protest. "Thanks," she spoke quietly as she grabbed it from him. He took his own from the basket before setting it down on the ground with the sound of rustling paper as they unwrapped the sandwiches, filling the silence between them.

"Ria found letters in Kalec's study," Ivy offered in between bites, her gaze finding his. "They're from my mother."

"Letters? Really?" he asked, his brows raised in surprise. Ivy took another bite of her sandwich as she nodded. If he had known about the letters before, he was doing a good job of feigning surprise. Not that that proved anything; Theo was good at lying, too.

Ivy sat the rest of her sandwich down on the bench arm, bending down to grab the pine box before offering it to him. Zainiel finished his sandwich before grabbing the box and prying the lid off of it. His fingers glided over the aged stack of letters as his brows furrowed in confusion. "There's so many of them."

Ivy nodded. "She begged him to return in every single one of them." Some letters contained nothing but her scrawled pleas, raw and desperate.

"Theo knew?" Zainiel's question hung in the air, and Ivy knew by the hardened look on his face that he already knew the answer. "I didn't know, Storm. I swear it."

Ivy watched closely, searching for any sign of deceit as he thumbed through the letters. Her magic swelled in her chest, almost as if to confirm that she could trust him; but then again, she had spent years of her life thinking Theo was the most trustworthy person she knew.

"You truly didn't know about them?"

Zainiel shook his head, a shadow of frustration crossing his features. "When it comes to his personal life, Kalec is a secretive man. I didn't even know your name until after you arrived. Everyone is on a need-to-know basis with him, and at the time, I didn't need to know." A cool breeze rustled the leaves sending a shiver down Ivy's spine. It would be dark soon, and with the darkness would come a biting chill.

Zainiel stood from the bench and shucked his jacket off, wrapping it around her shoulders, before falling back down onto the bench beside her. She offered him a small smile in thanks before tugging the jacket closer to her, enveloped by his spicy, warm scent like cinnamon and cedarwood—the same scent that she had found herself thinking of to calm down earlier.

"My aunt blamed me for her death, told me she died in childbirth," Ivy started, her eyes glued to the box. "All those years I lived thinking she hated me because I was the one who brought on her sister's death." She shook her head, tears glistening in her eyes threatening to spill over again.

Zainiel paused sifting through the letters, his gaze set intently on her as she spoke.

"Sometimes, I even hated myself for it," Ivy continued, her voice trembling. "I could see why she would, too. But then I read those letters, and..." Her voice faltered, as she traced her finger along the seam of the jacket. The night before the ritual, Seraphina's gaze had been filled with such hatred—such revulsion. She knew Ivy had fae blood, and that knowledge sealed Ivy's fate long before she had failed to call upon Zaria's gift.

"The coven worships the purity of our—their blood, and to them, I am anything but," Ivy said, a bitter edge to her voice. "I get why Seraphina did what she did. But what I can't understand is why the man who condemned my mother to that same hatred could just abandon us." Her voice trembled, pain lacing her words. "She loved him."

Zainiel's grip on the box had tightened, and Ivy swore she could see the subtle flare of his shadows fluttering around him as she spoke. A flame of fury lit in his eyes.

"How can I trust a man who does that?" Ivy's voice cracked, a tear slipping down her cheek. The gentle breeze wrapped around them, filling the void with a soft whisper, while she nervously toyed with the seam of her jacket, fighting to keep her tears at bay.

Zainiel shifted, setting the box down beside him on the bench. He turned to Ivy, taking her trembling hands in his own, their fingers interlocking like pieces of a delicate puzzle.

"The worst part is," Ivy continued, her voice barely above a whisper, "I'm so angry with her. She was strong—she should have been able to protect herself. Instead, she spent her days begging a man who abandoned her to come and save her." Her eyes glistened as she spoke. "When I read those letters and learned she survived childbirth, a part of me felt relieved. But the harsh reality is, she was only in that position because she chose to keep me, despite everyone telling her not to. That choice... it cost her everything."

Zainiel traced his thumb up and down the side of her hand. "Do the letters say what she was afraid of?"

"My mother's husband. Or, I guess, ex-husband. They were separated when she and my father met, but divorce is unheard of on Salus. Most of our marriages are formed for the benefit of the elders. Not for love," Ivy explained.

"Why would she think he'd harm her?" Zainiel asked, his brow furrowing with concern.

"She claimed he had lost his mind. That he was furious about her pregnancy, and she feared he might have turned to dark magic. In her last letter, she mentioned finding Fennrick lurking over my crib while she slept. She was terrified he would hurt me, but I think he's the one responsible for her death," Ivy explained, a shiver running through her. If what he wanted was for Ivy to be gone, then why hadn't he finished the job? She would have been a defenseless baby, unless her mother had found some way to protect her even after death. It wouldn't be the first spell her mother managed to cast that outlasted her own life. The ring on her hand glimmered in the moonlight that snaked through the leaves.

Zainiel's body tensed, his grip on her hand growing tight. "What did you say his name was?"

"Fennrick. My mother always called him Fenn, but his name is Fennrick."

Zainiel's face had grown tight beside her, and the flare of his shadows danced at his back once again. "Where is he now?" Zainiel asked carefully, his voice almost cold and detached. The warmth and kindness that had been in his gaze just moments ago now vanished.

"I'm not sure. He disappeared after my mother's death." Ivy answered, furrowing her brows in confusion. Why had he suddenly become so cold?

A sour look passed over his features before he dropped her hand and rose from the bench, where he began to pace before her, shadows spindling up from the ground with each step he took.

"Is there something I'm missing?" Ivy asked.

"Is that all the letters?" Zainiel asked, nodding towards the box.

"I would assume so, but Ria would probably be the person to ask. Do you want to tell me what's going on?" It had to be something more she didn't know. Zainiel had been angry before when she had talked about her time in Salus, but this was something different. This wasn't anger on her behalf—it was deeper, a fury that had been simmering for ages.

"I'm starting to realize that Kalec has far more secrets than any of us realized."

A stone formed in her gut. "I don't understand."

"Fennrick is much more than a man your mother was married to." Zainiel stood rigid, his back turned to her, fists clenched tightly at his sides. "He's the man who killed my sister."

His sister? Zainiel had more than one sister? Ivy released a breath she hadn't realized she was holding. How was this even possible?

"I—I don't understand," she said, shaking her head. This didn't make any sense to her. How could Fennrick have killed Zainiel's sister—a sister he and Ria never talked about?

"I'm not sure I do either," Zainiel admitted, as he turned to move back to the bench, falling back onto it with a sigh.

"Are you saying Fennrick was somehow in Arbor?" Ivy asked. It would explain why he disappeared, but why come here? And how? Theo had told her the gates were impenetrable—that unless you were a child of Arbor, or with someone who was, you couldn't access them. So how did Fennrick?

Zainiel scrubbed a hand down his face as he released a frustrated sound. "All this time, we didn't understand why Fennrick was so hell bent on destroying Kalec. I thought Kalec was just as clueless as the rest of us, but it turns out this is all a feud over a woman who isn't even breathing anymore."

Ivy flinched at his words. She knew he was upset— and he had a right to be, after all. He had been lied to about the man who killed his sister and his connections to a man Zainiel devoted himself to. But it was still her mother.

"I'm sorry, I just..." Zainiel spoke through a sigh, letting his words trail off. "She died a horrible death for your father."

Ivy reached out, placing her hand over his. Her heart ached—not just for him, but for Ria, and for herself. She had seen the anguish in Ria's eyes, had recognized the haunted shadows that flitted across her face—it all clicked into place now. Her father's choices had led to this torment, and where was he now?

Chapter Twenty-Eight

I vy, her determination like a flame in her eyes, marched to the dining hall. It was where Ria had last seen Theo, and she needed to talk to him before she lost the nerve. She wasn't prepared to talk to him after she had read the letters, but now, knowing what she knew, she needed to know just how entangled he was in her father's plans.

She hadn't been able to sleep at all the night before, her mind racing with all the truths she had uncovered in the letters. She and Zainiel had remained in the garden well after the sun had set. He had asked her to read the letters to see if there was anything in them that could help puzzle together how Fennrick had become such a big threat to Arbor.

She shoved through the large double doors with an echoing thud as they clanged into the wall. Theo sat alone in the empty hall, flipping through a book while he ate. His gaze shot up to hers in surprise as she strode towards him.

"Iv—"

"I need to know everything you know," she demanded as she placed her hands on the table. "No more lies, Theo."

He shifted uncomfortably in his seat as he closed the book while eyeing her wearily.

"Do you know where he is? My father?" Ivy asked.

"I don't." He shook his head, averting his eyes from hers as he drummed his fingers on the table.

She narrowed her eyes at him. "Are you sure?" She would have thought that someone who spent such a long time lying to her would be better at it.

"I don't know where he is," he repeated. "Not exactly, anyways," he added with a defeated sigh.

"For once, can you just be straight with me. Stop trying to beat around the bush, Theo, just tell me what it is you know." She was starting to think it was next to impossible to get a straight answer from him.

"A few months ago, I received word that he was responding to a breach on the Western wall. He was concerned that Fennrick had found a way into Arbor. He told me to continue with the plan and that he would meet us at the cabin the day after your twenty-first birthday. That was the last time I heard from him," Theo explained.

"Did you have contact with him regularly?" Ivy asked.

Theo's grim face was enough to tell her that he did. "Spelled letters," he paused, rubbing his hand across his chin, "like the ones your mother sent to him. He would write one, and it would just appear. When I needed to respond, I would do so on the back of the letter he sent, and it would return to him. Using modern technology wouldn't work; it was too risky. Besides, those sorts of advancements weren't readily available in Salus, and most people in Arbor choose not to use them. Your father was one of them."

Ivy didn't know why it was so shocking to her that they communicated with each other. She supposed it made sense, but knowing that Theo was talking to her father regularly somehow made all the lies that much worse. Part of her believed that maybe she had fallen for his lies with so much ease because maybe for a while he started believing them himself, but if he was reporting back to her father—well, that changed a lot of things.

"He knew what was happening? All of it?" Ivy asked, letting the unspoken words hang heavily between them. He knew the hell

Seraphina was putting her through and still ordered Theo not to act?

Theo averted his gaze from hers once more as he gave her a small nod. She sucked in a sharp breath as she let herself slip into the seat across from him. Her mother had spent her last moments pleading with her father to find Ivy, to keep her safe, to *love* her; and instead, he had left her on that island, fully aware of the torment she was experiencing. Had he ever truly loved either of them? Her mother believed her father to be a good man, that much was clear in the letters she had written him. And even though he failed to come back to her, failed to even respond, she continued to have faith in him. Ivy was beginning to believe that perhaps her mother was just a lovestruck fool who had fallen in love with the first mysterious man she crossed paths with.

"What about Zainiel's sister? Why wouldn't my father tell him the truth about who Fennrick really was?" Ivy asked, trying to shake off the ache that had settled in her chest. She came here for answers, not just for herself but for Zainiel as well.

A look of indifference settled on his face at the mention of Zainiel's name. He shrugged. "He didn't need to know."

Ivy scoffed. She couldn't believe what she was hearing. She knew that Zainiel and Theo had their problems but this... this was just cruel. "You can't be serious. It was his sister, Theo. He deserved to know the truth just as much as I did."

Anger sparked in Theo's eyes as he abruptly stood up from where he was sitting, the chair dragging across the floor with a resounding scrape. "Why do you suddenly care so much about him?" His voice dripped with bitterness and his eyes burned with an unspoken accusation.

"He, unlike you, has been helping me," Ivy shot back as she too shot up from her seat.

"Zainiel? Helping you?" Theo barked an incredulous laugh that echoed through the empty dining hall.

Ivy recoiled slightly in surprise. Why was it so hard to believe that Zainiel would help her? "He is," she insisted.

"Really?" Theo jeered. "Is that what you call destroying the gardens and nearly losing control at the bonfire?"

Ivy flinched at his words. It was a low blow for him to throw that in her face, and he knew it. "That was weeks ago. And if it hadn't been for Zainiel teaching me how to control it, it would've happened all over again yesterday. The only difference is this time, you would have been the target," she seethed. Her magic was writhing inside her, waking with the pulsating anger that rushed through her veins.

"I had a duty, and I fulfilled it. I kept you safe!" His voice thundered, echoing off of the dining hall walls.

"Safe?" she spat. "You and my father stood by while my mother was murdered. Then you let me believe for years that it was my do-ing, all the while pretending to be my friend." She was incredulous at his self-righteousness. Could he truly not see the wrong that he had done?

"If you want to be angry with someone, then be angry with your father."

"Oh, believe me, I am, but there's enough anger here for the both of you," she replied bitterly, the blackening skies outside a testament to her budding fury.

Theo let out a harsh, mirthless chuckle, a sound that sent chills down her spine. "You're something else, you know that?" He gazed at her with a mixture of disbelief and disdain. "You give me crap for lying to keep you safe, but here you are, cozying up with Zainiel. If you think the lies I have told are so bad, then I can't wait to see what you think of him once you learn about who he truly is—what he has done. He's dangerous."

What was that supposed to mean? Ivy rolled her eyes. "Zainiel is helping me, Theo, which is more than I can say for you, since you've practically avoided me since we got here."

"I was giving you space," he shot back, his voice rising as he threw his arms up in exasperation.

"Right. Space instead of answers. So don't blame me for seeking them elsewhere," she retorted, her eyes narrowing as she struggled to keep the power within her at bay. Thunder crashed outside, and the rain hammered against the windows with an almost furious intensity.

"You do what you want. But hear me when I say this, Iverlyn," he spat her name with venom, "Zainiel is no good, and if you aren't careful, you'll end up hurt, or worse, dead. He will destroy you. Just remember that I warned you. Don't come crawling to me when it ends badly," he warned.

Ivy shook her head. She couldn't believe the man standing before her was the same man who had once been considered her best friend. He was nothing like the Theo she knew, and arguing with him was pointless. She sighed, raking her hand through her hair as she tried to keep her magic at bay. She was angry with him, and a part of her would always be angry with him because he had betrayed her trust more than she ever thought possible. But to him, she wasn't a friend, she was a job, and he owed her nothing. No matter what she said or how much she yelled would change that.

"I can't keep doing this with you, Theo," she admitted, her shoulders sagging in defeat. "I know it wasn't all real to you, but it was to me. And I'm so *angry* with you, but I just..." she ran her hand down her face, "I can't do this anymore. I can't keep fighting a fight I will never win."

Theo let out a long, heavy sigh, his hands pressing down on the table as the tension in his body began to dissipate. "You hate me, don't you?"

"I don't hate you," she replied, pausing for a moment. "At least, I don't think I do. But every time I see you, I'm reminded that I don't really know who you are anymore. It feels like all those

years we spent as friends were just a facade, and that hurts. I just...
I need some time to sort through this."

Theo opened his mouth as if to respond, but the words fell
away. Instead, he bowed his head, letting out a defeated breath.
"You want me to leave."

"No, it's not that I want to drive you out of your home," she
clarified. Because after all, this place had been his home way longer
than it had been hers. She had no right to ask him to leave.

"But you don't want me around either." He completed her
thought, a note of bitterness creeping in.

She averted her gaze to her hands, the weight of the moment
pressing down on her. Why was this so difficult?

"I have some friends I need to check on. I can leave tonight
and come back in a couple of weeks," he said, each word laced with
finality.

"But Ivy..." he began, pulling her gaze back to his. "I need you
to understand. When he tears you apart—and trust me, he will—I
won't be here to pick up the pieces. Don't count on me to save
you." With those words hanging heavily in the air, he turned and
stormed out of the dining room, leaving her with only the sound
of his retreating footsteps.

Chapter Twenty-Nine

"Y ou're improving," Zainiel remarked from behind Ivy as she struck yet another target with a bolt of her magic, smashing it into splinters. She couldn't sleep and found herself in the training area at sunrise, eager to burn off some of the restlessness that had kept her up all night. It had been three weeks since Theo's departure, and he had yet to return. Nor had her father, and the more time she spent with Ria and Zainiel, the more she began to notice that his absence didn't just affect her. They were feeling it too.

"I've been practicing," she grunted as she threw another burst of lightning toward the third target, hitting it dead center. Every spare minute she had, she found an excuse to come out to the training grounds to practice, even skipping her training with Zainiel a few times when she felt herself growing too comfortable in his presence. Which, she realized, was an easy thing to do, and resulted in her practicing so much some days that she was too exhausted to even eat before collapsing in her bed at the end of the night. Not that her exhaustion made sleep any easier to come by.

"I noticed," he mused, "so much so that I've begun to wonder if you are avoiding me."

Ivy ignored his comment as she fastened her loosened hair tie. She had always loved her long hair, finding it to be one of her favorite qualities, but as she practiced and sparred more, she found herself becoming annoyed with its length and how it never seemed to stay put.

"Storm," Zainiel called out, a teasing lilt to his voice, "*are* you avoiding me?"

She let out a sigh and rolled her eyes, though her mind was racing. "Don't flatter yourself. You said I needed to improve, so I'm working on it." She knew there was truth in those words; she did need to get better, and she had. But she wasn't ready to reveal that her early mornings and sleepless nights were often caused by thoughts of him invading her mind. "Why, do you miss me?" she teased, flashing a grin over her shoulder.

"That depends," Zainiel grinned with one eyebrow cocked, "do you want me to?" He seemed to be enjoying this little game of flirtation they had developed over the past few weeks, and if Ivy was being honest, so did she. But she couldn't quiet that little voice in the back of her mind reminding her of Theo's words before he left. Now that she had spent enough time with him, Zainiel seemed harmless enough; but then again, so had Theo.

"What are you doing here, Zainiel?" she asked as she settled on a fourth target.

"I'm leaving for a few days. I thought you should know."

Ivy whirled around to face him, "Leaving? Why?"

Zainiel smirked. "I knew you cared." He tucked his hands into his pocket as he leaned against the outer fence of the sparring ring. "I need to go check up on something on the Eastern wall."

Ivy's shoulders tensed. "The same something that my father left to check on and never returned from?" She had been trying to keep her distance the past couple of weeks because she wasn't sure she could trust herself not to grow too comfortable around him. But the idea of him not being there and potentially finding himself in danger settled in her stomach with a rotting anxiety.

Zainiel just stared at her for a moment as if he were deciding whether or not to tell her the truth. "Honestly, I don't know. Some people have gone missing, and a friend has asked me to come help."

"So, this has nothing to do with Kalec or his orders?" she asked.

Zainiel shook his head. "No. I'm not doing this for him. I'm doing this because there are people missing and a friend asked me to help."

Ivy nodded as she studied him. Theo had been so sure that Zainiel was a horrible person, but the man standing before her seemed far from that. She didn't know if it was because of her magic that almost seemed to beg to be near him, or the fact that he was selflessly about to leave the safe confines of the estate and put himself in potential danger just because someone asked him for help. If he truly was a bad person, wouldn't he have said no?

"Take me with you," Ivy blurted out, startling both of them.

"No," Zainiel replied firmly, his tone leaving no room for argument. "Absolutely not. I have no idea what I'd be walking into."

"And that matters because?" she shot back, frustration bubbling over. "You've had me training for weeks to learn how to defend myself." Deep down, she longed to escape the confines of the estate. It was beautiful, sure, but there was a whole world of Arbor she was dying to explore—a world that could have been hers to call home.

Zainiel shook his head, his expression resolute. "I won't be the one to put you at risk."

"I won't be at risk, not with you there," Ivy insisted, her voice rising with determination. "Besides, we don't even know what we're walking into. And remember, you're the one with all the skills." She hoped that appealing to his inflated sense of prowess would be just enough to at least make him consider taking her along.

"*I* don't know what *I* would be walking into. There is no we, Storm. Not for this." Zainiel pushed up from where he was leaning against the fence and stood firm.

"Zainiel, please. I need to get off of this estate. We have no clue when Kalec is returning, or what he even has planned for me, but I can't just be locked up here like a prisoner. How am I ever going to be able to learn how to protect myself if you won't let me leave this place?" she pleaded, all but begging for him to take her with him.

Something like sorrow flickered across Zainiel's face before he shook his head. "Storm, I can't—"

"I'll do everything you say, and if it turns out to be too dangerous, I'll find somewhere safe and I'll stay there until you return. Please just let me come."

Zainiel sighed as he stood before her pondering what she had just said.

"If it helps," she added with a tentative, hopeful smile. "I promise not to burn down any more gardens."

Zainiel's lip twitched, a barely-contained smile flickering on his face. Progress was being made. "If I agree to this, you follow my lead. No wandering off on your own. You stay right by my side at all times," he instructed, his tone firm.

Ivy's eyes sparkled with excitement, a grin spreading wide across her face. "I can manage that."

"Above all, no one can discover your true identity. No one can know you're Kalec's daughter," Zainiel emphasized, his gaze steady and unyielding.

She felt the question bubble up inside her—why did it matter who she was?—but the thought of him reconsidering made her bite back her curiosity. Instead, she nodded, determination shining in her eyes. It didn't matter if she had to masquerade as someone entirely different; escaping this estate was worth any sacrifice.

"I can't believe I'm about to say yes to this," he murmured, almost to himself.

Ivy's smile widened, her excitement bubbling over. "When do we leave?" she asked, struggling to keep her eagerness at bay. She didn't want to seem too eager. After all, the reason they were going was grim, but the thought of being able to see more of Arbor, to learn more about the place part of her belongs... It was hard not to be excited.

"Tomorrow at first light. The trip will be a long one, so be sure to get some rest tonight." He paused, giving her a once over before saying, "I know you haven't been sleeping at night. Or at least not as much as you should be. But you need your rest, especially if we end up running into danger."

Ivy avoided his inquisitive stare as she grabbed the water canteen at her feet. It was true. She hadn't been sleeping well at night.

Part of that was due to her mind racing over all the information she had learned in the past few weeks. But even when sleep didn't elude her, she was left prey to an onslaught of nightmares that seemed to have the sole purpose of reminding her of the horrors she narrowly escaped in Salus.

"I know this has all been a lot for you to take in, and I'm not saying you have to talk about it if you don't want to, but you need to find a way to let go of some of that stress. What you've been doing to yourself the past few weeks is not healthy, Ivy."

She continued to avoid his gaze, but she could feel his stare piercing through her as if he were reading her as thoroughly as Ria could. She didn't think anyone had noticed, had thought herself to be slick, but she supposed that was foolish to believe. After all, Ria probably felt it through her empathic abilities and went straight to Zainiel about it. Ivy didn't blame her. They were twins, after all, and she would never expect Ria to lie to her brother on her behalf, but part of her wished she would have at least forgone some of what she picked up from Ivy during their daily strolls through the garden.

"Well then, I guess it's a good thing you're letting me come with you. Sounds like some new scenery is exactly what I need," Ivy said with a small smile as she walked past him. "You coming?" she called over her shoulder, but his only response was a disapproving stare that followed her all the way back to the estate.

Chapter Thirty

They didn't have cars. Not one single car. Which, now that she thought about it, she hadn't seen one since they entered this world. But who didn't have *cars*? Zainiel had seemed amused by her wide-eyed stare when he met her at the edge of the gardens with two massive horses in tow. She had never seen a horse, not in person. They didn't have a use for them in Salus, so they simply didn't have them on the island.

The horses towered above her, their muscles rippling as their chocolate-colored coats shimmered in the early dawn light. She had been so taken by their enormity and beauty that when Zainiel motioned to the one with the braided mane, instructing her to hop on—it looked almost silky to the touch, and had a tear drop of white nestled between its eyes—she had simply stood before him, her mouth agape like a fish out of water. There was no *way* she was riding that thing.

Zainiel claimed that she would get the hang of it over time, but they were over an hour into their ride and she still found herself slipping to the sides of the saddle, struggling to keep her feet in the stirrups.

"Seriously, Zainiel, why doesn't this place have cars?" she grumbled from behind him as she shifted once again in the saddle. The leather was slick beneath her thighs as the beast thundered through the forest, seemingly unbothered by her discomfort.

A deep chuckle rumbled from his chest as he turned his head back, amusement lit in his eyes. "Arbor wasn't meant for the modern world."

"Seriously? You have enough magic to hide an entire realm from the outside world, but you can't manage to pave a few roads?" Ivy asked incredulously. She knew she was being ridiculous and was thankful to have finally left the estate, but this wasn't exactly what she'd had in mind.

Zainiel's ears twitched into an unmistakable smile. "Many of us believe that our magic is a gift from nature. If we care for it, it cares for us in turn. Modern conveniences like paved roads and cars aren't exactly nature-friendly."

Ivy sighed, glancing around at the abundant forest. Above them was a blanket of lush greenery, different hues of color melding into the other as the leaves swayed in the gentle breeze, causing them to dance in the warm sunlight that trickled through the gaps. And if she listened hard enough past the sound of the clopping hooves, she swore she could hear the whispers of a nearby stream. A place like this would never have existed in Salus. "So, does that mean your—our magic is weaker in the modern world? Is that why I never felt my own until coming here?"

Zainiel eased his horse to match pace with hers. "I suppose you could say that it's easier to exhaust our resources outside of Arbor, but it's still there. You would think that after all these years, we would understand our magic, but the truth is, we don't. It works by its own rules. Some believe it's more of an essence attached to our souls. Others believe we draw energy from our surroundings, and some believe both. So, if the forest is healthy, we have more energy to tap into. As for you not sensing your magic, I really can't say. It is possible, though. Theo, on the other hand, thinks your magic has been showing itself for years."

Ivy nodded vaguely, remembering Theo mentioning that he believed the storms in Salus might have been from her, but she was still unsure. In Salus, she had felt so utterly weak; even when she begged for her magic to come to her, to save her from Seraphina's wrath, it never showed itself.

"Is there anything you miss about Salus?" Zainiel asked, his voice cutting through the rhythmic thud of hooves on the earth and the symphony of rustling leaves.

The question took her by surprise. Usually, she was the one with the questions.

"Honestly..." she hesitated, her mind wandering through memories like the sunlight filtering through the canopy. "Other than the beach, not really. Theo was the one bright spot I had there, and well... you know how that turned out," she replied, her fingers absently twisting the reins as Bae, her spirited horse, reached for some of the tender green leaves dangling from a low-hanging branch.

"You guys were pretty close," Zainiel observed, his voice reverberating softly through the vastness of the forest, mingling with the whispers of the wind.

"I thought we were," she replied, a wistful smile gracing her lips.

"Do you ever find yourself wishing for a different life?" he asked, his eyes locking onto hers with an intensity that suggested there was more behind his words.

She gave a small shrug. "Sometimes, I imagine what it would be like to have a normal life—a mom who cared, a dad who wanted me, a sister I could share laughs with like you and Ria do, maybe even someone to share this life with," she said, her shoulders lifting again as she strummed a hand down Bae's silky coat. "But these last few weeks in Arbor have been as liberating as they've been challenging. And that sense of freedom... well, I don't think I could ever give it up."

Zainiel adjusted himself in the saddle with effortless grace, his body naturally leaning towards her. One hand firmly grasped the reins while the other dangled loosely by his side. As she spoke, his gaze bored into her with a weighty intensity, making her feel as though he was peering into the depths of her soul.

"What about you?" she asked, her voice tinged with curiosity. "Do you ever think about what your life might have been?"

Zainiel let out a mirthless chuckle. "I might have, once. But it's far too late for that now." A bit of darkness flickered through his eyes, and she wondered if he was thinking about his sister, the one who had died at Fennrick's hands. Ivy realized they didn't talk about her at all. Ria hadn't either, and that was the precise reason she had stopped herself from asking about her in the past. It was almost as if she had never even existed.

"What was your sister like?" Ivy asked, the words slipping from her grasp before she had time to stop them.

Zainiel's shoulders tensed at the question.

"I'm sorry, I shouldn't have—"

"No, no, it's fine," he said with a shake of his head. "I should probably talk about her more, I just…" he trailed off, shrugging his shoulders. "I don't know how."

Ivy remained silent as she watched, his entire face darkening with grief. She couldn't imagine that type of loss. She had lost her mother, and that was a grief that would always follow her through life, but this was a sister. Someone who he had grown up alongside and was meant to have many years with. If his relationship with her was anything like the one he shared with Ria… she couldn't blame him for not wanting to talk about it, and she shouldn't have even asked.

Silence hung heavy over them, only punctuated by the rhythmic crunching of the leaves under the horse's hooves. As much as she wished, they did have some modern accommodations, like cars. She had to admit it was beautiful here as she took a deep breath, and the scent of the earthy woods assaulted her senses. It was peaceful.

"You remind me of her," Zainiel began quietly. "She was so kind, but she had this fire in her." He paused, shaking his head with a somber smile.

"Her name was Ellie. She was six years younger than me, and she was my favorite person in this dreadful world. She was willing to do anything to spare anyone from harm, and it annoyed me so much because even if it meant putting herself in harm's way, she'd do it. Sometimes, I like to imagine what she'd be like if she had survived that night. I don't think I ever saw her without a smile on her face, even when she died."

Even when she died. He had watched his own sister die? Her heart cleaved in her chest. How could a person move on from a loss like that?

Zainiel stroked his fingers up and down the horse's neck as he spoke. "She loved horses. I used to catch her sneaking out of the estate to ride when she thought no one was paying attention. She used to tell me that there was nothing more freeing than riding with her hair blowing in the wind."

"She sounds like she was a beautiful person," Ivy mused.

"She was the type of beautiful that made everyone and everything around her a little brighter. She was too good for this world, and I tried to shield her from that, wanted to protect her from anything that could harm her." The somber smile he had slipped into washed away as his brows pulled together in grief. "Sometimes I wonder if I hadn't done that, then maybe the night she died, she would've been more prepared, and maybe she would've stood a chance at surviving."

He blamed himself for his own sister's death. That explained so much, the way this darkness almost seemed to follow him everywhere he went. He was burdened with so much grief.

"What happened to her?" Ivy asked tenderly.

"Theo and Kalec thought they could use her to get close to Fennrick's supporters," Zainiel started, his voice thick with the weight of the past. "They'd taken root in Arbor, some of them familiar faces from our past, people we'd never suspected would betray us. We never understood how he twisted them against us, and Kalec was desperate to find out why. We all were. They insisted she was the key, saying we had kept her so sheltered at that cursed estate that no one truly knew her or her ties to Kalec." He paused, the reins gripped tightly in his hands, knuckles white against the harness.

"Theo was meant to protect her. Fennrick... he was cunning, more cunning than we ever realized. He shared just enough to keep everyone guessing, never revealing all to a single soul. The plan was simple. If multiple trusted figures infiltrated his circle, earned his confidence, perhaps we could gather the pieces we needed to dismantle his schemes."

Ivy felt her heart constrict as she saw the burden etched across Zainiel's face.

"But it all went wrong," he continued his voice barely above a whisper. "They were discovered. Theo and the others managed to flee, convinced Ellie had escaped with them. But she didn't. Fennrick found her... tortured her... and sent two of his lackeys to dump her body outside the estate walls." His lips quivered, and Ivy's heart ached for him, hating that she had forced him to dredge up such a harsh memory.

"She was still alive when I found her. I had just returned from handling a situation that had arisen in a nearby village. She was so beaten, so battered, that I didn't even recognize her. My own sister." A mirthless sound escaped his lips, something akin to a sob. "When I got close enough, and I realized it was her... I was *shattered*. By the time I got her into the estate and to someone who might have been able to help her, she was gone. I think she knew she wouldn't make it." He ran his hand down his face and shifted in his saddle.

"She tried to tell me. But I wouldn't listen. I refused to because there was no way that *my* sister—*my Ellie*—was leaving this world, and I told her that. I told her she needed to be strong, just for a little while longer, but she just smiled and... and then she was gone. "

Ivy didn't know what to say, or if there was anything she *could* even say. There was so much pain in his voice, etched into his face, in the air. Ivy found it almost hard to breathe because of how overwhelming it was. How did he manage to live with all of that on his shoulders? She understood now why he hated Theo so much. He had entrusted Theo to care for his sister, and Theo had left her behind.

Chapter Thirty-One

The air hung heavy with an unspoken weight as they traveled in silence, punctuated only by the soft rustle of leaves. Ivy felt the ache of Zainiel's sorrow radiating like heat from a forge, and she knew nothing she said would help lessen that burden. He had trotted slightly ahead, and she fell behind, allowing him the time and privacy to pull himself together.

She surrendered to the gentle sway of the saddle as Bae plodded steadfastly through the lush embrace of the forest. In just three short hours since departing the estate, the vibrant tapestry of life around her had unfolded in astonishing richness, far beyond what she had ever glimpsed in Salus. Birds darted from branch to branch, their cheerful melodies weaving through the air like strands of silk. Squirrels, those little acrobats of the woods, scurried energetically up and down the sturdy tree trunks, their playful chases painting a picture of unrestrained joy. And then, in a quiet corner of the thicket, her gaze caught the delicate sight of a fawn awkwardly bounding after its mother, each faltering step a dance of innocence and wonder. It truly was an amazing sight.

A soft melody danced through the air, the echo of whimsical laughter following it as Ivy forced herself to sit tall in the saddle, trying to see where it was coming from. "Where is that music coming from?" Ivy called out the Zainiel.

He tugged on his horse Luther's reins, slowing his pace to match Ivy's. "There's a settlement not far up the road. It seems they are having a festival of sorts," he explained. The sorrow from his eyes was mostly gone now, and Ivy felt a tug of relief as he offered her a small smile. "Those pastries you and Ria love so much are from there. May—I think you met her at the bonfire—learned how to make them from her mother. Her mother still resides there."

She recalled meeting the rotund lady with cherry cheeks and brunette hair tied back into a messy bun atop her head. She hadn't been able to speak to her much before Zainiel showed up and dragged her away. Ivy's stomach grumbled at the thought of May's cooking. She had been so excited to leave the estate this morning that she had skipped breakfast.

"Do you think we could stop?" Ivy asked timidly. "Just for a few moments?" The past two hours had dragged on, and while she was finally growing comfortable with Bae, every jolt of the saddle had sprung through her, making her legs feel leaden. The idea of being able to stretch them, if only for a few minutes, was tempting, especially with the vibrant festival growing nearer.

Zainiel's shoulders tensed in response, and Ivy tried not to let her disappointment show. Of course he wouldn't want to let her stop. After all, he still warned the others away from her at the estate even though she could control her powers now.

With a resigned sigh, Zainiel shook his head. "You know what? Yeah. I think the horses could use a break, too." His smile was resigned as he spoke, like he was holding back from saying something, but Ivy couldn't help the flutter of excitement in her belly as the small village came into view.

Quaint cabins formed a gentle arc, each snugly nestled against its neighbor. The air buzzed with the irresistible scent of warm bread and sweet treats, drawing her in. It caught her off guard to see a few storefronts scattered about, and one in particular stood out: a weathered sign swaying gently above the door, bearing the name *Prune's Diner* in faded, cracked letters.

At the heart of the village, a magnificent tree stretched towards the sky, children darting around its base. They wove vibrant streams of wildflowers around its trunk, petals liberated by the playful wind dancing before finally carpeting the ground in a mosaic of color. Laughter erupted like bubbles in the air, stretching Ivy's mouth into a joyful grin. Was this what her childhood could have felt like?

"Is it always like this?" she whispered, awestruck by the enchanting scene that had unfolded before her. She hadn't ever seen anything like it. Festivals in Salus were all dark and brooding, more about the display of one's power and what they could offer to the town than about having fun.

"Pretty much," Zainiel answered with a nostalgic grin as he reached over and grasped Bae's reins, pulling her to a stop. "Ellie and I used to sneak over to the festivals when we could. She loved the music."

"But not Ria?" Ivy asked as she watched Zainiel swing his leg over the saddle, dismounting in one swift movement.

He guided the horses toward a sturdy tree, where he tied their reins to a low-hanging branch. "Crowds used to be really tough for Ria. Back then, she struggled with her empathic abilities. It overwhelmed her too easily." Ivy had never thought about what it must be like for Ria in large crowds. She seemed so sure of herself all the time that the idea of her—or any of them, really—struggling with controlling their powers just as Ivy had, was something Ivy had never considered.

With a gentle air, Zainiel extended his hands towards her, hovering just above her waist, his brow raised in a silent question, asking for permission to touch. She nodded, a warmth rising to her cheeks as he carefully lifted her from the saddle and set her down on the ground. It crossed her mind that she could have climbed down herself, but with her legs feeling as heavy as they did, she doubted she would've been able to with the same amount of grace he had. More than likely, she would have tumbled to the ground.

"You go ahead. I'll tend to the horses," he said, nodding toward the bustling village.

"You aren't coming?" Ivy asked.

"I think I should hang back," he said. Ivy eyed him as he stroked his horse's mane, noting the apprehensiveness in his posture. What was it about this town that made him so uneasy? Was it because it reminded him of Ellie? Maybe she shouldn't go after all, she could come back another time.

"Go on, we don't have long." He smiled, giving her a reassuring nudge.

She watched him, saw how the smile he offered her didn't quite meet his eyes, and realized that he hadn't hesitated about stopping because he was worried about her causing trouble, but because this place was a reminder of something he lost that he'd never get back.

"Go see Arbor, Storm," he said again, sensing her hesitation.

She opened her mouth to speak, to tell him that she'd changed her mind, but he just shook his head and gave her another gentle nudge forward. "Go."

With one last look, she turned and started walking towards the village. As she stepped onto the petal-covered ground, three children ran towards her, one of them handing her a flower before they ran back to the other group playing underneath the tree. Ivy beamed. Everything was so joyous here that it made her feel like she too was floating through the air.

"Would you like a pastry, dear?" an elderly voice called out over the clamor, drawing Ivy's attention to a stall that was nestled next to the storefront and titled *Prune's Diner*. This must have been what she had smelled. Her mouth watered at just the sight of it. The woman had an array of decadent pastries strewn across the table.

"These smell amazing," Ivy exclaimed, practically salivating over the assortment of treats spread before her.

The woman smiled warmly and picked up a box from her left. "You look like a traveler. Let me put together a take-away box for you."

"Oh, I don't have any money," Ivy admitted, her cheeks flushing with embarrassment.

"Nonsense, dear," the woman replied. "I don't want your money. Just promise me you'll enjoy them."

Ivy smiled broadly. Was everyone in Arbor so welcoming?

"Can I take one for my friend?" Ivy asked, glancing over her shoulder at Zain, who was still waiting with the horses, as the woman placed the pastry in a box.

"Of cour—" The woman cut herself off abruptly, her eyes narrowing as they fixed on Zain. Her face clouded with a troubled expression. "What are you doing with him?" she hissed, quickly ushering the children playing in front of her shop inside.

"You mean Zainiel?" Ivy asked, baffled by the strong reaction.

"Zainiel," the woman spat the name as if it tasted foul. "As if he's just a harmless boy." She let out a bitter laugh.

"He's a good man. He's been helping me," Ivy protested. Her voice trembled with a mix of confusion and frustration as she saw the way the older woman and the townsfolk eyed Zainiel with suspicion and fear. It mirrored the very look she had often reserved for Seraphina.

The woman shook her head with a heavy sigh, her expression filled with pity. "Oh, you poor girl. You just don't see the trouble you've stepped into. Save yourself the heartache. Take these pastries and get as far away from him as you can. He's not worth the pain he'll bring you."

Ivy could feel her cheeks flush red with anger. Zainiel, despite his callous attitude at times, had been nothing but friendly to her. He had helped her when he could have easily walked away, and now he was trekking across Arbor simply because a friend asked for help. Yet these people saw him as the same monster Theo seemed to see. Was she really so blind? Or did they all have it wrong?

"You know," Ivy started, narrowing her eyes at the older woman, "I think I'll just go. My *friend* is waiting for me," she said coldly, ignoring the woman's extended hand with the box of pastries. She burned with anger as she turned to see that the festivities seemed to have paused as all the parents ushered the children into their homes, watching Zainiel with wary eyes. What had happened to cause these people to treat him this way?

Just as Ivy began to turn away, a frail hand clamped onto her wrist, halting her in her tracks. "Listen to me, dear," the woman's voice quivered with an urgency that was hard to ignore. "That boy will bring you nothing but trouble. Believe me, he's not worth it." Her eyes gleamed with a fervor that nearly compelled Ivy to question her further. However, before she could speak, a looming darkness enveloped them both, causing the woman to tense.

"Release her," Zainiel's cold and commanding voice cut through the air, sending a shiver down Ivy's spine. The woman quickly pulled her hand away and took a few staggering steps backward.

"I was merely offering the young lady some advice," she said resolutely, her eyes burning with determination as she held Zainiel's unwavering gaze. Unlike the rest of the town, she showed no sign of fear.

Zainiel enveloped Ivy in a gentle embrace, his protective arm around her back, and looked down at her. "Are you okay?" he asked, his voice a soft whisper edged with worry, a stark contrast to the tone he'd used with the woman.

Ivy nodded slightly. "I'm fine. We should go."

Zainiel nodded sharply, his eyes glinting with cold fury as he cast one last withering glare at the woman, before turning to lead Ivy back towards the horses. As they made their way through the town, Ivy's gaze swept across the scene that had so recently been filled with joyous celebration. Now, she saw the townspeople standing stiff and wary, their postures rigid as they guarded their children, who recoiled in fear from Ivy and Zainiel. She glanced over at him, noting the tight set of his jaw and his fist clenched so tightly at his side that his knuckles had turned white. Was this the real reason he didn't want to visit the village? Did he know they would react this poorly?

As they reached the horses, Ivy cast one last glance at the villagers, who all remained gathered together, wary expressions upon their faces as they watched them closely. What had happened to make people think he was such a monster?

"What just happened?" Ivy asked, breaking the tense silence they had found themselves in for the past thirty minutes. Zainiel had ushered her back onto Bae and hadn't spoken a word as he began to lead them away from the village, which had remained eerily quiet as they retreated. All of their festivities had come to a screeching halt the second they realized who stood amongst the tree line waiting for her, and she couldn't help but want to understand why.

"It's a long story," he grumbled. His jaw was still set in anger, and his back was rigid. Even the horses seemed aware of the tense air that seemed to surround them, as they too moved with less grace than before.

"Perfect, we can use it to pass the time," she pressed. When Theo warned her off, she assumed it was because of whatever bad blood they had between each other, but now... an entire village seemed to be put off by Zainiel's presence, and she couldn't just ignore that.

Zainiel sighed. "Storm, this really isn't something—"

"What exactly is it that you do for my father? Is this because of that?" she asked, cutting him off. It was a question that had been brewing in the back of her mind for a while now, ever since her conversation with Ria the night of the bonfire.

Zainiel bristled at her question. "The things I do for your father are for the good of Arbor," he paused, his jaw ticking, "even if other people don't see it that way."

"And if you chose to leave? Chose to stop doing that job, would my father let you?" she asked as she fidgeted with the reins in her hands.

Zainiel tugged on his horse's reins, stopping abruptly before turning towards her, anger flaring in his eyes. "I do what I do because it's a job that needs to be done, and someone has to do it. I owe your father mine and my sister's lives. So if it means that I serve him until the day he sees no need for me or until the day I die, then so be it." His voice was harsh and unforgiving as his gaze pierced into hers.

He was expecting her to cower away from him, just like the people had done at the village, but she wouldn't. Instead, she met his stare with an icy one of her own. She had seen that pain in his eyes, how he cared for his sisters, and she refused to believe that someone who could care as deeply as that could be bad.

A sharp, resounding crack echoed through the forest, and the horses rocked back. Bae let out a nervous whine. Only then did she notice the eerie stillness that had overtaken the woods. The usual chorus of chirping birds and rustling leaves had vanished, the only sound being another *CRRRACK*.

Zainiel pressed a finger to his lips, urging her into silence as he grasped the reins of her horse. He guided them to a grove of trees that cloaked the ground in deep, dappled shade. An eerie sensation crept over her. Had it grown darker and colder, or was her mind playing tricks?

Her eyes widened in wonder as a thick shroud of darkness enveloped them, cocooning them in an even deeper shadow. This was Zainiel's doing. His power rippled throughout the air, and she longed to touch it, to feel its texture against her skin. It moved with the fluidity of water, and she envisioned it wrapping around her in a luxurious, velvety caress if she surrendered to its embrace. Ivy knew the darkness had hidden them in the shadows, molding them into the scenery, but she could still see through the veil he had cast around them.

A thunderous snap split the silence, followed by a guttural, sinister growl reverberating through the dense forest. The air was thick with the nauseating stench of decay and death. Ivy felt the hairs on her neck stand on end as her heart thundered in her chest. Her eyes darted to Zainiel, who was tensely focused on something to his left, his jaw set in determination, and his hand gripping a dagger she hadn't realized he had been carrying. The atmosphere screamed *danger*.

Then, she saw it. A grotesque and malevolent creature moved among the trees, its motions jerky and unnatural. Its flesh was charred and blackened, its fingernails twisted into talon-like claws, and its limbs grotesquely malformed as if they had been shattered and incorrectly reassembled. The creature bore an unsettling resemblance to a human, igniting dread within Ivy as she pondered what horrific force could have twisted a person into such a monstrous form.

The creature took another step towards them, its left leg caving backward with a sickening pop as the rest of its body jerked from the movement. Scattered patches of hair that remained atop the creature's head swayed with the movement, and she watched as a chunk of the frayed hair fell from the decaying creature. It advanced towards them with an unnerving persistence, each step marked by a sickening crack that Ivy now recognized was not from breaking branches but from the creature's own brittle bones shattering under its weight. Ivy's breath hitched in her throat as it halted, now just a few feet away. Its mouth hung open as if it had been frozen in a silent scream, and rotted teeth stared back at her as a black liquid ran from the creature's mouth and down its lips. It shifted, leaning towards them, and elongated its neck as it twisted its head too far to the side, the bones in its neck creaking from the movement.

A shiver went down Ivy's spine as she wove her fingers through Bae's mane. Now standing directly before her as if it had sniffed her out, the creature's unnaturally blue-silver eyes, the only semblance of life in its otherwise deathly form, settled on her. Her breath halted in her throat. It couldn't see her. She knew it couldn't see her, but the way its eyes pierced through the shadowy veil, she wondered if somehow it knew she was there. It raised a gnarled finger, curved and twisted so the sharpened talon that used to be fingernails was parallel with its palm and reached out towards her, the tip of it brushing against the dark wall that Zainiel had built to shroud her.

It let out a crackling snarl, its upper lip curving upwards as it jerked its head to the other side with another resounding crack that sent Bae nervously twitching beneath her. With one last snarl, the creature flicked its rotted tongue before turning and stalking away, its bones snapping with a resounding *crack* with each step. She watched the creature disappear back in the direction it had come, taking the biting chill and darkness along with it, but leaving behind a heavy stench—a smell Ivy feared she'd never be able to wash off.

Chapter Thirty-Two

I vy remained motionless, frozen in the saddle, as Zainiel
dropped the cloak of darkness he had summoned around
them. *What was that?* She had never seen anything like it, not even
in her studies in Salus. Seraphina had journals, and some of them
consisted of entities that could be summoned during a ritual, but
nothing like this.

Zainiel remained in his saddle beside her, his fist still tightly
enclosed around the dagger as his eyes bored into the spot where
the creature had stood.

"What. Was. *That,*" Ivy breathed, her heart still hammering in her chest. Even though the biting chill that had settled over them dissipated with the creature's retreat, the sour stench of decay still lingered heavily in the air, searing itself into Ivy's memory. Her hands trembled at her sides as she wove them into Bae's mane in a soothing caress as the horse restlessly stirred beneath her.

"A Mortifer," Zainiel growled, the cadence of his voice rippling through the too-quiet forest.

"A what?" Ivy asked, craning her neck towards him. She was going to need a lot more of an explanation than that.

Zainiel didn't respond. Instead, he just sheathed the dagger with one angry thrust before he dismounted from his saddle in a fluid swoop. There was something different about him, something darker; he began to pace before her, clenching and unclenching his hands at his sides, his jaw set and brows furrowed. Darkness almost seemed to emit from him, clinging to his movements as it draped around him like a cloak.

"Zainiel, are you okay?" Ivy called out to him as he continued to pace before her.

He didn't bother to look her way; it was as if he couldn't even hear her. The darkness that clung to him only grew, forming into inky, spindly tendrils that lashed out anxiously at the air.

"Zainiel," she called out again, this time a bit louder as she studied the forest floor that now seemed impossibly far away. She could get off the saddle herself. She had watched him do it so gracefully each time; she just needed to keep a steady hold on the pommel, swing a leg over, and then descend. It wasn't that complicated. Only, it was, and as she brought her leg to the other side of the saddle, her foot became tangled in the stirrup, causing her to meet the solid ground with a loud grunt.

Zainiel still paced before her, seemingly unaware of the tumble she'd just taken, but it didn't stop her cheeks from heating up as Bae looked down at her almost comically. She stood, brushing off the debris of fallen leaves and dirt that now clung to her clothes. The shadows around continued to grow as he shook his head in dismay, the tendrilled phantoms writhing around him in a panic. Was he losing control? Panicking just as she had those few times at the estate? And if he was, what on earth could she do to ground him, to bring him back to reality, back to her?

"Zainiel," she took a tentative step forward, halting when his magic lashed out towards her. "Zainiel, I think you need to take some deep breaths."

He continued to pace, twigs underneath his boots snapping with each step he took. He dragged his hand down his face. "I should've never agreed to this," he mumbled, almost too quietly for her to notice. "I should've never let you leave the estate." Was this because he was worried for her safety?

"Zain, look at me." She took another small step, trying to calm her nervous heart as his magic surged forward, nearly colliding with her. Zainiel wouldn't hurt her, she knew that with a certainty that she didn't quite understand. But she also would never have destroyed the gardens, would have never lost control the night of the bonfire. But she wasn't in control those times, just as he seemed to not be in control now.

"I should have known better," he said, still unfazed by the fact that she was approaching him. The tendrils lashed through the air with increasing harshness as the seconds passed. One whistled past her ear in a whip-crack motion, causing her to stumble to the side in surprise. She needed him to realize what was happening, needed to reach him somehow.

At the estate during their training, he had used his magic almost as if a way to nullify hers. She had never tried to cancel out his with hers, but she supposed it could work... maybe. But if it didn't...

Bae let out a nervous whine as Luther rocked back and forth, the energy emanating from Zainiel unsettling both of them. Another tendril of darkness snapped through the air, smacking into the ground with an ear-splitting crack, sending Luther rearing up on his back legs before darting off into the forest. She had to do something.

Ivy held her hand out, calling to her magic. She imagined it being warm and calming as it flickered to life in her palm. She didn't want to hurt him, just needed to reach him. Zainiel had once told her that her magic didn't have to be destructive, that she could mold it into whatever she chose.

She glanced over her shoulder at Bae, whose nervous eyes were planted on her. "It's okay, girl," she soothed before turning back to Zainiel, who still paced back and forth before her. With an outstretched palm, she took a small step forward, her heart hammering in her chest as his shadows loomed above her. It was just Zainiel. She didn't have to be afraid. *It was just Zainiel.*

Ivy took a bolder step forward, feeling the shadowy tendrils encircle her like an eager embrace as though they sought to either draw her to him, or ensnare her. But she clung to the belief that his magic recognized hers, just as her own seemed to recognize his. The cool blue light flickering in her palm spiraled up her forearm and floated through the space between them, weaving towards his dark shadows. With wonder, she witnessed their magic entwine, almost as if they were two long-lost friends joyfully reuniting.

The icy blue strands of her magic danced gracefully through the air, seamlessly blending with his dark phantoms in a rhythm that spoke of familiarity as if these forces had once shared an intimate bond. It was... *beautiful.* The familiar tug she'd sensed during her weeks at the estate, training beside Zainiel, intensified, drawing her ever closer.

"Zainiel," she murmured softly, taking another step towards him.

"You could've died," he seethed, halting abruptly with his back still facing her. She saw his shoulders slump, a clear sign of surrender. "You could've died," he repeated, his voice quivering with emotion. Her heart wrenched in her chest seeing him like this, seeing him so *broken*.

"I'm okay," she whispered, taking another step towards him, letting that dark aura that had encased him envelop her. It didn't feel like she expected. The night of the bonfire, it was biting and cold as it leeched the magic from her, but now it was just cold... and heavy. *So heavy.* As if the weight of his anxiety and panic had actually manifested itself in his magic.

She placed her hand on his shoulder, letting the light of her magic wash over him, imagining it embracing him as she promised him that she was okay and safe. Ivy tugged him towards her, making him turn to face her as she grasped his hand with her other hand.

"I'm safe." She pressed his palm over her thundering heart. Looking into his eyes, she saw panic and fear and, underneath all of that, grief. She never broke eye contact with him, nor did he with her. Slowly, his breathing slowed, his shoulders softened, and the weighted cold from the darkness that had surrounded them dispersed, leaving them standing in the forest where Bae grazed a few feet away; but at that moment, Ivy saw nothing but him.

"I'm safe," she repeated, brushing a thumb along his cheek.

Zainiel sighed, closed his eyes, and leaned into her touch, his hand still pressed firmly against her chest. This was the closest they had been outside of the training grounds, and despite the way Ivy's stomach flipped and her heart stuttered, she felt safe.

Chapter Thirty-Three

ZAINIEL

What the fuck was wrong with him? First, he agreed to this foolish request of Ivy's that he bring her along, and then... he nearly lost control of his powers? He was too old for this. Too skilled with his magic for this to have happened. He pulled away from her abruptly and probably too harshly, considering the faltering look of hurt that flashed through her features before he turned towards the horses; or, well, horse, as Bae was the only one left grazing a few feet away. *Fuck, fuck, fuck.*

"Where's Luther?" he asked, not turning to face her. He couldn't stand to see the worry that was stricken over her face. *He was supposed to be helping her.* Not the other way around.

"He got spooked," she spoke softly behind him, her voice washing over him like a soothing melody. "I—I should've tried to grab him, but..." *But he was too busy losing control of his magic to leave that as an option.*

Zainiel loosed an irritated sigh as he raked his hands through his hair. Ria would never let him live this down if she knew about it. She had been after him for years about keeping his emotions pent up too tightly, had even warned him just weeks ago that if he didn't start facing them, he would lose control; but he was too prideful to listen to her. After all, he was over a century old. His time for losing control of his magic was long past.

"We'll have to ride the rest of the way together. It's not too much farther," he called back, then knelt to pick up Bae's reins from the ground where they had fallen as she nibbled happily on the grass. A slight grin tugged at the corners of his mouth as he stroked the spot between her eyes. Bae had always been more interested in her next sweet treat than in any potential fright. The clover she was feasting on now was, without a doubt, her favorite.

"What was that, Zainiel?" she breathed.

He turned to find her still rooted to the spot where he had left her. Her eyes were firmly planted in the direction the Mortifer had skulked off in, and the usual rosy color that dappled her cheeks was gone. He imagined that to her, the foul creature was a walking nightmare; but that was only the tip of the iceberg, and that was precisely the reason he should never have agreed to her coming along.

"A Mortifer, or at least that's what we call it. They showed up about twenty-one years ago, and all we know for sure about them is that when one shows up, death soon follows." The truth was, they really didn't know enough about them; just that whatever it was, it tended to hop from body to body, devouring the souls of their captives before moving onto their next victim.

"Was it," she paused, her brows furrowing as she dragged her gaze to meet his, "alive?"

"It was, once. And I suppose whatever is inhabiting the bodies is alive, but not in the same sense you and I are."

Ivy nodded as she glanced back in the direction that it had retreated. "Can they be killed?"

Zainiel raised his brow in surprise. Most people, Theo included, had sought to find a way to save the poor creatures, refusing to believe that killing them was the only option. "If you kill the body it is inhabiting, it will simply move onto another. There's only one way that we have discovered works to kill the creature itself."

"How?" she asked.

Zainiel tried to conceal a grimace. She had already encountered his ability to consume one's magic, but he was hoping to shield her from this truth just a little while longer, for his own selfish reasons.

People tended to look at him differently, to cower away from him just as the townsfolk in the village had done, and he wasn't ready to see that fear in her eyes every time she looked at him. Not yet. But he had promised her to be truthful, to answer her questions as she asked them, and he wouldn't become another person on the long list of people who betrayed her trust.

He cleared his throat, stroking his hands down Bae's chestnut mane as he met Ivy's emerald gaze. "Me."

Chapter Thirty-Four

"M e," Zainiel said, eyes boring into hers with an intensity that almost held her captive.

"You?" Ivy asked with a furrowed brow. How was he the only way to kill those creatures? *Zain's magic is powerful and at times, if he wishes it to be, consuming.* Ria's words sounded through her mind. "You consume them," she said breathlessly as she stared at him in shock.

A flicker of pain flashed through his eyes as he turned his gaze back to Bae, and he raked his fingers through the horse's mane.

Your father, he expects a lot from Zain, and it's a heavy burden to carry. Ria's words sounded again in her mind. Was that the job her father had pinned him with? Did he truly expect Zainiel to take on that sort of evil by himself? *Using his magic in that way... it does things to him, takes him to a dark place.* She couldn't begin to imagine what that sort of burden must've felt like. She could barely stand to be in that creature's presence for more than a few minutes, but to consume them? How could her father expect that of him?

"We need to leave. My friend will be waiting for us," Zainiel said, breaking the silence. His voice was clipped as he fidgeted with the saddle, tugging at the leather straps to ensure its security.

Ivy wanted to ask more questions. To learn more about the creature. To ask how they knew Zainiel was the only option. To ask him if her father would ever allow him to walk away from this burden, if he chose to. But as she looked at him and saw the ripple of his jawline as he clenched it, she chose to stay quiet and instead walked over to Bae, where he helped her into the saddle.

The silence had found them again. Neither of them uttered a word as they rode through the forest. Zainiel's body pressed tightly against hers, his arms wrapped around her waist as he held the reins. He seemed tense, so tense that Ivy could feel the rigidity of his muscles as they rode. Had she upset him with her question? She hadn't meant to, but she supposed she could understand how it would have upset him. After all, he didn't know how much Ria had shared with her. That she had told Ivy just how burdened he was with this... power.

She wanted to tell him she was sorry—sorry for always asking the wrong questions, for making him stop at that horrid village, and for her father, who she was beginning to think was not the great man everyone made him out to be. But she didn't speak out of fear of saying the wrong thing.

"You have leaves in your hair," Zainiel grumbled from behind her. "Why?"

Her cheeks heated with embarrassment. "I, uh... I fell when trying to get off the saddle earlier."

Zainiel shifted in the saddle, craning his neck to peer at her face as he raised a brow. "You fell?"

"The ground is a lot further down than it looks, and you made it look so easy..." she answered with a shy shrug. A deep chuckle sounded from his chest, vibrating against her back. It was a sound she was happy to hear, one that brought a calming wave over her as she felt it wash away some of the tension that had built between them.

"Alright, Storm, let's add how to dismount a horse to our training regimen. Can't have you tumbling and breaking any of those pretty bones of yours," he teased, though there was something still heavy in his voice. Like he was simply putting a mask on to play the part he always played with her. And she hated it, but now wasn't the time to hash that out.

"Do you think the Mortifer is the reason your friend called for your help?" Ivy asked hesitantly as she traced her finger along the rim of the pommel. The last thing she wanted to do was upset him by mentioning their encounter with the Mortifer, but it was a question that had been sitting on the tip of her tongue as she found herself wondering what other vile creatures haunted these woods.

Zainiel hesitated for a moment, and Ivy felt a puff of warm air brush against the back of her neck as if he were about to say something and then chose not to. She craned her neck and looked at him with a raised brow. "I'm not sure. I suppose it could be, but something about the message made it seem more urgent."

Ivy's palms slickened with nerves. More urgent than a soul-devouring parasite whose only weakness was the one person she was pressed up against on this horse? She knew he expected her to ask what he meant by that, and she supposed she should have, but the way her heart hammered in her chest at the idea that there was something worse than that vile creature they encountered was bone-chilling enough to make her simply nod and let the forest melodies fill the air.

They rode in silence the rest of the way, neither of them uttering a word until Bae trotted them out from under the heavy blanket of leaves that canvassed them above and into a sun-dappled clearing. Wildflowers carpeted the ground with specks of purples and pinks, and in the center lay a shimmering body of water, the surface rippling from the fish that spiritedly skipped atop the surface. She was beginning to think that there wasn't a place in Arbor that wasn't breathtaking.

"This is..." Ivy was at a loss for words. Zainiel had dismounted from Bae and now strode beside her as he led them further into the clearing.

"I know," Zainiel mused, nodding as he stopped and began to tether Bae's reins to a nearby post, being sure to allow enough slack so she could reach the water.

"We used to live not far from here. Before our parents died," Zainiel began, as he offered his hands to help guide her down from the saddle. "Ria and I used to sneak away with some of the other kids in the village." A smile glinted in his eyes as Ivy's feet landed softly on the ground.

"It sounds like it was a special place," Ivy offered with a small smile. She took a few steps forward, letting her fingers brush against the petals of the flowers as she watched the way the lake before her shimmered in the sunlight, reflecting the cloudless sky that lay above them.

"It was," Zainiel answered somberly as he knelt beside her, plucking one of the smoothed stones littered around the shore. He turned the stone around in his hands a few times, inspecting it as he ran his thumb over the surface. Cradling the stone in his fingers, he sent it skipping across the lake. Each skip sent ripples through the glassy surface.

Ivy plucked a flower and folded her knees beneath her, sitting on the soft ground as she watched Zainiel pick up another rock before sending it skipping across the water again. She smiled to herself as she watched him. The tension that had sat so heavily atop his shoulders the whole ride here was now nearly gone, and he seemed so... relaxed.

"Ria and I used to have contests to see how far each of us could skip rocks," he started as he tossed a rock in the air, catching it in his palm. "She always hated that I beat her. I know she doesn't seem like it now, but she used to be so competitive," he chuckled to himself as he shook his head.

"We used to spend hours here finding the perfect rocks to skip." He paused as he let himself fall into the grass beside Ivy, his shoulder brushing against hers. "You want them to be smooth. The smoother they are, the better." Zainiel passed the stone that he had in his hand to Ivy. She twirled it around in her hand, letting her fingertips brush over the cool, smooth surface.

Zainiel smiled as he talked, the corners of his eyes creasing and a slight dimple appearing on the left of his cheek. "Sometimes I wish those days never ended," he admitted.

Ivy let her hand fall to his knee. She had days like that. Days when she and Theo had managed to sneak away and she could be carefree for just a little while. In the moment, she would have done anything to make those days last a little longer. But now, as she sat before the water, surrounded by the blooming colors of wildflowers, watching as the wildlife around her buzzed with a beauty she never dreamed existed, she wasn't sure she'd ever give this up. Even if staying meant she had to face the horrors housed in these woods like the Mortifer.

"About what happened..." Zainiel started bringing his hand to rub it across the back of his neck.

Ivy shook her head and waved a dismissive hand. "You don't need to explain yourself, Zainiel. I understand." And the truth was, she did. He lost control of himself because he panicked. Something she wasn't in the place to judge anyone about.

Ivy twirled the flower in her hand, watching as the petals' colors seemed to bleed together in the air from the movement. She knew what he was trying to do. He lost control around her, and now he felt the need to explain himself, to make her understand that she was still safe with him, as much as she had been before. But Ivy didn't need that reassurance from him. She knew with everything she had that he wouldn't hurt her. She didn't quite understand it, but she just *knew.*

"I need you to know that that usually doesn't happen. Not to me." He shook his head as his brows furrowed in guilt and confusion.

Ivy nudged his shoulder with her own as she gave him a teasing grin. "That's what all the men say."

A loud, unexpected laugh barked from Zainiel as he looked at her with both shock and amusement. "Oh, so you have jokes now, do you?"

"I've always had them." *A lie.* She had rarely been one to joke before. But now... well, now she'd do just about anything to see the way his eyes lit up, dimple on display, chest rumbling as he laughed. *Truly laughed.* Not the forced laugh she had seen him do so often at the estate.

She watched as the smile faded and his gaze fell to the scar creeping up her neck. She hated that scar.

"I didn't hurt you, did I?" he asked hesitantly as his gaze still bored into that imperfect patch of skin. "The shadows, sometimes they can be a bit... brutal," he added with a wince.

She tugged at the collar of her shirt, shaking her head. "No. I'm not hurt." She remembered the way his magic had seemed to embrace hers as if they were each one half of a puzzle that had been separated for too long. "I think our magic recognizes one another," she added sheepishly, feeling a slight blush rise to her cheeks. She didn't know if he felt it too; if his magic pulled him towards her, as hers did to him.

Zainiel raised a brow, "What do you mean?"

Ivy looked at the flower in her hand, plucking a petal and rolling it between her fingers. This was ridiculous. She was going to sound crazy. "I—I don't know how to explain it. I noticed it before at the estate. It was almost like my magic was drawn to you somehow..." she trailed off, shaking her head with a sigh. "This sounds crazy, doesn't it?" She peered up at him through the hair that had fallen across her face, expecting to find judgment, but instead, he just stared at her with that intense expression that made her stomach flip.

"I've heard crazier. Continue," he pressed.

"In the forest, I tried calling you, but you wouldn't answer. You were trapped within yourself, and I knew that I needed to find a way to reach you. I remembered what you told me a few days after the bonfire. That my magic could be whatever I wanted it to be, that it didn't always have to be so destructive." She plucked another petal from the flower, watching as the breeze carried away in a dance. "I don't really know how to explain it. When my magic met yours, it was like they became one." *Like they were two halves of a whole.* "And then when your magic wrapped around me, it wasn't like that night in the field at the bonfire. It was *caring*, soft almost."

"It wrapped around you? And you didn't get hurt?" Zainiel grasped her arm in his hand, turning it over as if he were looking for some sign of injury.

"No, I didn't get hurt." Her brows furrowed as she watched the disbelief etch onto his face. He had used his magic on Theo and Ria that day, and neither of them had been hurt. "Why do you seem so shocked?"

"I—It should've—" he shook his head, his brows furrowing further as he examined her arm again.

"Zainiel?" Ivy asked as she placed her hand over his, still holding her arm. "What is it?"

"When I first came into my powers, and then again after Ellie... I would lose control like that. And when I did," he paused, shaking his head again, "When I did, people got hurt, Storm. *Really* hurt. One night after Ellie died, I had a nightmare. Ria felt it. I lost control while I slept and blew the windows out in my room, and Ria said by the time she found me, the shadows had taken over the whole room and were beginning to take over the hall. She tried to reach me, and I almost killed her. My own sister."

It was Ivy's turn to look shocked. If Ria's own empathic abilities couldn't reach him, then how had she been able to?

"You shouldn't have been able to reach me." He traced his fingers over her palm as he spoke, his brows still creased as he tried to puzzle out what exactly this meant. A look of dawning realization flashed across his features as he met her gaze with wide eyes. "Unless..." he trailed off, looking at her as if *she* were the puzzle he needed to figure out.

"Unless what?" she asked.

His lips parted as if he was about to answer her question, but before he could, he yanked his hand from hers and whipped his head around, his eyes narrowing to the dense forest that surrounded them. He abruptly stood, motioning for her to do the same.

"I'll explain later, but we have company," he said hurriedly, keeping his voice low. "Remember what I said. No one can know who you really are to Kalec." He gave her one more pointed look before turning and walking briskly towards the tree line, as if he were trying to place as much space between them as possible before whoever they were meeting showed themselves.

"I was starting to wonder if you might bail on us," a sultry voice sounded from behind Ivy. She turned to see a striking woman emerging from the thick blanket of trees, her physique reminiscent of Ria's but notably more muscular. The sun caught her golden, pin-straight hair, which fell just below her chin, shimmering as she moved with a confidence that commanded attention. Clad in snug leather that accentuated every curve, she left little to the imagination. Ivy noted the four weapons she carried: two daggers sheathed on her upper thighs, a third tucked securely at her hip, much like Zainiel's, and a bow clad across her back, peeking up above her shoulder.

Zainiel's usual playful grin tugged across his lips as he walked towards the woman and reached a hand out to clap her on the shoulder in greeting. "You know I would never. Plus, Ria would never let me hear the end of it."

The woman's full lips spread into a warm smile as she greeted Zainiel with a similar clap on the shoulder before bringing her forehead to his. "It's nice to see you, Z."

"Likewise, Maron," Zainiel said as they broke from their embrace.

Maron's eyes dragged over to Ivy as she raised an inquisitive eye. "I see you've finally taken on a travel companion."

"Training," Zainiel answered with a nonchalant wave over his shoulder. Ivy tried not to flinch from the disinterest in his voice. No one was supposed to know who she was. That's all it was. He was just trying to protect her.

Maron's gaze hovered over her for a little longer, her eyes sweeping up and down Ivy's body as if she were trying to determine if she was a threat or not before just shrugging her shoulders and returning her gaze to Zainiel. Ivy walked over to Bae, pretending to busy herself as she peered at the woman. How did she and Zainiel know each other? And why was she so comfortable around him, unlike everyone else?

"We encountered a Mortifer on the way here," Zainiel said.

Maron's shoulders tensed, and her lips tightened into a thin line before she nodded. "I was afraid that might happen." Ivy plucked an apple from the satchel hanging from Bae's saddle and offered it to the horse, feeling her lips tickle against her palm as she ate it.

"Is that why you asked me to come?" Zainiel asked.

"Not exactly…" Maron trailed off, her eyes flickering to Ivy before returning to Zainiel.

"She's fine," he assured her with another dismissive wave.

Ivy ran her hand down Bae's mane as she peered at Maron, whose gaze had fallen back on her as if she knew she wasn't just some new girl Zainiel was training. As if she didn't buy the dismissive act that he was putting on for her.

"There's been multiple sightings of Mortifers in the area, and it's not just one. They seem to have arrived in a group. We are still trying to pinpoint where they are coming from, but…" she trailed off again, her eyes flicking back over to Ivy. "But the people that have gone missing. There's no trace of them. At first, we thought the Mortifers had taken them, but I don't think they did. I think there is something else—something worse—coming."

Zainiel's shoulders tightened as he cast a glance to Ivy over his shoulder. "Any idea where they are coming from?" he asked as he turned back to face Maron.

Maron's lips thinned again as she gave him a curt nod. "They are coming from the human realm."

"You're certain?" Zainiel questioned, his fist tightening at his side.

"I saw them myself, Z. A group of three walked right through our border gate." Ivy still didn't know exactly how this world worked, or how it kept itself hidden from the outside world, but she knew enough to understand that if those monsters could walk through the gate like she and Theo had, it wasn't good.

"We haven't seen the magic at our borders falter like this since Edwin passed." *Edwin... who was Edwin?* "Is Kalec—"

"Kalec is fine." Zainiel cut her off, but there was a bit of unease in his voice as if he were trying to convince himself just as much as he was Maron; and, judging by the haunted expression that lay on Maron's face, she heard it too. "For now, let's focus on figuring out exactly where they are coming from. Perhaps there's something we can do to strengthen the gates. In the meantime, let anyone in the area know to remain in groups and report any suspicious activity."

Maron inclined her head. "We've set you up in the usual cabin nearby. How long do you plan to stay?"

"Until we resolve this situation," he asserted, his voice carrying a weight of authority. "Do you have enough personnel stationed at the gates? Instruct them not to engage, but we need to keep track of how many are coming in and where they're headed."

"I've assigned two guards here and alerted the teams at the other gates to do the same," Maron replied. Ivy observed the dynamic between them, noting how Zainiel effortlessly took command and how Maron followed without hesitation.

"Excellent," Zainiel said, nodding in approval. "I would like to meet with your team tomorrow morning, if that's agreeable. I trust that allows you sufficient time to arrange things?"

Maron nodded with a knowing smile as if she had anticipated this request all along. "They'll be there two hours after first light."

Bae nudged Ivy's hand, pulling her focus away from the pair as they discussed their next steps. With a playful nip at Ivy's palm, Bae urged her to reach back into the saddlebag still secured at her side.

Ivy let out a soft chuckle. "Alright, I get the hint." She fished another apple from the bag, offering it to Bae while lovingly rubbing the spot between the horse's eyes, a smile blossoming on her face.

"You know, those apples were supposed to be for us," Zainiel's voice rang out playfully from behind, catching her off guard.

Ivy turned, her cheeks flushing a delicate pink. "Oh, I didn't realize," she admitted, noticing for the first time that Maron had vanished from the field. "Where did Maron go?"

"She headed back to her village. Nightfall's coming soon, and we need to get to the cabin," he replied, untying Bae's reins from the post.

Ivy nodded, casting one last glance at the field. The flowers danced in the gentle breeze, their sweet fragrance enveloping the air, while the birds flitted playfully through the orange-tinged evening sky. A wish formed in her heart—she hoped to return to this magical place one day.

Chapter Thirty-Five

"I owe you some answers, don't I?" Zainiel asked as he let himself fall back into the chair that was nestled in the corner of the room. "I can practically feel the questions swarming around in that brain of yours," he added with a heavy sigh.

The ride to the cabin had been brief, and while Ivy wanted to finish the conversation they had started before Maron interrupted, she decided then wouldn't be a good time. Zainiel seemed tense. Like that slight respite he'd gotten from the weight he carried returned tenfold after his conversation with Maron.

Ivy sat on the small bed, snuggled tightly in the opposing corner of the room. The cabin was small: only housing the bed, barely large enough for someone of Zainiel's stature, the chair he had fallen into moments after walking through the door, and a small bathroom with only a toilet. There was no shower, but she was glad to see that there was at least some form of plumbing. The walls even remained bare, only being adorned by one cloudy mirror with a thick layer of dust atop the copper frame. It was clear Zainiel didn't visit here often, and when he did, he came alone.

While it wasn't shocking to her that he often traveled alone, something about it tugged at her heart. She knew how quickly loneliness could creep in with its suffocating hold, especially when one had a past as haunting as his.

"Storm?" Zainiel called, pulling her from her thoughts.

"I don't know where to start," she admitted. And it was the truth. It seemed with every passing moment she uncovered something more about this world that she didn't understand. She wanted to know what Zainiel had been about to tell her in the field. Wanted to know who Edwin was and how his passing had affected the borders. Wanted to understand how their borders even worked, what it meant now that these monsters were able to seamlessly cross over them, and most of all what any of this had to do with her father. Zainiel had tried to stop Maron from speaking further about it, but Ivy knew she was about to say something that Zainiel didn't want Ivy to hear. Something that left the both of them uneasy, even as the words remained unspoken between them.

Zainiel nodded knowingly. "Your father, then?" he suggested, catching Ivy by surprise. She had half expected to have to pull the information from him.

"Maron was about to say something, and you stopped her. I want to know why," Ivy said. "And I want to know who Edwin is and why his death had anything to do with the borders and my father." Ivy added before she lost the nerve.

"I stopped her because there's something I haven't told you about your father, something that I wanted you to hear from me," Zainiel answered as he leaned forward, resting his elbows on his knees. "Your father is a very important man to Arbor."

Ivy nodded. This much she did know. No one seemed to allow her to forget it. *He's an important man. He's a good man. He's a busy man.* It was a shame he was also an *absent* man.

"Edwin was your grandfather. He passed shortly before you were born. It was why your father had to leave your mother so abruptly. I guess you could say he was sort of our..." Zainiel paused, searching for the right word, "King. And when he passed, that responsibility fell to your father."

King. Was he trying to tell her that her father was the *ruler* of Arbor?

"There are gateways in each realm, connecting to the others that exist. Similar to the one you and Theo passed through to get here. When Edwin became sick, and his magic began to elude him, and those gateways became weak, allowing anyone or thing to pass through. When he died, the gates were left open, and we were left vulnerable."

Ivy's stomach churned as she listened to the words leave his mouth and an eerie chill settled over her shoulders. She knew that there was something more that Zainiel and Ria had been keeping from her these past few weeks. Anytime she had asked about her father, Ria had gotten this look in her eyes that made her think something more was going on. But she had simply thought they were all covering for him, making him out to be a better man than he was, but this... What did it mean for her father?

"When your father assumed his place, he tied his life and magic, just as his father had, to the gates. Sealing them off from other realms, protecting Arbor from anyone who might wish to cause us harm. When Kalec did this, it was nearly impossible for him to leave Arbor without leaving us vulnerable. That is why he never returned for your mother. He couldn't leave," Zainiel explained.

Ivy loosed a breath as she stared into the empty fireplace before her. Her father was a *king*. "Why haven't you told me before now?" Ivy asked.

"Ria wanted to. I asked her not to tell you. You had so much thrown at you all at once, I didn't think the whole 'future Queen of Arbor' tidbit would..."

Future Queen... Zainiel's lips kept moving but Ivy could hear no sound coming from them. The only thing she could hear were the words "future queen" on a loop inside her head. *Future Queen ... she was to be the future queen?* Ivy didn't think she could breathe. She knew nothing of what it meant to be a Queen. Gods, she knew nothing of this *realm,* let alone how she would one day go about *ruling* it.

"Storm? You still with me?" Zainiel asked. He gotten up from his seat and now knelt before her, placing a warm hand just above her knee as he peered up at her, the last bit of the evening sunlight filtering through the one small window and sparking in his eyes.

"I—" she stopped herself short, shaking her head. She was at a loss for words. Her father was a king, so it would only make sense that she would have some sort of future claim to Arbor, but this was the last thing she had expected. And if the magic that protected Arbor was failing, what did that mean for her father? For her? "Do you know where he is?" she asked, her eyes glassy from the emotion swelling within her.

Zainiel cast a look downward as he moved to sit next to her, the bed creaking under the newly added weight. "No one does."

Her heart stuttered anxiously in her chest as the next question she asked left her lips in a whisper. "Is he alive?" She peered up at Zainiel through a curtain of hair as she searched his face for some sign that what she feared wasn't true. That somehow, she had read into this all wrong. Tears began to well in her eyes as he gingerly reached out, lacing his fingers through hers.

"I'm choosing to believe that he is." *But there was no way of knowing, especially now that the magic has begun to fail.* A tear rolled down Ivy's cheek as the unspoken words hung heavily between them. He was alive. He *had* to be alive.

"And if he isn't?" Ivy asked, unsure if she was ready to hear the answer, if she was ready to face that possibility.

Zainiel gave her hand a reassuring squeeze. "We will cross that bridge when we get to it."

Ivy nodded, her mind still reeling from the idea that she would one day be expected to rule this realm; and not only rule it, but tie herself to it.

"So, you, Theo, Ria, are... what? A part of his court?" Ivy asked. If she was being honest, she didn't understand much about the politics that went into ruling a kingdom, which was an entirely other reason on her own as to why she would never be fit to be a queen.

Zainiel chuckled softly before shaking his head. "The title of king is applied to your father in the loosest term possible, and I don't think he'd ever refer to us as his court, but I suppose that is one way of viewing it. We are indebted to your father, all of us. We pledged ourselves to him when we all became old enough, before he became king. Arbor governs itself, mostly. Us, your father, we are just here to ensure that it remains that way."

"And the other realms? There's more than one?" Ivy asked.

"There's many, many more. But let's save that conversation for another time. I think we have enough to discuss right now," Zainiel answered with a warm smile.

Many more... Gods, she must seem so clueless to him. "So, what does all of this mean? The Mortifers coming in through the gates?" Ivy questioned.

Zainiel's jaw ticked slightly as his lips pulled into a thin scowl. "Nothing good. It means that either they have found a way to become immune to our magic, or your father..." Zainiel trailed off, letting the words hang between them. It seemed she wasn't the only one who refused to believe that something might have happened to him. "But I intend to figure this all out and find your father. I won't rest until I do," he pledged, giving her hand another tight squeeze.

Night had fallen quickly, and with it came an unforgiving chill that seeped into the cabin. It hadn't seemed to bother Zainiel, but all it took was one shiver running its way through Ivy before he knelt before the fireplace, teasing the small logs that had been stacked nearby into a fire.

They hadn't spoken much, not that Ivy minded. She found silence with Zainiel oddly comforting, and she needed time to sort through everything she had learned before asking him any more questions; though now, if she was being honest, most of them seemed trivial compared to the looming problem that awaited them tomorrow.

"Zainiel?" she asked as she watched the flames dance before her, casting a glance in his direction where he sat in the chair, his long legs stretched out in front of him, his head thrown back onto the chair's backrest.

"More questions?" he asked with a smirk as he peeked an eye open.

She smiled sheepishly. "Maybe a few."

Zainiel pushed up from where he had reclined in the chair and stretched his arms above his head before giving her a quick nod. "Let's hear them."

"I want to know exactly what you do for my father. Theo and Ria, too. And why those people at the village treated you so horribly," she started, forcing the words out before she lost the nerve to ask. "And also, who is Maron?"

Zainiel heaved a heavy sigh. "You aren't going to let this go, are you?" he asked. She knew he was referring to her question about what he did for her father, and perhaps she should let it go. After all, it didn't really affect her directly. But after Ria's words, Theo's warnings, and the entire village's reaction to him, she needed to know.

"I'm not trying to pry," *maybe she was a little,* "but I need to know. After what happened in the village, and Theo—" she paused, catching herself. He didn't need to know that Theo had warned her off of him, or that Ria had spoken to her. "I just feel like I should know why, and I get the idea that it has something to do with what you do for my father."

Zainiel sighed and scrubbed his hands down his face. "Anyone ever told you that you can be quite persistent?"

"Only when I know I'm not being told everything," she shot back with a shrug and a baiting stare.

"It's not that I'm trying to keep it from you, I just..." he trailed off as he let his gaze wander to the crackling fire before him. The room was dark, but she could see enough from the light cast by the fire to tell that he was struggling with something, debating with himself whether to answer her question or find a way to dance around it again.

"You just what?" she pressed.

Zainiel cast a penetrating stare in her direction, shadows of sadness and guilt dancing in his eyes. "I don't want you to see me like the rest of them do." Ivy's heart felt heavy in her chest. She didn't want to upset him. She just wanted to *understand.*

She offered him a teasing smirk. "Afraid I won't see you as the insufferable, big-headed, taunting—"

"Okay, okay, I get it," he cut her off with a dismissive wave, as a small smirk pulling at his lips, but just as quickly fell as he admitted, "I know what Theo told you. The day he left."

Ivy's brows lifted in surprise. She hadn't told anyone what Theo had told her, not even Ria. "Well, then you also know that I didn't listen to him."

Zainiel raised a brow. "Didn't you, though? Or was there another reason you began skipping our lessons and avoiding me around the estate?"

Ivy let her gaze drift away from his accusing stare and to the small window that framed the dark sky in soft, weathered wood. Her lips parted to explain, but no sound came out; how could she tell him that she was avoiding him because the way he made her feel scared her more than any warnings Theo could have ever given her?

"I guess I thought that if I answered your question, you would decide to heed his advice," Zainiel added. "Maybe it was selfish of me, but I wanted whatever this had been between us to last a little longer."

Ivy's gaze snapped back to his. So he felt it too? That unexplainable pull that she had to always seek him out, to always be near him? "I wasn't avoiding you because of what Theo said, at least not entirely," Ivy admitted. "The only other person I have allowed myself to grow close to in my entire life was Theo, and... well, when I started feeling safe with you, I guess it scared me."

Something unreadable flashed in his eyes. "I don't want to be a villain to you, Storm. But I also can't stop what it is I do to keep Arbor safe." His words pierced through the air, laden with a tempest of unspoken emotions. As his gaze met hers, Ivy longed to pierce the veil of his secrets that seemed to cloak him in this suffocating darkness. But more than that, she needed to wrap her arms around him, to convey that in her story, he was no villain. The time for that had passed. The line between then and now felt blurred, and she wasn't sure she knew when or how the shift had happened. But the thought of him causing her harm felt like a sure impossibility.

"I don't think I could ever see you as a villain, Zainiel. Not even if I tried," she admitted gently as she pushed herself further back onto the bed, motioning for Zainiel to come sit with her. She wanted him near, wanted to be able to reach out and grasp his hand, to show him that she wasn't afraid of him, that he wasn't alone.

He moved over to her, falling back onto the bed so his thigh brushed against her knee. "I'd be willing to wager that once you would have said the same thing about Theo, and now you can barely manage to speak his name."

Ivy took a breath. He was right. If someone had asked her three months ago, she would have told them the same thing about Theo. But it was different with Zainiel. She didn't understand why, but it was, and she knew with certainty she'd be willing to bet her own life that he would never cause her any harm.

"I did," she admitted, nodding slowly, "But I also know you better than I ever knew Theo. I was gullible with him, so blinded by my desperation for someone to care about me that I think I would have said the same thing about anyone who showed me kindness while I was on that island." She reached out, letting her fingertips brush against his, hoping she wasn't about to sound stupid as the next words left her lips. "It's different with you, though, and I think you feel that too."

His eyes clouded with vulnerability as he let his fingertips mingle with hers. "Promise you'll let me finish, even if you don't like what I am saying."

Ivy grasped his hand tightly, pulling it into her lap as she traced soothing circles on his hand. "I promise."

Zainiel turned his gaze towards the fire, staring so intently at it that Ivy could see the flames dancing in his eyes. His shoulders were drawn in a tight line while his jaw tightened. They sat like that for a few moments, so long that Ivy began to believe that he had decided not to answer her after all. Just as she was about to let go of his hand, having given up on getting an answer, he looked back at her, grief and guilt etched deeply in his features.

"I've killed people. Good, honest people who I knew, maybe even loved. People who others thought were worth saving, and even though they begged me not to," he paused, his tone flat as he swallowed hard. "I killed them. And I would do it all over again."

Chapter Thirty-Six

ZAINIEL

"I killed them," he admitted, his voice flat. "And I would do it all over again." He knew he should feel remorse, maybe even utter an apology for the lives he had ended, but he couldn't. Because with that came the guilt and grappling with the acceptance that perhaps he was just as much a monster as the ones he had pledged to eradicate from this world. He held his gaze steady with the flickering flames before him, watching as they ate away at the logs, just as the lives he consumed ate away at his soul. He didn't want to see the same look in her eyes that all the others had when they beheld the monster he had transformed himself into. When they looked at him and he saw the fear and hatred in their gaze, it was a means to an end. It was a sacrifice he was willing to make, whether or not they were willing to accept it. But if she looked at him that way... he didn't think he could bear it.

The bed shifted beside him, and his heart plummeted from his chest. She was leaving. She couldn't even bring herself to be in the same room as him. But he was surprised when, instead of hearing her retreating footsteps followed by the slam of a door, he felt her leg brush against his. He loosed a shuddering breath as she slipped her hand into his, weaving their fingers together. She didn't speak, but he didn't need her to. He knew what she was saying. That she was there, ready to listen, and she wasn't going anywhere. He liked that. Even in silence, they seemed to be able to converse with each other.

"A few months after the first Mortifer, we had tried everything to stop them. Nothing worked. Once the body they were inhabiting decomposed, they just moved on to the next," Zainiel started with a shake of his head.

Ria and Ellie had pored over every book in the archive, searching for the answers. He and Kalec had captured Mortifers, trying to extract information from them. Theo and some others had even traveled to other realms with the hope that they would hold some answers. Everything they tried had failed.

"The only thing we learned was that for the Mortifer to enter a body, it had to make you bleed, and no one ever lived through being taken by one." There was a time when Zainiel had hoped he could find a way to save the people that the Mortifers had possessed; but once the graves, both unmarked and marked, continued growing all through Arbor, he and Kalec were forced to face the truth that there would be no saving them, only showing them mercy.

"Your father knew I didn't like using the darker side of my magic, but after months of searching without finding a cure, and no way to kill them, he asked me to try, to see if consuming them would work. It did." He remembered the look on Ria's face when he told her, the fear in her eyes, the desperation in her voice as she begged him not to do it. She had feared that if he consumed the monster, he would allow it to take control of him just as it had everyone else. But they were all desperate, and he was willing to do anything if it meant not having to bury another friend.

Ivy's thumb moved back and forth on his hand in soothing strokes as he talked. She didn't ask any questions, didn't pull away from him. She just sat and listened, letting the crackling fire fill the silence as Zainiel willed himself to tell her the rest of the story. She deserved to know, and he knew it was only a matter of time before she heard it from someone else.

"There was this girl, Liola," Zainiel started, his throat bobbing with a hard swallow as her name passed through his lips. "She was like you, and didn't know she was fae until someone found her, recognized what she was, and brought her here to Arbor. Kalec offered her a place at the estate, and before long, she had become a part of our little family. She and Ellie were nearly inseparable, and she and Theo spent nearly every waking moment together."

Zainiel didn't think he had ever seen Theo so enraptured by a woman. He had always been one to follow the rules, but when it came to Liola, Theo was willing to break every single one of them if it meant that they could be together. Especially on the night she died.

"One morning, about a year after the first Mortifer came to Arbor, Liola didn't return from patrol." Zainiel could still remember the panicked look in Theo's eyes when he had barged into his room, and the way he pleaded with Zainiel to help him find her. He had been a desperate man who had lost the one thing that meant the most to him in the world. He had been even more desperate when they had found her and realized what she had become.

"Liola!" Zainiel called out into the dense green foliage surrounding him. His fingers grazed against the dampened leaves as he pushed aside the thick brush. The sky was a clear sea of azure as the sun hung high above, casting a warm golden glow over the forest floor. A soft breeze blew, rustling the leaves, sending the forest into a dance around him, but still, something seemed... off. The hairs on the back of his neck lifted in warning as his magic began to stir inside of

him, as if it, too, could feel that there was something different about the forest today. Something darker.

He knelt down, allowing his fingertips to glide over the cool earth, his gaze scanning the ground intently. She should have come through here on her patrol. He searched for any sign she might have passed this way. But all he found were the usual fallen leaves and the trampled grass left by the forest's wildlife—nothing to indicate her presence. Yet, this was nothing unexpected. He had trained her meticulously, instilling in her the necessity of moving stealthily.

A cold draft settled over the forest, and with it came a heavy, almost suffocating silence. Even the earthy scent of the remaining morning dew seemed muted. Something wasn't right here, and it was more than the anxiety he felt from not knowing where Liola was or why she hadn't returned.

A chilling whisper flitted through the air, followed by a guttural moan. Zainiel's magic was heavy in his chest, ready with the anticipation of a fight. Whatever had made that sound wasn't human, that much he was sure of. It was a sound he had heard many times before, but he refused to believe it. Refused to believe that a Mortifer had wandered this close to the estate.

A scraping sound echoed through the air, followed by the loud crunch of leaves to his right. He wasn't alone. Zainiel whirled around to find a form folded into itself, kneeling on the forest floor. A cold breeze blowing the leaves that had nestled into the ground around it. The figure was shrouded in a long auburn cloak, a hood pulled over its head, and blonde ringlets peeked out of the bottom of it—the same blonde ringlets that had belonged to Liola.

Zainiel took a cautious step forward, reaching out to her. "Liola? We've been looking for you. Theo's been worried." She didn't respond, just remained hunched over and completely still as he placed a hand on her shoulder. She was cold, so cold that he could feel it through the cloak that blanketed her body.

"Liola?" Zainiel asked again gingerly as dread settled into his stomach. It couldn't be. There was no way the Mortifers had reached her, no way they had taken her. Another cool breeze blew around them, causing the hood of her cloak to fall back, exposing the back of her neck, a thin red line etched into it.

Zainiel stepped back, shaking his head as his gaze pierced into the cut. That was all it took for a Mortifer to take you. One small cut and you were theirs, a puppet to have at their disposal until either your body gave out or they decided they were done with it. His heart clenched in his chest as Liola placed her all-too-pale hands on the forest floor and pushed herself up. She had always been tan, so much so that he often teased her that she must have spent her time sunbathing rather than training all those mornings. But now, it was like the color had been leached right out of her.

She straightened her spine, slowly dragging her head up to meet his gaze. A large scrape adorned her face, beginning at the top of her temple and working its way down to her lips, which lay in a twisted grin—an evil, vile grin—a grin she never would have worn herself.

"Liola," he breathed, hoping to see something in her eyes to prove him wrong. Something that told him he was just paranoid, that the girl he had come to care for as a sister was still there. But instead of finding her icy blue gaze, he was met with a cold, stagnant glare. One that told him what he had feared. She was gone.

He had hoped that this day would never come. Hoped that he wouldn't have to end the life of someone he cherished. He could tell himself that he was showing them mercy by giving them a quick death, that the other option of letting them live out the rest of their days held captive in their own body was more hellish than anything he could ever do to them, but it never helped. Not when he could feel their life draining from their body as he consumed them.

Liola—no—the creature took a hesitant step forward, as though it were still trying to find its footing within the confines of its new host. The early morning sun pierced through the lush canopy overhead, casting a golden glow that danced among the blonde curls framing its face. Once vibrant and alive, those strands now fell lifelessly, weighed down by the darkness that had overtaken her body. Even the gentle morning light struggled to breathe life into those dull locks. They hung flat and heavy, silent witnesses to her transformation.

He closed his eyes, reaching deep within himself to summon his magic. Shadows erupted around him, weaving a veil of darkness over the forest floor, swelling with tense anticipation. This part always repulsed him—not the impending danger, but the grim eagerness of his own magic, ever-hungry to devour and destroy. Dark *tendrils surged through the scattered leaves, reaching, arching toward Liola—the creature's feet. An inhuman growl erupted from its throat, exposing glinting teeth as it hissed menacingly at Zainiel. He watched in horror as the once elegantly manicured nails belonging to Liola elongated grotesquely, breaking off as long, jagged talons thrust out from her fingers. Her lip curled in a primal snarl, a chilling sound that sent the remaining wildlife skittering from their perches in the branches above.*

His magic coiled around the monster's feet, snaking its way up her body. For a fleeting heartbeat, he could have sworn he glimpsed a flash of fearful blue in the creature's gaze before it vanished, replaced by darkened eyes. She was still in there, fighting, clawing, against the Mortifer's hold on her. If only there were some way he could help, some way he could free her from its hold... but Zainiel knew there wasn't. The only thing he could do for her now was to show her the mercy of a quick death.

Another guttural scream erupted from the creature's throat as his magic continued to swell around it. The beast swiped at the shadows coiling around its waist, a maddened fury in its eyes. He could feel the shadows' insatiable hunger surge as they tightened their grip, relishing each agonizing moment. Ecstasy flooded through the connection he shared with his magic as the creature thrashed in pain, helplessly swiping at the tendrils that ensnared it.

"*No!*" *Theo's voice echoed through the trees, propelled by sheer panic. His eyes were wide, a look of horror etched across his ashen face.* "*Zainiel, please!*"

"*She's been taken. I have no choice,*" *Zainiel replied, another surge of his power lifting the creature higher off the ground.*

"*We can save her! She's still in there! I can feel it, Zain. Please... PLEASE!*" *Theo's voice broke as he reached out toward the woman he loved, flinching from the bite of Zainiel's shadows.*

Zainiel's heart twisted at the sight of his friend's anguish. This wasn't how it was supposed to be. Theo shouldn't have to witness her like this, shouldn't have to remember her as the beast she had been transformed into, shouldn't have to watch as the life was drained from her. But Zainiel couldn't stop, even if he wanted to. The shadows were in control as they feasted on the creature before them.

The beast's face contorted in pain. A piercing scream echoed through the forest. A scream that sounded too human, too familiar.

"*Please,*" *Theo pleaded through a choked sob as he fell to the ground, tears slickening his cheeks.*

A frenzied bliss flooded Zainiel, coursing through him like an intoxicating tide as the shadows encased the creature fully. He watched as they danced through the air, feeding on whatever essence was left. Felt the hatred from its soul weaving its way into his. Felt the fiery spirit that Liola always had clawing against his magic's grasp as it too was consumed, ripped away from her body.

His heart pounded in his chest as the shadows dispersed before him, and he watched as Liola's body crashed to the ground like a discarded doll. The talons that had ripped through her skin were gone, leaving bloodied fingers in their wake. Her skin was gray, lips left agape in a silent scream, eyes wide in horror.

Theo scrambled over to her, pulling her into his lap as he cradled her, rocking back and forth. "No, no, no, no," he muttered, tears falling from his cheeks and onto hers.

The euphoria that had filled Zainiel left with his shadows, leaving hollow guilt as he stared at the girl he had once thought of as family. Theo had been right. She was still in there, still fighting, refusing to lose against the creature that had taken her body. If only she could have also fought against him.

Chapter Thirty-Seven

"I knew she was still in there," Zainiel admitted in a whisper, his voice heavy with regret. "I felt her. But I couldn't stop, couldn't risk the Mortifer escaping, so I just..." he paused, taking a shaky breath. "I killed her."

Ivy didn't know what to say, so she sat beside him, his hand still tightly woven into hers as she listened to him tell his story. Her heart ached—not just for Zainiel and this unbearable burden he had to carry, but for Theo and all the others who had lost people they loved to these monsters. She now understood why the grief

Theo had shared with her in Salus had seemed so real. He hadn't been grieving for his parents. He had been grieving for the woman he loved. And the hatred he had for Zainiel, as misplaced as it might've been, she could understand that too.

"And do you want to know the worst part?" Zainiel asked, swallowing hard. "The worst part is the way it feels. When I tap into my powers like that, I get this rush..." He paused, shaking his head as he wrestled with his thoughts. "It's almost addictive. Honestly, if there was a way to draw just the Mortifer's energy, I doubt I'd even want to stop." His voice was thick with emotion, guilt spilling out between the words, so overwhelming that Ivy struggled to grasp their full weight.

All she could think about was the slight tremor of his hand in hers, the quiver that accompanied his confession, and how the moonlight poured through the window, painting shadows across his furrowed brow—his expression a heavy blend of sadness that left her unsure if she could ever truly comprehend it.

"I've never shared that with anyone," Zainiel murmured, his tone barely above a whisper. "Not even Ria."

Ivy still didn't know what to say or how to respond to everything she had just learned. It explained so much: how the entire village seemed to shy away from him, how Lilli and Luka were so afraid to go against his orders, and how Theo was so certain that her trusting Zainiel would lead to nothing but hurt.

When they looked at him, they didn't see the man she saw. They didn't see a man who had put this world before himself. They didn't see the sadness that always lingered in his eyes no matter what mask he wore. They didn't see this crushing weight he carried on his shoulders. All they saw was a face that they could blame for the loss of their loved ones. And it made her so... *angry.*

Ivy grunted as she threw another bolt of magic at the wooden stake yards away. Zainiel would be furious with her if he knew she'd snuck out, but hours after he had fallen asleep, she still lay in the bed next to him, their fingers still woven together, while her magic thrummed beneath her skin. They hadn't spoken, had simply just fallen back onto the bed as the silence wrapped around them. She knew she should have said something. But what was there to say? That it was okay? No. Because none of it was okay, and there would never be a world in which it was.

Her father asked him to do the unimaginable, and because of this overwhelming sense of loyalty they all seemed to hold for a man who wasn't even present, he did it. He carried around this burden, letting everyone see him as this monster when, in truth, Ivy was beginning to wonder if her father was the real monster.

The moon hung high in the night sky above her, its reflection shimmering in the puddles of water scattered about the field that she had created earlier when conjuring rain storms. She didn't know how long she had been out there, but judging by the thin layer of sweat that crested her brow and the fading pulse of her magic, she imagined it would be dawn soon.

Ivy extended her hand before her, watching as her magic whirled to life. Icy blue tendrils swirled in her palm, winding around her wrist. She weaved the magic between her fingers, relishing the warmth as she closed her eyes with a soft sigh. It was astounding how accessible it was to her, how eager it was to answer her call after all these years of nothing. She sighed, closing her fist and letting the magic dwindle between her fingers. She should head back before Zainiel realized she left.

"That was quite the impressive show." A low, steely voice cut through the night air. Ivy froze. The hairs rose on the back of her neck as she turned to find a man, shrouded in a cloak of darkness, stalking towards her.

"Please," the man rasped, "don't stop on my account." He took another menacing step forward. Despite straining her eyes, she still couldn't pierce the darkened veil that had fallen over him. But that voice... There was something familiar about it.

She withdrew a cautious step, her heart quickening as she stole a glance over her shoulder at the cabin, now a distant silhouette fifty yards behind her. The warm flicker of the firelight that had earlier danced in the window had faded into darkness, leaving the space eerily still. Zainiel was still sleeping, but if she could reach him, she knew she'd be safe.

"Who are you?" Ivy called out as she took another tentative step towards the cabin. Each step felt like a dance with danger as Zainiel's words from their training rang in her head. *Turning your back on an enemy you don't know enough about can be the difference between whether you live or die. Never take your eyes off of them.*

The man clicked his tongue, shaking his head as the shadows danced in sync with his movements. "You don't remember me?" The voice dripped with malice, sending a chill racing through Ivy's veins. Where had she heard that sinister drawl before?

"What do you want?" she demanded, searching for any clue that might reveal his identity. With every cautious step back, the cabin felt painfully far away. She should never have left. How could she have been so stupid?

"I want what was promised to me," he spat, the darkness surrounding him twisting into crimson tendrils fueled by his fury. "I want what was *taken* from me." With a deafening roar, he surged forward, moving so swiftly that it seemed he had blinked into existence just inches away from her.

With his face now visible with the fiery glow from the aura that surrounded him, a nearly silent gasp escaped Ivy's lips. *It couldn't be.* His hair hung limply, a disheveled crown of ashen strands that seemed to absorb the light rather than reflect it. The pallor of his skin was unnervingly ghostly, as if he had long been separated from the sun's warmth. His cheekbones protruded sharply, carving deep shadows into his sunken face. While his eyes had been cold before, they now glimmered like cold obsidian—dark and laced with a sinister hunger. A tremor coursed through her as his thin gray lips peeled back into a wicked grin, exposing his rotting teeth.

"Alastair," she gasped, her heart pounding as she stumbled back, shock coursing through her veins. How could he have tracked her down? What had transformed him into this?

"My beloved wife," he responded with a venomous bite, his upper lip curling into a menacing sneer.

"I'm not your wife," she retorted sharply, retreating further. Desperation clawed at her as she focused on reaching the cabin, on reaching Zainiel.

"Oh, but you will be," he whispered with a dark promise that made Ivy's skin crawl. He wouldn't be leaving with her, that much she was sure of.

She tried to still her trembling hands as she reached for her magic, only to find a mere trickle of it remaining. She doubted she'd even be able to summon more than a spark, and judging by the knowing grin on his face, Alastair knew as much, too. How long had he been watching her, waiting for her to use up all of her resources?

She considered her options. Running seemed futile; the speed with which he moved suggested he'd snatch her up long before she could reach the cabin door. Fighting was out of the question—his dark, writhing tendrils warned her that they had a life of their own, and she was painfully aware of how little progress she'd made in her combat training with Zain. Even in the best of circumstances, it would be a struggle for her to gain the upper hand. She could scream for help, praying Zainiel would come to her aid, yet that might only provoke Alastair's wrath further, and if Zainiel didn't hear... well, she couldn't face that truth.

"How did you find me, Alastair?" Ivy asked, trying to keep her voice steady. She needed to buy herself more time and figure out how to get out of this situation. If she remembered anything about Alastair and the rumors she had heard from Salus, it was that he loved the sound of his own voice.

"You thought your little friend could steal you away without me noticing? That you'd be safe here?" A callous chuckle rumbled from his chest as he circled around her. "I have some very powerful friends, darling. And they just so happen to owe me some favors. There's nowhere you could go where I couldn't find you."

Ivy's heart raced. To him, she was merely a plaything, a target to be manipulated. The dark energy surrounding him now glimmered, an almost-black midnight blue, while the once-vibrant red streaks dimmed as it extended toward her. She instinctively recoiled as it reached out, almost brushing her cheek. She had to find a way to escape—had to find a way to stun him long enough to sprint to the cabin. If she could just get to Zainiel...

"Why me?" Ivy questioned, taking another step back. "What's the point of all this trouble just to find *me*?"

Alastair's grin spread wider as he materialized right before her, gripping her chin with a vice-like hold. He traced a sharp fingernail down her cheek, smirking with dark allure. "Because, my darling, with you by my side, nothing could stop us." Was that why he wanted her? For her power? Had he somehow known what she was capable of in Salus?

Ivy suppressed a shiver as she roughly tore herself away from his grip, his nail clipping her cheek, causing a thin line of blood to appear. She quickly took a few more steps back, desperately needing to create space between them. Alastair didn't advance toward her. He only watched her as the aura around him swelled, lashing out towards her, reflecting the same hunger that shone brightly in his eyes the night they first met. He wanted her, and he would stop at nothing to get her.

Silver threads of moonlight filtered through the clouds, shimmering in the puddle just a couple of feet away—where Alastair now stood. A spark of hope ignited in her gut as she reached for her magic once more. She knew that what she had left wouldn't be enough to stun him outright, but if she could channel her power through the water, it just might work. With determination, she summoned her energy, silently thanking Zainiel for those targeting lessons, and unleashed a small bolt of electricity, watching as it sizzled into the puddle. Without pausing to gauge his reaction, she turned and sprinted towards the cabin doors, urgency propelling her forward as her heart hammered in her chest.

"Zainiel!" she yelled, willing her legs to pump faster. *Almost there. She was almost there.* "Zainiel, help!" she cried again, hoping he heard her.

As she neared the cabin, an unexpected force yanked her backward, sending her flying backward and sprawling onto the ground. It wasn't just any force. It was Alastair. He had caught up to her, seizing her long, braided hair, and now loomed over her with his boot pressing hard into her shoulder, pinning her in place. His darkened irises swirled with shades of red and blue, giving them an almost purplish hue, and a wicked, triumphant grin stretched across his face.

"You know," he started, leaning over her, his stagnant breath brushing against her cheeks as he dragged a cold finger down her face, his sharpened nail biting into her skin. "I wasn't supposed to claim you tonight, but when I saw you—saw how glorious you were with all that power—" he chuckled darkly. "Well, how could I say no to that?"

He grabbed her arm, his touch cold as ice, sending a chill racing through her whole body as he yanked her to her feet. Ivy strained against his hold, determination pushing her to escape, yet his grip was unyielding. She stifled a cry as a searing, burning pain cut into her arm. No way would she grant him the pleasure of her screams.

"I suppose my brothers won't be too happy, but what's done—"

His words were abruptly cut off as they were both thrown forward by an explosive force, splintered wood raining down around them as they crashed toward the ground. A cushion of woven darkness softened Ivy's fall before the shadows dispersed and raced back to their master, who stood where the cabin wall had once been, a fire in his eyes as he zeroed his gaze onto Alastair. Shadows pooled at his feet, each deliberate step he took producing another, ready to act on his command.

In an instant, Zainiel closed the distance between himself and Alastair, looming menacingly over him. The air around him crackled with an eerie energy as his shadowy phantoms writhed and danced. Their dark forms stretched like ominous specters, poised to strike. Alastair, desperate to regain his footing, struggled to rise, but his leg, viciously speared by a jagged shard of the cabin wall, buckled beneath him, sending him crashing back to the ground.

Ivy stood frozen, her wide eyes absorbing the cruel elegance of the scene unfolding before her. Zainiel's shadowy vines slithered around Alastair's throat, lifting him off the earth until the tips of his toes barely grazed the floor. A malicious grin twisted Zainiel's features as he extended his hand and summoned his magic, molding it into an obsidian spear of darkness.

"You're t—too late," Alastair choked out, blood dribbling from the corner of his mouth as his eyes shot over to Ivy. Her arm burned, as she met his gaze. "Sh—she's mine."

A guttural growl escaped from Zainiel's throat as he bared his teeth and hurled the dark spear into Alastair's gut. Ivy's heart raced as she witnessed the impact send Alastair careening backward, crashing to the earth in a crumpled heap. Zainiel advanced toward him with deliberate, predatory grace, his shadows following behind him like a small army. Alastair lay motionless, blood seeping from the jagged wound, his dark aura now a mere whisper as he gasped for breath, his chest heaving in desperation.

Kneeling beside Alastair, Zainiel's lips moved in a low murmur, a wicked gleam dancing in his eyes. Before Alastair could even muster a response, Zainiel's phantoms lunged forward, lifting Alastair's body into the air, his back turned to Ivy. With a sickening crack that shattered the stillness of the night, she watched in horror as his neck snapped, leaving his lifeless gaze to bore into her soul. Zainiel released his grip, and Alastair's body crumpled to the ground with a resounding thud.

Chapter Thirty-Eight

"Are you hurt?" Zainiel's voice sliced through the cabin as he paced back and forth before her in agitation. He hadn't uttered a word to her until now, just stalked over to her, his phantoms still writhing around him as he helped her stand, before guiding her to the cabin. Not that she would have been able to speak or even hear him over her pounding heart. She could barely tell her legs to move as they trembled beneath her.

Alastair had tracked her down. And despite all the training she had undergone with Zainiel, she felt utterly defenseless, as if she had willingly presented herself on a silver platter, ripe for the taking. The memory of Zainiel's wicked grin while he dispatched Alastair invaded her thoughts—so cruel, so delightfully sadistic, that it sent chills racing down her spine.

"Storm, I need to know that you're alright." He knelt before her. The cold fury that had blazed in his eyes was replaced with a softness as his gaze swept over her body, assessing her carefully. He reached out a hand toward her cheek, but instinctively, she recoiled, pulling her knees up to her chest to shield herself from his touch. It was only Zainiel, she reminded herself. He would never cause her harm, but that darkness she had seen from him... that wasn't the Zainiel she knew. Yet, he still saved her, still cared for her as he tenderly guided her towards the cabin.

He withdrew his hand, hurt flashing through his eyes as he took two large steps backward. "Are you hurt?" he repeated more of an edge to his voice before. She shook her head, pulling the blanket that Zainiel had draped around her shoulders tighter around her body. The scratch on her face stung, and her arm still burned from where Alastair's touch had seemed to sear into her, but she was breathing. She was *safe*. Safe because of Zainiel.

"You're sure?" he asked again. Ivy nodded, not trusting her voice to answer.

"Good," he said with a clipped nod. "Then what the *hell* were you thinking?" he roared, as he began pacing before her again. "You could have been killed. You almost *were.*" His shadows danced above him as if they, too, were chastising her.

"I—I couldn't sleep. I thought some air might help," she answered as she wrapped her arms tighter around her knees, wincing slightly as the blanket brushed against her arm. Zainiel continued to pace before her, splintered wood crunching underneath his shoes as moments passed and neither of them spoke.

The cabin was in complete disarray, and judging by the gaping hole in the Western wall, she was surprised to find that its structure remained steady enough for them to be inside. Why he wouldn't have just used the door was beyond her.

Zainiel sighed, exasperated, as he perched on the edge of the bed, his back turned to her. He let his head fall into his hands. "You do realize how badly that could have ended, don't you?" he asked as he peered over his shoulder, his eyes blazing with raw emotion.

Ivy swallowed hard as she nodded, causing strands of her hair to tumble over her shoulder and into her face. The same hair Alastair had gripped with possessive cruelty as he caught up to her, the same hair he had praised on the night her family had offered her to him. Her hair used to be one of her favorite qualities about herself, but now? Now, it was one of *his.* She wanted it gone. No. She *needed* it gone.

"Can I see your dagger?" she asked, her voice quavering with the weight of emotion, forcing back the tears that threatened to spill. She refused to allow herself to cry over this—over him. She had to be stronger. Zainiel rose from the bed, cautious as he faced her. "My dagger?" he inquired, a hint of wariness lacing his tone.

With a firm nod, she pushed herself up, letting the blanket cascade down to the bed. "Please," she added, extending a shaky hand toward him. She was certain he still had it; she hadn't seen him part with it since their encounter with the Mortifer in the woods.

He grasped the handle of the dagger, drawing it from its sheath. With a swift motion, he flipped it around, offering the handle to her. Concern deepened in his brow as he watched her stalk over to the mirror that miraculously still stood intact amongst the rubble.

The weapon was light, its handle warm from where it had rested against Zain's side. The blade was a deep, shadowy black, almost as inky as the conjured spear that had run Alastair through. She grazed her fingertip along the edge, assessing its sharpness, before turning her attention to the mirror, meeting her gaze.

She was a wretched sight, with grime clinging tenaciously to her temple like a stubborn shadow. Dried blood traced a cruel path down her cheek, a vivid reminder of Alastair's grasp. Her chin bore the faint outlines of bruises, little crescent moons etched into her skin, the ghosts of his fingertips lingering far too long. Her eyes, however, were the most haunting aspect—void of their usual luster, they stared back vacantly as if she were merely gazing at a specter of her former self, trapped in a fragile shell. He had done this to her in just a matter of moments. She couldn't even fathom what would have happened had she been left with him for a lifetime.

She felt Zainiel's piercing eyes following her every movement as she gathered a section of her hair into her hand, pulling it taut. Without allowing herself even a moment to reflect in the glass, she swept the blade through her hair in a decisive act, then did the same to the other side. She stared intently as the remnants of her hair fluttered delicately to the ground. Each strand seemed to fall in slow motion, forming a sorrowful halo around her feet.

Her shoulders drooped, arms hanging limply as she gazed at her freshly cut hair, now just grazing her shoulders. Tears threatened to spill from her eyes. This was meant to be liberating, a step away from that dreadful man, yet the stain of him still clung to her with a relentless grip. He was dead. He couldn't hurt her.

Zainiel approached her carefully, placing his hand softly around her wrist before retrieving the blade from her fingers. He intertwined his fingers with hers, gently guiding her back to the bed. A wince escaped her as his arm brushed against the spot where Alastair had held her, and she felt Zainiel stiffen beside her.

"I thought you said you weren't hurt?" he challenged, his voice a blend of concern and disbelief as she perched on the edge of the bed. With a gentle grip, he took hold of her arm, turning it to scrutinize the skin.

"I'm fine," she replied, her gaze drifting toward the spot where Zainiel's fingers had lingered, her heart sinking at the sight of a blistering handprint seared into her flesh—his handprint, Alastair's mark. *I wasn't supposed to claim you tonight.* Alastair's voice echoed in her mind. Was this his way of claiming her? Some sick way of branding her as his own?

A wave of nausea crashed over her, twisting her insides as panic surged. She felt the bile rise, teetering on the edge of throwing up. *He's dead. He's dead. He's dead.* The mantra played on repeat as she clung to the only truth that could anchor her. *He's dead. He's dead. He's dead.* She had seen it with her own eyes.

"Yes, Storm, he's gone. He's dead and can't hurt you anymore." Zain's voice was a tender balm as he enveloped her in his strong arms, pulling her close. She hadn't realized she was speaking out loud, hadn't been aware of the violent tremors shaking her body or the tears that were now falling freely down her cheeks, hadn't even noticed when he nestled her into his lap, holding her with a protective warmth.

The first light of dawn crept over the horizon, and Ivy felt the exhaustion crash into her like a torrent. She didn't know how long Zainiel had cradled her against him, or how exactly she had ended up lying in the bed, his heavy arm draped securely around her waist, their legs tangled together and her head on his chest with his fingers woven through her short hair. Neither of them had spoken a word. He had simply held her, rubbing soothing circles into her back as she cried. She felt pathetic. After all, Alastair was dead—he couldn't ever come back for her—but she couldn't help this foreboding feeling that somehow, some way, he would.

"Ivy?" Zainiel asked softly as he shifted, craning his neck to look at her. "I don't want to ask this of you, but I need you to tell me everything that happened. I need to figure out why this man was so intent on taking you."

Ivy's heart thrummed in her chest as she pulled herself from Zainiel's grasp and shuffled backward onto the bed to lean against the headboard. He did the same, his arm brushing against hers on the narrow bed. She pulled her hands into her lap, nervously twisting the ring that adorned her finger as she took a shuddering breath.

"I know—I *knew* him," Ivy said quietly as she let her gaze wander to the empty hearth before them. The small stone mantle was cracked, and pieces were crumbled and scattered amongst the rest of the debris, no doubt from Zainiel. "I was to be his bride."

A soft exhale sounded from Zainiel as the bed shifted beside her. He had sat up and turned himself around, so he was facing her. "His bride?" Zainiel asked incredulously as he arched a brow.

Ivy was surprised that he hadn't already known about Alastair; she assumed Theo would have told them, or at the very least Ria. "In Salus, once you fail the ritual, you are either exiled from the island or married off with the expectation of producing heirs to continue the family name."

Zainiel's jaw clenched, and she watched all kindness seep from his eyes. "You mean to tell me that your family was going to force you to marry that man?" A shadow fell across the bed as his phantoms began to swirl above him in agitation.

She nodded gently, her eyes drifting down to her hands as she anxiously picked at the skin surrounding her fingernails. "He was the last of his line. His first wife was unable to bear children. So when I failed the ritual, my family arranged for us to marry, hoping my children would possess the magic I didn't."

Zainiel clenched his fists at his sides. "They were going to force you to bear his children?"

"That's just how things are in Salus. I failed, and even worse than that, I was the first in my family to fail. A marriage to him was the only way I could prove my worth to my family—to the coven."

"Why wasn't I told about any of this?"

"I—I thought you were aware. I thought Theo would have shared it with Ria..." Ivy's voice faltered. She had always believed Theo knew about Alastair, and that fateful night when he found her in her room... She thought he was rescuing her from him, but in truth, he was merely trying to whisk her away from the island—to bring her home. "He didn't know," Ivy murmured, more to herself than to Zainiel. "I assumed he knew. He found me right after, and—" she shook her head.

"Found you after what?" Zainiel pressed, his gaze darting between her freshly cut hair and the raw mark on her arm, as if trying to assemble a puzzle without all the pieces. So, Ivy revealed everything—the harrowing details of the night she had failed the ritual. She recounted how her family almost seemed eager to surrender her to Alastair, despite their suspicions about his first wife's death. She shared her desperation to escape that life, how far she would have gone to avoid it.

"None of them should have been left alive," Zainiel growled, and his phantoms writhed around him almost in agreement. Ivy's eyes found his and within them there was a promise that nothing and no one would ever harm her again. He wouldn't allow it. "What happened before I found you out there?" Zainiel asked.

"I was practicing, working out some of my magic. I guess I lost track of time, or just got too caught up in it, because before I realized, I had pretty much run myself dry. I was coming back to the cabin to sleep when he came out from the shadows. There was something different about him, something dark." Ivy paused as she remembered the way his magic responded to his every move, almost as if it were a cloak he was wearing. "The magic was new, and it looked like it was draining him. He was always so... put together, but the man I saw last night was not the same Alastair that everyone knew on Salus."

Zainiel nodded, intently listening to her, "Anything else?"

"He moved fast, *really* fast. I thought that maybe if I stunned him, it would give me enough time to reach you, but..." she shrugged letting the words trail off. *But she wasn't strong enough.*

"You used your magic on him?" Zainiel asked, a flicker of pride flashing through his eyes.

"I tried. I knew I didn't have much, but he was standing in a puddle, so I thought maybe if I threw a spark of my magic at it, it would slow him down." And maybe it did, but not long enough for her to get away. "I almost made it to the door, but he caught up to me, grabbed my braid, and pulled me back."

Zainiel's eyes faltered as his gaze darted to the hair still scattered on the floor before the mirror. Understanding flashed through his eyes as he squeezed her hand.

"I think he was watching me, and I don't think he was supposed to confront me yet," she admitted, the last words he had spoken to her echoing in her mind.

Zainiel straightened, alarm igniting in his eyes. "Why do you say that?"

"After I shocked him, when he caught up to me, he told me he wasn't supposed to claim me yet." The handprint on her arm burned.

"Did he say anything else?" Zainiel pressed, urgency laced through his voice.

Ivy was about to say no, but then she remembered what he had said before Zainiel exploded from the cabin. *My brothers won't be too happy.* But he didn't have any brothers. Hell, aside from his mother and his deceased wife, he had no relatives. The Proctor family was coming to an end with him.

"What is it?" Zainiel asked.

"He was saying something right before you—" she glanced at the gaping hole in the wall. "Well, right before you blew a hole in the cabin. He said his brothers wouldn't be happy with him. But he doesn't have brothers." Ivy's brows creased in confusion. This made no sense to her.

"You're certain?"

Ivy nodded. She didn't know Alastair personally and hadn't even been in the same room as him until the night of the ritual, but everyone knew that he was the only child of the last living witch in his bloodline. She supposed that was why he was so eager for an heir to continue his family's name.

"What do you think it means?" she asked.

Zainiel clenched his jaw, his eyes locked on the field outside. "Nothing good," he muttered, rising from the bed with a determined air before striding out of the cabin. Ivy leaped up, carefully navigating the splintered wood littering the floor as she hurried after him.

"Where are you going?" she called, trying to match his pace.

"Get back inside, Storm," he shot back, not bothering to look back. But Ivy was resolute; she wouldn't retreat to the cabin, not when she sensed that whatever was drawing Zainiel out to the field had everything to do with her.

She kept close behind him, even as he suddenly halted, bending to inspect something on the ground. What could it be? Ivy edged closer, peering over his shoulder to glimpse a heap of crumpled, bloodsoaked clothes and something that resembled clay. The same bloodsoaked clothes that Alastair had worn last night, but no body. A chill coursed through her as the mark on her arm burned as if to remind her that it was still there. Alastair's body was *gone.*

Chapter Thirty-Nine

"Where is his body?" Ivy breathed, trying to calm her racing heart. There had to be a reason it was gone. Bodies didn't just disappear. *Right?*

Zainiel stood frozen in front of her, his body rigid, tension coiling in every muscle as he stared down at the heap of clay and tattered clothes littering the ground. Ivy recognized that look. She had seen it before when they had come face to face with the Mortifer. That angered dread. But it couldn't mean what she feared. It simply couldn't.

He was dead—she had seen it with her own eyes. She remembered the moment his chest caved in, that final, shuddering breath escaping his lips, the life fading from his eyes as his neck hung lifeless at an unnatural angle. He was dead. No one could survive that.

But now, as she focused on the pile of clothes illuminated in the morning light, the blood she had seen seep from him last night appeared disturbingly dark—almost black. It was the same shade that had oozed from the Mortifer in the woods. Dread washed over her, draining the color from her face. It couldn't be true. She refused to accept it.

"Zainiel," she said, her voice pitched with panic as she wrestled to calm herself. "Where is the body?"

"I told you to stay in the cabin," he answered, not even bothering to turn to look at her.

"Yeah, well, I didn't," she shot back, "Where is—"

Zainiel whirled around her, a fire in his eyes that she had never seen directed towards her before, not even at the estate when they'd fought with each other. "Go back to the cabin," he demanded, his shadows flaring behind him in a warning. Something was wrong. Something was wrong, and he wasn't telling her what.

"No." She had spent her entire life being told what to do and when to do it. She had been kept on an island and away from this world that was to be her home, that her mother wanted to be her home, and she would be damned if she'd continue hiding away now. No. She refused. "You need to tell me what is happening." She pulled her arms across her chest defiantly as she narrowed her eyes at him. His shadows grew darker behind him. It was a scare tactic, and one she wouldn't fall for. He wouldn't hurt her, and she was willing to bet that his magic wouldn't either.

"Storm, now isn't the time. You need to go back to the cabin and stay there until I return." His eyes flared with authority.

"I'm not doing anything until you tell me what this means." She planted her feet firmly on the ground, refusing to waver from his stare. Those looks might've worked on other people, but she saw the Zainiel that was behind them. The Zainiel that just wanted to keep everyone safe, even if that meant forfeiting himself.

"Storm," Zainiel warned, his hands clenched at his side. "It's not safe. I need you to go back now."

"Zainiel, *please.*" She couldn't just go back to that cabin, not now. Not when the evidence before her was screaming that Alastair somehow didn't die last night. If he was alive... she shook off a chill that settled over her shoulders. "He won't stop until he has me," she whispered. Her heart hammered in her chest, and her palms began to quake. He would never stop. She knew that with a bone-chilling certainty.

Zainiel's gaze softened on her for a fraction of a second before it hardened again. "I can't do this with you right now. I need to think, and I can't do that with you here. Go back to the cabin. You'll be safe there until I can come back for you."

Ivy scoffed and reeled back. Clearly, he had lost his mind. "You mean the cabin that has a gaping hole where the door used to be? That cabin?" She knew her response was snarky, probably more so than necessary, but she would be damned if he thought he could just shove her away in that cabin while he stayed out here trying to hunt Alastair down.

His shadows flared in aggravation, and his jaw worked as he clenched his teeth together. "Ivy," his eyes narrowed into blackened slits. "Go back, now."

She was pushing her luck. She knew she was pushing her luck. But despite the glare he had pinned on her, she couldn't bring herself to be afraid. So instead of giving in and turning back to the cabin like she should have, she placed her hand on her hips and said, "No."

A low, resonant growl emanated from his chest, vibrating like distant thunder as he closed the gap between them with a single, fluid step. His hands clasped around her waist, tugging her forward with a swift motion that stole the air from her lungs, sending her heart racing. Before she could fully process what he was doing, he hoisted her effortlessly over his shoulder, the pressure digging uncomfortably into her midsection.

"Put me down right now!" Ivy exclaimed, her fists clenched tightly in frustration. She pounded them against the solid expanse of his back, muscles like granite beneath her touch. "You can't just keep manhandling me like a sack of potatoes!"

"I wouldn't have to if you'd actually listen for once in your life," he retorted, his voice a low timbre as he adjusted her weight, raising her higher on his shoulder.

"That's rich coming from you," she scoffed as she twisted in his grip as he marched toward the cabin, seemingly indifferent to her struggles. Here he was lecturing *her* about listening to others when she was fairly certain he had never listened to anyone other than her father his entire life. *And look where that had gotten him.*

Zainiel paid no heed to her words as he crossed the threshold, the weathered floorboards groaning with each purposeful step. It wasn't until he reached the bed that he carelessly threw her onto the firm mattress. Only then did he meet her gaze, one finger hovering just before her nose, before commanding, "Stay."

Without uttering another word, he turned on his heel and exited the cabin, with only the creak of the floorboards filling the silence. With a careless wave of his hand, Ivy watched as a flickering fire ignited in the hearth, casting light across the room before a wall of darkness enveloped the cabin, sealing her inside.

Tick. Tick. Tick. Ivy jolted awake to the rhythmic sound. Her surroundings were cloaked in a darkness that stretched on as far as she could see. The firm mattress that she had dozed off on while waiting

for Zainiel's return was gone, replaced with a cold, hard surface. Rock? Had Zainiel returned and moved her somewhere else?

Tick. Tick. Tick. It echoed, almost seeming to swallow her, sounding from in front, below, and above her all at once. Where was she? She moved her lips to speak, but no sound came out. Her heart beat frantically in her chest as she stumbled to her feet, holding her hands out before her as she tried to navigate her way through this darkness but was only met with cold, damp air.

Tick. Tick. Tick. "I've been waiting for you," a voice hissed, coiling around her. Chills raced up her spine, and she halted, frozen in fear. She knew that voice. That voice would haunt her dreams for months to come, maybe even years. A whisper of a touch brushed across the back of her neck, her hair swaying from the movement.

"You cut your hair," Alastair tsked, his fingertip trailing around her neck and across the bottom of her jaw. She could feel his hot breath hit her skin, could smell the stench of his rotting teeth; but still, she could see nothing but absolute darkness. "I rather enjoyed your long hair. But you knew that, didn't you?" he mused, winding a lock of hair around his finger.

Ivy tried to suppress a shudder as his other hand trailed up her arm, lingering on the spot where his handprint had been branded into her. "Out of all of your little imperfections, this one is my favorite."

She could hear the cruel smile in his voice as he spoke. She clenched her fist at her side, digging her nails into the palm of her hand. This *wasn't real. It couldn't be real. It was a dream. Some sick twisted dream that she had brought onto herself. But it wasn't real.*

"Have you figured it out yet?" Alastair asked, the rough skin of his cracked lips brushing against her cheek as he whispered into her ear. Her clenched fist trembled at her side as her nails tore into her skin, and tears threatened to swell in her eyes.

Tick. Tick. Tick. The sound seemed to grow louder with each beat of her heart, making her head throb from the sheer volume of it. She just needed to wake up. Wake up. Wake up. Wake up! Her lips traced over the words as she chanted them to herself, yet no sound left her. Why couldn't she speak?

"This mark," Alastair's fingers worked their way back up her arm, weaving beneath the hem of her sleeve as he traced over it, "binds you to me. There is nowhere you can go, no one you can run to, that would prevent me from finding you."

The spot on her arm burned. She didn't know if it was from Alastair's lingering touch or the strange magic that seemed to thrum beneath her skin in response to him, but whatever it was—dark and not her own—felt like a parasite trying to weave itself into her very being. And try as it might, Ivy refused to let it win—to let him win.

Ivy shot up in bed, a scream clawing its way from her throat, drenched in a cold sweat. Her heart raced wildly, pounding against her ribs as she took in her surroundings. She was back in the cabin—entirely alone. The suffocating black wall of Zainiel's magic obscured all exits, sealing her off from the outside world. Yet the thick stench of rot and decay lingered in the air, as if Alastair still stood before her, his fingers ghosting over her skin. She trembled at the thought, forcing herself out of bed and hastily wiping away the tears that had marked her cheeks.

It was just a dream, a nightmarish figment of her mind. And the smell? Merely a trick her imagination played on her. That's all it could be. Because the alternative—that somehow Alastair had survived and could invade her dreams at will—was utterly insane.

She paced anxiously before the fire, its light flickering in the growing shadows of the cabin. How long had she been here? Zainiel had not only sealed off the only means to exit the cabin, but he had also shrouded the single window in darkness. She couldn't even tell if it was day or night. The dwindling flames and the growing pile of ash hinted that it had been at least a few hours. Surely, his magic would grow tired at some point and fail. It was just a matter of how long it would take.

Chapter Forty

"What the hell, Zainiel!" Ivy's voice echoed in the cabin as the obsidian curtain fell. Zainiel, seemingly oblivious to her distress, strode into the cabin and collapsed onto the bed. His once-sleek hair was now a tangled mess, plastered to his head with a gritty gray, mud-like substance, a twig protruding from it. His breathing was labored as he sank further into the bed. Was he injured?

"What happened?" she demanded, her voice tinged with worry as she approached him. His boots, once a deep black, were now a dull gray, caked in mud that had left a trail across the cabin floor. His pants were torn at the knee as if something with razor-sharp claws had tried to grab him. Her heart raced. Had it succeeded?

"Are you okay?" she asked.

"I'm great," he mumbled sourly, tossing his forearm over his face, a sharp wince following. He wasn't great. She had begun to suspect that it wasn't possible for him to look bad, but as she walked closer, she noticed his pale face, split lip, a hint of a swollen eye hidden beneath his arm, and the smell of rot coming off of his body.

"Well, for someone so great, you look pretty awful." She wrinkled her nose. "And you smell pretty awful, too."

He shifted, moving so he was reclined on the backs of his elbows. His jaw ticked as he winced at the movement, but that didn't stop the cocky smirk from spreading across his lips before he said, "By all means, next time, I'll be sure to shower before returning, princess."

Ivy narrowed her eyes. *Princess?* She thought they had moved on from that insufferable pet name, thought they had moved on from him deflecting every question she had with this cocky arrogance. "Just tell me what happened, Zainiel." She wasn't in the mood for his games. She needed to know what happened while he had her locked away in this god's forsaken cabin; needed to know if there was even the slightest chance that Alastair was alive.

He shifted beside her, pushing himself off the couch. He cleared the room with three long, slow strides, stopping just before the fireplace. "I let myself become too distracted," he said, his voice cold and detached as he left his back to her. His shadows flared, agitated from whatever was bothering him.

"What happened?" she repeated, trying to keep the bite from her voice. She was growing tired of him dancing around the question. It wasn't that hard. She just needed to know if there was even a sliver of a chance that this burning dread inside of her that Alastair was still alive was more than just her overactive imagination.

Zainiel turned, meeting her gaze through dark and... *accusing* eyes. Whatever glimmer of kindness she had seen in them in the days leading up to this were gone, and she was left facing the Zainiel she had compared to Seraphina all those times. *He'll destroy you.* Theo's voice echoed in her mind as she remembered his warning.

"You," he growled, his voice trembling with barely controlled anger. His shadows loomed behind him. "You happened."

She resisted the urge to flinch under the weight of his accusing glare and the reverberating anger in his voice. *He'll destroy you.*

"I was fine before you," he spat, shaking his head. The shadows around him grew larger, now nearly blanketing half the cabin in their darkness, but instead of lashing out toward her, they beat against his skin in steady waves. "I did my job, and I was good at it. But then you showed up with your feelings, and your words, and your *truths*," a mirthless laugh escaped his lips. "You wrecked me.

Now, all I can think about is you—keeping you safe, destroying anyone who would ever dare hurt you, your laugh, the feel of your skin against mine, the way your voice almost seems to pull the darkness out of me, and how I would do anything... *anything* to hear your voice every day for the rest of my life."

His voice softened as he spoke, and the tension in his shoulder seemed to drain away, the dark aura of his shadows retreating along with it. Ivy's heart thundered in her chest, and she hated herself for ever comparing this man to Seraphina. She hated that she ever thought for a second that Theo's warnings held some truth.

"And now, because of that, because of *you,* I allowed myself to get distracted. And do you know what happens when I get distracted, Storm?" his voice cracked ever so slightly, his brows furrowed as his gaze bore into her. "People die. Good, innocent people die, and last night, that could have been you."

Ivy didn't know what to say. How was she supposed to respond? She knew going out there like that was stupid and he was right. It could have ended much worse, and it would have if he hadn't been there to save her.

"Zainiel, I—"

"Alastair is alive." Ivy's blood ran cold, her breath seizing in her lungs. *Alive.* He was alive. Did that mean the dream... no. *No,* it couldn't.

"I was so blinded by the rage that that man had his hands on you—that you had even found yourself in that position to begin with—" his accusing stare turned her blood to ice. "I missed it. I missed the signs. While I was lying here, holding you, he escaped."

Ivy felt like her world was collapsing around her. *Alastair was alive.* She had watched him draw his last breath, had seen Zainiel's magic impale him. How could someone survive that?

"I—I don't understand," she mumbled. Alastair was alive somehow. And that dream—that dream had been *real*.

"A Mimic," Zainiel answered gruffly, falling back into the chair beside the fireplace.

"A Mimic?" Ivy parroted, realizing she still needed to learn more about Arbor and the creatures that inhabited it.

A sigh of frustration left him, leaving Ivy with a stabbing reminder that she was still just as helpless here as she was in Salus. That here all she was was a distraction, a *burden*.

"A creature that can be conjured to take on the features of whoever controls it. But they age and break down at an accelerated pace. I've never known one to last more than a week," Zainiel explained in a monotone voice as if reading directly from a passage.

"Alastair was here, in mind and soul, but not in body. I didn't kill him. I couldn't have, even if I tried. The coward ensured he was far enough away that by the time I tracked him down, he would be long gone."

Ivy's blood was ice as her hands trembled in her lap. *There is nowhere you can go, no one you can run to, that would prevent me from finding you.* She fought off a shiver as Alastair's words echoed in her ears. He was alive. Her heart thundered, each breath coming harder and faster as panic settled in.

It was supposed to be just a dream—a silly little trick her mind had played on her. But now... *Nowhere you can go...* Ivy tightly wrapped her arms around her legs and pulled them against her chest. Zainiel was still talking. She could see his lips moving, but the frantic beating in her ears was all she could hear.

"He'll come back for me," she said, her voice barely a whisper over the stale wind circling in the cabin. The mark on her arm burned almost as if in agreement. He would come for her, and when he did, he had no intention of leaving without her. That much she knew for sure.

"I need to be prepared next time. I need to train more, read more about Arbor," she said, the words tumbling out in a frantic rush. "I need to learn how to fight against him, how to make my magic last, how to protect my—"

"Storm, just take a deep breath for me," Zainiel said, placing a hand over hers as it nervously ticked on her knee. You aren't alone here; we will keep you safe." His voice was a gentle caress as he knelt before her. All the anger and accusation his eyes had held earlier were gone, only concern glimmering in them now.

"No," she refused, shoving away from his touch before standing to place some distance between them. She couldn't think clearly with him so close. "You don't understand. He will come back for me. I need to be prepared." Zainiel had been right. She was a distraction, and she would continue to be one if she didn't start taking this a little more seriously.

"You'll be safe with me."

"I'll be a *distraction* with you," she shot back, using his earlier words against him. It was a cheap shot. But necessary.

"That's not what I meant, Storm, I—" he stammered, his confidence crumbling beneath the weight of his own words.

"You were upset because you missed something. And you missed it because of me," she finished for him, watching as his gaze dropped in guilt. "You said so yourself, Zainiel."

His eyes locked onto hers again, the previous chill creeping back into his expression. "You know I didn't mean it that way," he growled, his voice a low whisper of pent-up frustration.

"You were angry, and you blamed me. Whether you meant to say it or not." Ivy started, pausing to kick a piece of debris out of her way. "You said it, and it's the truth."

A frustrated sound ripped from his throat. With two swift strides, he closed the distance between them, forcing her back against the remnants of the cabin wall. His arms caged her in, his hands placed firmly on either side of her.

"You're right. I was angry," he confessed, lowering his face until it was mere inches from hers, electrifying the air between them. "But you have no idea how wrong you are about everything else."

Ivy swallowed hard, her heartbeat hammering in her chest. "Oh yeah? Care to enlighten me?" she challenged, her voice catching slightly.

He wore a smirk that sent Ivy's heart racing, a chaotic dance of emotions she found hard to rein in. It infuriated her how effortlessly he stirred her feelings. Even covered in mud, with bruises marking his skin, the intoxicating blend of sandalwood and the briny essence of the sea lingered around him, pulling her in like a spell.

"You drive me wild, Storm," he whispered, his voice a shadow of a breath against the charged silence surrounding them. No man had ever fixed his eyes on her with such fervor, as if she were the sun in his universe. The floorboards protested softly beneath them, their creaks echoing like secrets shared in a dimly lit room as Zainiel drew closer, his hips pressing her against the cool, unyielding wall.

"You've become my obsession," he confessed, his head dipping low. His warm breath ghosted over her ear, sending shivers cascading down her spine as a flush of warmth bloomed in her chest. The familiar flutter of her magic sparked to life, begging her to lean into him and confess that she felt the same.

"I've never felt this way about anyone," he continued, the weight of his words hanging in the air. "So yeah, I was angry. Furious that I let myself get lost in this—" His voice trailed off as he nuzzled into the crook of her neck, the soft tickle of his unruly hair brushing against her skin, causing her breath to catch in her throat.

"In you. The worst part is, I wouldn't change a single moment if it ended with you in my arms."

He pulled back just enough to meet her gaze, tenderly tucking a wayward strand of hair behind her ear. His fingers lingered close to her cheek, emanating warmth that beckoned her to lean into the gentle caress. It didn't make sense, but everything about him screamed *home*. The longer she stood there breathing in his scent, his breath mingling with her own, the warmth of his skin brushing against hers, everything else seemed to melt away. There was no debris-ridden cabin, no crushing weight of panic, no Alastair, no *dream*.

The dream. She still hadn't told Zainiel about the dream.

Ivy pressed her back further into the wall as she ducked underneath his arm. If she was going to think clearly, she needed space between them, and clearly, so did Zainiel. He remained silent, his gaze tracking her as she walked back over to the bed and perched on the corner. He leaned against the wall, his hands shoved in the pockets of his pants.

She reached up, brushing her fingers over the swollen skin on her arm. "This mark, whatever it is, connects me to Alastair," she admitted into the silence. A stark breeze flitted through the cabin, causing a rough shiver to rack its way throughout her body.

Zainiel's brows furrowed as his gaze remained glued to the handprint. "What do you mean?"

"He—he said that I'm bound to him." *Nowhere you can go.*

Zainiel's spine went straight, and she watched that cold, detached stare slip back onto his face as he pushed off the wall. "When did he say this?"

Ivy clasped her hands together, picking at the skin around her thumb. "When you were gone, I fell asleep, and somehow..." she trailed off. How could she explain this without sounding insane?

"He got into the cabin? Why are you just now saying something?" His eyes were wide with panic as he scanned her body up and down, undoubtedly looking for signs of injury.

"No. He—" Ivy sighed and shook her head. This was unbelievable, absolutely ridiculous. She would tell Zainiel that she thought Alastair visited her in her dreams, and he would reassure her that wasn't possible, and then they would laugh about it together months from now, as if her naivety of this world was a punchline to a joke.

"He what, Storm?" His words were laced with the bite of frustration as he stood before her.

"I think he visited me in my dreams," she rushed out, a blush creeping up to her cheeks when she realized just how crazy she sounded. It felt so real, and when Zainiel had returned and told her that Alastair was alive... she let the panic consume her.

"Visited you in your dreams?" Zainiel's brows were furrowed, his eyes searching hers for answers. He wasn't laughing; in fact, no part of him looked like he didn't believe the words that left her mouth.

"I—I don't know how to describe it. I must have fallen asleep, and then suddenly, I was in this dark room and couldn't see anything. But then he was there, and he told me that this mark binds me to him." The hairs on the back of her neck stood on end as she felt the ghost of his touch and heard the cool whisper of his promise never to let her go.

"It was real, wasn't it?" she asked. She didn't need to see the tense line of Zainiel's jaw or the subtle clenching of his fist to know his answer. No matter how much she wished it to be, the dream wasn't just a dream. Alastair was alive, and she was bound to him.

Chapter Forty-One

Ivy's fingertips glided over the rough, jagged edge of the gaping hole in the wall, the splintered wood biting into her skin as she gazed at the soft lavender hues draping the world around her. Dusk enveloped them, painting the sky with a fleeting warmth that stirred an unsettling vulnerability within her. Nightfall had once been a familiar friend, a gentle cover that whispered comfort to her, even in her darkest moments. Yet now, with the encroaching shadows came the heavy promise of sleep and the chilling awareness of who awaited her on the other side of slumber, that comfort was nowhere to be found.

The floorboards groaned as Zainiel approached her from behind. He had been silent, but she knew he was waiting for her to say something, do something. After all, he had just confirmed that her greatest nightmare was real. But honestly, what was there for her to say, or to do? She felt numb, like no matter what she did or where she was, something would come along to remind her that she was just as weak and pathetic as Seraphina had seen her to be.

"What's next?" she asked quietly, still staring out at the field, watching a large bird fly in circles above them.

"First, we get some rest. Then we go back to the estate, where it's safer."

Ivy tried to withhold a scoff. *Safer.* As long as Alastair was still out there, something told her she'd be in just as much danger at the estate as she would be anywhere else.

"He won't stop. It doesn't matter where I am or who I'm with."

"The estate has wards up around it, stronger ones built into the framework of the grounds. They'll be strong enough to keep you out of his reach." Zainiel started to explain, but Ivy shook her head and turned to face him.

"I don't want to be locked up at the estate," she declared, her voice firm with defiance. She hadn't endured everything she had gone through the past couple of months to hide away.

"You won't be locked away. You'll be safe."

"Just like I was safe in Salus? Or out here with you?" She knew it was a cheap shot, regretting it the minute the words passed through her lips, but it was the truth. Alastair would find a way to reach her, no matter where she was. Even now, she could feel that dark magic writhing underneath her skin.

"You would have been safe with me had you listened," he glowered, his jaw ticking.

"Yeah, well..." Ivy started her words trailing off. There was nothing she could say to that. He was right. Her own stupid decision had put her in the situation she was in now. But the idea of being locked at the estate waiting to see if Alastair could find her... it made her feel like a mouse caught in a trap. "I just can't be locked up there, Zainiel."

"You won't be. Besides, there must be something about that mark at the estate library. There's a good chance Ria has even read it."

"Fine. So we go back to the estate and see if we can find any answers, and then what?" Ivy asked.

"Then I find Alastair, and I—"

"We." Ivy cut him off, throwing her arms across her chest and jutting out a hip. "*We* find Alastair."

She was challenging him, and by the subtle flare of his nostrils, Ivy knew he wasn't happy about it.

"I won't be the one to put you in danger." He shook his head.

"Good thing it's not your decision, then."

His jaw ticked with annoyance as his eyes darkened. "Until you can learn to protect yourself, it is my decision."

This time, she didn't bother to hold in her scoff. "I know it was stupid of me to go out there alone, but let's be honest. Something is happening here, and until my father returns, I need to learn more about this realm. How am I supposed to do that locked up at the estate?"

"Will you stop saying that?" Zainiel growled. "You won't be locked up. I would never leave you to be locked away."

"Yeah? Didn't stop you from sealing me in this cabin."

An inhuman growl ripped from his throat as he raked his fingers through his hair, sending specs of dried mud flaking around him. "You are insufferable."

Ivy shrugged. Maybe so. But she knew one thing for sure. She was done letting others decide for her. "You would be, too, if you were in my shoes."

Zainiel paused for a moment, contemplating her words. "What would you have me do, Storm?" he asked with an exasperated sigh.

She paced towards the hearth and drummed her fingertips against the small mantel above it. They needed to find Alastair. Something told her he was involved in whatever was happening here, and maybe if they could catch him, Zainiel could get some answers. There was only one sure way to lure him out.

She turned to face Zainiel, knowing he wouldn't like the words about to leave her lips. "Use me."

"No," Zainiel said almost as immediately as she spoke the words.

"Zainiel, it makes sense. We know that for whatever reason, he seems to have this sick obsession with me, and this," she paused, motioning to the blazing handprint on her arm, "connects me to him. So *use* me."

Zainiel's jaw ticked as he shook his head. "I will not put you in danger."

"I'm already in it. All we would do is use it as an advantage to get some answers." Alastair obviously had a powerful friend who knew about Arbor. Maybe if they found him, he could lead them to some answers about her father.

"Ivy," Zainiel warned in a clipped tone.

It was odd hearing her name on his lips. As much as his pet names annoyed her in the beginning, Storm had grown on her.

"I need you to hear me when I say this. I cannot put you in danger." He spoke slowly, emphasizing every word.

"I know my father ordered you to—"

"This has nothing to do with your father." Zainiel cut her off as he cleared the space between them.

"Care to enlighten me?" She tried to keep her voice steady but couldn't help the little flutter in her stomach as she met his gaze.

"Do you really need me to?" His fingertips brushed against hers, sending tingles up and down her arm.

She shuffled backward, falling into the chair behind her. Even covered in filth, looking like he was fresh out of a bar brawl, he still had this effect on her.

"Alastair has someone that helped him get into Arbor. If we can find them, maybe we can get some answers about where my father is. Using me is—" Zainiel's finger pressed against her lips.

"It's not up for discussion."

Ivy rolled her eyes and shoved off of the chair, pushing past him. "You're right. It's not up for discussion because it's not your choice."

Another irritated growl tore from his chest as he raked his hands through his hair again.

"We obviously aren't getting anywhere with this. Why don't you get cleaned up? You're filthy." She waved her hand up and down in a sweeping motion as her eyes swept over the mud trail on the floor. Not that it mattered much. The cabin was still in complete disarray.

Zainiel raised a brow as he glanced down at himself, almost as if he hadn't noticed the state he was in. He waved his hand, and with it, a black cloud settled over the room, dispersing almost as quickly as it appeared.

Ivy gawked at the sight before her. The gaping hole that had been left in the cabin wall was suddenly repaired, and any signs of debris were gone. The hearth even housed a healthy fire, the sounds of the crackle and pop of the wood filling the room. And Zainiel... he was clean, the clothes he had been wearing were replaced with a worn pair of jeans and a fitted black t-shirt. His hair was no longer caked in mud, and even the bruises and cuts that marred his face looked better.

"H—how?" Ivy asked with wide eyes.

"I just imagine what I want, and then it appears." Zainiel shrugged.

Ivy shook her head in bewilderment as she fell back onto the bed that was now covered in warm, clean sheets. Every time she felt like she understood this world a little better, something else would happen to remind her that she knew nothing.

"Could my magic do that?" she asked, as she propped herself up on her elbows.

"Much of our magic tends to evolve, developing into something greater as time passes. Ria possesses the ability to nurture plants and herbs and Theo has the gift of light manipulation." The image of the blast that had left Theo when they were trying to escape Salus came to her mind. She hadn't ever thought to question it before she didn't know enough about how their magic worked, and she hadn't thought of it again since then.

"And I... well, I can do this." He extended his hand, conjuring a swirling ball of shadows that danced through his fingers before dissipating into the air. As the darkness vanished, a single flower emerged in his grasp—strikingly similar to the blossoms she had admired at the lake only the day before. Leaning closer, he hovered over her, tenderly pushing her hair back and tucking it, alongside the flower, behind her ear.

"Stunning," he breathed softly, and warmth surged through her, a wild rhythm of excitement thrumming in her chest as their eyes locked. He was barely inches away, his fingers brushing the delicate curve of her cheek, their breaths mingling in the charged space between them. His gaze sparked a tantalizing flicker toward her lips, only to swiftly return to her eyes. *Was he about to kiss her?*

Ivy felt her gaze drift from his, tracing the strong line of his jaw, sculpted and striking, which contrasted intriguingly with his full lips, slightly parted as he edged closer towards her. His fingers left her cheek in a gentle trail, threading themselves into her hair, sending tingles down her spine. She held her breath, feeling the electrifying closeness as their noses barely brushed against each other. She found his eyes once again, a mesmerizing depth in them as they swirled with emotion, reminding her of the storms she would so often run to in Salus.

Zainiel closed his eyes, resting his forehead against hers, his fingers pressing gently into the nape of her neck. But just as suddenly, he unwound his hand from her hair and pulled away, leaving a cold ache blooming within Ivy's core. *What had just happened?*

The bed shifted beneath him as he cleared his throat and rose, retreating to the far side of the room as though he needed to create an expanse between them. Ivy remained anchored in her place, grappling with the whirlwind of emotions. He had almost kissed her, had described her as stunning, and then, just like that, was *gone*. Had she done something wrong?

Ivy pushed herself up, bringing her unsteady hand to her cheek, brushing it over where his had just been. Zainiel stood with his back to her, both hands braced on the mantle in front of him. Had she read the situation wrong? No. He was about to kiss her, that much she was sure of. So what had stopped him?

"We should try to get some rest. We'll leave tomorrow to go back to the estate." His voice was husky as he spoke, but he still remained with his back to her. He clearly wanted to pretend that whatever it was that had just happened, hadn't.

"What about Maron? Doesn't she still need your help?" That was the whole reason they had come all this way, after all. And Ivy's problem with Alastair didn't change the fact that other people were relying on Zainiel's help.

"I did my part while I was out." He moved to the chair in the corner of his room as he spoke, unlacing his boots before tossing them to the side. "Maron can handle it from here."

Is that what had taken him so long? Had he left to track down Alastair and then dealt with the Mortifers on his own?

"So that's where the bruises and cuts came from? You went after the Mortifer we saw in the forest?" It seemed so long ago, as if that hadn't just transpired a little more than twenty-four hours before.

"I had to," he nodded curtly. "I couldn't leave unless they were taken care of." *Because her father made it his job to eradicate these creatures from this realm.* She couldn't help the sour twist in her gut at the thought. She wanted to believe he was a good man, but what man left someone else to fight a war that was not entirely their own? *Unless he truly was in trouble.*

Chapter Forty-Two

The forest was oddly quiet, and that did nothing to settle the unease building in Ivy's gut. Alastair was out there somewhere, watching, waiting. Zainiel was a few yards away, standing at the waterhole with Bae.

They had left before the sun crested the horizon to start their trek back to the estate. Ivy had been restless all night—afraid that once she closed her eyes, she would awaken to find herself locked in her mind with Alastair again. She'd sleep when they caught him. Until then, she'd do anything it took to stay awake.

Ivy picked up a small purple flower that peeked over the side of her boot. The tiny dewdrops glistened in the sun as she twirled it between her fingers. Her gaze lifted to Zainiel as he strummed his fingers through Bae's mane. Luther had never been found after he had been spooked in the forest that day. Ivy's heart clenched at the idea of him wandering the woods, scared and alone; but Zainiel had assured her that he was probably already safely back at the estate, awaiting their return.

Ivy's heart raced as a sudden rustling pierced the stillness around her. She spun on her heels, her senses heightened, to see the dense underbrush shifting ominously behind her. Gripping the dagger that Zainiel had entrusted to her only moments earlier, she braced for whatever might emerge. The pungent scent of Mortifer was absent, but the thought of an unknown creature lurking just out of sight sent a shiver down her spine.

Another rustle echoed, followed by a chorus of frantic chirps—a symphony of panic unfolding within the thicket. Ivy's breath caught in her throat as she released a shaky breath, her tension ebbing slightly. It seemed the sounds belonged to a creature in distress, likely ensnared by a cruel trap set by one of the nearby villagers. A pang of sadness gripped her heart as another bout of desperate chirps echoed from the brush.

Looking around, she grasped a large stick nestled on the ground just a few steps away, using it to push aside the bundle of barbed branches. Her hand, slick with sweat, trembled as she sank to her knees, bracing her hands in front of her on the dampened ground. With the brush clear now, she could see a small ball of movement, jerking and twisting as more panicked cries left it. A trap with a large chain connected to it ensnared the creature.

"Shh, it's alright. I'll take care of you," she murmured gently, her hand reaching into the space she had cleared. She seized the chain, pulling it towards her, the creature trailing along with it. Ivy observed the animal as it writhed to free itself from the snare. Its wings resembled a bird, thickly coated in mud, perhaps from its frantic attempts to escape. Yet, this was no bird. Birds didn't possess fur or ears—one stood erect while the other drooped, resting precariously above its left eye. It had four legs, delicate paws, and a long, bushy tail that thrashed wildly as it struggled to release its hind leg from the trap. A fox, Ivy realized, or something akin to one, if foxes had wings. She had never encountered such a creature up close, but a memory flickered from a book she had once discovered in Isodyl's room.

It was remarkably small. She imagined it could easily fit into the cradle of her hands. The only large thing about the creature was its ears, nearly the same size as its head, and the vast, violet-hued eyes that stared up at her in panic. Just a baby, she thought, though a baby with sharp teeth, she soon learned, as she extended her hand towards it, only to recoil with a bloodied finger.

Ivy swore under her breath, pulling her finger close to her chest. "I'm trying to help you," she scolded.

The creature paused in its struggle and tilted its head to the side, its ear folded over its left eye flopping over. Its wide eyes blinked at Ivy as if trying to figure out what, or who, she was.

Ivy tenderly reached out a hand, pausing just inches before the animal's face. She allowed it to study her scent, just as Zainiel had instructed her to do with Bae. Its lips curled upward, a rumbling snarl coming from the creature. It bared its sharp teeth, and its whiskers twitched with a warning.

"I'm not going to hurt you," she cooed. She held her other hand out, moving it to rub the creature's head between its ears. It cowered away, another snarl sounding, the fur on its back and tail standing straight up. But after a moment, the creature relaxed and pushed its head into her palm as if finally understanding what she was offering.

"I leave you alone for five minutes, and you manage to find yourself a familiar?" Zainiel chuckled amusedly from behind her.

Ivy craned her neck to look over her shoulder as she raised a brow. "A familiar?"

Zainiel moved, squatting beside her as he examined the trap the creature was caught in. "Some believe they are spiritual guardians, meant to help guide us through hardships. Others believe they are what's left of species who used to roam the worlds long before we did," he explained as he reached a hand towards the trap, only to withdraw it when the creature snarled and bared its teeth at him.

"Do you have one?" she asked, eyes scanning his face.

"No," Zainiel replied, shifting to crouch behind the familiar to avoid getting bit. Its tail, now nearly double in size, swished angrily. "They're actually quite rare," he added, a glint of knowledge sparking in his expression. He carefully placed a hand on either side of the trap, pressing down until it released with a soft clink.

Suddenly, the creature lunged forward, its hind leg drawn up against its body. Ivy stumbled back, caught off guard, as it collided with her chest, burying its face into the crook of her arm. A soft purr churned from it as it buried itself further into her hold.

"It should be fine. They heal almost instantly from most injuries," Zainiel assured her, a grin spreading across his face as he gathered the trap, careful to avoid the sharp prongs jutting from it, tossing it over a nearby branch.

"Kind of like you?" Ivy teased, her curiosity piqued. She marveled at how little evidence remained of the battle he had fought the day before. The only remnant was a faint bruise marking his lip.

"Faster," he replied, nodding toward the creature nestled against her, still burrowing into her arm.

Ivy tilted her head, gazing down at the tiny being. To her astonishment, there was no sign of injury whatsoever. Where she expected to see a gash or some blood, there was only its soft copper-blonde fur. Cautiously, she ran her fingers over the leg, confirming her suspicion—it was fine.

It peered up at her, its large violet eyes shining in the sunlight that filtered through the canopy of leaves above. A mixture of soft purrs and chitters sounded as she strummed her fingers down its back.

"You'll need to name it," Zainiel said as he secured the saddlebag back onto Bae. Giving it a swift tug to make sure it was secure.

"Name it? I can't keep it," she shook her head. It was a wild animal, albeit cute, but wild nonetheless.

"It chose you. That's what familiars do. You found it in that trap, but it wasn't a coincidence. You wouldn't have found it if it didn't want you to."

Ivy's brows furrowed. "Are you trying to tell me it purposefully let itself be ensnared by a trap so I could find it?"

Zainiel shrugged. "Maybe it was some sort of test."

A test. Ivy eyed the creature as it looked up at her with a cocked head, its one floppy ear laying over its eye. Soft chirps sounded from it as its tail swished, wrapping around her arm.

"So? A name?" Zainiel asked, his arm stretched across the saddle as he leaned against Bae with a raised brow.

Ivy studied the creature. She had never been great with names. When they were younger, she and Theo used to play a game where they'd create stories of another world, pretending they could escape and be free. Now, she realized that most of his stories must have been about Arbor.

"Foxy?" she offered, her voice wavering with uncertainty.

An amused smile stretched across Zainiel's face, and the creature's lips drew back as it swiftly shook its head as if it could understand her.

"You're right. I can do better than that." She sat it down on a nearby rock, watching as it walked itself in two circles before settling onto the rock, wrapping its tail so it rested on its paws.

She glanced over at Zainiel, "Any suggestions?"

"Don't ask me. She's your familiar."

"She?" Ivy hadn't even thought to ask what gender it was.

The creature swished its tail as it chirped, almost as if she had confirmed what Zainiel had said.

Ivy scratched the back of her head, and her familiar let out a tired yawn as it stretched its wings out before chirping again.

"What about Cricket?" Ivy offered.

The creature's ear perked up as she shot up to all fours and started prancing around, flapping her wings and wagging her tail in excitement. A series of excited chitters sounded from her.

Ivy laughed as she stood. "Cricket it is, then."

Chapter Forty-Three

"What the hell happened!?" Ria demanded as she burst through the stable doors. They had just returned to the estate, and Ivy was leaning against the stall as she watched Zainiel brush down Bae, with Cricket curled up on a bale of hay nearby.

"Good to see you too, Ria," Zainiel muttered as he sat the brush down, patting Bae before exiting the stall.

"No. You don't get pleasantries until you explain to me why Luther showed up here without you three days ago! How dare you not send word that you were okay?" She stomped up to him, her ponytail bouncing with each aggravated step. "You better have a good explanation for this, or so help me," she seethed, jabbing her finger into his chest.

Ivy was surprised. She didn't think Ria could lose her temper like this; she had always seemed so calm. But Ivy supposed that if she lost a sister like Zainiel and Ria did, she'd also be worried and angry.

Zainiel held his hands up, his lips tugging into that infuriating smirk he got right before he was going to say something equally as infuriating.

Before she could stop herself, Ivy sent a swift kick to the back of his knee. "She's just worried, don't be an ass about it."

He and Ria both turned towards her, the same slightly amused expressions on their faces. Gods, they looked so similar. She wondered if Ellie also shared the exact uncanny resemblance.

"We ran into some trouble. Luther was spooked and took off. But we are okay," he paused, his eyes settling on Ivy's arm. "Well, mostly okay."

Ria's gaze shifted to Ivy's hair. Her brows creased with worry, and her lips parted. She was undoubtedly about to spring a torrent of questions upon them, but Zainiel held up a hand and shook his head before she could.

"Let us get changed, and then I promise we will fill you in. Meet you in the dining hall in an hour?" Zainiel asked as he hoisted the saddle bag onto his shoulder.

Ria opened her mouth like she was going to object, but her eyes swept over Ivy and Zainiel, and with a long sigh, she nodded.

"Fine," she grumbled before spinning around and stomping off.

The soft clicks of Cricket's paws against the stone floor echoed through the hallway as Ivy followed Zainiel into the dining hall. Ria stood in the middle, pacing up and down the length of the room between two tables. Luka and Lilli sat near the large bay window, plates of steaming food before them, watching her with curious eyes.

The heavy wooden door swung shut with a thud, causing Ria to stop and whirl around to face the two of them.

"Took you long enough. I know something bad hap—"

Zainiel held his hand up, silencing his sister as he turned a steely gaze toward Luka and Lilli.

"Leave," he commanded, leaving no room for questions.

Ivy glared at him and then shot Luka and Lilli an apologetic smile as they both scampered out of the dining room, leaving their plates of barely-touched food behind.

"You don't have to be so mean to them," Ivy chided. She hadn't been able to spend as much time with the pair as she would have liked, but they were just kids. Sweet kids. She'd be sure to find them later and apologize.

"We needed the room."

"You could've asked. Or we could have gone somewhere more private," Ivy argued.

"We also need food," he shot back as he walked over, grabbing the two plates they had left and placing them down on the table. He pulled out two chairs, falling into one and motioning for Ivy to sit in the other.She rolled her eyes but obliged. Cricket padded off to the cushioned chair in the corner.

"Are you ready to tell me why waves of anxiety are coming off of both of you? Gods, I'm so anxious I'm ready to pull my own hair out." Ria tapped her foot nervously in front of them.

"What do you know about a mark that binds one person to another?" Zainiel asked as he shoveled in a mouthful of food. Ivy didn't know how he could eat at a time like this. Her stomach twisted at just the thought.

"Binds how?" Ria asked, her brows furrowing as she looked between them.

Zainiel looked at Ivy, motioning for her to explain as he shoveled another mouthful of food.

"I—I don't know exactly. He can get into my dreams, I think, and control them. It was like I was trapped in my own mind." Ivy fought off a shiver as the mark on her arm tingled.

Ria's brows furrowed, and she shook her head, "I'm going to need more information here. Who is he, and how did this even happen?"

Zainiel sat his fork down with a clang and shoved the plate before Ivy. "Eat," he demanded before turning his attention back to Ria. "His name is Alastair. He's someone that she knew from Salus. He found her here and approached her when she decided to sneak off while I was sleeping," he paused to send Ivy an icy glare.Clearly, he was still upset about it.

"I thought I killed him and realized too late that it was a Mimic. I was distracted."

Distracted with caring for her. Ivy fiddled with her hands in her lap as she stared at the plate of food before her. The more they talked, the less appetizing it seemed.

"I sealed her in the cabin, and while I was go—"

"You sealed her in the cabin?" Ria exclaimed, cutting him off.

Zainiel met her incredulous stare with a hardened one. "She kept trying to follow me. It was the only thing I could do to ensure she didn't."

"She had just been attacked, and you left her alone?" Ria said, as if repeating the question could help her somehow understand.

"I wouldn't have had to if she would've just listened."

"*She* is right here," Ivy said, tired of listening to the two bicker back and forth as if she wasn't.

"Sorry," Ria mumbled. "What happened next?"

"I fell asleep while Zainiel was gone, and I was in this darkness. Alastair was there. He told me that this mark," she paused, yanking up her sleeve so Ria could see, "binds me to him."

Ria drew in a sharp breath as her eyes widened. She walked around the table, stopping beside Ivy.

"Does it hurt?" she asked, studying the mark.

Ivy shook her head. "Not really. I mean, it did, but now it's like..." Ivy trailed off, searching for the right words to describe it. "It's like he still has a hold of me." She felt ridiculous as the words left her mouth and waited—*prayed*—for Ria to laugh and tell her she was wrong, that it was all in her head. She'd rather be crazy than right.

Ria's brows knitted together as she continued studying the mark, reaching her hand toward it. "May I?" she asked, lifting her gaze to meet Ivy's as she waited for permission.

Ivy nodded and stood from the table, hoisting the sleeve of her shirt higher onto her shoulder. Ria worked her fingers over the mark, the crease in her brows deepening.

"Dark magic," Ria breathed, the words barely audible as they passed through her lips.

Ivy's breath caught as a wave of panic flooded through her. Panic that was not her own.

Ria yanked her hand away, stumbling backward with a yelp as Cricket barreled between them, fur bristling, teeth bared, emitting a fierce chittering snarl.

"I—I'm sorry," Ria stuttered as her gaze flickered between her hand and the familiar that still stood, teeth bared between them. Her usual golden complexion drained, a ghostly pallor overtaking her features as a haunted look settled in her gaze.

"What is it?" Zainiel demanded. He stood behind Ivy now, his towering frame casting a shadow over her as the evening light filtered in the window.

Ria's gaze flickered between her brother and the mark. "Do you remember the stories that Mother used to tell us?"

Cricket flicked her tail, sending one more snarl in Ria's direction before curling up on top of Ivy's feet.

Zainiel scoffed. "Do you?"

"Only a few," Ria started. "There was this one about a ritual a couple could do that would bind their souls through their magic. Mother and Father did it. I remember Mother had this mark over her heart, and I always dreamed I would find that type of love someday. It's not really he—"

"Get to the point, Ria," Zainiel snapped, growing impatient with her rambling.

Ria's gaze flickered to Ivy's. "You said he told you the mark binds you to him?"

A sinking feeling struck Ivy. She hadn't completed a ritual with Alastair and didn't leave a mark on him. Surely, Ria couldn't be suggesting that they were—that their souls were bound together?

"But I didn't complete a ritual," Ivy objected, turning to look at Zainiel, whose brows were furrowed, eyes fixed on the mark that stained her arm.

Her hands began to quake at her side. If Ria looked this scared... Ivy's heart thundered in her chest, this time the panic solely hers.

"Is there a way to break it?" Zainiel asked.

Ivy didn't know how he could remain so calm.

Ria shook her head, and her shoulders fell forward. "I—I don't know."

Ivy collapsed into her chair. What did this even mean? And if they couldn't find a way to break it... Her heart quickened in a frantic flutter, the room's edges dissolving into a haze. Sensing her panic, Cricket moved into her lap, nuzzling her head into Ivy's shaky palms. She just needed to breathe. *Inhale. Exhale.*

"I'll find a way," Ria said, her voice more steady now as she knelt before Ivy. "I'm sure some books or old journals in the library have some answers." She moved to place a hand on Ivy's knee but stopped short when Cricket bared her teeth in warning.

Ivy nodded, or at least she thought she did.

"In the meantime, the wards around the estate should lessen whatever hold he has on you. But I'm sure I can come up with some sort of tonic to make sure he can't reach you." Ria added, casting a glance over to Zainiel. Something in her expression told Ivy that there was more to it than what Ria was saying, but she didn't think she could handle anything else. She'd pick that battle later, when she could breathe again.

Ivy stared at the folded letter in her hand, her heart racing with a mix of curiosity and dread. Ria had offered to walk her back to her room once they left the dining hall. Zainiel looked as if he were going to object, but after a sharp snarl and a snap of Cricket's teeth, he rolled his eyes, threw his hands up in defeat, and sulked off in the other direction—no doubt heading to the stables to check on Luther. He had tried to play it off, but Ivy knew part of him had been concerned for his horse, and that he wanted to check on Luther himself.

Once they had reached Ivy's room, Ria pulled a letter from the fold of her dress and pressed it into Ivy's palm. She didn't need Ria to tell her who the letter had come from as she spotted her name scribbled across the parchment in Theo's messy handwriting; the same scrawl she used to tease him about in Salus.

"He came back to the estate the day you and Z left." Ria started as they settled onto the couch. "He couldn't stay, but he asked me to give you this letter if you made it back before he did."

"Did he say where he was going, or when he'd be back?" Ivy asked, her brows furrowed in concern. She knew the way they had left things hadn't been great, but the idea of him out there on his own sent a wave of worry washing through her.

Ria shook her head. "All he said was that the letter would explain everything."

Ivy shifted in her seat, pulling her legs onto the couch as she looked at the letter in her hands. What else could there possibly be to say? They had said it all when he left.

"What do you think it says?" Ivy asked, peering up at Ria through the curtain of hair that had fallen across her face.

Ria shrugged. "He wouldn't tell me. But whatever it is, I got the sense that it was imperative to him that you read it." She paused, her eyes settling on the letter. "I would've given it to you earlier when you first arrived, but, well..." Her eyes trailed up Ivy's arm and to the blazing mark. They had more pressing matters than a letter.

Ivy ran her fingers around the edges of the letter. "I'm nervous to open it," she confessed. "Things weren't great with us when he left."

Don't count on me to save you. Theo's parting words echoed in her mind.

"If it helps, he didn't seem angry when he gave it to me," Ria offered.

Ivy brushed her hair back, tucking it behind her ear. She didn't know why she was so nervous. Cricket chirped as she hopped onto the couch, nestling between Ria and Ivy and placing her head in Ivy's lap.

"Did you want me to leave you alone to read it?" Ria asked.

"No," Ivy rushed out, "I mean, yes, but not right now. I—I don't want to be alone right now." Just the thought of it made her stomach twist. She was safe here but had also thought she was safe at the cabin.

"You know, if you want to talk about it—any of it—I'm here for you. Right?" Ria's gaze had fallen to Ivy's hair, her brows knitted together in concern.

Ivy knew she still had questions about what happened with Alastair. She had caught her studying her newly-cut hair on more than one occasion since they returned. "In Salus, once you fail the bloodstone ritual, you are either exiled from the island or betrothed. Alastair was my betrothed. He thinks he has some sick claim over me. That's why he followed me here."

Sadness shimmered in Ria's eyes, "So, your hair?"

"He liked it long. He caught me by my braid that night at the cabin. I thought maybe if I cut it—if I took the part of me he seemed so infatuated by..." Ivy sighed, shaking her head. How could she explain it? At the time, it felt like the only answer to the spiraling chaos she had found herself in.

"It would free you."

Ivy nodded, tears swelling behind her eyes. How silly must she be to think that a simple haircut could free her from the man who now, quite literally, haunted her dreams? A man she was now bound to, with no apparent way of escape.

"What you did isn't pathetic, Ivy. You took control the only way you knew how to." Ria reached across the sofa, giving Ivy's hand a reassuring squeeze.

Cricket nuzzled her head deeper into her lap as Ivy offered Ria a small smile. She didn't think she'd ever get used to the fact that Ria was so skilled at dissecting someone's emotions that she could practically tell what they were thinking.

Silence fell upon them, the soft purrs of Cricket's slumber filling the space between them as Ivy worked up the nerve to read the letter still clutched in her hand. "I think I'm ready to read it," Ivy said, breaking the silence.

"Would you like to be alone?"

Ivy nodded, feeling a twinge of anxiety. "If you don't mind?"

"Of course. I'll be in the library if you change your mind. Come find me after?" Ria asked, giving Ivy's hand one final squeeze before rising from the couch.

"Ria?" Ivy called after her as she walked toward the door.

Ria paused, glancing over her shoulder with a raised brow as she placed her hand on the doorknob.

"Thank you for sitting with me."

Her lips curved into a soft smile. "One day, you'll trust us when we say we are here for you. You just have to let us in, Ivy." And with that, she was gone.

Dear Ivy,

I know you asked me not to call you Ivy moving for-
ward, but I can't do that, because you aren't Iverlyn
anymore. Iverlyn was that scared little girl I met in
Salus that day on the beach. The one that kept looking
over her shoulder, afraid of what her aunt would do
if she saw her talking to someone rather than reading
that ridiculous book. You haven't been that girl for a
while, and now that you're here, you never will be that
girl again. Everything that I have done was to ensure
that. No matter what happens, I need you to remembert
hat.

I was hoping to do this in person, but maybe it's a good
thing I'm writing this letter instead. You would think
that after all my years, I would have learned to be
better with my words, like Zainiel or Ria. But the truth
is, I'm pretty awful at saying what I mean, especially
when it comes to you.

I never meant to hurt you, Ivy. Never. When I agreed
to do this for your father, we made a pact that bound

me by my magic: I would not show myself to you or anyone else until the time was right. I wasn't lying all those nights we spent dreaming about the day we'd escape Salus. The first time I heard about Seraphina striking you, I wanted to take you as far away from that place as I could. I tried to tell you the truth once but couldn't. Kalec made it so I wouldn't be able to.

I suppose I could have told you this sooner, but you needed to be angry with someone, and I was worried that if I wasn't that someone, your father would be. I know you, and I know you need to place the blame somewhere, but your father does not deserve that blame. He was only ever trying to do right by you. We both were. I just didn't expect it to be so hard. I didn't think I would grow to care for you as I did.

The last time we spoke, I was unfair to you. Zainiel and I will always have our differences. We have too much of a history for things to change between us. A history I'm sure you have figured out by now. You never were one to let things go easily. But if he is the person you need to help navigate this world and find your place in it, then

I understand. I don't like it—I will never like it—but I understand. Just promise me you'll be careful. We've all seen him change over the years, watched his dark side grow a little darker each day, and I can't bear to see that darkness consume you, too. But if it does, I will be here. I will always be here. Fighting for you, waiting for you.

In the weeks since I left, I've been searching for Kalec, tracing his last steps, and hoping to understand why he hasn't returned. I'm growing closer to finding him, I can feel it; and when I do, I'll bring him to you. We all deserve answers, but you deserve them most of all.

Stay safe, Ivy. We'll be home soon.

Your Friend, Theo

Chapter Forty-Four

I had orders. Theo tried to tell her the truth, but he couldn't. All this time she thought he chose the orders Kalec had given over sharing the truth with her, but he couldn't have told her anything even if he'd wanted to. Cricket padded slightly ahead of her, her tail swishing with each step down the corridor, almost as if she knew precisely where Ivy intended to go.

She needed to talk to Ria; to find out what she knew about this pact Theo had made with Kalec, and if other pacts like it existed. How was she supposed to trust them if Kalec could simply bind

416

them in a way that made it impossible to defy his orders? What if he had also ordered Zainiel to grow close to her? For all she knew, they all could be under his influence in some way or another.

Ivy pushed open the doors to the library, and the smell of aged leather and polished wood washed over her like a gentle tide. Bookshelves lined either side of the room, a warm glow from the mounted lights illuminating the space. Ria sat hunched over one of the long oak tables, stacks of books littered around her in disarray. She was alone. Everyone else was more than likely at dinner, but since she had learned of the mark branded into Ivy's arm, Ria had hardly left this room. Ivy's chest swelled with appreciation; back in Salus, no one would have devoted themselves to helping her the way Ria had.

Cricket chirped as she launched herself onto the table. Ria gasped, startled.

"Sorry," Ivy muttered sheepishly as she scooped Cricket up and placed her on one of the chairs. "She seems to really like you." Which was more than Ivy could say for Zainiel. Anytime he came around it usually elicited a harrowing stare and bared teeth from the familiar.

"I don't mind it. She just startled me is all," Ria smiled as she placed a hand between Cricket's floppy ears and patted her, eliciting a chorus of chirps and purrs as her tail enthusiastically thumped against the chair. "Is something wrong?" she asked, her eyes darting to the folded letter in Ivy's hands.

Ivy moved around the table, slipping into the chair across from Ria. "I need to know more about bonds. Specifically, pacts made between two people and bound by magic." She slid the letter across the table. "Theo had one with Kalec."

Ria's eyes widened in shock, but there was something else in her gaze that Ivy couldn't quite read as Ria grasped the letter and scanned it.

"I need to know if this is something he does regularly," Ivy said as Ria continued scanning the letter. She couldn't explain why the pact bothered her, but it almost seemed *cruel*, as if Kalec had taken away Theo's free will.

Ria passed the letter back to Ivy, her brows furrowed, her bottom lip pulled in between her teeth as if she were trying to carefully choose her next words.

"The pacts that Kalec makes are for the good of Arbor. And no one enters into one with him without consent," Ria said after a few moments.

"Has he made ones with you and Zainiel?" Ivy pressed.

Ria's eyes shimmered with an uncertainty as she twisted a lock of her chestnut hair around her finger. There was something she wasn't telling Ivy. Or was it that she wanted to tell her but *couldn't*?

"Ria, I need to know the truth here. *Please*." She was a job to Theo, one that he couldn't have walked away from even if he wanted to. She didn't want to be that to Zainiel or Ria.

"If you're asking if your father made sure we would accept you and look out for you the same way he did with Theo, then the answer is no. He didn't and would never have to," Ria answered after a few moments.

Ivy didn't know why she was disappointed. Ria's answer was what Ivy had wanted to hear—that whatever had happened between her and Zainiel hadn't been the product of some twisted pact made by Kalec. But she couldn't help the knot of growing unease in her stomach. Ria hadn't actually answered the question that Ivy had asked her.

"Zainiel cares for you, and no pact or bond that he made with your father could ever change that," Ria added, sensing Ivy's unease.

Ivy drummed her fingers on the table as she nodded slowly. Deep down, she knew that Ria was telling the truth and that the connection she had felt with Zainiel was real and untainted. But the idea that Kalec—her father—felt the need to bind people in a way that stripped them of their free will didn't sit well with her. What type of man was he, that he felt the need to do that?

"Doesn't it bother you?" Ivy blurted out. "That pact he made with Theo, took away his right to make his own choices. I know you all say he's an amazing man, but Ria, what type of man does that?"

Ria sighed, and a sort of sadness glimmered in her eyes before she said, "When you have lived a life as long as your father's, people you least expect can cause you pain. As time's worn on, he's become guarded; these pacts are his way of learning to trust again. They not only bind us to our promises but also tether him to *his*."

Ivy hadn't thought about it that way, yet the idea of her father binding people in a manner that could prevent them from making their own choices or acting upon their own desires continued to gnaw at her. Regardless of his reasons, it still felt inherently *wrong*. Cricket hopped onto the table, padding over to Ivy and nuzzling against her cheek before dropping into her lap, curling into a ball.

"Do you think he intends to do the same to me?" Ivy asked, gently running her fingers through Cricket's soft fur. She had witnessed the power that words could wield over a person; Seraphina was a master of manipulating others, even without the use of magic. Ivy couldn't shake the thought that perhaps her father shared this trait with her aunt, only his method was amplified by magic, rendering it far more dangerous.

"You're his daughter, Ivy," Ria offered softly, as if that could answer her question. Ivy knew those words were meant to put her at ease. And perhaps they should have, but she couldn't shake the feeling that there was something else Ria wasn't telling her—something that would do nothing but make her suspicion towards her father grow.

Chapter Forty-Five

I vy found herself back at the lake. The moon hung above her in a crescent, and the stars shimmered in the clear night sky. She had told Zainiel she was going back to her room to try to sleep. But the moment she closed her eyes, she could feel Alastair waiting for her, eager to trap her inside herself once more. Besides, she hadn't seen much of Luka since her return and missed their nightly conversations.

"I figured I'd find you here." Luka's voice shattered the night air as he settled down beside her. "Zainiel was looking for you.

Something about you needing to sleep?" Luka raised a brow at her, smirking slightly.

Ivy sighed and shook her head. Of course Zainiel checked to make sure she was sleeping. He didn't think she had noticed, but he had even moved into the room across the hall from her. He gave Ria some half-baked excuse that his room was farther from the library, and he didn't want to lug books to and from it; even though he could conjure them, and they'd appear.

"I can't sleep," she offered with a weak shrug. She didn't feel like diving into the whole *"I'm terrified if I fall asleep, I'll fall victim to Alastair's control and never wake up"* thing. They all knew about the mark. Ria had recruited Lilli and Luka to help them scour the library for answers. So far, the closest thing they had come to finding anything was a fable about a fallen consort who tried to bond himself to a powerful fae woman to regain the immortality his goddess had stripped from him. He had failed.

"I've known Zainiel for a few years, and I've never seen him act like this about someone. I don't think he would ever come out and say it, but he's worried about you. We all are. You need sleep, Ivy."

She appreciated what he was trying to do, what all of them were trying to do. But these dreams were more than just dreams. She didn't understand it, but Alastair was *there*, and if he could take control of her dreams like that, then what was to say he wouldn't be able to control more in the future? She wasn't willing to give him the opportunity. Right now, at least for the time being, she was in control as long as she was awake.

"Did I ever tell you how I ended up at the estate?" Luka asked as he adjusted his glasses.

"Just that Zainiel found you and brought you here when you were twelve."

Luka nodded. "He was tracking a Mortifer from a nearby village. We kept to ourselves mostly—my mother, father, and I. Not everyone took too kindly to the idea that my mother had chosen to mate with a human, so it was easier that way. She was resourceful, always finding odd jobs in return for supplies we couldn't forage on our own." A faint smile crossed his face, though it didn't quite reach his eyes.

"The last job she took was to help find a missing girl. I knew something was wrong when she didn't come home that night. She always came home." He cleared his throat and picked at the hem of his rust-colored shirt.

"My dad left the next morning. He told me to stay behind, but I didn't listen. Sometimes, I wonder if maybe he knew what we would find."

When I saw her, I knew something was wrong. She used to have this effortless grace about her; my father used to call her his Kari, which means grace in Finnish. But when we found her, I knew it wasn't her; and I think he did too, but she was the love of his life, the woman who saved him, so he tried to do the same for her. Only there wasn't a cure for what my mother had. She was already lost." He drew his bottom lip between his teeth, and his eyes glistened in the moonlight.

"And when she killed him," Luka paused, his voice catching over the words, "he told her it was okay, that he loved her, and that he'd find her again in another life."

Ivy's heart ached for him. He was so young and had already been through a lifetime of loss.

"Zainiel found us right after. I don't know if she was the Mortifer he was tracking, but she was the one he found, and he had to kill her. I had nowhere to go. No family to turn to. So he brought me here."

Ivy opened her mouth to speak, but she didn't know what to say, or if there even was anything she *could* say. He had watched his mother kill his father and then had to watch as Zainiel killed her. She couldn't fathom that kind of loss.

"Luka, I—"

"You don't have to say it," he shook his head, cutting her off. "That's not why I'm telling you this. It happened a long time ago, and as awful as it is, we all have a tragic story following us. One day, when my time has come, I'll join them in another life, too."

A twig snapped in the distance, filling the silence between them. No doubt a curious animal roaming the estate forest. Luka pushed up and angled himself so he could face Ivy.

"What I'm getting at, though, is that I used to have these awful nightmares. For a long time, I refused to talk about it, refused the help anyone was offering. But all it did was add to my hurt. It's lonely, pretending you're okay when you aren't." Luka gave her a pointed look, and Ivy knew what he was getting at.

"It's not that I don't want the help that has been offered," Ivy started, pausing as she tried to find the right words. "But I can feel him, Luka. It's like... this creeping darkness. When I close my eyes, I'm back in that place with him, and I just—" She let out a resigned sigh, shaking her head.

Luka leaned forward, bracing his arms atop his knees. "You're worried the tonic Lilli and Ria made won't work."

Ivy nodded, picking at her nails nervously in her lap. "I *know* it won't. I can feel it, and I'm terrified of what will happen. He could manipulate me there, and what if this mark," she traced her fingers over the fabric that concealed her arms, "what if it grants him power beyond just my dreams?" She hadn't voiced that fear to anyone, not even Zainiel. If she did, she feared he might start perceiving her as a threat, and she selfishly didn't want to risk losing the fragile connection that had blossomed between them at the cabin.

Luka inched closer to her, his arm hovering awkwardly as if he were trying to determine whether it was appropriate before he draped it across the back of her shoulders. "Lilli is better at this than me," he admitted, chuckling softly. "But I promise you, Ivy, no one here will give up on finding the answers we need."

She smiled softly in return, leaning slightly into his reassuring embrace. She knew Zainiel and Ria would stop at nothing to find the answers they needed, but she couldn't help the gnawing dread building in her core that maybe there were no answers.

Chapter Forty-Six

RIA

R ia shifted in the chair, rubbing the sleep from her eyes as she studied the pages before her. *The earliest record of the binding ritual occurred when Zaria, the Goddess of Night, bound herself to her consort, giving him the gift of...*

She slammed the book shut, tossing it onto the growing pile of discarded books as she let her head fall to the desk before her. This was useless—utterly useless. She had combed through every historical text in the library that mentioned the binding rituals and had now resorted to reading journals of those who had deemed themselves scholars in the past. There had been nothing of use. She had found plenty of text on completing the ritual, but nothing on *breaking* the bonds once they were formed.

Ivy's panicked face flashed through her mind. The poor girl was still so young, yet had already suffered unimaginable things—and now this. She looked haggard when they arrived, and Ria could feel the fatigue rolling off her in waves. She suspected Ivy hadn't slept since the dream at the cabin. Not that Ria blamed her; sleep wouldn't come easy to her either, if she had been in Ivy's shoes.

The door to the library flew open with a resounding thud that could have only come from one person—her brother. She sighed, lifting her head from the table and turning to meet his gaze. He thought he hid it well. But she knew better than anyone how panicked he was under this calm facade he always wore. She'd need to remember to thank Kalec for warding the library against magic when he returned—*if* he returned. It would be insurmountably harder for her to focus if she was constantly bombarded with the emotions her brother always clamped down.

She stood from the desk, drawing her hands over the top of her head and stretching out her back. How long had she been here? Five or six hours?

"Tell me what you didn't want to say in front of Ivy," Zainiel said, skipping the pleasantries. Not that she could blame him; after all, he had seemed to take a liking to her, and the panic Ria felt rolling off him when they returned—well, that wasn't just any panic.

"That mark was imbued with dark magic."

Zainiel raised a brow in question and motioned for her to continue. She sighed. Clearly, he had never read the books she had left for him over the years.

"Dark magic works differently than ours. With our magic, there's a balance that keeps us from abusing power; it's why we can burn ourselves out if we try to pull on too much of it at once. With dark magic, it doesn't care how the cost is paid. It'll either devour the host or anything the host offers. It's like a parasite or a drug. Once it has a grasp on you, the need to use it is overwhelming. It can drive people mad until eventually there's nothing left of them: mind, body, or soul."

"Get to the point, Ria." Zainiel's jaw ticked, his hands clenched into tight fists as he braced himself on the table.

"When I touched the mark, it felt alive," Ria began, a shiver creeping up her neck as the memory washed over her. "It was angry, ancient—nothing like I've ever experienced before." She twisted a lock of hair around her finger, her foot tapping an anxious rhythm against the floor.

"What else? I can tell there's more," Zainiel prompted, his gaze fixed on her restless movements.

Ria shifted her eyes away from him, focusing instead on the cobwebbed corner of the shelf. "I'm not sure there's a way to remove it," she admitted, a hint of uncertainty in her voice.

Silence lingered for a heartbeat, then broke abruptly with a resounding bang as the desk Zainiel had been leaning against flipped over, scattering books across the room. He began to pace, fury radiating from him, and Ria sensed the dark shadows he usually commanded were close to overwhelming them, if not for the room's protective wards.

"How did I let this happen?" He slammed his forearm against the wall, pressing his forehead against the cool surface and remaining there, defeated. "She's supposed to be—" His voice trailed into a sigh, his shoulders slumping heavily. "I swore I would keep her safe. Why can't I ever keep them *safe*?"

His voice broke, a jagged shard of anguish lodging itself into Ria's chest. There were no wards that could protect her from an emotion this profound. She knew this wasn't just about Ivy. This was about Ellie, Liola, and all the others he thought he had failed.

"Zainiel, you can't—"

"Please don't, Ria. I don't need to hear that this isn't my fault. I just need to know what I can do to *fix* it." He turned to face her, letting his back fall against the wall. "Just tell me what I can do to save her."

Ria studied her brother. She had never seen him like this. She had witnessed his sorrow before, moments when the weight of the world seemed to press down too hard, but this—this was a different kind of despair.

"You love her," Ria breathed, suddenly seeing it with such clarity that she was surprised she had missed it. She had felt the electric tension between them buried beneath layers of anxiety and panic, but she had pushed it aside. After all, Ivy was beautiful and wouldn't be the first beautiful girl her brother had paid special attention to. "Z, you *really* love her. Don't you?"

"No." Zainiel's eyes drifted to hers, filled with a raw, desperate emotion she hadn't seen in him for what felt like an eternity. "I'm utterly consumed by her."

Chapter Forty-Seven

Three days. That's how long it had been since Ivy slept, and every nerve in her body screamed at her to relent and close her eyes, even if it was only for a few seconds. But that was all he would need. Alastair was waiting; despite the tonic that Ria and Lilli claimed should keep him at bay, she could feel his anticipation through the bond as his dark magic writhed inside her.

The words on the page before her were beginning to blur together, and her body swayed in the seat as she fought to stay awake. Everyone else had left hours ago, and she was sure if she walked over to the small window on the other side of the shelf, she'd be able to see the faint colors of the rising sun bleeding into the horizon.

Make that four days since she last slept. How long could someone go without sleep? She had already felt its effects on her magic, which Zainiel had noticed today during their training. He had even suggested she take a day off. Ivy refused. The last thing she needed to do was slow down on honing her magic so she could protect herself.

"Have you been here all night?" Ria's voice sounded from behind her as the door to the library creaked open.

"I couldn't sleep." Even her words felt weighed down with exhaustion as they passed through her lips. She knew she couldn't fool Ria. With or without the wards, she would see right through whatever excuse Ivy gave her.

Ria sighed as she pulled the chair out across from Ivy and sat. Cricket peeked one eye open from where she was curled up in the corner, only to go back to sleep with a lengthy yawn when she determined Ria wasn't a threat.

"Ivy, you *have* to sleep. This isn't healthy," Ria chided, shaking her head.

"What isn't *healthy* is this mark on my arm and the fact that every time I close my eyes, I'm terrified of what will be waiting for me." Ivy snapped. The words left her lips more sharply than she had intended, but she was growing tired of the same daily lecture.

"The tonic I ga—"

"It doesn't work." Ivy cut her off, slamming the book shut. There were no answers in it anyway.

"Did something happen? Did you try to sleep?" Ria asked.

Ivy sighed, covering her face with her palms. How many more times would they have this same conversation? "I can feel him waiting for me."

There was silence, then the scraping of Ria's chair as she pushed up from the table before Ivy felt her hand rest on her arm. "I know this is scary for you. But you'll be safe. And even if the tonic doesn't work, Zainiel and I will pull you out of the dream."

Ria's words washed over her like a warm wave of complacency, soothing Ivy's frayed nerves. She *could* sleep, and despite the gnawing feeling in her gut that promised her the tonic wouldn't work. It could just be anxiety worsened by sleep deprivation. After all, she hadn't slept for four days. Her judgment was slipping, and Ria was just trying to center her. She just needed to get some sleep. She'd feel better when she woke up.

"Let me take you to your room. I'll even sit with you while you sleep," Ria offered, tugging gently at Ivy's arm.

Ivy felt herself nodding, but the exhaustion weighed so heavily on her shoulders that she felt like an extension of herself. It wasn't until Cricket barreled towards them, her hackles raised as she jumped on the table, nipping at Ria's arm, that Ria stumbled back in surprise. The fog in Ivy's mind dispersed as soon as Ria's hand left her arm, and while the exhaustion lingered, the comforting thought that she would be safe vanished.

Ria had used her magic on her. She had tried to trick her. Ivy stepped back, increasing the distance between them. This room was supposed to be warded. How had Ria even managed to use her magic?

"*Never* do that again," Ivy seethed, feeling Cricket's angry swish of her tail as she positioned herself at Ivy's feet. Heat flooded through her veins as she felt the familiar tingle of her magic at her fingertips.

"I'm just trying to help you," Ria exclaimed, holding her hands up defensively.

"Then help me find a way to get this thing off of me," Ivy motioned to the mark on her arm. "And in the meantime, keep your hands to yourself."

"I'm sorry, I shouldn't ha—"

"How *did* you? I thought this room was warded against magic," Ivy interrupted. It was the reason she had remained here all night, away from other parts of the estate. She didn't want Ria to sense she was still awake.

"The wards only work when the door is shut," Ria explained, motioning to the barely cracked door.

Ivy scoffed and shook her head. *Of course.* Just one more thing to add to the growing list of mysteries surrounding this place.

Would there ever come a time when she understood how things worked here?

Tick. Tick. Tick.

No. *She hadn't fallen asleep. She couldn't have. She had just finished lunch with Lilli and sat on her bed for a moment. She didn't even remember closing her eyes. Ivy tried to summon her magic, but it was out of her reach—eager to answer her call, yet restrained by an unseen force.*

Tick. Tick. Tick.

Her heart thundered in her chest as she spun around, only to find darkness—the same as before. She stumbled forward, surprised when she came into contact with a cold, damp wall. Running her fingers over the jagged surface, taking a step, then another, then another. Was she in a cave? Maybe if she could find an exit, she could wake herself up before he could realize she had found herself in his trap agai n.

Tick. Tick. Tick.

The rigid grooves in the wall gave way beneath her touch, causing her to stumble to her knees. She winced as the stone floor bit into her palms.

"I'm glad to see that you've finally made it. I was beginning to think you might have been avoiding me," Alastair's voice echoed. Ivy watched as the darkness lifted and the cold stone beneath her palms morphed into mounds of plush grass.

He loomed over her, towering with a wicked smile stretching across his face. "I like the sight of you on your knees before me."

Her stomach curled in on itself as she shoved up from the ground, stumbling backward, creating whatever distance she could manage. Behind her stood an intricate black gate adorned with swirling golden accents, and rows of trees swaying in the chilling night air as the sky dimmed from day to night. It was a scene she had been captivated by before, one that belonged to the estate entrance.

He knew where she was, and this was his way of showing her that he really could find her anywhere she went. No wards would keep her safe.

"What do you want?" Ivy demanded, trying to still her wavering voice.

"Haven't I made it obvious? I want what was promised to me." Alastair took a step forward, his eyes gleaming with hunger.

"I won't be your bride." Ivy refused it. Mark or not. She would not be his to claim.

"No," Alastair mused, "You'll be so much more than that." He took another menacing step forward, and Ivy tried to step back, only to find she was frozen in space, unable to move. He controlled this dream; she was just a puppet for his amusement.

Her heart thundered in her chest, but she refused to let him see her fear. "Let me go," she demanded.

Alastair chuckled, his smile broadening, revealing rotting teeth. "Where's the fun in that?" He took another step closer, now standing barely a foot away.

Ivy closed her eyes, forcing herself to breathe. This was a dream. He was controlling it, but it was still just a dream if she could just wake herself up.

"You know, I've rather enjoyed this little game of ours." He circled around her, a predator stalking its prey.

Ivy clutched her hands into fists, digging her fingernails into her palm. Wake up!

"But I must admit, I'm growing impatient." The ticking had stopped, and in its place were the thuds of Alastair's steps as he circled around her, just like he had done the night her family presented her to him.

Ivy could feel the magic thrumming beneath her skin, begging for release; yet an invisible chain remained, keeping it from answering her call.

"I would hate to have to hurt another one of your friends to get the point across."

Another. *Who had he hurt?*

Alastair bent closer so his lips brushed against the tip of her ear while his body pressed against her back. "But, oh, how I love to hear them scream."

The hairs on the back of her neck rose, and her hands began to tremble. "Who?" *Ivy asked, struggling to keep her voice from quaking.* "Who did you hurt?"

Alastair began circling her again, letting his fingers brush through the hair that hung just above her shoulder.

"You know, he never betrayed you. Even when he begged me for his life."

He. *Ivy's blood ran cold. Alastair couldn't be talking about Zainiel. He would never beg anyone for his life. Luka was safe on the estate grounds. But Theo, he was searching for her father. He was alone. No. No, she hadn't had the chance to make things right with him. He couldn't be gone.*

"What did you do? Where is Theo?" *Ivy seethed, her fear turning into a torrent of molten anger as her magic flared beneath her skin. If he had hurt Theo, she didn't think she could ever live with herself.*

"Theo?" *Alastair grinned, malice sparking in his eyes, shaking his head,* "Oh no, I have far better plans for Theo."

Her breath froze in her lungs. If he wasn't talking about Theo, then who was he talking about?

Alastair trailed his fingertip along the scar that branded her collarbone. "Would you like to see?" His grin broadened into a prideful smile, the stench from the rotting decay of his teeth puffing out with each word. "I'm rather proud of it. I think it may be my best work yet," he mused.

Ivy's voice was caught in her throat, her hands trembling at her side. This wasn't real. He was just trying to get into her head. She just needed to wake up.

"I was planning on waiting, letting you and your friends discover my little treat in the morning. But, well..." he paused, wrapping his hand around the brazen mark on her arm that almost seemed to hum from the contact. "I've never been a patient man, now have I?"

The scene around them dissolved, twisting and warping like shadows dancing in a dying light. The moon loomed high, a pale, watchful eye hidden by the fleeting clouds. They stood atop a hill, Alastair's hand still wrapped around the mark he had brandished into her skin as he stood beside her, gazing down at a lake that glimmered beneath the moon's ghostly caress. A hair-raising chill crept into the air as Ivy realized it wasn't just any lake they stood before. No. It was the lake where she had met Lilli and Luka. The one she and Luka often found themselves walking to during one of their many late-night strolls. Their laughter now echoed like a distant whisper in the dark. Something awful had happened here. She could feel it in her bones, could smell it in the air.

"Well, go on," Alastair splayed his hand on the small of her back, giving her a shove. "I know you aren't a stranger to this place." He leaned down, his cracked lips brushing against the top of her ear. "That's why I chose it."

Ivy's heart dropped into the pit of dread building in her core. He had been watching her. Knowing what the estate gates looked like was one thing. But knowing what the lake buried deep inside the estate wards looked like? Knowing that she had come here? No.

She stumbled away from his grasp, her eyes widening in horror as she shook her head. No. She refused to believe it. It wasn't possible. They were behind the wards. They were safe. No.

"Yes," Alastair purred. "You've begun to figure it out, haven't you?"

Her hands grew clammy as she fisted them at her sides. There was another explanation. This was some sort of trick he was playing on her, and she'd wake up to find everyone safe.

"Wrong," Alastair taunted. "The time for tricks is over. Now the real game has begun."

He was in her head. Hearing her thoughts, toying with her as if she were his own personal puppet.

"Walk," he ordered.

She fought against it—tried to stop her legs from moving at his command, but this was more than just a dream he had invaded. This was a trap he had constructed perfectly for her. One that left her completely at his mercy.

The night was still, and aside from the thundering beat of her own heart in her ears, it was eerily quiet. Each step echoed through the night as she walked down the small hill, Alastair following behind her, ordering her to stop as she neared the lake.

"Are you ready?" he whispered in her ear, placing a hand on her shoulder as he stood behind her.

"Why are you doing this?" Her voice trembled as she spoke, and her magic flared beneath her skin in defiance, fighting against the invisible restraints that kept it chained like a dog on a leash.

His breath washed over the back of her neck as he released a sinister chuckle. "Because I can."

He waved his hand before her, and once more, she beheld the scene warping and shimmering into an unsettling new reality. They remained by the lake, yet now they turned their backs to its tranquil waters, directing their gaze toward the dense rows of trees that stretched back to the estate. Shadows clung tenaciously to one particular tree, and an involuntary impulse tugged at her, compelling her to move closer, her stomach twisting with dread at each hesitant step as those shadows began to reshape into something all too tangible—a form, a body.

No, no, no, no! This couldn't be real. It had to be a trick. He was just trying to break her. She attempted to shut her eyes—yearned to break away from the gruesome tableau unfolding before her—struggled against the cloying, metallic scent of blood as it invaded her senses. A scream, sharp and piercing, sliced through the stillness of the night, and it was only when she started gasping for breath that she understood the chilling truth: that scream was hers.

Chapter Forty-Eight

RIA

Ivy's blood-curdling scream echoed through the trees as Ria dropped to her knees before a crumpled body—Luka's lifeless body. Ria was going to be sick. When did this happen? *How* had this happened? They were on estate grounds. No one should have been able to breach the wards.

His wrists jutted out at grotesque angles as if the bones had been twisted until they shattered from the pressure. His fingers ended in bloodied stumps, smeared with congealed blood where his nails had been torn from his body. His face was a mask of crimson, the freckles that dotted his cheeks and nose no longer visible underneath the blood-speckled swollen mess that remained—so disfigured that it teetered on the edge of inhuman. His wild, curly tufts of hair were now matted with dark clots and draped over his forehead like a macabre crown. Save for the remnants of his wire-framed glasses, catching in the glow of the early dawn, embedded into his right cheek, Ria feared that he would have been left unrecognizable.

A torrent of guilt and anguish flooded Ria, slamming into her so fiercely that it knocked the breath from her lungs. Ivy's shoulders jolted with uncontrollable sobs as she gathered Luka's lifeless body into her embrace, her fingers weaving through his hair as though she might somehow mend what had been so cruelly broken.

"I'm so sorry," Ivy wailed, her grip tightening around his body. "I'm so sorry." Again and again, she repeated the words, cradling his bloodied form into her chest as she rocked back and forth in despair.

Ria was frozen by the sheer volume of emotion radiating from Ivy. She could hear Zainiel's pounding footsteps approaching, yet the brazen panic emanating from him paled in comparison to the deluge of emotions holding Ria hostage. How did Ivy know he would be here? Ria had found her wandering the estate and assumed it was a side effect of her refusing to sleep for so many days—she had assumed she had been sleepwalking.

Zainiel's face came into view. He crouched before Ria, gripping her shoulders tightly. His lips were moving, and his eyes were wide with a terror Ria hadn't seen from him in years. Still, she couldn't hear anything over the deafening wails coming from Ivy and the pounding of her own blood in her ears. She struggled against the sheer agony that was crashing into her wave after wave, scream after scream.

"Get a hold of yourself! What happened?" Zainiel said, his fingertips digging painfully into her shoulders as he shook her. A cloak of darkness shrouded her, severing her magic's connection to Ivy. Ria's whole body trembled. Luka was dead. *Dead.*

"Ria," Zainiel's voice cut through the air, sharp and commanding. "What. Happened."

"I—she," Ria stammered, her voice quivering as she struggled to gather her thoughts. The events felt jumbled, like fragments of a nightmare. "When I found her, she was wandering in the gardens. I thought she was sleepwalking. I followed her here and... Oh. Oh gods, Luka." The words slipped from her lips, and a sob erupted from her, shaking her frame.

Zainiel's jaw tightened. Within the depths of his eyes, she glimpsed a flicker of darkness as he steeled himself, embodying the weapon Kalec had forged. Did he suspect Ivy was responsible for this horror?

"She didn't do this," Ria blurted out, desperation lining her voice. "I followed her here, and when she saw his body, she just—" Her voice cracked, her head shaking in disbelief as tears streamed down her cheeks. *Luka was gone.* She hadn't been able to feel any emotion from Ivy when she found her in the garden, almost as if she were in a trance, or as if something was shielding her from Ria's power; but when she found Luka, it was like a floodgate had been opened.

"I need you to return to the estate. Get inside and ensure that no one leaves. Do you understand me?" Zainiel's tone remained steady, almost soothing, acting as an anchor amongst the chaotic storm surrounding them. She always envied how he managed to stay so composed, even in a crisis. "Ria, do you understand me?" he pressed again.

Drawing a shaky breath, she nodded, her heart pounding.

"Repeat it back to me."

"Go to the estate, stay inside, and make sure no one leaves."

With a curt nod, Zainiel released his hold on her shoulders. "Go."

Chapter Forty-Nine

ZAINIEL

Ivy trembled as sobs continued to quake through her body. Zainiel had heard her screams on the other side of the estate. He couldn't explain how, but the moment the shrill noise had pierced the early morning air, he knew it belonged to Ivy. Finding her was easy. All he had to do was allow his magic to lead him to her. So many scenarios had crossed his mind as he rushed across the estate, crashing through the brush and trampling over a few of

Ria's flowers, but he had never once suspected that this was what he would find.

Ivy's front was drenched in blood, clutching Luka's lifeless body to her chest, screaming, sobbing, *apologizing*. Ria had been on her knees in the grass, tears streaming down her face, fingers woven through her hair, screams ripping from her throat as she was no doubt taken over by the emotions leaving Ivy. He had only been able to pull her out of it when he used his magic as a shield. Sometimes, he wondered if her powers were more of a curse than the gift that Kalec had preached them to be.

When Ria finally composed herself and told him she had found Ivy wandering the estate gardens and followed her here, he had allowed himself to assume the worst. After all, how else could Ivy know that Luka's body was this deep into the estate? And, coincidentally, in the same place where she and Luka often spent time together?

Ria was positive that it couldn't have been Ivy, but the truth of the matter was they knew next to nothing about the mark on her arm and how exactly it bonded her to Alastair. As much as he didn't want to admit it, he might have unquestionably allowed an enemy of Arbor into the estate walls—that the woman he had grown to care for was no longer the woman he knew at all, but instead a shell of who she once was with Alastair as the puppeteer. And if that were the case—if she was no longer in control of herself, and the magic coursing through her veins fell under the control of corruption—she'd be considered a threat to Arbor. A threat so dangerous that she couldn't be allowed to live.

No matter how much he'd grown to care for her, or the yearning that his magic felt to be near her, he was bound to eliminate all threats to Arbor by whatever means necessary. Kalec had made sure of that.

The wails from Ivy quieted. Zainiel watched her back go rigid as she laid Luka's body on the ground, carefully arranging him as if she were worried she'd hurt him. She pushed herself up onto unsteady feet, turning slowly to face Zainiel. The warmth that had always been in her eyes was dulled. Tears mingled with Luka's blood, creating small scarlet rivers that ran down her cheeks, beneath her chin, and onto her neck. Her black shirt—one of his, he realized—now clung to her, stamped to her skin from where she had cradled Luka's bloodied body in her arms. She took a wavering step forward, her hands trembling at her sides before she collapsed back to her knees.

"I did this," she whispered, her voice raw from the screams.

Zainiel's heart stuttered. *No.* He was torn in two, forced to look with suspicion at the woman who had wholly consumed his every thought over the past months. He knew she didn't have this type of horror in her. He had followed her a few times during her nightly strolls with Luka. At first, it was to make sure she kept her powers in check; then, somewhere along the way, it had turned into something more. Something he couldn't quite explain. He had seen how she interacted with Luka—her radiant smile that seemed to make those little golden flecks in her eyes burn even brighter, the way her nose crinkled when she laughed—each moment igniting sparks of jealousy and longing.

She cared for Luka and clearly cherished the bond they had built during her time in Arbor. So, if she really had done this, the woman he knew—the one he had admired from the shadows all those nights—was gone. Or, at the very least, she was corrupted beyond return.

"This is all my fault, Zainiel." She peered up at him, her hair hanging in tangled locks, dark circles under her eyes. When was the last time she had slept? "He killed him because of me." More tears swelled in her eyes, cascading down her cheeks.

He. A fleeting wave of relief flooded him before it was replaced with a gnawing sense of dread. They were on the estate. If Ivy hadn't done this, then that meant...

"It's all my fault." Ivy's voice trembled as she fell forward, palms digging into the earth. Zainiel could feel the raw energy of her magic pulsing around her like a storm. Her breaths came in sharp, labored gasps. "He warned me this would happen. Told me that if I ran from him, he'd find me, and he would hurt someone I cared about."

Despair twisted her face as she shook her head, tears spilling forth. She dug her fingers into the grass, her knuckles white with effort as tremors radiated through her arms, struggling to contain the torrent of power building within her.

"Ivy," Zainiel warned. "Your magic."

"He took it." A blue light flickered to life beneath her palms. Was she channeling without even realizing it?

She was in shock. Did she even notice him standing a few feet away from her?

Zainiel readied himself, shadows poised on either side of him, prepared to take action if she lost control, or worse, burned out. He wanted nothing more than to go to her. To pull her into his arms and promise her he'd fix it all. But empty promises would do neither of them any good right now. Not until he knew exactly what had happened, and whether or not he would be bound by his oath to Kalec.

"He won't stop." Ivy's voice broke; she rocked back on her knees as she raked her fingers through her hair, leaving trails of blood in their wake. "He's in my head," she sobbed, her hands gripping her temples before she collapsed forward once again.

"Just make it stop," she wailed. Another flare of blue light erupted from her hands, this time so bright it was nearly blinding.

The ground trembled beneath his feet, and his shadows flew out to his side, steadying him against the quakes. This was Ivy's doing—her magic manifesting into something more. The earth continued to tremble in tune with her panic. Trees groaned in the distance. Birds squawked as they fled. The lake rippled with frantic waves.

Another piercing scream shattered through the air before the trembles tearing through the ground ceased just as abruptly as they had begun, leaving the forest wrapped in silence.

Zainiel's shadows drew back, revealing Ivy lying in a heap before him, completely still.

He's in my head. Zainiel dragged his hands down his face. Ivy's cries had been haunting his every waking moment. Two days had passed, and still, all he could hear were the sounds of her wails as she fell apart before him. He should have gone to her and told her it wasn't her fault. Told her it was okay. But he *couldn't.* Even now, as she lay ten feet away from him, all he wanted to do was hold her— but no matter how much he tried to fight it, his bond with Kalec prevented him from doing so.

Until they could figure out what had happened to Luka, and how Ivy had known where to find him, she was a hazard, a possible seed of corruption that he had allowed into the estate, blinded by the feelings he had so recklessly allowed to take control. That mark and the power it allowed Alastair to have over her were a threat that he could no longer ignore, and one that he was a damned fool for not expecting far sooner.

The creak of the bedroom door opening pulled Zainiel from his thoughts.

"She still hasn't woken up?" Ria asked in a hushed voice as she slid into the room, the door clicking shut behind her.

Zainiel let his hands fall into his lap, twisting his seat and resting his back against the desk. "Yeah," he sighed. "The healers said she should wake up soon."

She had been unconscious since she collapsed onto the forest floor. The healers had suspected it was from her not sleeping for so many days, and then channeling such a large amount of magic. The quake she caused had stretched so far that villages miles from the estate had felt it. But Zainiel couldn't help but wonder if she was still unconscious because she had finally succumbed to the hold Alastair had on her.

"She didn't do it, Zainiel," Ria said, throwing her arms across her chest as she leaned against the back of the couch.

"Stay out of my head, Ria," he growled. This had to be the fifth time she had muttered those same words to him in the past twenty-four hours, and he was growing tired of hearing them. Of course Ivy didn't do it. But he was forced to consider that Ivy was no longer in control.

"Maybe if your emotions weren't so *loud,* I could," she shot back, rolling her eyes.

Zainiel sighed frustratedly. "You know that I can't just *believe* that she's innocent in this."

Ria was the only other person who knew about the bond he and Kalec had made. She wasn't meant to, but she had been able to sense it and eventually had pieced it together on her own. Kalec ensured that Zainiel could not tell others of the bond. He had claimed it was for the good of Arbor that no one knew about it, and Zainiel had blindly agreed.

"I told you she's still in there," Ria insisted with a piercing glare. "This isn't the same as with the Mortifers. That," she gestured towards Ivy, "is still Ivy."

"How can you be so sure?" Zainiel snapped, rising so abruptly from the chair that it tumbled backward and clattered onto the floor.

"Because!" Ria exclaimed, wincing slightly at her raised voice before glancing over her shoulder at a still-sleeping Ivy. They wouldn't wake her. Zainiel wasn't sure anything could. "I can *feel* her."

Zainiel's eyes darkened, a bitter laugh escaping his lips. "And you think I can't feel *them* when the Mortifers take control? You think they aren't still alive, trapped within their own decaying flesh?"

His words were harsh, and a wave of regret crashed over him the moment they left his lips. Ria recoiled away from him, her eyes brimming with unshed tears.

"I'm sorry, I just..." he sighed, dragging his fingers through his hair as the weight of his words settled heavily over the room. "She told me that he was in her *head*. What else am I supposed to think?"

"You're supposed to think that she was a girl who was traumatized by finding her friend's mutilated body. You're *supposed* to believe me when I tell you she didn't do this, Zainiel." The anguish in Ria's gaze tore at him. He knew she would never dare to say it out loud, but it was times like these, when she looked at him with that fury and hurt in her eyes, that he couldn't help but feel like he was also failing her.

"She is not the enemy here. Don't try to make her into one."

He narrowed his eyes at his sister, his shadows flaring behind him. "Do you think I want to?" he asked darkly. "Do you think I want to think about how this may very well end with *me* having to end her life?" He turned, slamming his hands down on the desk, the pile of books he had been studying toppling over and spilling onto the floor.

He closed his eyes, drawing in a few breaths. "I don't want to see her as a threat. But you and I both know that isn't my choice. It stopped being my choice the moment I agreed to Kalec's bond."

"You can't honestly believe that Kalec would expect you—"

"It's not that simple, Ria. He wanted to be sure that I couldn't be biased. That *he* couldn't be biased." There was only silence, filled with the low purrs sounding from Cricket as she carelessly slept, curled in a ball on Ivy's chest.

Ria shuffled behind Zainiel, her voice barely above a whisper. "But she's—"

"Enough, Ria," he barked, pivoting to face her with a steely gaze. "Kalec ensured that no matter their connection to me—or to any of us—any threat to Arbor would be neutralized."

Ria's mouth opened slightly as if she meant to respond, but she let out a heavy sigh instead, shaking her head as she shifted her focus toward Ivy. "Do you honestly believe she could have done it?"

Zainiel's eyes were fixed on Ivy's still form, where she appeared troubled even in slumber. Her brows furrowed delicately, her lips pressed into a thin line, and her fists clenched tightly by her sides.

"I've checked the wards," he said firmly, breaking the silence. "They're still secure. If she didn't, then someone within the estate grounds did." As much as he wanted to believe Ivy's innocence in all of this, the thought that there was a traitor amongst them—someone who could commit an act like that—was chilling.

"For all of our sakes, I hope you are wrong," Ria said; and Zainiel, for the first time in his life, found himself wishing the same.

Chapter Fifty

Ivy shot up from the bed with a sheen of cold sweat clinging to her skin. She wasn't sure how she had gotten here, why her head and body ached, or even what day it was. The last thing she remembered was—*what was the last thing she could remember?*

Cricket was curled in a tight ball at her feet, deep in slumber, seemingly unaware that Ivy had woken up. She knew she was at the estate. The golden-flecked mantel above the fireplace in her room gleamed in the warm sunlight that filtered through the curtains. But how had she gotten here?

"You're awake." Zainiel's voice, rough and low, drifted from the far corner of the room, where he was hunched over her desk. Books littered the surface chaotically, a matching pile on the floor beside him towering so high that it threatened to topple over.

"I'm awake," she said, offering him a weak smile that faltered when she noticed the lack of warmth in his expression.

Tension visibly coiled in his jaw, and his brow furrowed deeply as he scrutinized her. *Had she done something to anger him?*

His hair gleamed in the soft sunlight as he shifted in the chair, slick with an oiliness that betrayed days of neglect. Shadows hung heavily beneath his eyes as if he hadn't slept in days. The stubble on his jaw accentuated its sharp angles, making his rugged features appear even harsher.

"Is something wrong?" she asked, slowly pushing herself higher on the pillows, her arms quaking beneath her.

"Do you not remember?" He rose from the chair, the wood scraping loudly against the floor. His gaze pinned her to the bed with a piercing and accusatory intensity.

"I—" Ivy faltered. Her heart hammered in her chest as she tried to filter through the hazy memories. Something had happened, something so terrible that she couldn't bring herself to remember it.

"Tell me what you remember." The command rang out like a blade cutting through the silence. It wasn't merely a request from a worried friend. *No.* It was an order from the man who had been tasked to serve as the protector of Arbor—a decree from someone who now saw her as a threat.

Her head throbbed with a pulsating ache, and her hands began to tremble at her sides. She could feel her magic stir within her, but it was distant, out of reach. Had she lost control again? Hurt someone? Anxiety twisted in her stomach.

"Iverlyn," Zainiel snapped, pulling her from her thoughts.

Iverlyn. The use of her full name cut deep. He never called her Iverlyn. He barely even called her Ivy.

"What do you remember?" he repeated. His voice seemed detached, and that subtle pull she always felt from his magic was dulled. Instead of the tingling warmth, it was replaced with a chilling coldness, as if it itself had withdrawn from her.

"I—we." She shook her head. The last clear memory she had was leaving the estate with Zainiel. The rest was like a jumbled puzzle she couldn't quite piece together, like pieces were missing. She remembered finding Cricket, but was that on the way to where they had been going or on the way back? She remembered Zainiel holding her, soothing her, but why? She had been angry with Ria in the library. They were all searching for something—an answer she knew they needed to find, but *what was it?*

She leaned forward, clutching her head in her hands. What couldn't she remember?

"Do you really not remember?" Zainiel asked, disbelief in his voice.

"I know you and I left the estate, and after that..." She pulled her head out of her hands and met his gaze, "I *know* something happened. I can tell by the way you are looking at me, but I—I can't piece it together."

For a fleeting moment, his gaze softened before it was replaced with the same cold, stoic stare he had before.

"Did I—" Ivy took a shaky breath, tears brimming in her eyes. "Did I hurt someone?"

Zainiel's jaw ticked, and his fist clenched and unclenched at his sides, the only signs that he was holding something back. "Do you remember what happened at the cabin?"

Visions surged through her mind. Zainiel's strong arms wrapped around her trembling figure. The inside of a cabin, debris littering the floor, a gaping hole where a door once stood. Her hand, steady yet trembling, gripping the hilt of a dagger, the metal cold against the clammy warmth of her skin. Her hair drifting to the floor like petals in the wind. A gasp left her lips as she brought her hands to her hair to find it had been chopped, now resting just above her shoulders.

"I cut my hair?" she asked with wide eyes.

Zainiel eyed her, a brow raised in suspicion as he nodded slowly. "With my dagger," he answered.

"Why?"

Zainiel cocked his head to the side as he leaned against the back of the couch, arms crossed, studying her, as if he were trying to determine if she was telling the truth. "What *do* you remember?"

He wasn't answering her questions. Why wasn't he answering her questions?

"I remember finding Cricket, but I don't know how or when," she paused, running a shaky hand through her hair. "I remember being angry with Ria, but I don't know why. I—I think that happened after I found Cricket."

"Anything else?" he pressed.

"I remember you holding me. I was crying, or scared, maybe both." Her cheeks flushed as another memory flashed before her eyes. She was caged between his arms as he dipped his head down to hers, his fingers deftly brushing back strands of her hair. *You drive me wild, Storm.*

What had happened between now and then that caused him to look at her so differently? What had she done?

"Anything else?" he pressed.

"We were looking for something," she motioned to the stack of books spilling over the table. "in the books. Did we find it?"

"No." His tone was clipped as she shoved off of the couch. At least he answered her question that time.

At the foot of the bed, Cricket stirred, extending her paws and elongating her body. Her wings shuddered as she stretched. A gaping yawn left her before her violet eyes fluttered open. Her tail wagged happily as she noticed Ivy was awake.

"What about the mark?" Zainiel asked, causing Ivy's hand to freeze in midair as she reached to stroke Cricket's fur.

The mark. An image flashed before her eyes, blistering red skin in the shape of a hand, the cruel rotting smile of a man cloaked in darkness. Her heart thundered in her chest as she scrambled off the bed and rushed to the mirror beside the mantle. She tugged at the sleeve of her shirt, exposing her arm, gasping as she stared at her reflection to find the same blazing mark upon her skin. Who had done this to her?

"What's going on here?" Ivy heard Ria's voice, but her eyes were still trained on the scarlet handprint stamped onto her skin. When did this happen?

"She doesn't remember," Zainiel responded gruffly.

Ivy's heart raced as she traced the outline of the print with trembling fingers. It was obviously a man's, but whose? A jarring vision struck her: Zainiel stood in a moonlit clearing, a man suspended above him, a spear of darkness impaling his gut.

"...possible she suppressed the memories." Ria's voice continued to weave through Ivy's thoughts, but the words barely registered. A cold dread seeped through her, encasing her bones.

"Or maybe she's not herself anymore." Zainiel's response snapped Ivy out of her thoughts as she turned to face him and Ria.

Not herself? Why would he say that?

"What is going on?" Ivy demanded, but neither of them answered. Instead, they stood in a tense standoff, eyes locked in a fierce exchange.

"You're wrong," Ria shot back as she narrowed her gaze at Zainiel.

Zainiel's stare mirrored the cold intensity of his sister's. "Am I? Because we have a body that suggests otherwise."

A body? Ivy's stomach churned. Did he think she killed someone? She stumbled back, the haunting memory crashing over her—a bloodied figure draped across her lap, their features obscured in a haze, her own screams piercing the silence, taunting laughter swirling around her like a sinister storm.

Her breaths were coming in quick bursts, and a cold sweat broke out over her skin as she was hammered with an onslaught of memories. The field, Alastair, the mark, the dreams, and—oh gods. Oh gods, she was going to be sick. *No.*

She darted into the bathing room, crashing to her knees as she heaved. This couldn't be—it couldn't be right. Her mind was betraying her, weaving a cruel tapestry of despair, complicit to Alastair's cruel tricks. But if it wasn't real, if she hadn't just been cradling Luka's limp body against her chest, why were her hands stained red with his blood?

Waves of nausea assaulted her again, each one more relentless than the last. Beside her, she could hear Cricket whimpering softly, the gentle brush of her whiskers as she nudged Ivy's trembling hand. Zainiel and Ria's voices drifted in the background, their words lost in the fog of her anguish, their argument feeling like echoes from another world, distant and detached.

He never betrayed you, even when he begged me for his life. Alastair's sinister voice, slithered through her thoughts, tightening its grip around her heart. A sob tore free from her chest, raw and unrestrained.

Luka was dead, and Zainiel—oh gods, Zainiel thought she had killed him.

Epilogue

NAMELESS

Bound tightly in iron-clad shackles, he felt the damp stone behind him soaking through the back of his shirt, the cold biting into his skin. He sucked in a ragged breath, wincing as pain laced up his side, squinting into the darkness that enveloped him. The air was thick with a metallic musk that stung his eyes and choked his throat with each labored inhale.

Beside him dangled a man, his arms suspended and bound, his head hanging limply. The only signs of life were the ragged movements of his chest with each wheezing breath. A cut marred the side of the man's face, swollen and oozing, while matted, overgrown hair clung to his temple, concealing much of his features. Yet, he couldn't shake the unsettling feeling that there was something familiar about this man—something he needed to remember but couldn't grasp.

"Do you know who you are?" A booming voice surged through the silence, echoing off the cavern walls. A towering figure loomed above him, obscured by the engulfing darkness, but his size was undeniable. A stray shaft of light swept across his broad shoulders, illuminating the cruel curve of his lips and revealing a jagged scar that slashed from the corner of his mouth down to his sharp jawline.

Of course he knew who he was. Why wouldn't he? Except—anxiety clawed at him. He didn't. He didn't know his name, didn't know the contours of his face, the color of his eyes, wouldn't be able to recognize his reflection. He knew nothing. Nothing but pain and humiliation from the certainty that, at some point, he had soiled himself. Still a deep-seated panic surged within him—he needed to be somewhere, to reach someone. But who?

"Do you know your name?" the man bellowed, punctuating his question with a sharp kick to his ribs.

"N—no," he gritted through clenched teeth, struggling to search his mind for anything that could tell him who he was or how he had ended up here.

"Good," the man cooed, a wicked smile spreading across his face. "From now on, you'll answer to the name Maliki and do as I say. Understood?"

He wanted to spit in the man's face and tell him he could go to hell, but before he could act, his head nodded involuntarily, the muscles in his neck straining as he tried to stop the movement but failed. His lips parted despite his struggle to gain control.

"I am Maliki," he said, the words spilling from his mouth. He wasn't the one speaking, nodding, and bowing his head submissively to the towering figure above him. He wasn't Maliki. He was... trapped. Not just against the cold cave wall, but within his own body and mind.

The clang of iron against stone reverberated around them as the man unhooked his shackles from the wall, leaving the cuffs in place before letting his hands fall roughly into his lap.

"Stand," he ordered.

His teeth ground together, fingernails biting into the palm of his hand as he curled them into tight fists at his side. He would not stand. He refused. But as the defiance sparked within him, his legs curled beneath his body, and he pushed himself up. Pain tore through his side, a wave of fire that made him want to curl inward and scream, but he couldn't. His body wouldn't allow it. Maliki wouldn't allow it.

Beside him, the man remained in an unconscious heap, propped up only by the shackles binding him to the wall. Would he, too, wake up to find himself stripped of the memory of the man he once was? The thought sent a chill racing through him, a whisper of dread curling in his gut. This man was nothing more than a stranger to him. But for some strange reason, he was certain that they would all be doomed if he didn't wake soon—if he didn't find a way to escape.

Acknowledgements

Writing a book has always been a dream of mine. I remember fourteen-year-old me, sitting in math class, scribbling away in my notebook—the teacher always thought I was a devoted note-taker, and *of course*, I was. But I was also a fourteen-year-old girl with the dream of one day becoming a published author. I just never imagined the road I would take before I arrived there. If someone had told me of all the bumps in the road— that felt like mountains at the time— that I'd have to face before this dream came true, I would've been crushed. Because there's just no way that hurt and pain could lead to something so amazing. But I suppose that's just the naivety of a fourteen-year-old girl. As hard as it may have been, I wouldn't change a thing. After all, what is a good story without conflict?

All those bumps led me to an amazing guy who saw me when I felt like no one did and eventually would become my husband and the father of our two beautiful children. While he may have never shared my love for writing and literature, he supported me when I needed him to. If it weren't for that support, these pages you just read would be nothing more than empty dreams.

I don't know what possessed me to pick up that pen for the first time in years and start writing again. Maybe I was bored. Perhaps I was lonely. Or maybe I wanted to prove to my girls that it's okay to dream big, it's okay to stumble, and that they can be whoever they want to be. I hope that when they are old enough to understand, they know that none of this would have been possible without them. While my husband may have given me the support I needed, they gave me the courage.

I'm fortunate to have the community that I have now. Not everyone is so lucky. To my family, who stood by my side throughout this, it means the world to me. To my friends who cheered me on from the sidelines on the days when I needed that extra pep in my step—David, Bridgette, Zach, Michaela, Ruby—you are all truly amazing. To the Burning Pages book club, while I haven't known many of you long, you have become such a huge part of my community. To my amazing editor, Grace Fabbri, thank you for being so easy to work with. And to Devyn Shank, you helped me bring all of this to life with the beautiful artwork you created.

I am truly grateful for all of you, and I couldn't have done any of this without you.

About the author

Haley Davis, along with her husband, two children, and pets, calls the coast of North Carolina home. She enjoys surrounding herself with friends and family. Haley has always been captivated by reading and writing, but it wasn't until she had her second child that she decided to take the leap and write her own story.

A Dance of Light and Shadows is her debut novel, and the sequel is already in the works. It explores themes of found family, hidden heritage, and a slow burn that'll have readers kicking and screaming. She loves bringing others into the worlds she creates and seeing the joy it brings them. Haley loves connecting with her readers and seeing the wonderment the world she has created brings them. You can find her on most social media platforms @authorhaleydavis, or her author webpage at www.thestormyqu ill.com